Sabrina & T... f
The Sev...ıı Sea

Guy Sheppard

SOCCIONES

ISBN-13: 978-1981883660
ISBN-10: 1981883665

Cover design © Socciones

Design & formatting by Socciones Editoria Digitale
www.kindle-publishing-service.co.uk

'And I will give thee the treasures of darkness.'
Isaiah 45:3

Prologue

As Tina leaned closer, she wondered if the buoy would do what it did the last time it resurfaced.

It was so cork-like on the water, so alive. Not so easy to dismiss as rubbish. At first sight.

But when would it leave them alone?

She was annoyed with herself for staring. Why not simply go on with her eel fishing? For mere flotsam that came with the tide, the float's sinuous ripples not only signalled something wrong but insistent. It positively swam in their boat's wake as if it would gain their attention.

The hellish glow that fired the horizon half an hour ago was already a dark, ominous smudge above the disused nuclear power station as the sun set lower. She watched ribbons of water turn from pink to black, like blood, for miles.

'Don't tell me a big boy like you is afraid of the dark?' said Tina.

Randal shivered on the sailing dinghy's transom. It was typical of her ten-year-old friend not to realise how wild and empty it would be on the river in April.

What teenager in her right mind chose to hang out with such a fussy child, anyway, even if he could steer the tiller quite well?

'But, Tina, the tide's turning. What if we get caught by the bore?'

'A simple 'no' will do.'

Shivering, she chewed more gum.

'How far now, Tina?'

'We're past Narlwood Rocks already.'

'I thought you said I could navigate?'

'Well, you thought wrong.'

Icy air froze her pimply white kneecaps where she had torn fashionable holes in her faded jeans.

She had at least thought to wear her woolly hat tonight, if only she could pull it further down her face like a proper balaclava? It was okay for posh little Randal. He might moan, but it was only thanks to her that he was clad in her father's windproof shooting jacket. He looked a real toff in the hopelessly over-sized tweed cap that she had, at the last minute, thought to lift from a hook on their way out of the farmhouse.

She banged against the dinghy's transom, wedged her feet inside its hull as the shrouds groaned midway on the mast. She ought to adjust the tension with the lanyards. Instead she left the links to protest on the chain-plates while she rushed to balance the boat.

That sudden bump to the stern was like a kick in the buttocks.

Quick to tack left or right, she fought not to be dragged right over.

She fought quite a while.

'I'm scared,' said Randal.

'Shut up and give me a hand here, will you?'

Alarmed, Tina tried not to alarm.

Meanwhile black-backed gulls marched like sentries along thin, shingly islands. They ruffled their feathers. Mocked the boat's erratic progress. With shrieks and cackles.

Next moment a lamp winked at them from the darkening riverbank.

Not police, thought Tina. The police wouldn't give themselves away quite so easily.

Most likely it was elvermen. Sure enough, she soon made out the large, square aluminium box-nets that hung from long poles resting on their shoulders. They formed striking silhouettes against the skyline. They looked, in this light, like bizarre butterfly hunters.

Tina sank lower on her seat. Of course, being fifteen years old, she should have been in possession of a valid fishing licence. Some of those people on the bank might actually recognize their dinghy. One of them might be Randal's stepdad come to look for the boy who ought to be in bed by now.

She did not fancy arguing with brawny men who fiercely guarded their 'stumps' at the edge of the river.

Fishermen on the Severn could be a funny lot, not least because they, too, wanted to cash in on its treasures, albeit legally. Glass eels were fetching £150 per kilo. Like caviar they were. Smugglers could earn millions in Hong Kong, if they could get past GO at Heathrow.

Why else had her father just been 'detained' trying to smuggle live eels on board a plane bound for China?

'Quick, Randal. Take the tiller while I dip my net in the water.'

Randal skidded from gunwale to gunwale in his green, plastic Wellingtons.

'Where do they all come from again?'

Tina began slopping elvers by the gallon into buckets. Plop, plop, plop went the living slurry. She could make out the two pretty, parallel black bands along their slippery sides.

She scooped the transparent snakelike fish in her hands where, glassily, they sparkled against her wet palms. They twisted and tied themselves in ever tighter knots.

She could see why so many people said that they came from dead men's skulls. They were no more than three inches long and not much thicker than curls of human hair.

By the time they were adult eels each one would grow lots of white, needle-sharp teeth; they'd be ferocious. On a damp night like this they were known to leave the river. Cross the land.

'They swim three thousand miles from the Sargasso Sea. They spend two years floating here as babies on the Gulf Stream in order to grow into adults in our rivers…'

But Randal was no longer listening. That buoy, more tangled weed than ball, had reappeared in their boat's creamy wake.

His heart began to pound as the river flexed its dark spine. He felt no need to prove anything to anyone, but he bit his tongue in case he cried.

Tina looked hard, too.

'I'd say it's part of a net used for bottom trawling the ocean? I reckon that's one of those hollow metal balls designed to bounce off rocks on the sea floor.'

Randal screwed his cap back to front for a better view.

'But there's something else with it.'

Tina seized anchor and rope from the floor of the dinghy.

'Okay, so now I have questions.'

'What can we do?'

'Stay back, I'm going to hook it with this.'

'You don't want to do that, Tina. That's not a good idea, at all.'

She kept her balance as the dinghy's keel grazed a sandbank. Then she launched her metal hook at the river. The big ball of seaweed advanced at them with the same unstoppable buoyancy as it did when it had bumped them before.

'Wow, it's big.'

'Leave it alone, Tina, it looks alive.'

'Stay out my way.'

'Do you even have a plan?'

'Running out of time here.'

'We should go home like I said.'

'Trust me, Randal, I know what I'm doing.'

'What makes you so sure?'

'Is this you helping?'

He finally took hold of the tiller.

'What if it's from a shipwreck or something?'

'You asking me?'

Next moment, she was looking for the eight-metre high, steel tower that signified Berkeley Pill whose tidal entrance led to the nearby medieval fortress. She tried to see all eight green fluorescents in its white lantern house as she decided to make a run for it between Black Rock and Bull Rock Beacon.

In no sense did they intend to alert anyone at the nearby docks to their presence, but headed up the tributary towards Berkeley Castle.

Salt water brimmed at the bottom of the Pill's steeply curving banks, whose slippery black mud made beaching the boat very tricky.

But Tina let icy water flood her boots all the way up to her knees as she began to unravel the substantial piece of fishing net from its catch. It was a very large, leather suitcase.

Randal saw his boots sink into slime, too.

'Oh, bloody hell, there's something inside it. I see teeth. It looks like a monster.'

Tina used her knife to cut away more net. That was no monster, she thought. It didn't want to attack them. Instead, the suitcase wanted to disgorge something. Towards her. Towards land. Some horror. And she dreaded it.

But that didn't mean it had to stop her.

'A trawlerman has lost part of his gear, all right. That metal bobbin from some broken rock-hopper net has snagged the case and floated it to the surface.'

Randal let out a wail.

'Tina, what are you doing?'

She wrestled with the damaged suitcase's leathery folds – peeled back a flap despite its unseemly resistance before she turned her attention to the mummified contents inside. A skull's vacant sockets met hers with a stare of stupefaction. Latched on.

In dragging away more net and weed she revealed the voracious maw's last, frozen cry for help.

Randal followed her every move. Crouched down. The colour drained from his cheeks until he looked as shocked as she did with his popping pupils.

'Is that a hand I can see?'

'It's a black glove, certainly.'

Randal gave a whistle.

'Wow, Tina, that's great.'

'Damn right.'

'It's not, though, is it?'

'Give me a moment.'

Randal came closer.

'You got anything yet, Tina?'

'Do me a favour.'

With that, she shrugged him off her as a mother might her own child. She pushed him right away with an urgency that baffled him totally. Forgot all about any stupid elvers. Many a day she'd spent scavenging in river mud for objects of value, but this was something else. No self-respecting mudlark could pass up the chance to add to her collection back home.

They were looking at half a human skeleton with one arm. The rest was gone. The suitcase had recently begun to come apart and leaked its load. Whoever it was had been dead long enough to lose all their flesh but not yet totally dissolve.

'Do NOT tell anyone what we have here.'

Randal pouted.

'Why not? It's my find, too.'

'Consider it our secret.'

'What do I get if I do?'

'You get to look for more bones.'

Tina grinned. From the glove's unflinching grip came a glint of gold.

Chapter 1

'What could possibly go wrong?' thought Jorge Winter as he drove into the prison car park. He sat for a moment with the key in the ignition of his bright orange camper van while he contemplated breakfast.

Ever since Christmas, had he not set himself the modest target of losing twice as many pounds as he did in 2016?

But spring was already here and his dream weight was nowhere to be seen. The Bishop of Gloucester had already warned him that his size would hold him back in every aspect of his life which was why, from this morning, he had decided to cut out the Crunchy Nut Cornflakes, eggs, bacon, sausage and toast.

He gathered up a thin, black plastic file from the seat beside him. At thirty-six he was within sight of joining the eighty-three per cent of middle-aged people who were increasing their risk of liver disease and at least five types of cancer by making pigs of themselves, he reminded himself brutally, while he strode across the car park. He took a bite from his *ever so tiny* breakfast bar before he banged on the door of HMPL....

He could do this, he thought, he could reboot his battle not to be a glutton. Fat was such a little word it hardly did itself justice – he simply had to think of it as his own special kind of parole.

Dieting was not unlike the belief in heaven. To shed weight you had to aim ridiculously high.

Actually, it wasn't a spiritual thing at all, it was stress. Ever since he had agreed to hunt someone down who was supposed to be dead.

*

'You got a Mars Bar in your pants, at all, Inspector?'

Prison Officer James Pettifer was all grins, but still his look was glacial and so was Jorge's. When a man was only trying to go about Church business he should not be treated like some unwanted arrival at some soulless border control.

HMPL.... was a prison which held over five hundred men. More to the point, it was one of only two open prisons in England to accept sex offenders and in particular child sex offenders, who were serving life sentences.

'Really? Mars Bars? That the latest?'

'Last week I caught someone trying to smuggle in a mobile phone coated in chocolate. Relatives buy the phones for £25 but in here they sell for hundreds.'

'Really? In my pants?'

'Or elsewhere.'

'I don't want to know.'

'Could be worse, this could be a women's prison.'

'Sadly, arseholes and greed make perfect bedfellows.'

'Keep your eyes skinned, Inspector. Two staff rang in sick today.'

'Problem?'

'Do I really have to say it? Things are tense with so few officers on the wings.'

'I'm not here to upset anyone.'

'No? Those fancy silver diamonds on your epaulettes might make them think otherwise.'

'Am I that scary?'

'Your insignia are very like that of a regular police inspector from New Scotland Yard, you have to admit.'

Jorge squinted at each shoulder in turn.

'Look carefully and you will also see the City of Gloucester's crest of a red shield, two lions with broadswords and FIDES INVICTA TRIUMPHAT. It means 'Invincible faith triumphs'. I come from the cathedral's new private police force, not the Bill.'

Officer Pettifer arched one eyebrow.

'Since when do cathedrals have their own cops?'

'Since 1855 when the title of 'Minster Police' was first recorded. At York

2

Minster, where I worked for five years, I was in charge of eight constables.'

'If you say so.'

'Thanks to me Gloucester will soon be the fifth cathedral in England to have its own constables. The others are York, Liverpool, Canterbury and Chester, though Salisbury and Hereford also employed their own policemen until a few years ago. Our motto is 'In Deo Speramus'. In God We Trust. You happy now?'

'You have to forget all about that in here, Inspector.'

'Don't see how I can.'

'You have powers of arrest, at all?'

'Such powers are about to be granted to York and I'm sure Gloucester will soon follow suit. Otherwise the local territorial police force remains responsible for dealing with all major incidents and crime, but I do carry handcuffs and a baton in my van just in case.'

Once more Officer Pettifer regarded him as some peculiar blow-in.

'I meant what are you doing this far from the cathedral? Gloucester is twenty miles away.'

Jorge did his best not to feel conspicuous in his well-ironed white shirt, black tie and black trousers. He kept his black peaked cap with its blue and white diced band tucked neatly under his left arm.

'So what if I'm out of bounds?'

Officer Pettifer caught his tone.

'Just watch your step, that's all, Inspector. Some of the guys in here have been smoking 'Spice' sprayed on children's drawings.'

'Bold move. Usually legal highs get smuggled in on the soles of trainers.'

'You know about that?'

'I once served as a volunteer prison chaplain in Yorkshire. That was an open prison too.'

'Then you're a minister? Lay or ordained?'

'All that's behind me now.'

'What happened?'

'I moved on.'

This time Officer Pettifer eyed him even more sharply.

'No charger or USB card, Inspector?'

'That's funny.'

That true faith was now problematical to him only made someone like Pettifer more strident in his cynical insinuations. Even though some great light had recently grown dim within him the officer would not settle for so little, he would have him blinded like Paul on the road to Damascus before he would believe that turning up here today could do any good.

'So you must know by now, Inspector, that some prisoners will consider all visitors to be a soft touch. They'll give you some sob story or they'll try to pretend that they've found Jesus. At best they'll get you to wangle them a job in the kitchen.'

'That it? You can't just wish me good morning?'

'Please move against the wall for the dogs to go past.'

'Got it.'

Two Labradors nuzzled the bottom of Jorge's voluminous black trousers with noses that were two thousand times stronger and fifty times more sensitive than his own. They detected the existence of something but ignored the smell detected. It was sweat. Neither animal dug and pawed at him in any aggressive alert, however.

These drug dogs were absolutely bloody marvellous but he carried no Mamba or Spice on him this morning, easy enough though it was to pass it off as rolled tobacco.

He decided to risk a bit of banter with the handler, nevertheless.

'I hear that Dutch prisons have bought four sea eagle chicks. They want to train them up to attack rogue drones.'

'You got that right, Inspector. We had a drone crash into the roof only last week. It tried to deliver drugs to a cell window in West Block. Now we've been told we might get a specialist unit of our own to bring them down.'

'Don't tell me, it's going to be called the 'flying squad'.'

'Seriously, two men have just been jailed at Luton Crown Court for trying to flood prisons across Suffolk and Kent with contraband worth £50,000, including drugs and phones. They flew them over the prison wall. Mind you, eagles are pie in the sky if you ask me.'

'Oh, I don't know.'

'What kind of person thinks a bird can bring down a drone?'

4

'A birdbrain.'

It was his first visit to HMPL…. and already he felt shut off, shut in and enclosed, thought Jorge. It was like being confined on board a submarine.

Boots echoed emptily down corridors and doors clanged as though he had just joined the crew on some undersea voyage.

Such was the formidable change in sound between 'in' and 'out' that every noise was magnified tenfold in a world so stark and bright. He flinched at each step, or rather its prequel. It was as though just before each boot hit the floor along the metal tunnel every man in his cell held his breath. He did the same.

He took one look at the grubby chairs and declined to sit down.

'I really don't have much time to waste.'

It was a reassuringly rotund prison chaplain called Hammond who directed them into the wing office.

'That's what I thought you'd say, Inspector.'

'I'm here to speak to Frank Cordell, the child rapist who's due for release on licence tomorrow.'

'Damn right you are.'

'Is there a problem?'

'As you say, Cordell's free to go in the morning but here's the rub: his beloved grandchild died last night from a bleed on the brain.'

'Ironic, huh? But what's that got to do with the purpose of my visit?'

'I want to be honest with you, Inspector, someone has to break the bad news.'

'Don't tell me, that person is me?'

'Nothing you can't handle?'

'I love you, too.'

'I'd do it myself but as managing chaplain I have to meet the Governor for the daily briefing in five minutes.'

'I bet you do.'

Jorge felt perspiration pour down his chest. That was another problem with

5

being somewhat large and sartorially challenged, you could feel hot in all sorts of unexpected places. A lot of red, itchy spots began to prickle between his 'moobs'.

But Hammond wasn't finished.

'The thing is, Inspector, the guv nearly blew his lid when he heard you were coming. Never heard of a church detective before and doesn't like it.'

'Nor do I. I expected to be in charge of cathedral keys and security for VIPs.'

'Just thought I'd warn you.'

'Yeah, right. Heaven knows what that bastard Cordell will have to say to me anyway.'

Hammond, playful as ever, landed a heavy pat on his upper arm. His face quizzed him with the same suspicious smile that he had displayed on first making his acquaintance. The truly personable did not give that smile, thought Jorge. It put him on guard. He clutched his file of paperwork ever more firmly under his arm. Set off fast down the corridor.

'Hey, Inspector, guess what? Cordell has been asking after you.'

'Really?'

'By the hour.'

'How come?'

'It's not every day that someone agrees to pay a visit to a paedophile in prison. Actually, you could say you're the talk of the town.'

He might have guessed. News travelled fast in prison and even from prison to prison.

*

He was no fan of special care and segregation units but he did appreciate this one's surgically sterile, anti-septic atmosphere. The pronounced tenseness in his leg muscles, that so threatened to upset his equilibrium, eased as he stepped over the threshold.

He felt momentarily emboldened.

But the suggestion that he was here to depend on some sort of testimony from the old man who sat at the table in front of him seemed ludicrous. The hideously conspicuous scars on his forehead, the tattoos on his knuckles, the one good, hard green eye, lent him all the attributes of a pathetic old whaler no longer able to go after his quarry.

Before he sat down he wiped the chair with a tissue.

'Hallo Frank, my name is Inspector Jorge Winter.'

'You here about your brother, Inspector? Please tell me you are.'

'I'm terribly sorry, Frank, but I have bad news.'

Cordell's face fell. When someone was incarcerated for years they lost out on just about everything. Since they lost out on so much, there was always a lot to desire. They had to make do with wild promises to themselves and other people. But if they had someone special to look forward to when they were freed, they could at least reassure themselves that they had something to salvage *in the future*.

'Don't tell me. My grandson Alex is dead?'

'Last night. I'm so sorry, he collapsed at home in Bristol. An ambulance rushed him to Southmead Hospital, but to no avail.'

Cordell pressed both hands to his face. The horrible twist in his nose, the loss of an eye, only emphasised the physical manifestation of pure wretchedness. He rose from his chair, Jorge from his.

Cordell banged his fists on the table. He leaned straight ahead. Stared into thin air. Jorge took a step backwards and kept the table between them, as the other man tried to circle it and him – his sudden move caught him seriously off guard.

'Damn you, Inspector. May you all rot in hell for keeping me from him.'

'Really? It's my fault now?'

Any other person would have told him, 'Now you know what it feels like to see your own suffer,' but he didn't. Of course the grandson's demise was a cruel blow, but what was he to say?

Cordell was already out of breath. Having held cruel sway over children, a child now held sway over him.

He looked doubly unwell as he paled but refused to sit down.

'Everything I've done, I've done for that boy, Inspector. Now it's too fucking late. What's the point of getting out of here now?'

'It's God's will.'

'He told me he'd set things right. He promised me that he had a plan. And he did, but he fucking well let me down.'

'He?'

'That fucking priest who was the prison chaplain. Your brother.'

'*Brother* as in the church. We're not related.'

'He's betrayed me, Inspector. Oh, I can tell you a thing or two about him. You should go after him straightaway.'

'How come?'

'Are you not here to catch one of your own since he strayed?'

'That's not what I asked. I'm here to find out why you have the effrontery to keep writing such abusive letters to the Bishop of Gloucester. In them you swear that you'll go to the press if no one listens to you. You say that Reverend Luke Lyons isn't dead. So where in God's name is he?'

*

Most people simply forgot each other after decades apart. It was easier. But sometimes there was one person on whom you never quite gave up? Luke was like that, thought Jorge, walking out of the prison. Perhaps it had something to do with having known one another when boys. It never totally went away but resided in some dark part of your soul. The joy. The understanding. The sympathy. The forgiveness.

But how did anyone get back to it? To this shared beginning? Which ship took you home? Back into yourself? The most mysterious of voyages on the most secret of currents – into your own heart.

Chapter 2

It was Easter Monday 2016 and Rev. 'Lucky' Luke Lyons had just walked out of Wandsworth Prison on this, his last full day in London. It was his 35th birthday. Perhaps because he was skin and bone the sudden chill hit him hard.

One hour later he arrived home just as Storm Katie struck London. She tore up trees, felled power lines and diverted aircraft on her rampage to the North Sea while the Dartford Crossing in Kent had to be closed, as did the Severn Road Bridge in Gloucestershire. A roof blew off just round the corner from where he rented his flat in Vauxhall.

'Steady, Sasha. '*Sash*'? Do stop barking. It won't help.'

His miniature Bull Terrier flattened her ears. She left the windowsill and its panoramic view of the Thames. Let droop her thin, rat-like tail. She trembled at the strange mood in the air as much as he did.

Her small dark eyes stared straight at him with an anxious meanness.

Roused to fight or flight by all the thunder and lightning, it was difficult to dissuade her from constantly growling. He was used to that growl: she had been kept in a cage for three years by her so-called owners who had, one day, donated her to an unimpressed seller of The Big Issue outside Waterloo railway station.

Which was when he had stepped forward to make his modest donation to a cause close to his heart. She had followed him home in the pouring rain.

He still had to take her from place to place and show her things such as cars and pushchairs, because she had not really been out in the world. Her behaviour could be vicious in public, but no more so than was consistent with terror.

He had no cause to suppose she was beyond all hope, thought Luke. Had not so far regretted giving his fellow loner a fresh start in life.

Until he'd come along she hadn't even had a name.

He was not one to believe that weather could be demonic, but he did wonder if something akin to a malevolent spirit had set foot on land as he listened to two tenants squawk in the flat directly below him.

It had to be because of them that Sasha was so fidgety lately? She was shocked and unnerved, not simply by the fact that both young men were mentally disturbed (they had recently been rehoused by the local council and with them came the stink of vomit on the stairs), but by the desperation with which they howled.

It sounded like wolves.

Luke could share their fright, if not their plight, when he switched on his TV set to drown out their noise.

A face appeared on the screen.

Blue-black eyes, uncannily like his own, stared directly at him through a fringe of hair that was dyed bright purple.

Clearly some elderly expat was being interviewed via satellite link to Spain? The matriarch looked, by her relaxed attitude on the studio couch, very proud of herself and appeared to relish all the attention.

The eager young TV presenter fired questions at her.

'So, Ms Jessica Kennedy, you admit it's true that between 1971 and 1981 you and your gang stole pictures and antiques worth millions of pounds from English country houses, but only a tenth of it has ever been retrieved? How is that possible, by the way?'

'What the hell!' cried Luke.

Alarmed, he took to pulling at his clerical collar before it choked him. 'Hell doesn't even begin to cover it!'

He felt like a rabbit frozen in the glare of someone's car headlights.

The interviewee broke into a broad smile.

'Please, dear, call me Jess. As to your query you'd have to ask my ex-boyfriend. He buried the loot somewhere thirty-five years ago.'

He leaned closer to her in his horror.

'That'll be Rex Lyons? He's your lover and partner in crime?'

'Technically. He's dead.'

'So, Jess, how come Rex had the stolen goods and you didn't?'

Jessica blinked her false eyelashes for the benefit of the camera.

'Or maybe the fact that I got caught by the police a few hours before he did says something?'

'That'll be after your last raid in 1981? That was the night a pregnant woman was fatally wounded, was it not?'

'The thing is, dear, I should be plain with all those watching in the UK right now, with the toffs as well as the cops, that no one ever set out to take a pop at anyone...'

'Possibly Lady Sara Greene wouldn't agree with you?'

'Who cares? She died.'

'You say you never meant to kill anyone?'

'Okay, dear, it's just that if there was a need to protect ourselves when robbing someone's obscenely big house, then we would do so. Rex only ever reacted because Lady Sara gave us no choice. We had to defend ourselves against someone who thought nothing of shooting the likes of us simply because we'd invaded their home. I mean, everyone has the fucking right to kill or be killed, don't they, when some Sir or Lady points their shotgun at you?'

Still Luke refused to avert his gaze from the beaming face on the TV screen. With her absurdly coloured perm and brash sapphire rings on all her fingers, Jessica did her best to portray herself as a charmless but harmless old lady who smiled straight into the camera's lens and showed off her cleavage.

Her shamelessness shamed him. He quickly became conscious of how fast his heart was beating, how recklessly. The rise in pulse rate was not exactly inexplicable yet grew steadily more violent. He sat on a chair and the hammering in his chest subsided. When he tried to ease the pain in his side, it pounded.

The interviewer's face adopted a slightly bemused expression as he addressed his next killer question.

'Judge Alexander Bristow, when he sentenced you and your gang for the raids, was pretty damning, was he not? *This is one of the worst instances of aggravated burglary I have ever seen come before this court. Most of the property has not been recovered and is doubtless well concealed in the Gloucestershire countryside or passed on for disposal. Your mockery of the police is indicative of your contempt for the law. You have no respect for people's lives or property so I have no alternative but to impose very*

11

serious sentences.'

'Doesn't mean I'm a bad person, dear.'

'Just to recap, you also targeted shops, did you not? For instance, you and your gang stole a lot of Waterford crystal and Royal Doulton china from four stores in Warwickshire. That haul alone was worth £150,000.'

'It's not a good thing, dear. I mean we did an awful lot of thieving back then. But the judge didn't come down so hard on us because of a few shops, it's because of the rich people we robbed.'

'How's that?'

Jessica leaned back from the camera. Her long black, curving eyelashes blinked faster in the harsh studio lights as though she was, after all, nervous of being exposed to the media at her age. She was sixty-seven, she admitted sheepishly. Her picture had been in all the British newspapers lately which was how everyone, including him, knew her face as the onetime head of Britain's number 1 crime family of the 1970s and 80s, now living in exile on Spain's Costa Del Sol.

'Fuck you,' said Jessica. 'I can't have been such a bad mother, can I? Not when my daughter Ellie is about to get married and my son has gone into the church. So, Luke, dear boy, if you're watching this now, please know that mummy is coming home for your sister's wedding.'

Chapter 3

Jorge righted one of the segregation unit's hard plastic chairs and ordered Cordell to do the same. To his surprise the prisoner, wearing his regulation yellow vest, obeyed, but not before he exuded that peculiar smell of all those who were on HMPL....'s programme to come off heroin.

It was hard not to turn up his nose at the stench of methadone.

'You're messing with the wrong man, Frank. You hear me?'

'That's funny. Reverend 'Lucky' Luke Lyons said the same thing.'

'Don't call him that. That man is gone.'

'Really, Inspector? And if you catch up with him, dead or alive, how do you think he'll feel?'

'Redeemed.'

Cordell raised his head and his one good, bloodshot eye focused on his face.

'*Lay not up for yourselves treasures upon earth, where moth and dust doth corrupt, and where thieves break through and steal.* Matthew 6:19.'

'I'm not following you.'

'Now that I literally have your attention, Inspector, let's talk man to man. Stop me if you don't already know that Reverend Lyons's mother and father were fucking celebrities? They burgled the rich and famous. Rex Lyons and Jess Kennedy amassed themselves a fortune. We're talking national treasures worth millions.'

'It's all in my file.'

'Shocked, are you?'

'Should I be?'

'Your missing priest has a black heart. Want me to go on?'

13

'I'm not entirely sure what you're insinuating.'

'Rev. Luke must have found it very hard to grow up in the shadow of his parents' glamourous past, don't you think? His father, in particular, was such a hard act to follow. I bet he resented his old man something rotten. Now he's gone back to the Devil.'

'I doubt that very much.'

'But this is what you are here to determine, isn't it, Inspector?'

'In a very broad sense.'

Cordell changed tack most wilfully, Jorge noticed. His wall eye never blinked, but that settled nothing.

He narrowed his own chestnut coloured eyes and gripped his chair's seat to confront what he was sure would turn out to be total nonsense.

Back in the day he was always standing up for Luke's bad behaviour. The petty lies. The minor thefts. He'd do it now, if he could. Adults never understood his loyalty at the time. They hated it. What they couldn't accept was that a vicar's son could like someone so bad and vice versa. It broke all the rules.

Genes had to be a factor, though, in everyone. In his own case he had an unexpected ancestry via his mother's side, hence the spelling of his name. It was said that he was called Jorge after a famous seventeenth century Portuguese pirate who had been in the family. He doubted this version of events because not only did 'Jorge' derive from the Greek name 'georgos' meaning farmer, but he could find no record of any pirate named 'George', no matter what the spelling, in the history books. He liked to think, nevertheless, that his fiery temperament, if not his fastidious side, derived from his mysterious Mediterranean blood.

'You talk as if you knew the Lyons family very well, Frank. What were they to you, exactly? Was it strictly friendship?'

'It rarely is.'

'Business, then?'

'That's more like it, Inspector. Back in the 1970's and 80's, after each robbery, Rex brought me a 'parcel' of antiques for disposal and I'd try to get him a decent fix. He gave me mostly the shitty stuff, but he always gave me a bit of the cream as well. That way we kept the channels open, ready to pass on the rest of the stuff, the bit worth millions…. Much later on I did the same for Luke before he pretended to find God.'

14

'What does this have to do with Reverend Lyons now?'

'Fact is, Inspector, if anyone has that loot it has to be him.'

'These are the Devil's words.'

'That, Inspector, is because the Devil pays best.'

'Luke chose to give up crime years ago.'

'Keep reminding yourself of that.'

'Sorry, Cordell, but you're insane.'

'What if I told you I think I know where Reverend Lyons has gone? What if I told you that it's on account of me that he *isn't* dead?'

'You can learn a lot from a born liar but not that much.'

'They tell you what we all called him in here?'

'I forget.'

'We called him 'The Captain' on account of his passion for boats. Not any old boats, either. I'm talking about those real ocean-going ships that sail up the canal to Gloucester for the Tall Ships Festival every couple of years.'

'It's true that Luke once worked as a ship's chaplain on cruise liners.'

'He has sailed off with his old man's treasure, Inspector, I'll bet my life on it.'

Cordell's lizard's tongue flickered at the gap in his very long and twisted lips. His face was not merely cunning, it appealed to Jorge with a knowingness and malignant familiarity.

'So how do you account for the fact that the GPS signal on his phone ended at the River Severn? He left behind his hat and coat but his body has yet to be found.'

'And if the dead should ever resurface, Inspector? Do you have pen and paper, by any chance?'

'I do.'

Cordell wrote something with his shaky hand and thrust it at him across the table's scratched surface.

'That's where you'll find me, Inspector, after my release tomorrow.'

'You really have something to tell me about Reverend Lyons?'

'There's so much more that you don't know about your missing priest, believe me.'

'Until tomorrow, then.'

'It's safer. Thanks to that bastard my boy is dead.'

*

Back in his impeccably restored VW camper van, Jorge pulled pages from Luke's case file. He remained unconvinced that he would ever hear anything useful or reliable from Frank Cordell since everything about him appeared so wild.

Last year's disciplinary procedure against the missing man lay before him. He reread lines about his quarry, feeling a trifle unnerved in both body and spirit. He skipped paragraphs 1.1 to 5. Looking under 'Investigations', he reprised his role against the Rev. Luke Lyons in absentia.

5.1: The purpose of an investigation is for us to establish a fair and balanced view of the facts relating to any allegations against you, before deciding whether to proceed with a disciplinary hearing. The amount of investigation required will depend on the nature of the allegations... It may involve interviewing and taking statements from you and any witnesses, and/or reviewing relevant documents.

He moved on to 6.1: Where your conduct is the subject of a criminal investigation, charge or conviction the Church will investigate the facts before deciding whether to take formal disciplinary action.

More importantly his file contained a 'selfie' that Luke had taken one Christmas at a carol service at Westminster Abbey. In it he was in many ways still the boy he remembered, but being in his mid-thirties his black hair was, like his own, already beginning to recede across his scalp and he had acquired large dark circles round his eyes. His face was lean, much leaner than expected, his skin worn, his cheeks drawn, his chin badly shaved. His large blue-black eyes, with some exotic swirls of agate, granite and gold, burned with a fire that belonged to a visionary or former gangster, or both.

'Where have you been these last eight months, Luke, my old friend?' Jorge wondered as he turned the key in the ignition and heard the camper van's smoky engine cough into life. 'Are you really at the bottom of the river?'

Having been informed in writing of the allegations against him, the basis for those allegations, and what the likely range of consequences would be if the Senior Deacon decided after the hearing that the allegations were true, Rev. Luke Lyons, aka 'The Captain', had promptly denied everything by return of post.

A quotation accompanied his denial which was, appropriately enough, from Luke 12:34:

For where your treasure is, there will your heart be also.

Since then, nothing.

Chapter 4

Luke paced up and down before his TV set. Beside himself with anger, he watched as the camera in the Spanish television studio switched from distinguished guest to interviewer briefly.

'Admit it, Jess. You and your gang burgled people's homes because you liked it?'

Jessica gazed pleasantly into the lens.

'I never said we were saints. Besides, everyone has to make a living. Take Paul Colley for instance – he had a heroin habit to feed. Mel McAtree was a compulsive gambler. Couldn't go a day without putting a bet on the horses.'

Luke stopped pacing to listen.

'Well, Jess, okay, but that's not what you told The Tatler. In it you said that you were proud to be the best burglars in the business. You were, in fact, career criminals of the worst kind, were you not?'

'The real point is, dear, did we have a fair trial?' said Jessica, fanning herself with the folds of her black and gold fan. 'And my reply to that is no, dear, we didn't. I mean it suited certain people to demonise us. The way hundreds of police broke into my home and put a gun to my head just shows how the upper classes control everything. We were treated like terrorists. Quite simply all the bigwigs set the police onto us like a bunch of vigilantes – we were victims of a vendetta. I can't go shopping in Spain without feeling as though some security guard is following me everywhere. The whole business has left me with post-traumatic stress disorder. I should get compensation. Even Ellie, my daughter, suffers and she's never done anything bad in her whole life except kill her first husband in a car crash. I feel sorry for the rest of the gang.'

'You suggesting you were wrongly sentenced?'

'No, yeah, I don't know. Apart from Rex I got seven years, Paul Colley got ten, Mel McAtree got four years and three months, Slim Jim Jackson got the same, while Johnnie Hunt got five. Even Frank Cordell was given two years and six months and all he did was fence a carriage clock worth £10,000, though he's made up for it since. That doesn't make us malicious.'

'Is it true that you showed Rex how to break into caravans on a site next to Berkeley nuclear power station when you were both children? Did you come up with the name Severn Sea Gang all by yourself?'

'I really can't remember.'

There echoed in Luke's head a sudden torrent of crazy things. 'Like father, like son' it was normally said, but what about 'like mother'?

From the very beginning the Severn Sea Gang had been his father *and* mother. They were an inseparable team of two. They were first drawn to each other as far back as schoolchildren, alone and angry, by Johnny Kidd & the Pirates – rock n' roll that took the world by storm in 1960. Rex and Jess were a gang you could join only if you dressed up in pirate costumes complete with eye-patches and wooden cutlasses. While Kidd strutted the stage before an enormous backcloth of a buccaneer's galleon, his parents had acted out their own version of Clem Cattini on drums by beating the shit out of passing pupils. The fact that they grew up to be sweethearts only confirmed their common cause. What could be more exciting than to be the next Bonnie and Clyde in a small Gloucestershire town like Berkeley? They were eleven at the time.

The interviewer smiled faintly.

'What about the other members of the gang? They weren't exactly angelic, either. Mel McAtree attacked a man with a claw hammer in a pub in Gloucester.'

'He was provoked.'

'Consider this, then. Johnnie Hunt and Paul Colley smashed their way into factories. Stole lorry loads of precious metals. They also robbed two post offices. Frank Cordell still deals in stolen goods and has been convicted of grooming a thirteen-year-old girl online. After you were all locked up in prison reports of crime declined by sixty per cent in Gloucestershire, did they not?'

Jessica fanned herself vigorously in the hot halo of studio lights.

'It was a relief, in a way, to get away with it for so long.'

19

'So what made you graduate from a few smash-and-grabs to raiding a dozen stately homes?'

'Really we just got better and better at what we did. As the head of the Metropolitan Police's Art and Antiques Unit said at the time, *Give the Devil his due, they know their stuff*.'

'It took four police forces in Operation Gold to nail you, am I right?'

'That's because we were in and out of a place in minutes. Whenever the police took us on, we won.'

'Can't feel much like a victory now?'

'No. Yeah, I don't know, dear. That haul in Wiltshire alone was worth £35 million.'

'So, Jess, tell us. Where is it now? Out there somewhere is £100,000 million to the first person who can find it?'

Luke leaned in to listen.

Jessica giggled. The Gloucestershire burr in her voice betrayed all the excitement of a giggling girl.

'The figure gets bigger every time you mention it.'

'Well?'

'Honestly? You want the location?'

'Seems sensible.'

'All I can say is that *some*one knows where it is because Rex did leave behind a clue of some sort, I'm certain. Poor Rex, I loved him so. He read a lot, too. His favourite book was 'Treasure Island'. He read it to me three times. Smartest criminal I ever knew.'

*

That last part, at least, was true, thought Luke coolly. During prison visits his father would spend every minute telling him how he had loved to dress up as a Teddy Boy. His favourite garb had been his drape jacket with cuffs made from the same colour velvet as the collar. Not that he'd ever get to wear it again. Powder blue, it was and it went with his drainpipe trousers and Crombie overcoat. He told him stories of visits to London where he liked to buy his crepe soled shoes with one inch heels which he named Brothel Creepers. Or he'd tell him how he wore a pocket watch on a gold chain on his fancy waistcoat. Just like his own father had.

The next visit, it would all be about a threat from people 'we' couldn't trust, in case they ever came between 'us' and the as yet unspecified 'good fortune' that was to come Luke's way one day. These were all former gang members. By seven years of age he knew their names by heart. One name in particular. Frank Cordell.

'Never trust the bastard with whom you have to share a cell, Luke, my boy. That one is slippier than an eel.'

Next minute Rex was all sweetness and light.

It had all seemed, at the time, a bit of a game. Now those last words came back to haunt him: 'In a few years' time, son, the world will be our oyster. Take care. Not a word to your mother or anyone else because I've got it all sorted.'

'But dad, I never see her. She doesn't want me.'

'Then it'll be you and me.'

Rex neglected to mention that, unlike Jessica, he was serving life for murder. Perhaps he thought he'd forgotten?

'What the devil?' thought Luke and went back to pacing the floor.

The interviewer had changed subject.

'So, Jess, you gave birth to twins in prison, did you not? That can't have been easy.'

'I'd rather not discuss it.'

'Why not?'

'Because they're not me, dear.'

'It looked for years as if your son Luke would follow in your criminal footsteps. He had nineteen convictions for burglary, robbery, fraud and dangerous driving by the time he was twenty. Did you ever worry that he might simply end up like you?'

Luke became aware of a tremor in his body, almost a fit at first, then more and more like simple fear. He stood motionless and watched the TV as he held his hand to his temple. Felt a rhythmical throbbing increase between his eyes. He squeezed his fingers and the blood momentarily stopped being propelled along his veins.

He had never before bothered to take stock of his heart's innermost working. Never considered its fragile existence, like glass. The beat of someone's pulse was forever the beat of their mother's womb, but this felt like a series of enormous hammer blows. He attributed it to her being an otherwise total stranger.

Jessica smeared the back of her hand idly across her lips. With her fingers went a bad taste.

'I can't say what my son did. Honestly, I can't say in my heart-of-hearts if Luke did those things or not because the where and when of his life I never knew until recently. I'm told he fell into wrong company while he lived in Chapel Cottage by the River Severn, that his grandmother found him to be a bit of a handful. Can't believe everything the youth custody centre said about him, either. That was a rotten place to be in the 1990's. My son has been made a scapegoat for a lot of other people's misdemeanours. It was the system back then. I have every reason to believe that he was abused and beaten. It was not his mother who made him violent, it was evil men he should have been able to trust. If I had raised him by myself he would never have committed a single crime.'

'So Jess, is it true that Luke has put his past behind him to become a man of God?'

Jessica snarled.

'It's not the worst thing in the world. No, I absolutely don't know of anything worse. He must be off his head.'

'Doesn't mean a criminal can't ever decide to go straight, does it?'

'I very much doubt it, dear. He must have had a total nervous breakdown to do what he's doing now.'

'So what did you say when your daughter told you that he's a priest?'

'What does anyone say about a religious crank?'

'Fuck it,' thought Luke and changed TV stations ready to look out the window again. A fallen tree had just sliced a parked car in two.

No signs yet that the Devil would desist in time for his departure tomorrow.

He glanced at the very large, half-packed leather suitcase on the table.

If he had his mother's eyes, he also had his father's beaky nose.

That harpy had to be wrong, though, because people's characters could sometimes change, if not their looks.

This was literally his last chance to return home and start over.

He'd spent too many years burning bridges already.

Pretty much.

In a fit of bravado he pulled off his clerical collar and undid a few buttons on his shirt. A serpentine tattoo reflected in the glass of the window.

Its red-headed water spirit curled her tail round the curve of his neck as he wondered how such a harsh reminder could still be his.

Her silvery sea-green eyes were not simply of the nature of a monster. Rather, she gazed back at him with a ravishing delight, a vindictive callousness, a viper's charm.

If only all hell wasn't about to break out, he hoped, braving the latest thunder. It was the strangest of times. According to the latest news a crocodile had just been seen swimming in the docks in Bristol.

Some things refused to stay at the bottom of the deepest water.

Five minutes later he switched back to the interview.

'So Jess, finally, what would you say to all your critics out there who might call you a heartless mother and incorrigible thief?'

Jessica tilted the best side of her face to the camera.

'I'd say it's all about context, dear. I grew up without a father. So did Rex. Until you know the whole truth about someone you shouldn't judge them. What I will say is this. That rat who grassed on us has a lot to answer for. So, you bastard, if you're listening to this right now, don't think I've forgotten about everything I lost on account of you, because one day soon I will find a way to get even.'

Luke took a quick step back as his mother jabbed her finger straight at him. He knew that he should not go so far as to believe a word she said. Should forget that's where he came from.

Yet he found himself staring at her like some terrible goddess of hell. The greedy-eyed Proserpine grinned at him with such a sly mouth and ironical grimace that he could not help but feel drawn to admire her vile nature.

There had been a time when he had dreamt of finding that treasure, too.

Chapter 5

If there was one thing of which he was acutely aware, it was the awful aftertaste of cabbage under his tongue.

Jorge was steering his camper van along narrow, frosty lanes out of Berkeley while reminding himself sternly that the Cabbage Soup Diet was NOT intended as a long-term solution to his problem.

Unlike The 3 Day Military Diet which had very quickly proved that he was no soldier, his latest quick fix solution billed itself as 'a bit of a miracle'. He gave his stomach a pat. Who wouldn't invoke divine intervention if they could?

The truth was that food took his mind off Selma, his Brazilian girlfriend, who had just called time on their five-year relationship. She had declared him an intolerable burden.

'What the hell?' he cried suddenly as an animal burst from a gap in the hedge right under his wheels.

Sickened, he tried not to be sick. There was one advantage to being large: the folds in his belly cushioned the impact in his replacement Saab 9000 front seat and its belt quite nicely.

The creature's oddly intense observation of him now sent his thoughts in a new direction. Its bold stance struck him as pugnacious and not a little contemptuous, while its entirely superior air he could attribute only to something vaguely human.

Worse still he'd failed to hit it. He could always put fresh roadkill to good use. In the kitchen.

The pre-Christian landscape had been full of plants and animals that had held peculiar significance, he recalled as he drove more carefully along the lane towards Berkeley Castle. He fought to slam the camper van into a higher gear as if he would rearrange his own thoughts just as easily. Horses, wolves and ravens all had their spiritual importance, along with trees and flowers such as oak, holly, willow or yew.

That hare he had just met would once have been deemed sufficiently powerful as to belong to a mysterious otherworld of the supernatural.

'See some animals and you see shape-shifters,' he told himself aloud. 'When the Irish warrior Oisin hit a hare with his arrow, he followed it to a door in a wood that led far below ground. He arrived at a large subterranean hall. Found a beautiful young woman who sat on a throne and who was trying to stem the blood that flowed from her wound. The Celtic peoples thought that a hare had such supernatural powers that they forbade anyone to eat it.'

If only people endowed more animals with that sort of respect, then he would, de facto, have less to eat. It would be like not eating cows in India.

Papers from his file landed loose at his feet. A warning hand could not have scattered them better all over the handbrake.

He wriggled about in his long black coat and took firm hold of the faux leopard skin steering-wheel. Since 'Martha' had most likely been stolen, 'scrapped', exported or flagged as otherwise unroadworthy, he had been able to acquire her six months ago for a very few pounds – no questions asked – from a very nice woman in a backstreet in County Londonderry. He had been on an interfaith pilgrimage to Holy Mountain at the time but had ended up drinking Guinness with the locals in a pub. He fell in love with the offer of his very own 1974 Hippie wagon.

Jorge belched. Never before had he emitted sounds so loud now that he had decided to go on his skinnybitch low-fat, high-fibre diet. Never had it occurred to him that day after day of consuming cabbage could turn anyone into a giant rabbit.

Nothing was that therianthropic?

Was it?

*

Next minute Jorge could not deny that he was somewhat astonished, or wondered in fact if he had come to the right place. His satnav, however, thought it correct. The sun had bleached the brick walls of a scabby Gothic fantasy, apparently – two castellated turrets resembled those of a very small castle or folly.

25

His jaw dropped as he settled his black cap on his head.

'You come about the bitch, Inspector?'

'Good question.'

Jorge stared at the tall man in the doorway. Began to suspect that he was about to be rather unpleasant or uncooperative. Instead he levelled his eyes thankfully on his.

'You are the head constable from Gloucester Cathedral, aren't you? You are Inspector Jorge Winter?'

'I am.'

'At last! I must have rung the dean a dozen times and asked what they wanted to do about her. This way, Inspector. She's been going crazy all cooped up. She'll be delighted to see you.'

'Interesting.'

It was not the intention of his investigation to interview any animal as such.

'The local police have been no help at all, Inspector. They told me to call the RSPCA. If only dogs could talk, eh? This one would soon solve your murder for you, I bet.'

'Who said anything about a murder?'

'What are you doing here, then?'

'Do me a favour, hurry it up.'

The huntsman pulled his tweed cap low over his eyebrows. His face was pink with a sense of rightful injustice, Jorge noted. His guide squeaked in his tight green Wellingtons as he led the way through the mini-castle. He explained on the way that he came from a family who had tended to the foxhounds here for many centuries.

'As I said, Inspector, I rang the Church as soon as our vet saw that her ear had been chipped, but no one has done a bloody thing about it. Then out of the blue you call to say that you're on your way over. Why all the delay and indecision? It's been eight months.'

'What can I tell you? Perhaps it's ecumenical.'

*

A row of stables with green upper and lower doors lined the wall at the back of the mock castle. Beyond that lay two more stables in an adjoining building with a pitched roof outside which lay brushes, scoops and barrows for clearing out muck and straw. It was to the last, shut door, that the grey-eyed huntsman led him.

'I'm Andy Bridgeman by the way.'

'Well, Mr Bridgeman, what's up with all the hounds? What's set them off?'

'Can't understand it, Inspector. It's not time for their raw meat yet.'

Andy bellowed in vain at the noisy, restless animals nearby. They had the run of a paved yard all of their own; they were putting their paws up to the wire mesh that kept them captive in order to press their white muzzles and brown heads together while they tried to get a better view of their mystery visitor.

'I never would have been able to put her in with them,' said Andy. 'They would have torn her to pieces.'

Jorge tried to close his ears to the awful baying.

'Torn?'

'We're talking about hounds, beagles and harriers. They're not pets, they're here to do a job.'

Andy slid back the bolts on the upper and lower doors to the stable. At once a strong smell of stale bedding filled the air.

'Time's up, Sasha.'

Jorge looked in uneasily.

'This her?'

'Correct. Name and address are on her microchip. That's how we discovered that she belonged to Reverend Luke Lyons. You'll have to ask the vet to change the records.'

'I'll come to that in due course.'

At rest on the straw lay a black and white bitch whose large egg-shaped face immediately indicated to him that she was some sort of Bull Terrier.

'Here, girl,' said Andy, clapping his hands.

'Is she well?'

'Perfectly well, Inspector. Come, Sasha, come and say hallo to your new owner.'

'You got that wrong.'

'Dogs like her were bred to fight other dogs after the ban on bull-baiting in 1835,' said Andy, approvingly. 'Bulldogs were too slow to fight, so breeders crossed them with terriers for that aggressive, ruthless streak.'

'If you say so.'

'You not convinced?'

'I'm just not sure there's enough dog there to fight anything.'

'That's because she's a miniature, Inspector. Bred for ratting. She comes from the runts of Bullterrier litters. Oh, and there's some Dalmatian in her for extra power and stamina.'

'Is she safe?'

'Bullterriers were ferocious fighters but the modern dog has a gentler side. Can be damned hard to dissuade if they do decide to act, though.'

'That's not massively reassuring.'

He studied Sasha's small, dark eyes and the scissors bite of her jaws. She gave a few welcoming flicks of her short, black tail. He was struck mostly, though, by her loneliness as he took out his notebook and pencil.

'You found her when and where exactly?'

Andy's face expressed surprise.

'Oh, no, I didn't find her, Inspector. She was given to me.'

'By whom?'

'It was the day after Reverend Lyons disappeared on the 31st of July last year. A woman marched into the yard. Stood right where you are now. Said I must take Sasha off her hands there and then because she was going away that very day.'

'She give a name at all?'

'No.'

'But you remember her face?'

There followed a not very coherent list of attributes. Ask two people to describe a person and they would invariably give different accounts, but Jorge wrote everything down on his pad anyway.

'Some say she was staying in Berkeley Castle. No one knows for sure, Inspector. But I can say that she was tall and thin and her hair was exceptionally red. Very striking. Spoke with a strong Welsh accent. Oh, and she wore black lipstick. Said she found Sasha running down the road and wanted to be rid of her.'

'You believe it was a fortuitous act of self-interest?'

'So now you want me to give you a better reason?'

'I'm interested in discovering who last saw Reverend Luke Lyons alive. Might it be this redhead, do you think?'

'I have absolutely no idea.'

'Still, you must have some clue where I can find her?'

'Trust me, she won't help you, Inspector.'

'On the contrary, I very much need to speak to anyone who might know whether some person or thing drove Reverend Lyons to kill himself.'

'She won't care.'

'He might have been in trouble and it might not have been his fault.'

'So he's dead, then? I knew it. I've been telling everyone in The Mariners Arms it was foul play all along.'

'You really don't want to do that. Believe me. That's a very bad idea.'

'You mean the Church is scared of a scandal? You've not come for the dog, have you Inspector? You've come to cover it all up?'

He made no response since the conversation threatened to go down a very difficult path indeed. He was suddenly at a loss to explain himself in anything like agreeable terms.

'Has your mysterious visitor ever shown her face again?'

'No, absolutely bloody not.'

'Can you be certain?'

'Yeah, I think I can.'

'I'm sorry to hear that.'

'So am I, Inspector.'

'Are you? Are you honestly?'

The hounds, by now, were becoming increasingly disturbed. They were hurling themselves angrily at their wire fence as though some demonic compulsion drove them to attack, even though all their attempts proved fruitless.

'About Reverend Lyons's bitch?' said Andy, holding open the stable door.

'What about her?'

'Don't forget to take her with you.'

'Oh no.'

'Fact is, she's a provocation to the hounds. You know what will have to be done if you don't…'

'Fact is, I can't lose sight of my mission.'

*

Safely ensconced in his camper van, Jorge eased off the brakes and let its 2ltr twin carb engine take him back to his B&B in Berkeley.

Which still begged the question, why in God's name was he really here?

It was to do, in part, with Church politics. The recent welcome appointment of a woman as Bishop of Gloucester remained controversial among certain members of the Church. The last thing she needed right now was some zealot or other stirring up trouble, she did not want any scandal on her watch to give them any ammunition against her.

But he had to tread carefully because he was on a very tight budget. While he personally was only being paid a little over twenty thousand pounds a year, it represented a significant cost to the diocese to fund the additional Security Manager and several constables that he was going to have to hire to keep the cathedral safe. So far he was on his own. That meant managing the safety of cash and artefacts, maintaining fire and intruder alarms on properties belonging to the Chapter, as well as patrolling the old Abbey grounds and providing security for VIP visits.

He had also to respond to enquiries about the Memorial Books from members of the public.

Hence, Frank Cordell's letters had come his way marked Strictly Confidential.

He had been provided with the file on disciplinary measures concerning Rev. Luke Lyons just prior to his disappearance. Such a process was started by a formal written complaint which was made to the diocesan bishop. No anonymous complaints were accepted. The complaint contained certain prescribed information, was signed and verified by a statement of truth and had written evidence in support.

As such, he had some facts and names to go on but there had to be more to it than met the eye?

Somebody in the Church was obviously very worried since he had been given carte blanche to investigate.

He felt certain of one thing. Andy had known the name of the redhead who had left Sasha at the castle kennels, in what he would have him believe was a simple act of kindness.

Of course no one wanted such a dog.

What fool would?

At which point something very wet and slithery licked his chin.

He could discount the feeling of brief discomfort, but not of revulsion.

'Wow, that was unpleasant.'

Sasha sat up on his lap. She tried to look out of the camper van's windscreen. Behaved as though they were already the best of friends.

'Yeah, most likely it'll never happen but we've got to try, I suppose.'

The first day of his investigation had given him no reason to doubt what he already knew.

1. Luke vanished without explanation one Sunday last summer.

2. Police had investigated his clothes left at the riverside and had concluded that it was most likely suicide.

3. Luke left behind him a dog named Sasha.

Jorge stared at the river, its dark currents swirling past his window, and thought equally dark thoughts. He wondered whether it knew where Luke had gone. And what he'd run from? Or to?

Or whether he was ever coming home?

Chapter 6

Luke drove over Chelsea Bridge with Sasha on the seat beside him, even as intrepid people searched the Thames's beaches below him. With the storm tide came all sorts of relics and their hunters.

Acquisitive himself, he understood their acquisitiveness.

He, too, was a mudlark who loved to comb for coins, wig-curlers, Georgian jewellery or even the iron balls and chains once used to shackle condemned pirates that occasionally emerged from among all the used condoms and pebbles. Every river was the perfect depository for everyone's rubbish, losses and secrets.

And skeletons.

Every week at least one decomposing cadaver washed up with the tide in London.

'Don't worry, Sash, you'll love it where we're going now, you really will.'

Sasha sat shivering on her cushion in their very old Land Rover while behind them bumped a sailing dinghy on its four-wheeled metal trailer. She cocked her head on one side and eyed him suspiciously. Anyone could tell a dog a thing or two, but tone of voice was one of those fundamental prerequisites of the man-dog relationship. That's why the inability to lie took such special talent.

Suddenly the latest weather bulletin crackled over the radio.

Another turbulent front was expected to make landfall in the early hours after crossing the Atlantic.

The London to Penzance railway, meanwhile, had fallen into the sea at Dawlish. It was not without precedent. Such acts had once been deemed more spiritual than meteorological. Contemporary pamphlets had said of one such storm in the seventeenth century, it was *'God's warning to the people of England by the great overflowing of the waters or floods'.*

Severed branches littered the roads after such a tempestuous night. Fog turned to icy rain as the savagely split sky lit up and blinded him every few seconds. Or, as Adele's song would have it, thought Luke, with a shiver: 'There was something in the water, now that something's in me.'

He lost sight of reassuring suburbs that fast dissolved into nothing.

There was snow on the hills and the temperature plummeted the further west they travelled.

The way the sleet pursued the Land Rover fuelled some apprehension on his part – it was the lashing, scaly swipes of something serpentine and living. Violent strokes of head, limb and tail spat at him against his windscreen. Hissed a challenge.

'What the hell. It's just a shower.'

Three hours later they stopped at a layby high on the Cotswolds, two thirds of the way to their destination. A dark red bus-cum-café offered him All Day Breakfast.

He had just sat down with some coffee at a table next to a steamed up window, when his phone rang.

'Listen to me, Luke, I can't stand it any more! Molly, my grey mare, has collided with a wall. Nearly knocked her fucking eyeball out. It's too fucking much, I tell you, what with this stupid wedding and the farm going to pieces. Did you order the flowers yet? All I've done so far today is milk the cows.'

It was his twin sister Ellie.

'Relax. For £3000 the wedding reception tables will be covered with crystal vases filled with fragrant white blooms just you as you want.'

'Doesn't mean you have to sound so cynical.'

When one sibling called another he ought not to behave like a pious fraud in his godly clothes.

He ought not to attempt to sound too soothing like the saint he really wasn't, thought Luke, as he fed Sasha a sausage.

'No, well, yeah, it seems an awful lot for a few lily of the valley and ranunculus.'

He was dressed in his clerical collar which he had found so hard to earn, but realistically he could only aim to offer advice that was unlikely to be fulfilled.

33

'Please, Luke, do you think the silver and white tea-lights will be all right?'

'Don't ask me, ask mother.'

'Very funny.'

'You saw her on TV, then?'

'It would be nice to be able to cut her out of the preparations altogether.'

'From the way she was talking she could fly home from Spain at any moment.'

'That's just it, I'm already the talk of the town which is *so* embarrassing. The whole of Berkeley suddenly remembers I'm Jessica Kennedy's daughter.'

'So what? It's not as if *you* were ever the criminal.'

'That TV broadcast has brought it all back just when I thought I'd put it all behind me. Jeremy, my fiancé, is being quite good about it, but really, can I expect him to marry me now he knows I was born in prison?'

'You hadn't told him?'

'What do you think?'

He should have sympathised. Had he not chosen to be known as Lyons instead of Kennedy, in order to live up to the notorious family legend?

That tattoo on his neck, half woman and half dangerous water spirit, was like his father's – it signified his honorary, if posthumous, membership of the Severn Sea Gang. It was his way of picturing what might have been.

His much more sensible sister wished to forget all about it.

'Of course you must go through with your wedding, Ellie. You owe it to your son, Randal. And me. This is a whole new beginning for us all.'

'I thought that last time.'

'You couldn't predict that your first husband would die in a car accident.'

'How do you know? You weren't there. I was drunk, depressed. Having my loving brother in my life might have made all the difference.'

'I very much doubt it.'

'Doesn't mean you can't be there for me now, Luke.'

'How many times must I say it – I will officiate at your wedding.'

'We haven't exactly been a proper brother and sister, have we?'

'No, but that's over now.'

34

He could tolerate the awkward pause but not the underlying awkwardness.

'You staying at grandma's house?' asked Ellie suddenly. 'You'll find the key in the greenhouse.'

'Thanks but I have other plans.'

'You'll still need the keys.'

'Fine with me.'

'Jeremy says that if Gwendolen only appoints one attorney we won't be able to sell Chapel Cottage over her head. Is that true?'

'I'll explain when I see you.'

'Good luck with that.'

Ellie abruptly announced that she was suffering from a headache and rang off. It was but a temporary reprieve. Even the most dysfunctional families had to sort out awkward things sooner or later.

He turned off the M5 at a sign that pointed to Berkeley Castle. The coming of the motorway had redirected the bulk of the traffic elsewhere during his years away, until the wider world had ceased to impinge on this forgotten and sparsely populated hinterland.

Now most people only came to see where King Edward II was murdered so horrifically with a red-hot poker?

He was determined but truly this last turn proved daunting. The long straight road was littered with storm-tossed twigs that struck loud blows on his Land Rover's rusty chassis.

'Not to worry, Sash. We're nearly there.'

When a reformed person decided to return home, however diffidently, he should not have to creep along to the town where he was born like some sort of rat anxious to get back to its ship. He was looking ahead for the first signs of Sharpness Docks.

Memory played tricks on him, however. In order to see all the way to the River Severn he first had to see over the brow of the next hill.

Whatever else may have happened, no matter how many wrong turnings he had taken in the recent past, his real roots lay here.

Besides, only a man of God had the right to claim might on his side and such a person alone could raise his avenging hand. That he could do so, now he was so morally armed, gave him the chance to reflect on the true nature of good and evil.

He gave Sasha a pat even as he felt his heart pound. Surely that TV broadcast by his so-called mother wasn't going to start a hare, ruin everything?

Chapter 7

It was all a vile conspiracy, thought Jorge, as he paid a pound to cross Clifton Suspension Bridge into Bristol.

A newspaper headline had just confirmed his deepest suspicions: Diet Health Drinks Warning.

Ever since switching to sugar-free fizzy drinks he had begun to drink more *because* it was healthy.

Nobody of his admirably impressive bulk should suffer from so many tasty choices that turned out to make things worse, not better, for the sake of someone's else's profits?

He tossed his empty can into a box in the back of the van; rattled its pyramidal pile.

Sasha gave him a significant stare. Clearly she was not impressed. As a result, he drove straight ahead and said, 'I'm entirely confident that I can lose a stone in a month. That's the plan.'

A silver ribbon of water flowed hundreds of feet below him. Some sensation of floating in the air naturally entered his head so high in the sky. He mentally signed himself with the figure of the cross, secretly urged cars in front of him to go faster.

'Mother of God, why aren't we moving?'

Drivers began to leave their stationary vehicles. They stood about on the bridge's decking. All looked one way.

Jorge and Sasha did the same but first he donned his peaked cap with its white-diced band.

Sasha's head was high and her black ears were erect. She asked for more reassurance than he could possibly give her as they walked up to a taxi driver who was reaching urgently for his phone.

'What is it?' asked Jorge. 'Why have we stopped?'

'There's a jumper.'

'Man or woman?'

'Does it matter?'

Sure enough, a distant figure was doing his best to scale the bridge's safety barriers. Jorge looked down. Gnarled trees, thorny roses and rampant elder clung to the vertical sides of the gorge dug by feuding giants. This was an ancient place once revered by superstitious people where wolves, wild boar and bears had roamed many thousands of years ago at a bend in the river called the Coiled Dragon. The monster's steamy breath still bubbled through the mud in the form of a spring just below them at Hotwell. It made the perfect place for people to worship wind, earth, fire and water. He could not describe the deadly chill that gripped his heart. It was a feeling of absolute dread.

Another few feet and the climber would outdistance all his helpers – he was behaving like someone chased by devils.

'How absurd is this? Must it really be me who has to talk him down?'

Sasha stared at him quizzically, narrowed her eyes. She looked directly ahead without comment.

He glanced at his watch. He could spare a minute.

*

Young men and women smiled, pointed and made kitten noises to exclaim what was to them almost an epiphany. Astonishment was no less infectious. The peculiarity of it all held them spell-bound. It was a base alloy of fascination, curiosity, jeopardy and joy. Like him, though, they still couldn't quite believe their eyes.

'Bet you he does it?' cried a ginger-haired youth.

'Shit,' said another, inspecting his phone. 'Would you believe it, my battery's dying.'

'Never thought I'd live to see the day this happens.'

'Please stand aside,' said Jorge firmly with a wave of his black leather glove.

He cast his eye up and down the barriers that had been erected since 1998 to help stop this very scenario.

From here he could see the climber's shabby blue business suit.

Already the would-be jumper resembled a fly in the sky. It was not all bad. In 1885 the billowing skirts of the young Sarah Ann Henley had acted as her parachute. She had jumped off the bridge and hit soft mud at low tide, only to survive to go on to live into her eighties.

Or, to put it another way, what was it about bridges that so inspired people to do something so utterly stupid? He was mostly thinking about himself at this critical juncture. He hated heights.

Sasha stopped to scratch her head. She was not so ignorant. There were all sorts of connections to things he'd never see.

'Hi there, my name is Jorge Winter. What's yours?'

The frightened man had his back to him but he could see how much he was shaking.

'You can't help me. No one can.'

'Please come down, you're holding up a shitload of traffic.'

Jorge began to climb. He clawed at the wire and dug at it with the slippery toes of his boots. Shifted his weight from hip to hip as well as shoulder to shoulder. Each step took him a little further up one side of the safety cage while the man clung to the other by his nails.

He could feel the bridge's decking move slightly beneath him in the strong wind, or he imagined it. But why should he worry? Such sideways play might shake a braver person's faith in himself, but a good, sound bridge was the safest way to pass the otherwise impassable? People had used ropes, stones and logs to make this world their own ever since humankind had first colonised the Earth. Iron, steel and concrete had been but the natural developments of the same desire. In that way, one person relied on another to build them something that could be used without question. It was a matter of trust – people built bridges for each other and it was unbelievable that they should ever fail.

'Now, sir, please listen to me carefully. I want you to look me in the eye and then do as I do. We're going to descend together.'

'Why should you care?'

'That's why I'm here.'

Jorge learnt later that the fifty-year-old man had enjoyed a very good job until recently. He had travelled the world, been married twice and had a nineteen-year-old daughter from his first marriage. He had once driven a top of the range BMW, worked for foreign charities and co-authored a report on artesian wells in Africa where he witnessed the death of a friend in an ambush in Congo. Then, after the collapse of his second marriage he had returned to Bristol where he had suffered a total breakdown. Just after Christmas he had ended up homeless. It was a fact that he had been abused as a child. A place was found for him in a boarding house but in March he had moved into a hostel. By his own admission he had a drink problem and was prone to bouts of extreme violence to others and also self-harm, but they never got to talk about any of it.

That man was gone.

*

There stood at ninety degrees to the Avon Gorge an impressive terrace of Georgian houses, Jorge discovered, as he checked the address on his piece of paper.

House number one literally hung off the edge into the air but was massively constructed from great blocks of stone five floors high. Four tapered pillars at its front formed classical embellishments that enforced the verticality of the windows, all very elegant or otherwise proportionally disposed.

However, a sign said SOLD on the railings that fenced off the house's boarded up basement while internal white wooden shutters hid all its windows.

This was not the sort of place in which he expected to find an ex-con like Cordell.

'What the devil!' he thought, suddenly afflicted by a feeling of uncertainty and disappointment.

This time he left his cap in the van.

Sasha raised her right paw to the front door of the house. Found it open. She vanished through the gap with a more or less instant wriggle.

He, too, placed his gloved hand on the door and gave it a push, although he was overcome by a greater reluctance to follow.

'Yeah, I mean, should I even be here?' he wondered aloud.

That instant he felt his reluctance turn to aversion as he examined the names on the bell-pushes. It was Cordell's daughter's door on which he expected to come banging and she had moved on?

Caustic tiles led into the reception hall with its impressive old staircase.

Fine paper hung on striped walls as Jorge prepared to tread in the footsteps of those elegant ladies and gentlemen who had once come to sample Clifton's rival version of the spa at Bath.

From one ceiling hung a great chandelier in the shape of a glassy octopus. He blinked and the gloriousness of it all disappeared.

He was, in reality, standing in a building site earmarked for total renovation.

'Cordell! Are you there? It's Inspector Jorge Winter. I'm here on behalf of Rev. Luke Lyons.'

He had always admired Luke. They had been on the same wavelength. The way of thinking that others so misunderstood.

The reckless way. The ruleless way. The free way. The wild way.

Cavernous spaces echoed to his footsteps and felt undeniably deserted and cold. It was the chilling effect of so much stone. Or he couldn't stop thinking of the man who had just vanished off the bridge into the void. That broke all the rules, too.

Sasha growled. She had neither person not object in sight but her nose remained pressed to the bare floorboards.

Suddenly she whined and pawed the floor at his feet.

'You got something?' asked Jorge.

Sasha turned her head. Watched him with her baleful eyes. Sighed.

There could be no doubt. On the bare boards by the window lay a great many discarded cigarette butts. He gathered up all the crumpled remains in the palm of one hand and held them briefly to his nose. They smelt warm.

'Come out Cordell! It's me, Jorge Winter. Don't be alarmed. I come alone.'

As it happened, there was easy access to the roof from one of the bedrooms on the fifth floor.

A crumbling stone balustrade ran right round the top of the house, Jorge discovered somewhat cautiously.

Here elegant partygoers had once promenaded beneath the stars on balmy summer nights to behold the view of Bristol's pretty red and brown roofs and its docks.

Although the River Avon bypassed the Floating Harbour in a very unprepossessing, muddy ditch at low tide, there was something about it that still enthralled with a sense of legend. That was because it had taken its name from a Wiltshire-born merry belle called Avona. Thus had ancient people invested dangerous but life-giving waters with a human name that was an embodiment of the inexplicable mystery of their lives.

The vista inspired a new dizziness in him, something akin to a sour dismissal of all things mythical.

Within the docks floated a tall ship, half lost in shimmer and appearing like some Fata Morgana, so like an illusion did it seem on the sunlit water. Something else about it appealed to him – a dangerously fascinating allurement whose siren call he would have done well to resist.

Jorge could admire the vessel's elegant lines but not her colour. It was entirely black. The three-masted schooner struck him as incongruous and a trifle sinister. Its whole presence he could recognise only as somehow disturbingly ominous.

Suddenly Jorge became aware of a frightening turmoil in his stomach, a sort of vertigo, barely worthy of notice at first but making him feel sicker and sicker. He looked away from the view and it passed.

It was what he had felt when trying to save the suicide.

'Well, I'll be damned!' he said aloud and gazed back into space.

The gorge plunged before him with its healing steam from its dragon's nostrils. The river's serpentine strip of mercurial liquid lapped the mud on its way out to the Atlantic Ocean. He had, from up here, a god-like vista, he was Vincent the giant as he hewed out the gorge with his pick-axe while his rival Goram slept off the effects of strong ale. Poor Goram. After he had failed to win the hand of fair Avona he had run like a mad dog to Weston-super-Mare; he had thrown himself down in the mud at Whorle Down ever since when the water of the Severn had recoiled twice a day with a roar. Terrified witnesses called the portent the bore.

Next moment all thought of a giant hitting the ground with a splat took on special significance.

His increasing giddiness was difficult to deny since at first his eyes did their upmost to deceive him.

As he dared to lean over the parapet, he observed far below him several smashed terracotta pots which lay in a little, paved garden that was fenced on three sides by black railings.

A sack hung off the wrought iron spears.

Not long, though, could he deny what he saw.
That was no sack, it was human.

Chapter 8

'The devil!' cried Luke.

He braked hard to bring his Land Rover to a slippery stop just in time to see two elegant black horses turn across the road right in front of him.

Whoever made very stately progress did so as if they owned the entire road out of Berkeley. He felt the blood rush to his head. They blocked his path as they pulled a boat-shaped coffin through the gate that led to the nearby castle.

Sasha leapt back on to her seat. She placed her front paws on her cushion. Looked to see what was happening.

'Sorry, Sash. Not my fault.'

Black roses spelt the name STEPHEN inside the hearse's glass sides, but otherwise he had no idea who the deceased was or how he'd come to die.

Never one for delays, Luke gave everyone a quick toot on his horn. The leading mourner, a tall, thin, red-haired woman in a long black gown turned very slightly his way and lifted her papery veil.

She wore broad black lipstick while at her throat hung avian claws in a necklace strung with blue crystals and black beads on baroque swirls. Below the claws hung three large pearls from some distant ocean.

Her face disappeared again, with a slow turn of her head, behind her wide brimmed, black lace fedora. The hat was topped by a felt fascinator with waxed satin ribbons that had been cut and sewn, sprayed and stiffened to create a conch or shell-trumpet of a Triton. It resembled some witty, surrealist cocktail hat of the 1930s.

Or it was the sort of thing worn by Lady Gaga at MTV Video Music Awards – think steak hats and telephones, he decided.

He admitted defeat and switched off the Land Rover's engine.

There walked beside the redhead a younger, dark-haired woman also in mourning. Small but athletic, she wore 'widow faux fur' on her coat as well as square, cat-eye sunglasses and black crosses for earrings.

The fascinator on her large black hat had been fashioned into some immoderate but appropriately marine shape, too. Serpentine ribbons and beads resembled a black seahorse round which had been woven the lilac funnel-shaped flowers of sea-lavender.

The two mourners processed towards the parish church of St. Mary to which he himself had just been appointed. Next minute, there came the awful ruckus of some quarrelsome and unkind dirge, for which there seemed no earthly reason. He could scarcely credit it but a great many nesting birds appeared profoundly upset among their budding branches, which very much upset him too.

He gave Sasha a pat on the back.

'Relax, it's just some ghastly rookery overlooking the castle walls.'

He risked another look at the procession.

With it walked a man dressed in black who was sobbing his eyes out.

Suddenly his phone rang in his coat pocket. It was Ellie again.

'How about you tell me where the hell you are?'

'I'm stuck outside Berkeley Castle.'

'Please come to the farm right away. Mother called from Spain. Didn't I say she would?'

'What does she want now?'

'Can't trust me to plan my own wedding.'

'I see.'

'No, you don't. You don't know what it's like having her try to muscle in like this.'

Luke sighed.

'We've had this conversation once today already.'

'Doesn't mean she can sail back into my life just because I'm getting married.'

'Listen, Ellie, Jess is my curse. She doesn't have to be yours, too.'

'It's a curse, all right, it's who we are.'

'But what does she really want, that's what I want to know?'

'She says she feels left out. Not because she screwed up the past but because of the future.'

'Is there a difference?'

'So, when am I, like, going to see you, brother? I'm cooking chicken for dinner tonight.'

'Give me the rest of the day to get settled.'

'That's not fair. That's not kind.'

'Don't forget I start work tomorrow.'

'So?'

'As well as your new parish vicar I'm the new visiting chaplain at the local prison.'

'Listen here, Luke, don't try to be clever.'

'But I have a pile of paperwork to get through.'

'Do what you like, then.'

'What's that supposed to mean?'

'You're stalling, I can tell.'

'Don't give me that, I'll see you on Tuesday.'

'Damn right you will. It's been thirty-five years.'

'Makes sense.'

'Wait, Luke.'

'What is it?'

'Welcome home.'

Moments later the last of the funeral procession filed into Berkeley Castle's tree-lined grounds on the way to the church.

Presiding at such funerals would be his job from now on, thought Luke optimistically, as he restarted the Land Rover's engine and drove into town.

A newsagent emerged from his shop's doorway. He hurriedly unclipped the freestanding, wire billboard on the wet pavement. Displayed the latest newspaper headline for all to see: **Second Gruesome Find On Severn Shore.**

Luke did a slow circuit of Berkeley's once familiar streets as he became aware that his horizon was lit by a visible presence of a different sort. He saw wink at him down narrow streets some intermittent but insistent flashes in a strange Morse code whose true nature he had thought to forget.

Each dot and dash, each long and short flash were the tell-tale signals of some living creature which tried to awaken his attention?

He could purposely shut his eyes, if not ignore the silvery snake so close by him. It was high tide on the River Severn.

There was something about so much water that gave an impression of magnificence, but not necessarily of magnanimity. He felt himself clench the Land Rover's steering wheel more firmly than he could explain.

For as long as he had known it the Severn had been a source of both brightness and darkness, as he recalled not only how it had nearly drowned his best friend but had actually killed his grandfather.

It was said that rivers always gave up their dead, but this was not simply him honouring the family hero, this was the river as reminder.

He'd always thought that one day that old Sean Lyons would walk back out of the water.

So strong were the tides that flowed east as far as Gloucester or ebbed west to Bristol that until Tudor times the estuary had been known as the Severn Sea. It still was in Welsh where it was known as Mor Hafren and in Cornish, Mor Havren. The ancient riverine frontier seemed to him to have unfinished business with all manner of people and matters as yet unspoken.

It was strangely compelling, as if it promised to invite feelings he never knew he had.

No, he had invited it.

So here he was.

He towed his boat past a few houses across the otherwise uninhabited flood plain. They were in an ancient Manor once included in a grant of the Barony of Berkeley, bestowed upon Robert Fitzharding by Henry II of England after he assumed the throne in the twelfth century.

Sasha sat up beside him and sniffed the air.

'What is it, Sash? You want a wee or something? Not to worry, this is the place if I'm not mistaken.'

With that he stopped the Land Rover at the end of a long, curving driveway high above the village of Hill and jumped out.

Sasha followed, not flinching from what they might find.

Bushes had been allowed to encroach on all sides.

He did not baulk at the prospect of being challenged, although the chilly silence was sufficient hindrance.

A bird table stood somewhat incongruously on an oval island dense with small trees and shrubs, right outside a gloomy old house's front entrance. Sasha barked. It appeared that her nostrils alerted her to some invisible presence to which he was not yet privy. She could uncover the trail of footprints, if not the actual revenant trailed – she was retracing his childhood footsteps.

A large lake lay at the base of a grassy slope where yellow marsh marigolds shone like cups of gold along its shore. Elsewhere in the grounds stood a dovecote and stables. He was confused and surprised not simply by the number of paths he had to follow, but by the high brick walls that encompassed him on all sides.

That's because whenever he had been here before, his friend Jorge had been obliged to sneak him in and out to avoid his cantankerous father.

At last, there stood Hill House's very old sundial in the middle of an overgrown lawn just as he remembered it, overlooked by a raised stone terrace.

Next minute he heard a voice.

'You the new reverend, at all? You Reverend Luke Lyons?'

'I am.'

A man in blue overalls descended the terrace's broad steps with a clipboard in his hand.

'Removals. We've brought all your stuff from storage in London. A weird lot it is, too. Like a bleedin' museum, innit? Never moved a stuffed shark before.'

'Bravo.'

That everything he needed to begin his new life was in that lorry, there could be no doubt, thought Luke. But how past and future would fit together was still a big puzzle to him.

Chapter 9

'Sasha, with me!'

Jorge was alarmed and sickened, not simply by what he had already seen from the roof of No 1 Windsor Terrace but by the confirmation that came with it.

Whoever wriggled on the spear-point fence did so like a pig on a spit. They had fallen backwards on to the iron railings from a great height.

On one side the victim's feet barely touched the garden slabs while on the other his head and arms dangled above the sheer drop into the Avon Gorge. Agony caused him to gasp for breath, but barely could he utter a single intelligible plea for help. His duffel coat was torn at its toggles to expose a hideously twisted hip from which white bone protruded through his ripped trousers.

And, horror of horrors, Jorge observed, the brow above his one good eye oozed brain. It was Frank Cordell.

'Careful Sasha. Don't get blood on your paws.'

So saying, Jorge donned a pair of white plastic gloves from his pocket. In no way was he going to ruin his black leather ones.

He mounted the brick wall at the base of the railings. He reached out to the victim, frantic and fumbling.

'Frank? Can you hear me? It's Inspector Jorge Winter.'

Honestly, he feared the worst. Cordell suddenly choked. Spat a few words. How long he had been hanging there he could not be sure, but it seemed likely that he had only just regained semi-consciousness.

'What's that, you say? Speak up Frank, damn you.'

'The Bible? You have it, Inspector?'

'For God's sake, since when does that matter now?'

'It's all on account of… Revelation 15:2.'

'Are you mad?'

Of course he had *a* Bible somewhere back in the camper van, but this hardly seemed the time.

But what else was he to do? Cordell had hold of his wrist. He seemed possessed by the Devil.

'In Rex Lyons's Bible… Gold.'

Next moment the stricken man groaned and from the corner of his broken mouth poured more blood. A spear had punctured a lung.

'Go easy, Frank. What are you trying to tell me?'

'Beware, in the river: *and before the throne there was something like a sea of glass, like crystal; and in the centre and around the throne, four living creatures full of eyes in front and back…*'

'That's from Revelation. What about it?'

'Find it before anyone else does. Do right to negate wrong…'

'Not my call.'

'Then burn that Bible before it burns you in hell.'

Cordell lapsed back into unconsciousness. When someone talked blasphemy it could not be good news.

'Listen to me Cordell, we had a deal. Wake up, you bastard. You said you know why Reverend Luke Lyons has disappeared? You say he isn't dead. Why?'

Cordell opened his mouth but not his eyes.

'*She will give you the treasures of darkness.*'

'Who is 'she', Frank?'

'Know this, Inspector… Reverend Luke Lyons never walked into any river.'

'Don't be ridiculous. The police did a full investigation. There is absolutely no evidence of foul play.'

Something avaricious burned in Cordell's good eye as he uttered a few feeble syllables with his reptilian tongue.

'He's gone to the Devil, Inspector, thanks to his greed. I should never have told him what I knew… I had no idea what he'd do with it… But you can still make it right, you can stop him before he goes any further. Go get the fucker back. Get rich in the process if you must.'

'That's insane.'

'Luke was your best friend was he not, Inspector?'

'That was a long time ago. What can you possibly stand to gain if I do what you say?'

'The cheating bastard gets to make amends.'

'And if he really is dead?'

'You believe in Lazarus, or what?'

'So you literally think that Reverend Lyons can come back from the dead?'

Cordell slid another inch down the railings before either of them could realise what was happening.

'That bastard said he was my friend. I thought him an honest person who loved his fellow humans. I hope right now he's in a living hell. Whatever you do, Inspector, take care. Remember Rex's Bible: *For where your treasure is, there will your heart be also.*'

He recognised Luke 12.34. Had not Luke himself quoted those very words in his written riposte to the Church's preliminary enquiry into his conduct? On Cordell's face came a smile. Not that it did him much good. He died.

*

Jorge tore off his white plastic gloves. Made a call on his phone.

'My name is Jorge Winter. I need an ambulance and fire brigade. There's been a terrible accident….'

Tearing loose the knot in his black tie, he breathed hard to fill his lungs. He did his best to calm his heaving chest. Looked past the stone lions on the prettily decorated loggia and terrace. Saw again the black sailing ship far below in the harbour. He had the impression that it had just come a long way.

Which was when a prayer suddenly entered his head which he used to give Cordell some sort of blessing:

'Be merciful to me, O God, be merciful to me,

for my soul takes refuge in you;

In the shadow of your wings will I take refuge

Until the storm of destruction has passed by.'

He reconsidered the inauspicious ramblings of the dead man as he took care to withdraw his highly polished black boots from drips of red. There ended his sympathy. Very little that he had been told so far squared with what he knew of 'Lucky' Luke Lyons, but then he hadn't spoken to him for decades. The best loved person could change a lot over time.

Rather than solve any queries, that mention of a Bible only posed more questions.

*

Part-way through his statement to the Avon and Somerset police Jorge confessed that he was a policeman, too.

The officers looked blank.

'Sorry to ask, sir, but what does that mean, exactly?'

'Want to ring Gloucester Cathedral? Check out my identity? I'm Inspector Jorge Winter.'

'If it's all right with you, sir, DI Thompson wants a word.'

'You do what you have to.'

A short, balding man dressed in a creased grey suit came straight over.

'I don't even want to think about what you are doing here, Mr Winter.'

'Just doing my job, Detective Inspector.'

'Not right now you don't.'

'As I've told your men, I spoke to the deceased in prison only yesterday.'

Jorge noted the critical contradiction of the smile on the lean man's face and registered the cold look in his eyes. Those same eyes grew greyer, as grey as his badly pressed suit, as their gazes clashed.

'You have to forget about interfering in things that don't concern you, Mr Winter.'

He looked down at his toes. There was one ugly spot of blood on his boot after all.

'Don't see how I can, Detective Inspector.'

'This is a matter for the Bristol police now. You have no jurisdiction here in Clifton or anywhere else.'

'I know your arguments already. I don't need to hear them again.'

'Here's a thing. If I find you poking your nose into matters that don't concern you, life will go very badly for you.'

'Tell yourself that.'

'I don't like people who masquerade as cops.'

'Come on. Admit it. You love it.'

'Now we have all your details, Mr Winter, we'll be in touch if we need to speak to you again.'

'Fact is, the deceased just left HMPL... not too far from here. His name is Frank Cordell. He may have run into someone who bore him a grudge. Many a newly released prisoner meets his match from a former enemy as soon as he walks free. Some people wait years to settle old scores.'

'Might mean nothing.'

'He was a convicted paedophile, remember.'

'This is my case. You got a problem with that?'

'Why would I?'

'Goodbye Mr Winter.'

'Then I'm free to go?'

'Take my advice. Stay out of it. I've enough on my plate today already. A man just jumped off Clifton Bridge.'

Jorge turned his back on the death scene.

'I'm having quite a day, too. You hungry, Sasha?'

Sasha looked up. It was not a very friendly look but he made no comment. A dog was entitled to her own opinion.

With that, he decided to walk down to the harbour. To hell with his diet. He felt a sudden need to eat like an Olympian.

*

A poster on the wall of a floating restaurant at the dockside advertised a performance of Das Rheingold as Jorge ordered lunch. That tale was all about lost gold, too. All you had to do to find it was to renounce love.

'Is that what you've done, Luke, my friend? Or has love renounced you?'

53

It sounded such an impossible thing to do, like forgoing good food. So saying, he was very conscious of his shaky hands. He did his best to keep tight hold of the spoon with which he stirred his coffee.

Rattled himself, he tried not to rattle.

Whereas someone else might have sought professional help for their problems, Luke had chosen oblivion? Sought the mad maelstrom, the unfathomable whirlpool? To leave home.

The tall ship that had attracted Jorge's attention from the top of the gorge lay berthed just across the water at Baltic Wharf. The black iron hull with its single funnel amidships was extremely elegant, almost streamlined, with one square-rigged and two schooner-rigged iron masts as secondary sail power. The ship cast its long shadow on the Floating Harbour's silvery surface while a row of false gun ports along its side gave it the semblance of a warship from long ago.

There was absolutely no sign of any crew. Its combination of smoking funnel and absolute stillness he could only admit was mildly mysterious.

'Don't see many ships like that, I must say,' commented a spiky-haired waitress with black eyelids and matching fingernails. The badge on her shirt said Lucy.

'What's she doing here?' asked Jorge.

He did not much feel like eating after all.

'They do say she's crossed the Atlantic.'

'Who's her captain?'

'Dunno. But the police are crawling all over her as we speak. There's a dead body on board, apparently. Don't know much else about it so far. No one does.'

'Got you.'

'As I said, she hit a storm and sustained some damage.'

'Does she have a name, at all?'

Lucy studied the silver diamonds on his shirt's epaulettes.

'You a cop, too?'

'Inspector Jorge Winter.'

'Never had a real cop in here before.'

'Am I that convincing?'

'I think being a cop is sexy.'

'What's that ship's name again?'

'Search me. It's a long walk round to that side of the docks or you can take the bridge across Cumberland Basin.'

She was positively drawn to one thing in particular, Jorge noted, so much so that her frequent returns to his table became quite rude, not to say unnerving.

'They do say it's the Devil's ship, Inspector.'

'You serious?'

'Makes my flesh creep,' said Lucy and fled back to the kitchen.

An hour later Jorge stopped to button his coat as he stepped back on shore. He had, from here, a clear view of the black ship across the harbour.

The inquisitive Lucy had a point because something about it made his flesh crawl.

It was the ship's figurehead. It was no pretty lady but a grinning human skeleton that hung on chains by its head and pelvis from the vessel's bowsprit. A hideous curvature of the bony spine lent the abominable thing a semblance of sinuous life as it flexed its empty ribcage in the breeze.

Bones and chains rattled horribly whenever the leering cadaver raised or lowered its calcified arm in order to proffer its drinking cup to the sea. With its other hand it clasped a hawser. The skull's fleshless jaws gaped with delight at its awful toast to the waves.

He was outraged and amused, not simply by the novelty of the figurehead, but by the unsettling audacity of whoever had put it there. How could anyone be unaffected by this gloomy harbinger of death so plain to see in the bright spring air? On the doomster's back danced three much smaller skeletons like children.

Lucy was correct, it looked to be a long walk round the harbour via the bridge. Sasha sat up on her cushion in the camper van to greet him. She pressed the tip of her nose to the window as he started the engine.

Clifton Suspension Bridge had reopened as police concentrated on recovering the body of the jumper from the mud below.

Too much to hope that he survived?

Tried to settle the flutter in his heart.

His thoughts focused again on Rex Lyons's Bible as he drove out of Bristol.

There was no mention of it in the notes in his case file but that particular copy of the Good Book held special significance for Rev. Luke's disappearance, according to Frank Cordell. What if that's what the killers wanted when they showed him the view from the roof?

There could be but one explanation – the most unfavourable one.

'Consider this a warning, Sasha. Somebody wants to know the same thing we do?'

Worse, what if Frank blabbed before he flew?

Chapter 10

'What do you mean, you have something to tell me *in confidence*?' said Luke, declining to shake the prisoner's hand. It was Tuesday, March 29th 2016, his first day at work in HMPL…. 'I'm your new chaplain. What else?'

'Don't be such a fool, reverend.'

He again tried to turn away. To ignore the other man's iron grip on his wrist was dangerous, though. He stopped moving. He had not been able to believe his luck when he saw Cordell's name on his list of prisoners for counselling today. It was like someone's idea of a bad joke.

'I don't have time for your silly mysteries.'

'Surely you remember who fenced those jewels for you in London not so very long ago?'

'How can anyone ever forget the great Frank Cordell?'

'My point exactly.'

'Believe me, I've done my best.'

That was not to say that he didn't feel some sympathy for the old man as he sat down in his office, thought Luke. The gap-toothed felon had a wall eye, courtesy of a cellmate's razor and dislike of child abusers at his previous jail. His cheeks, too, had the unhealthy pallor of someone who had, as a consequence, avoided the exercise yard for his own safety.

But now he was in an open prison things were a little more relaxed in preparation for his eventual release back into the community.

Cordell smiled.

'I am still your friend, Luke, believe me.'

'Hardly.'

'Yet you answered my call.'

'I didn't have to. Okay, it's good to see you alive, Frank. Never expected you to make it this far. I sure as hell didn't expect to make it myself.'

'Happy times, eh, Luke?'

'Is that what this is about?'

'Listen to me, reverend. Your father and I did time together on and off in prison, as you know. I was in jail when Rex Lyons died because of that deadly brawl in the showers. I saw Paul Colley stab him in the throat with a sharpened pencil, as a result of which Rex contracted sepsis which the doctors failed to detect in time. It killed him. End of story.'

'Amen to that.'

'Except it isn't.'

'Paul later hanged himself in his cell.'

'That's because Rex had powerful friends.'

Luke stared out of the window for a moment to the prison gates beyond.

'Is this why you wanted to see me, Frank? To dredge something up? Well done, you.'

'Believe me, reverend, I'm on your side.'

'Somehow I doubt it.'

'Yeah, long story.'

'I'm past all that now, anyway.'

'Are you, reverend? Then why are you here?'

'I'm here to do my job.'

'Doesn't mean Rex died for no reason.'

Luke left the window and faced the table; he was both horrified and fascinated to meet this ghost from the past.

'Listen, Frank, I've said it once and I'll say it again. I'm the Reverend Luke Lyons now. What do I care about what you think about my father's murderer? It's one crook's opinion of another.'

'Oh no, it's more than that.'

'You don't say.'

'Rex Lyons died to keep his secret.'

'Secret? What secret?'

'You know that very well.'

'I don't have time for this, I really don't.'

'Perhaps you know more than you realise.'

Cordell's cyclopean eye bore into Luke. It reminded him how everything concerning his father's death had forever been shrouded in the unnatural fog of incarceration.

'Don't mess with me, Frank. You hear me?'

'Honestly? You don't want to know?'

'As a Christian I feel I should turn the other cheek.'

'You? The 'Lucky' Luke Lyons who wouldn't hesitate to settle a score with his own gun?'

'What can I tell you? In London every gang had to look after its own.'

'Fact is, reverend, I'm prepared to give up my evil ways like you. What if God wants me to help you in order to save us both? Don't I deserve forgiveness, too?'

'Technically.'

'Rex Lyons speaks to me from 'the other side', reverend. I hear his whispers in my head from beyond the grave every day.'

'I'm really happy for you.'

'Damn it, Luke, will you listen to me or not? Do it as a man of God if not as an old friend?'

When a prisoner suddenly professed that he had seen the light in something like a spiritual conversion, then he had to wonder, thought Luke. If not risky the ploy was no less repulsive. It might help him to win coveted category D status, it might enable him to play with his kids in a special room when they next visited. In short, he was being set up?

'What is it you want from me, Frank? What is it you expect me to do for you?'

'I'm old and not a well man. True, I'll be out of here in twelve months but this is not about me, it's about Alex, my grandson. He's only six and very ill. I want him to have a chance of survival, to see him ride his bike like a normal child. All I need is the money because the NHS won't fund the operation. Time's running out, reverend. UK doctors say Alex is too far gone for surgery already.'

'What's wrong with him?'

'He has a brain tumour. It already affects his sense of balance but you can save him if you try.'

'Don't see how I can.'

'Here's the thing. For £100,000 my daughter can send her son to Prague for proton-beam therapy.'

This charmless conversation suddenly had Luke's full attention. This was not to be a gentle trip down memory lane after all. He was speechless for a moment, then he laughed out loud.

'Seriously, Frank, you think I have that kind of money to give to the likes of you?'

'You will when I tell you how to get it.'

'I doubt that very much.'

'I'm talking about all those antiques that were stolen by the Severn Sea Gang during the 1970s and 80s.'

'To this day no one knows where my father hid it all.'

'What have you got to lose, reverend?'

'My parents, Rex and Jess, did a very bad thing. A woman died because of that stupid treasure.'

'Damn right she did.'

He glared once more at Frank's cunning face and was momentarily really furious.

'That's not all. Because Rex and Jess were thieves I grew up to believe that I could have whatever I wanted. No laws of common decency applied to me and my sense of entitlement overrode all protest. I was born with a burden. An evil one. That same burden got Rex murdered, most likely. That treasure is cursed because it knows no rules. You're right, I did come here today in the vain hope that I might learn something about my father, but it has nothing to do with those lost antiques. I was going to ask you if he ever spoke to you about me. Ever say he loved me? Instead, you tell me that he has plans for me from the next world. Are you insane?'

The pain in his head eased. Rather, it became throb by throb the constant pulse of his strained heartbeat.

'Rex's burden doesn't have to be yours, reverend,' replied Frank and scratched his thin grey hair with his dirty fingernails. 'When I fenced goods for your dad I did it as a true friend. I owe him, big time. I don't like to see his memory trashed, is all. That's why Paul Colley got what was due to him. Thanks to Rex I fenced a fortune in gold, diamonds and sapphires. I can do so again, for you. Why let everything go to waste? Rex owes it to you as his beloved son. Think of it as your legitimate inheritance.'

Luke did not react beyond a contemptuous toss of his head. He found the other man's whole attitude daring but ridiculous. Had he not long ago given up any notion of honour among thieves?

Ever since then he had tried to distinguish between crime and a means to an end.

'You want me to fund your sick grandson's operation with stolen goods? Honestly? That's why you petitioned so eagerly to see me this morning?'

'That stash of antiques is the answer to both our prayers.'

'But I can't help you! Besides, it would be a sin.'

Cordell's good eye was no mere madman's staring orb. It looked inwards. With a treasure hunter's glint. A monomaniac's passion.

'*If thou seekest her as silver, and searchest for her as hid treasures; Then shalt thou understand the fear of the LORD, and find the knowledge of God.* Proverbs 2: 4-5.'

Luke paced about, his hands in his hair.

'You're absolutely wrong, Frank. It can't be done. My old man's been dead for twenty-six years and so are some of his gang. Not even my mother was entrusted with the secret of where Rex buried that loot.'

'What can I tell you? Someone is already after it.'

'Who?'

'Never mind who. If they can come after me, they can go after you.'

'Why bother about the treasure now?'

'All I'm saying, reverend, is this. If you're going to get it you have to move fast.'

'Love to chat but I have other prisoners to console today.'

'Hey, slow down. Listen to me, Luke. Rex and I did drugs together in our cell and he talked about a Bible in his dreams.'

'So?'

'Do you remember if he gave it to you as he laying dying in his hospital bed? I asked after it but it had already gone.'

'The prison chaplain gave my father a Bible at his request. Rex swore to him that he had found God. What's the point, here?'

'You still have it? You do, don't you?'

'It's all I do have of his. It was 1990 for Christ's sake. I was only nine.'

Frank's ugly eye lit up. His waxy cheeks, with the dull colour of a corpse-candle, positively crinkled and cracked with relief. Suddenly he appealed to him not like a wheedling, pathetic pensioner-cum-prisoner any more, but like a fellow conspirator.

'Good for you! Bring it to me. Can you do that?'

'You asking me for my father's Bible?'

'Just do it, damn you. I must look at it. So must you, Luke. It could be your salvation and my grandson's, too.'

He stood there so long waiting for some general explanation that he forgot the hour. It was 12 o'clock. Just time to fill in his chaplain's log before he had lunch.

'And if I still don't like the sound of it?'

Frank fixed him with his bloody eye. Even for a recovering drug addict he had a strangely cadaverous look about him. Skin on his cheeks shrank tightly to the bone. Eye sockets were dark and sunken. He looked from some angles like a scrawny vulture.

'Charity begins at home, reverend.'

'What's in my father's Bible that's so important to you? Is it a map?'

'You might say.'

'That's crazy.'

'Come again soon, Luke. Do we have a deal?'

'I don't know yet.'

'Think of it as God's gift. He brought us together so we can do great things.'

'It doesn't look like that to me.'

'This way you not only get to save a little boy's life, reverend, you get to set your family's record straight. Think of it as your own special redemption.'

*

Of course there was no map in his father's battered Bible, thought Luke or else he would have seen it by now? He'd been using that Bible for years. He felt certain that the sad aftereffects of his pathetic withdrawal from hard drugs could explain the all-enveloping delusion that was ready to invade Frank Cordell's life right now. Who knew what fog filled his addled brain? He glanced at the door that he closed behind him, but it was all right. Within the prison's bright blue and white corridors, shiny floors and merciless lights there was little room for any shadow. Nothing could be regarded as his inseparable attendant – nothing unsubstantial, unreal or counterfeit was allowed to live here where the truth was laid bare.

There was, in prison, literally nowhere for anyone's rotten soul to hide.

He locked the Chapel at seven p.m. Left the prison. Hurried home.

*

The sun had almost set as Luke walked Sasha round the grounds of Hill House vicarage and back into its big reception room. He was very tired, but after he had relit the fire he began to unpack his beloved possessions from their boxes one by one.

That removals man had been correct – he had here the beginnings of a veritable museum.

A dozen wooden crates were filled with stuffed fish all caught by his own rod and line. Ready for the walls of his new home. Sea bass, cod and salmon were all lovingly framed amid reeds, gravel beds and blue-painted lagoons in their pretty glass display boxes.

From another crate he took the bell that had once belonged to the full-rigged sailing ship MARY E. CAMPBELL. He put his hand to its bronze curves. Set it swinging. It was suspended from timber salvaged from the ship's actual wreck, he had been assured at auction. Inside its rim was a child's name. The baby had been christened on board the ship and her name etched into its bell for posterity but it had not brought the vessel good luck. An explanatory brass plate told how, years later, the collier's cargo had shifted in a sudden squall. So mysterious was it that the master was acquitted of all blame when the ship foundered in the Bristol Channel on the 13th September 1869 with the loss of seven lives. Its only survivor had been a stowaway woman.

How strange it felt to see the soul of a ship hanging there before his very eyes. It was like a revelation.

'This recalls my days as a ship's chaplain,' he said and grinned at Sasha who lay down by the fire. She stretched her paws before the enormous 17th century chimney piece. Flattened her ears. Growled.

A woman's head was carved into the front of the elaborately gilded overmantel, Luke noticed. Hair streamed red in the glow of the flames. Fiery eyes peered his way with the same intensity that someone might gaze out to sea.

He removed his copy of the Bible from his suitcase when a sudden chilling reminder came over him.

Had he not, in his great distraction, forgotten to visit Ellie at Floodgates Farm?

Meanwhile the Bible's aged, yellow pages exuded a rich, musty aroma as he took care to turn its brittle paper.

Still it remained his most prized possession, a last link to the otherwise bridgeless past that was his dead father.

Only, he could not then have predicted how soon this memento would so nearly destroy him.

Chapter 11

Luke woke up in alarm. He had to blink several times before he could make sense of anything.

He was still in his chair by the fire in Hill House's main reception room. He must have dozed off while doing his jigsaw puzzle, he decided. Sasha stood on his chest. Licked his stubbly face with her horribly wet tongue.

Meanwhile the clock on the wall said three minutes past midnight.

Sasha jumped to the floor and barked. Her small, sunken eyes urged him to hurry. Things literally didn't sound too good.

He hurried to switch on more lights. He laid a hand on a heavy brass telescope. Strode down the hall.

Someone wouldn't stop hammering on the front door.

So washed-up and stranded appeared the house, so full of his salvaged bits and pieces and nautical mementos of those who had died at sea, that he found himself horrified by the sudden summons.

There was no denying the terror of the hand that did the banging.

The dead could not have knocked any louder.

'Who is it?' demanded Luke and flung open the front door.

'Please, reverend, let me in.'

A panicky and completely naked young man stood before him. Wild, reddish brown eyes appeared drunk or drugged, or simply distressed; his entirely pathetic appearance was nothing short of ridiculous. He was also soaking wet, though there was no sign that it was raining.

'Whatever's wrong?'

'Please, reverend. Can you help me?'

'You hurt, at all?'

'If I could just come in and warm up a bit...'

'You alone?'

'Yes, I am.'

There came from the direction of the River Severn the noise of distant dogs along the shore.

'Tell me, how is it you're in such a state?' asked Luke, beckoning the caller quickly indoors.

It prompted Sasha to prick up her ears briefly at something, too.

'Just give me a moment, reverend...'

'Come from the estuary, have you?'

'Can you keep a secret?'

Their unexpected visitor stared anxiously all about him. He shivered as he walked, dripping, into the reception room. Panted. Held his sides in pain. He appeared too breathless from his exertions to talk any more.

Black hair stuck to his wet scalp and his bare feet were cut to ribbons.

'What's your name?' asked Luke.

'Richard Lambert. I work as a guide at the castle...'

'Okay Richard, first we need to get you warm and dry.'

They moved in the direction of the chairs by the fire.

'Please reverend, you won't tell them I'm here, will you?'

'Who's they?'

'For heaven's sake keep your voice down.'

'What have you done?'

'You're not going to believe it.'

'Sorry. What?'

'As a man of God you should know all about it.'

Luke fetched blankets and towels.

'So tell me, was it some skinny dip with friends?'

Richard began to rub himself dry then went to the window to peep out between its shutters.

'Never you mind, reverend.'

'You look as if you've been running for your life. Why would you do that?'

'Give me a minute.'

'At least let me pour you a whisky.'

'That would be helpful.'

'Take your time. Start at the beginning.'

Instead, the young man adopted a stubborn silence as he stared at the woman's face carved into the fireplace's gilded overmantel. He studied her with peculiar fascination. And horror.

He could only assume that it had something to do with being utterly exhausted.

The drink did little to loosen Richard's tongue.

'Should I ring the police?' asked Luke.

The fugitive would have none of it.

Next minute, men's shouts grew louder and louder, as did the sound of dogs, outside the house. The latter was somewhat chilling and confusing because it was not barking that could be heard exactly.

Those noises coming up the driveway were much more deafening – they were howls.

'Okay, damn it! I'm coming,' Luke shouted as fists rained down again on the vicarage's front door. 'What's your hurry?'

Even as he began to leave the room Richard touched his arm in a panic.

'I was never here, reverend.'

*

A very tall, very muscular individual filled the vicarage's porch.

'Have you any idea what time it is?' said Luke. 'Who are you and what are you doing at Hill House?'

His summoner smelt of rain and river. He was dressed in an olive shooting jacket with its collar turned up high, khaki tweed breeks and Wellington boots.

'Where's Father James? I must speak to him. Is he still here?'

'Should he be?'

'You a friend of his?'

'As of Tuesday I'm the new vicar at St. Mary's. I'm Reverend Luke Lyons.'

'Sorry reverend. My name is Andy Bridgeman. I work at the castle kennels.'

'So, please, can you tell me what's wrong?'

Andy glared. Hard grey eyes struck Luke as suspicious and antagonistic. His entire posture he had to accept was nothing short of disconcertingly menacing.

'Stand aside, reverend.'

'You haven't stated what it is you're after.'

'You seen a young man tonight?'

'No.'

'You sure about that, reverend?'

'As I said, it's late.'

'If I can just see inside with my own eyes?'

'You want to search my house this minute?'

'Please, reverend, it won't take long.'

'Really?'

'That's sensible.'

The arrival of more men clad in waterproof coats, gaiters and boots only stiffened Luke's resolve. Over one man's arm rested a 28 inch barrelled, 20-bore game gun while his moody companion carried a bird-decorated 31 inch barrelled pigeon-gun. These men were at the top of their game if they could use such powerful weapons, as opposed to a 12-bore gun – they could use the full nine-pin side-lock and pistol grip stock to their advantage.

He had to commit Hill House to violent vigilantes if not yet to any violence committed, it seemed.

Two black hounds followed the hunters. Luke promptly called Sasha to heel. One hound, the male, stood eighteen inches high and weighed fifty to sixty pounds. The other, a bitch, was nearly the same. Definitely hunting hounds. They could have been wolves but for their tightly curled tails set high over their backs.

Still Luke stood his ground.

'As I said, there's no one here but me.'

'Okay, Reverend Lyons, we'll take your word for it, but we still have to check the grounds,' said Andy. 'It might look as if we're intruding but we have our reasons.'

'Is there a thief on the run, or what?'

'That's none of your business.'

'The way I see it, you're on Church property.'

But Andy was no longer listening. Luke saw him suddenly follow the hounds into the gardens. Definitely hunting dogs, they filled his ears with more of their spine-tingling howls. As if some stricken soul called from hell itself. The squarely built animals nosed about with their powerful, wedge-shaped heads along the terrace. Their teeth met in a scissors bite while their wet, double coats bristled with thick, hard fur.

He was about to protest further when one hound started barking ferociously. It was a signal, evidently.

Sensing that they had their prey at bay at last, they ran back and forth among the hideously twisted, witch-like trees that grew in the nearby orchard. They saw Richard jump out of a ground floor window.

Weak at the knees, the fugitive exhibited all the appearance of pathetic and cruel vulnerability as he let himself be caught with only a blanket to cover him.

Luke ran across the driveway.

'Why him? What's going on?'

He was that stubborn.

'Don't concern yourself, reverend,' said Andy. 'He's a local lad who doesn't know what's good for him...'

'I don't care where he comes from. What has he done?'

'Sorry, reverend. Duty calls.'

'I still don't get it.'

'We have to go. It's just a bit of fun.'

'Make sure you treat him right?'

'He'll get what he deserves. At least the silly bugger didn't drown.'

'That's not what I asked.'

At which point Luke realised that his authority counted for nothing. It was little wonder that the previous vicar had resigned in such a hurry, little wonder that nobody had wanted to do his job in this particular parish? Nothing else was expected from him, not even his special pleading. Hounds and guns were too powerful. It literally made him furious. To say of someone's dog collar that he was now a man of peace was not necessarily very useful. He should have fetched a gun of his own.

But the laughing and joking captors clapped Richard on the back, as though he had been elevated to the status of some buck or other from the nearby deer park. Was it, then, all a misunderstanding on his part, Luke wondered? Was it nothing but a prank from some actual stag party? He followed everyone a few more paces down the lane. Saw them herd the young man back to the river.

No one mentioned anything about getting married.

On such a night of odd occurrences, one thing struck him as still odder: Richard might have been naked but someone had strung round his neck a thickly braided garland of seaweed and shells.

Chapter 12

Today was not a good day. Okay, it was a combination of Day 1 and Day 2 of his diet when he could eat as much fruit as he liked along with his cabbage soup, of course, but in that case why was he, Jorge Winter, forbidden to eat any bananas at all? He *liked* bananas.

He bit hard into his Granny Smith apple on his way into HMPL...., chewed it all up including its core and pips. Apple seeds contained a cyanide compound which the human body could detoxify in small doses, but in big ones? Such a poison killed by denying blood the ability to carry oxygen. Victims therefore died of asphyxiation because their lungs couldn't work, rather like drowning. It was always the unexpected that got the better of you, he thought, smiling.

It was imperative that he study Frank Cordell's prison record straightaway.

Multi-faith team leader Hammond disagreed.

'Sorry, Inspector. You know the rules.'

'But he's dead for Christ's sake.'

Hammond closed the door to the chaplain's office in a hurry.

'You'll get nowhere with the governor. Don't even try.'

'You mean he doesn't know what to do with me?'

'Okay, I admit it. He wants you to bugger off back to Gloucester. Doesn't think you have any jurisdiction in his prison.'

'Doesn't mean we shouldn't wonder why Cordell died.'

'Honestly, who gives a shit about him, Inspector? Leave it to the Avon and Somerset police.'

'Believe me, I won't.'

'Everyone's thinking suicide.'

'Oh no it wasn't.'

'Did you actually see the bastard fall, Inspector?'

Hammond's curiosity was blatant, his ghoulish concern for him tinged with relish. Even so he was unwilling to express to anyone his particular confusion of shock and indignation that he felt right now. He hesitated to call it disappointment.

'No, I *did not* see him fall.'

'Fact is, Inspector, you never should have gone to Bristol at all, you shouldn't have bothered. The guv got wind of it and he's NOT HAPPY.'

It was true. His attempt to see Cordell had met with disaster. It was his own fault, thought Jorge, for clutching at straws. Never was it a good idea to take someone's offer to help at face value. It was all about what was in it for them.

'Frank drew Reverend Lyons's attention to a Bible that once belonged to his father, Rex. You know anything about that?'

'Who cares? Everyone in Gloucestershire knows Rex for a callous murderer. If Cordell told you any different it was only to plant some evil snake in your ear for some twisted pleasure of his own. Really, he was not nice at all.'

'Nevertheless I'd like to know what made him tick, in his soul. I need to know if what he told Reverend Lyons influenced his subsequent behaviour in any way.'

'Men like Cordell have no souls, Inspector.'

'Without a soul what are we?'

Hammond went to pat him on the back as one might pat an upset child.

'You'll be telling me next that Frank Cordell played some direct part in the reverend's demise. You think that Bible somehow 'did' for him? You do, don't you, Inspector?'

'Cordell thought he could strike a deal with Luke to do an act of good. When a bad man feels the need to redeem himself, albeit for purely selfish reasons, I am at least prepared to give him the benefit of the doubt. Only by speaking the truth can we build a bridge between good and evil.'

'What bridge?'

'*Of Hope*. Now let's look at everything we have on Cordell's last stint in prison. I want to know all you do,' said Jorge.

Hammond studied red paint lodged under his fingernails.

'As it happens I do have something.'

They started along the corridor in the direction of the various classrooms. Jorge glanced up at a clock. This time last year Luke would have been going down this very same corridor, but to Bible study classes. Already he was treading in the missing man's footsteps.

*

'Art classes are usually held five evenings per week,' said Hammond. 'Special reference is made to landscapes but some men opt to specialise in subjects of their own choosing.'

Jorge let his eye settle on prisoners' competent but lifeless pictures that hung on the walls. Whether oil or water paints, chalk, pastel or charcoal they could be said to offer a brief window into a man's inner being. If daubs of paint could ever wholly express the yearning for freedom? Actually, he didn't know what they did. If not good the pictures were at least a welcome splash of colour in his present surroundings.

'What's not to like?' he said, impatiently.

Hammond opened a drawer and laid rolls of paper on the table.

'I'm surprised Cordell didn't apply to the Governor to take these home with him.'

'What are they?'

'Take a good look, Inspector.'

Jorge donned a fresh pair of white plastic gloves from his pocket. He picked a roll and spread it open to reveal a coloured drawing.

A wooden sailing ship looked ready to sink on a stormy ocean as a towering sea-serpent burst over its deck in a fountain of water. Part human and part redheaded dragon, the beast sought to crush the ship's fragile wooden hull with ever tighter constrictions of its coiled body. Already three men had been lost off the lee mainyard-arm at the flick of its scaly tail. More sailors had heroically cut away the mizzenmast but the fore stay-sail was split and the headyards braced back to little avail.

The vessel was doomed to a watery grave in the high and dangerous waves, apparently.

'Why this scene?'

Hammond laughed.

'Oh, bloody hell, Inspector, I'm afraid Cordell had a passion for William Falconer's interminable poem called 'The Shipwreck'. Always quoting bits by heart:

The horrid apparition still draws nigh,

And white with foam the whirling billows fly.'

'Okay, yeah, I get it. Not quite the evidence I was expecting but it's a start, I suppose.'

'See here. Cordell wrote a verse on the back of every drawing: 'The swelling stu'n sails now their wings extend…'

'I said I get it. Are the pictures all like this?'

'Shipwrecks, mostly.'

'Sea-serpents, certainly.'

'You any good at deciphering psychotic doodles, Inspector?'

'Why do you ask?'

'There must be at least a hundred depictions of 'The Shipwreck' here. Not all have lines from Falconer. A few quote the Bible. The man was obsessed by something.'

'Or possessed.'

'By what, exactly?'

'By fear of hellish retribution.'

'Really, Inspector?'

Written in a childish hand on the back of one drawing was the biblical quotation: *And I saw a beast rising out of the sea, with ten horns and seven heads, with ten diadems on its horns and blasphemous names on its heads.*

'Tell me more about Cordell the prisoner.'

'You really want to know, Inspector? In his last prison everyone lost count of the times he was off his head on legal highs. Once he was caught with homemade hooch. Just before coming to HMPL… he did his best to scratch out the tattoo of a sea nymph on his neck. Said it was trying to choke him in his dreams. Nearly scuppered his chances of coming here. All governors take a dim view of tattooing, don't they? Not only is it strictly prohibited but it's also dangerous. Then Reverend Luke Lyons joined us as chaplain. From that moment Cordell said not another bad word. He took up painting. Became a model prisoner. Blabbed a lot about how he'd be rich one day. Bored everyone half to death with tales of treasure. Suddenly people started to visit him, whereas before that there had been no one except his daughter, very occasionally.'

'These people have a name, at all?'

'Honestly, Inspector, you'd have thought that one of them had decided to rise up from his grave or something.'

'This oldie have a name?'

'Jim Jackson I think it was.'

'Not 'Slim' Jim Jackson?'

'You know him?'

'Damn right I do.'

'Sounds personal.'

'Back in the day Jackson went poaching elvers and salmon on the River Severn.'

'I see you come armed with information, Inspector.'

Jorge stuck with his line of investigation but felt obliged to explain.

'Reverend Luke Lyons and I grew up together just outside Berkeley. We gravitated to the river because we both liked boats. Luke was the wild one while I was 'Tubby Jorge', son of the local vicar. Because Jackson knew Luke's family he took him fishing and sometimes I tagged along, too. As a boy I thought Jackson was just one of those fishermen who tried to harvest the river's riches. Never saw him as a hardened criminal, but I was wrong.'

'Jackson was mighty anxious about something, Inspector. He was sweating. I heard him say to Cordell, "If you want us both to live, let alone get what's due to us, which I do, then you've got to tell me…" Cordell's face was an absolute picture. He went white. Nothing he said calmed Jackson down. The sight of those two talking themselves breathless in the prison's visiting room like a couple of old pirates was quite comical. Except now, of course, one of them is dead.'

'This visit happened when?'

'Early spring last year.'

'I see.'

Hammond's first reaction was to put the pictures back in the drawer.

'Not so fast,' said Jorge. 'I'll take those if I may.'

'As I said, what's not to like, Inspector?'

'So what else did Jackson have to say to Cordell?'

'Dunno. But not long afterwards a woman came to the prison and spoke to him, too. I distinctly remember that she wore a dark brown racoon gilet. She kept its furry hood up all the time she was here.'

'She got a name?'

'I haven't the foggiest idea. Cordell got really agitated as soon as she sat down with just the hard plastic tabletop between them. I really thought he was going to do a runner back to his cell. Instead, he went all defensive. *J, I ain't no fucking grass. Slim Jim could have stopped all such bollocks by telling the truth. I have always been there for you and Rex, but no one's ever been there for me. We are like family. Help me, because the truth will hurt.*'

'That it?'

Hammond shrugged.

'I don't know what the issue was between J and Cordell but it seemed to relate to their dealings years ago.'

Jorge nodded. Two people at least had been interested in Cordell's return to the real world.

'Whoever forced Frank Cordell to jump off the roof may have viewed him as some sort of traitor? Then again some people are so feral that they think the only way to resolve even a petty misunderstanding is to use violence.'

'You a full-blown detective now, Inspector?'

'Cordell mentioned a woman with his dying breath. He also said that Reverend Luke Lyons did not commit suicide.'

'What can I say? Cordell boasted about all sorts of things. He was a serial offender. Always in and out of clink. But as far as I recall, he was eager to salvage his reputation about something.'

'Could 'J' have been a redhead, at all?'

'Like I said, I wasn't the one who had to comb her hair for drugs on her way into prison. I didn't get the impression that she was a relative, if that helps? You can always tell the wives and girlfriends. After a while they look as if they're visiting the dead, but they're the dead ones. They are single but not single, free but not free, with their relationships on hold for as long as their partner stays inside. She wasn't the sort to have illicit sex in plain sight, nor was she there to deliver him a 'Dear John' letter. It looked like strictly business to me.'

'Thanks for the pictures, Mr Hammond.'

'Cordell was a right piece of shit. You hear me?'

'What do *you* think he meant when he said he would be rich one day?'

Hammond's lips curled in ever greater disgust since that was what he thought all interest in paedophiles merited.

'Wow, you're persistent.'

'Trust me, I am.'

'Shit. What's wrong, Inspector?'

The world had begun to spin as Jorge felt himself go pale.

'You ill, Inspector? Have you considered that you might be in shock after what you saw in Bristol?'

'Do me a favour, don't tell anyone we had this conversation. Do I make myself clear?'

'Why the fuss? The man was a fantasist.'

'These ships that Cordell drew are copied from medieval pictures of Spanish treasure ships. Galleon, serpent, gold, they're all part of a theme – he had you thinking he was madder than he was.'

'You don't want to bother about all that, Inspector.'

'Drawings can express heartfelt feelings. Only feelings keep one's soul alive.'

'You suppose?'

*

Jorge marched back to the prison chapel. It was 18.30. In half an hour Hammond would lock up and go home and he should, too. Instead, he straightway wiped clean a pew with a tissue. He sat down. Donned his gloves again. Examined Cordell's pile of pictures on his lap.

He stared at the red-headed sea-serpent in his hand. It could have been either the embodiment of greed or the retribution it deserved.

He studied the quotation from Revelation 13: 1. on the back of one of the rolls of paper.

Sat there undecided for a moment.

Then, holding the drawing up to his face, Jorge recognised subtle alterations deftly made: *And I saw a beast rising out of the sea, with ten horns and seven heads, with ten diadems on 'her' horns and blasphemous names on 'her' heads.*

To Cordell the beast was semi-human. How could he have been so careless as to have misread it before?

He turned over a second picture and there, too, was a biblical quotation on its back.

'Bold move, Cordell, but I have to ask myself why, even if I had been as obsessed as you were, would I have chosen Isaiah 45: 3?'

God was addressing Cyrus, the Persian King, whom He was going to help capture Babylon: *I will give you the treasures of darkness and the hoards in secret places.* The gold of pagans was usually concealed in the darkest of locations. A man would have to go somewhere that was without light, both factually and spiritually, to find it. Might that not be deep under the sea? Or river? In looking for hidden riches in such dark places, could he not expect to anger some guardian angel? Had Frank Cordell?

The doomed man had, with his dying breath, given him an actual warning; his plea for help had been no less real. Whatever it was, Jorge felt quite sure that he had said it to Rev. Luke Lyons, too.

*

He marched out of prison only to discover that someone had pinned a note to the windscreen of his camper van. Any such message could only be bad news?

Cowardice outstripped courage for a moment.

What was it going to take to find Rev. Luke Lyons, anyway?

He had to ask himself whether he was ready for all the discoveries that might lie in store for him?

Slowly and with great apprehension he eased the piece of paper from beneath its rubber wiper.

With heart racing, he examined its blood-red words.

It was a leaflet entitled 'Live happy with Slimming World'.

Chapter 13

The strangely white morning was as wet as a Scotch mist as Luke took Sasha for a walk by the Severn. Raindrops ran like beads round the rim of his black leather fedora while, with a shiver, he turned up his coat's furry collar.

If it was one thing that he had missed during his years away from home, it was this particular stroll along the riverbank.

Today, however, the drizzle had a peculiar way of misleading him. Like smoke. But for the seawall the fog was thick enough to lure them right into the water – each fresh step stressed the tide's musical proximity. He was drawn to the sound of its apparent singing, although in no actual singer did the waves result.

The mist drifted across sand and rocks in a series of castellated clouds. It built some sort of silvery palace. From dark currents rose turrets at whose every window shone a light.

The harder Luke strained his eyes to penetrate the haze, the more the palace retreated – the less and it returned. Next he became aware of a different chill, even sliminess, on his cheek – a sudden, violent change of feeling, hardly explicable for a moment, but whose touch could have been a scaly, fish-like hand. He rubbed his face with his glove and his alarm diminished – walked on and it returned.

'Am I not simply seeing a reflection of the actual castle at Berkeley?' he told himself, while he observed the clouds drift by.

There again, this Fata Morgana was most likely some ship's navigation lights severally refracted first by the fog and secondly by the water.

'Sash! Come! Time to go home.'

Someone swathed in a white coat and a scarf stood in Hill House's curving driveway. Luke could make out a few features, if not all the face featured.

His chest tightened and his breathing quickened. He felt an uncanny tingling electrify the hairs on the back of his neck.

Sasha growled and refused to move another inch, only drew attention to the mist that was coiling and uncoiling everywhere around them. Finding someone bar the way like that was confusing.

'Steady, now, Sash.'

Just because that phantom palace a moment ago had left him unsure whether anything this morning was real or unreal, or just plain wrong, did not mean that he should see more ghosts now, thought Luke. The spectre stayed where it was at his advance. Soon they were not six paces apart.

Whoever it was had very long red hair. Her face was angular and strikingly chiselled, her eyes very narrow, her cheeks rather bleached as if worn by care or weather. Her black painted lips breathed white snakes which writhed about her in the cold air with a life that was uncannily eel-like.

She could have been a Greek Hydra who kept two wolfish black hounds on tight leads while, with peculiarly grim and decisive smile, she put out her hand by way of greeting.

'Did I startle you, reverend? I like to walk my dogs early in the morning, too.'

'Oh no, I'm okay. I'm fine,' replied Luke. 'Absolutely I am. Do I know you?'

Hands met briefly glove to glove.

'My name is Sabrina ap Loegres. Don't worry, Varg and Freya won't hurt you.'

'Doesn't mean they didn't scare the shit out of me the other night.'

Sasha growled deeper.

'Forgive me, I've come to apologize. My companions caught someone poaching in the deer park and chased him down.'

'Doesn't explain how he came to be wet and naked.'

'Most likely he tried to ditch the smell of deer on his clothes so that my hounds couldn't track him.'

'By the look of him he almost drowned.'

Sabrina's sea-green eyes flashed silver.

'The Severn can be very unforgiving.'

'You got that right.'

'And whose fault was that?'

'Like it or not, the poor man was terrified.'

'Really he came to very little harm, reverend.'

The hounds grew restless.

Luke delayed rather than rush their parting.

The fear was not for himself but for Sasha's safety; he did not want her bitten.

There hung in the air the damp, iodized smell of some unusual perfume. Its aromatic scent of the ocean brought with it a hint of seaweed, rock pools and salt.

'Have we met before by any chance?'

'No, sir, but I'm staying awhile at Berkeley Castle.'

'Then please know that I'm Reverend Luke Lyons. I'm the new vicar for the local parish. I very much hope to officiate at my sister Ellie's wedding in St. Mary's Church this summer.'

'Then you will have chosen the castle for the reception?'

'Unfortunately she failed to secure a booking. Can't be helped, I guess.'

'You should let me put in a good word for you.'

'You can't be serious?'

'I don't know if I can but I have friends who might.'

'I remember now. I saw you at the head of a funeral recently?'

Sabrina dipped her head to one side...

Sasha snarled.

...even as her thick, flowing hair fell forward to expose one ear and its silver serpent.

Luke had not forgotten her beauty, yet how that beauty astounded him now! Never had such eyes anchored his with such depth of understanding, never before had anyone captivated him as she did, face to face. Thus was he inclined to believe all her blithe talk of poachers.

'That would be Stephen who drowned in the river,' said Sabrina.

'I saw his name spelt out in flowers. Who was he, exactly?'

'It makes no difference now. Varg. Freya. Come. We must return at once.'

81

'To the castle?'

Sasha fretted. She tried again to read his face. Decided how best to react to this stranger. Kept looking to him for her cue, Luke noticed. Or she couldn't believe that he was being so stupid.

Sabrina took a step backwards into the mist's confusing swirls.

'As you say – to the castle.'

'Did I say something wrong?'

'Good day, reverend. Don't forget. Let me help your sister.'

'Wait, at least tell me the breed of those hounds of yours. I've never seen such fine animals.'

'They're Nordic hunting dogs. These, however, are no ordinary Norwegian Elkhounds but the rarer black ones. It is a lighter, faster dog. They possess great energy, too. Most of all they are loyal by nature, more so than men and make good watchdogs at home. They are more biddable than Alaskan Malamutes, for instance.'

'I love the way they curl their tails forwards over their backs.'

'It is a trait bred into them. It means that at a distance hunters can tell them apart from wolves, since wolves always trail their tails behind their bodies at all times.'

'Do they howl, at all?'

'Why do you ask?'

'I heard a lot of howling last night from the direction of Berkeley Castle's kennels.'

'Really, reverend, I don't know what you heard.'

Sabrina signalled him good morning. She gave him a frown that verged on the abrupt. Perhaps frowns from her were always that spellbinding? Then she led her pack quietly away into the mist. Many a dog had to be restrained firmly from an early age or they could challenge you later. You needed to assert your authority right at the beginning, but she had. They had learned their place in the family hierarchy; they had been taught never to try to displace her at all.

He resolved to discover more about her as soon as possible if he could.

'Come, Sash. Time to take a drive into town. I don't know about you, but I need my breakfast.'

Less than an hour later Luke was sitting in some cosy tearooms just off the High Street in Berkeley, while Sasha sat outside in the cobbled yard where people parked their bicycles. He was eating his bacon and fried egg sandwich when an elderly man looked up from a neighbouring brown wooden table.

He stared back as openly as politeness could dictate. He did it with much slow spreading of marmalade on his toast. He only knew that at nine a.m. someone should be able to eat his meal in peace.

Instead, his rude scrutineer earned his wife's admonishments.

'For God's sake, Sam, stop staring. Your sausages will get cold.'

'I'm telling you, Sheila, it could be him. Look at the nose.'

Sheila dropped her fork with a clang.

'Don't be silly. Rex Lyons died years ago.'

Then the large, red-faced Sam again swivelled his head his way, Luke noted.

'Yeah, well, I dare say, but he is literally his spitting image you have to admit.'

More tense moments passed. Then Luke rose from his table and walked boldly to the counter. Smiled pleasantly at the waitress.

'Americano, please. Half a shot.'

'We don't do half shots.'

But he could be charming.

'Americano. Half a shot *only*.'

The whole atmosphere in the room they could all agree was discomfortingly charged. Two other elderly men were seated at a table by the fireplace. They stopped chewing panini. Observed what was going on.

Luke ran his hand over his oily, slicked black hair. His fists opened and closed several times as he regarded himself in the mirror behind the counter. Then he spun round. What could it cost to come clean if it helped him to be the person that he needed to be from now on?

'My name is Reverend Luke Lyons. I'm your new vicar. You have something to say to me?'

What occurred in the next few moments was not expressed in words. All four breakfasters, finding they had no more appetite, stood up together. They seized hats and coats. Crossed bare, creaking floorboards in a hurry.

Shut the door behind them.

Clearly his challenge was too scary to be challenged.

'You from around here originally, then?' asked the waitress, impressed, as she mopped the counter very hard. Her hazel eyes widened his way.

Luke sipped his coffee.

'It's been a while.'

Chapter 14

'You got a kiss for me then, Luke?'

From the look on his sister's face his arrival at Floodgates Farm was all the relief he could ever hope for.

'It's been too long, or what?'

Kissing, though, was not something he ever did.

'For God's sake, brother, let me hold you,' said Ellie, settling for a hug. 'I'm glad to say that you look so much less sallow in real life than you do on screen.'

'You on the other hand are just as bonny as I'd hoped. I know I'm late but "Happy Birthday".'

So saying, he produced a small, red velvet box from his coat pocket.

'So this is my long lost twin at last,' said Ellie, laughing.

'No more lectures?'

'It's so strange to think that last Sunday was your birthday, too.'

Luke watched her open the box. Saw her examine its silver bracelet engraved with entwined dragons.

'Hope you like it. It's modelled on something Anglo-Saxon.'

'Not nicked, is it?'

'No, it's not.'

'I'm not really a jewellery sort of person. It soon gets trapped in all the machinery round here. But thanks, it's very nice. I have an Easter egg for you back at the house. Hope you like dark chocolate?'

She must have felt very unsure that he would show up at all as she registered the look on his face.

'Don't tell me. You're a milk chocolate man?'

'Sorry.'

'But Jeremy, my fiancé, will eat anything.'

He had a strong sense of literally how childishly her complaint rankled. They might have spoken for weeks via Skype and phone ever since he had tracked her down on social media, but not in the flesh.

'Who's this with you?' asked Ellie.

'Meet Sasha. Or Sash, for short.'

'Dogs make me nervous ever since a Great Dane bit me in Spain when I was little.'

'No, yeah, I didn't know?'

'There's a lot we both don't know.'

'Don't worry, she won't hurt you.'

Sasha went off to hunt cats.

Ellie's blue-black eyes mirrored his. Again she clawed dark curls across her brow, since she really was very nervous beneath all the bravado. He felt the same. This was not going to be easy but very definitely would he try to enter into the occasion.

'You're so tall!'

'So are you, brother, but far too thin.'

'I've been this way a while now.'

'It's no bad thing, I suppose.'

Luke could recognise the strangeness of the situation if not the estrangement. Had it really been thirty-five years? Yet her whole foreignness could be said to be miraculously unalienable. Surely that was as it should be, however? A brother should know his own sister, even if they had only ever met once before in the womb.

Ellie giggled.

'Make yourself useful. There's a stone wall we need to patch with electric fencing.'

'Where's Jeremy?'

'Gone to the castle to pay the rent.'

They set off together past the wooden stables that smelt of freshly applied creosote. They stopped to collect some fencing stakes and a mallet in a wheelbarrow. It seemed the most natural thing in the world to do something practical together and yet there were so many questions that he still had to ask her about herself.

Instead he played safe.

'How's Molly doing now?'

'Her eye's still half shut but there's no swelling except for her lower lid which is still a bit puffy. The pupil itself is clear, thank goodness. There's no running, so there can't be any wound in it.'

'Sounds gory.'

'Doesn't mean she didn't collide with the wall with one hell of a bang. She tried to jump it at a real gallop, I'd say. Okay, she has cataracts. Doesn't mean she wasn't trying to escape from something.'

'Some *thing*?'

'Some trespasser throwing stones, very likely.'

'Why would anyone do that?'

'Some people get a kick out of frightening horses.'

Next minute a fair-haired boy charged across the yard with a wooden sword held high in one hand.

'Hey, Randal,' cried Ellie. 'I thought I told you to stay in the house? Mummy's busy right now.'

'Let him come,' said Luke. 'I've brought him the biggest chocolate rabbit I could find. It's in the Land Rover.'

'Randal, this is your Uncle Luke. You'll be seeing a lot of him from now on. He's just moved to Berkeley.'

Man and boy traded puzzled looks.

'Is this the gangster you spoke about?' said Randal, in awe.

'Ex-gangster, silly.'

'He has the family nose,' said Luke. 'And he's already very tall, too!'

Ellie straightened her son's blue jacket. Took his hand.

'He was ten in January. Really, just recently I've begun to think he looks more like his grandmother. 'Don't you think he has her almond eyes?'

'I forget.'

'As we all do.'

Ellie steered Randal round a pile of horse dung close by the gate to the field. Clearly the poor grey mare had been frightened out of her wits by something very unnatural. Horses shat a lot when terrified.

A hare suddenly jumped the breach in the wall on their side of the field; it passed close to them where fallen stones hid their approach. The leggy animal loped across the grass. Paused. Turned its tall black ears their way. It listened to them intensely from a safe distance. Next moment, its reddish brown fur gleamed in a blaze of sunlight that shone through a gap in the mist.

'First one I've seen this year,' said Ellie. 'I hope it's not the Witch of Berkeley.'

'Don't be silly, mummy,' said Randal. 'There's no such thing as witches.'

Luke raised his eyebrows.

'What witch is that exactly?'

'Sold her soul to the Devil in 1063. Suffice to say, she's a red-headed sorceress who sometimes goes about the countryside round here disguised as a hare. Aren't they always? I sometimes think redheads get a very raw deal.'

'Yeah. Definitely never happened, but you've got to admire the gullibility of some people, haven't you?'

His appetite for ridicule was somewhat checked by a clear sign that Ellie seemed deadly serious.

*

'This where it happened?' asked Luke.

He was surprised and mystified not simply by the wrecked drystone wall but by the brute force which had wrecked it. His gaze turned to the broken ground and frantic hoof prints all around them. Why did a half-blind pony charge headlong at this formidable barrier now so shattered in the sunlight? Sometimes animals could be so stupid.

Ellie offered him the stakes in one hand and the mallet in the other.

'You choose.'

'I'll hold, you bang.'

'Good choice.'

Each fencing stake carried an insulated slot for white electric tape. Once all four stakes were hammered into position, Ellie unrolled the tape as far back as a red solar-powered battery already positioned at the edge of the field. Her willingness to co-opt him emboldened him to break his self-inflicted censorship so far.

'So what did our mother ask you about me, precisely?'

Ellie connected the tape to the battery with a spark.

'Whatever do you mean, Luke?'

'Jess said on TV that she knew I was a priest.'

'You and she can talk about it when you meet.'

'You can say that again.'

Job done, Ellie gathered up her mallet and began pushing her wheelbarrow back to the farmyard.

'Please don't say that, Luke.'

'I worry she's up to something, that's all.'

'We'll know soon enough.'

'Not before she ruins everything else!'

'Do you good to cut her some slack after all this time, brother.'

'She hasn't nearly explained why she abandoned me, not you.'

'Or this is about you not wanting to forgive and forget?'

'You think?'

'Pretty much.'

There was nothing like jealousy to encourage someone in his not unreasonable resentments.

'When Jess got out of prison she tracked you down and re-established contact,' said Luke. 'She didn't do that for me. I lost out. I had to live with gran for years. I might as well have been an orphan. She didn't even visit.'

Ellie stopped by a grey mare in a stable.

'Honestly, you think Jess loved me more than you?'

'In a sense, yeah.'

'There appears to be some confusion about what the hell she ever felt for anyone. I never met a harder woman than our mother.'

'No, well, yeah, if witches exist then she's it.'

'Please, Luke, what did you lose, in your opinion?'

'I lost my childhood.'

'Doesn't mean you had to end up in a young offenders' home.'

'Jess didn't visit me there, either.'

'Don't punish yourself for nothing.'

'What was I supposed to do?'

Ellie unbolted the door to a stable and slipped a head collar over Molly's nose. She passed its strap up and over the pony's ears. Buckled it together against the side of her neck.

'Hold still while I give her this ointment, will you?'

'Got it.'

Next minute Ellie slid one hand under the collar's straps to open the mare's top eyelid and peel back the bottom one. That way her hand could move with the head. She shot him half a smile.

'Haven't broken my arm yet.'

It was the first time she had fully relaxed in his presence. With her other hand she carefully squeezed ointment from a little tube inside Molly's bottom eyelid which she then closed.

If only he wasn't mildly allergic to horses, thought Luke.

'Molly will have to stay in tonight,' said Ellie firmly. 'Look sharp, brother. Bring me two slices of hay from that blue barrel in the yard over there, will you?'

'Anything to oblige.'

Luke crossed the cobbles. Returned with an armful of soaked feed.

Ellie took him to one side.

'I know this isn't easy for you. It isn't very easy for me, either. And yes, I do think it's a bit odd that Jess should make that TV broadcast now? What is really behind it, do you think?'

'You heard what she said, she wants to dig up the past. Whereas I've decided to come home and make a fresh start, she hasn't changed a bit.'

Ellie pulled a face.

'So what else is new?'

'If I'm being honest I dread meeting her at the wedding.'

'I don't trust her, either.'

'After that she's on her own.'

'Okay, okay, but you don't get to spoil my big day.'

'That's a promise.'

'Moving on. Did you visit grandma's house yet?'

'Soon.'

'You'll find the key under the amaryllis in the greenhouse when you do.'

'I haven't forgotten.'

'Have you considered that selling Chapel Cottage will break Gwendolen's heart? It's been her home since the 1950s.'

'If we don't, someone else will.'

'That's not a good reason.'

Luke tried not to sneeze as Ellie brushed Molly's muddy back.

'You not told her, then?'

'A crazy old woman is what she is these days.'

'Okay, yeah, I don't know. Dementia can be managed. She's just ill. That makes her kind of special.'

'A lot of people are scared of special. Some nights she stands in her room and howls.'

'You really want to talk about this now?'

'Do please explain it to her as gently as you can, Luke? Won't you?'

'Damn right I will.'

'She seemed better yesterday, I must say. I actually had a decent conversation with her.'

'What about?'

'Oh, this and that.'

'It's not such a bad thing, Ellie. Thanks to this new nuclear power station that is going to be built, Chapel Cottage is prime real estate suddenly. What have we got to lose?'

'All the same, we don't want to do anything rash, do we? We could talk it over with Jeremy when he gets home if you like. He may not be my husband quite yet but he's worked this farm for years. He's well placed to gauge the strength of local feeling among the neighbours.'

'I'd better go. Things to do. Something's come up at the prison.'

Ellie stared after him.

'Never thought you'd want to see 'inside' again.'

'Think of it as my biggest qualification. Really, it's only two days a week at the moment as part of a multi-faith team.'

He sneezed and wiped red off his hand.

'You bleeding?' said Ellie.

'H'm, well, yeah, it happens.'

'Here, put my doctor's number on your phone at once. It could be high blood pressure or something.'

'Fine. Yeah. Whatever.'

'I mean it. Give them a ring today.'

Luke flinched. If she could be caring he could be terribly careless.

'Wait,' said Ellie suddenly. 'At least stay for lunch like a proper family.'

'Well, all right then.'

And so in her own way she gave him her blessing.

Chapter 15

Eat slowly. Fast intermittently. Such advice was sound, as advice went, thought Jorge. He was handing Sasha her breakfast bowl of dog biscuits on the cold stone floor of Hill House's gloomy kitchen. Dawn had broken and he had not slept well in a bed whose sheets he did not regard as sufficiently clean, no matter how much he sprayed them with air freshener.

He had dreamt that he was falling head first from some precipitous bridge – he was being driven to jump to his death by his irate landlady as he relived being caught trying to smuggle Sasha into his B&B, late yesterday evening.

Being a policeman cut no ice with her. She threw his peaked cap into Station Road. Told him to follow.

'Damned rozzer.'

The result was that he had been forced to retrieve the key to the vicarage from a drawer in St. Mary's Church in Berkeley in a bit of a hurry. It was not a good thing. He might have grown up in Hill House, but to be back in his old home made him feel like a squatter in his own sadly neglected premises.

'There you are, Sasha. Enjoy.'

At least today was the day he could eat as many bananas as he liked. He was also allowed skimmed milk and, naturally, all the bowls of cabbage soup that he could possibly bear to swallow. There was something portentous about Day 4 of his diet which was not helped by his miniscule loss of weight. So far he had shed one pound.

His stomach simply ignored the glass of water that he now drank before all his meals to invite a sense of satiety. Nor did chewing longer and savouring each bite of his fifth banana make much difference. His belly was in open rebellion; it was doing its best to test his resolution as God tempted Abraham.

He moved through the kitchen, observing the relative chaos. Luke had always lived so. Disordered, messy, out of control. Febrile. Urgent. Driven. He lived the moment before it could make him stop and think.

Sasha would not stop poking her wet nose into every corner. There could be no complacency until she had investigated everything absolutely thoroughly according to the custom of dogs in old places. After all, she had once lived here, too.

'Seriously? You can still smell him? How long does it take for someone's scent to vanish with them, anyway?'

*

Next minute, Jorge produced a pack of new Brillo pads from his shopping bag. He used them to polish four saucepans and their lids to a bright silver colour ready for cabbage, onions, peppers and celery.

How could anyone be blind to all those brown stains, so obvious to the most casual observer?

Such neglect was an insult to the disciplined mind, an indictment of the true believer, a disgrace before God.

Or it was his own Obsessive Compulsive Disorder, thought Jorge, scrubbing harder.

Meanwhile, Sasha went off to investigate spiders in the cellar.

*

'I don't know about you, Sasha, but it doesn't feel right. It's as if Luke hasn't strayed very far.'

Which also went for himself, thought Jorge. It felt very odd that he and Luke had eaten meals together as boys at this very table, not least because his father would permit 'that Lyons brat' no further than the kitchen.

A white china tea caddy was still full of teabags.

Elsewhere a ship's calendar from 2016 hung on the wall.

Each day had been crossed off until the fateful one – the Sunday on which his friend had unaccountably stepped off the edge of the Earth forever.

Among an impressive pile of receipts, bills, bank statements and junk mail, many copies of Sailing Magazine and Marlinspike Magazine for Schooner

94

and Tall Ship News, as well as Porthole Cruise Magazine stood piled on a Welsh dresser. He thumbed through a copy of the latter. Saw it fall open at its centre spread.

He could not rightly say what drew his attention to it, unless it was the strange name of a tall black schooner called Amatheia. Its owner, Welsh-born business woman Sabrina ap Loegres had built it as an enlarged, updated version of a classic 19th century barquentine design. Round its name was a ring drawn in red biro.

The magazines were both old and recent. Luke had renewed their subscriptions shortly before his disappearance? Here, then, was some thread of communication. Inside these magazines had to be a clue as to how and where he'd always wanted to sail, in his dreams. He'd left Berkeley for some desert island?

Whatever the truth, his friend's passion for all things nautical had kept his favourite publications coming even if he didn't.

Luke had left behind something of himself. Things he loved. Physical things. One antiquated item was a ship's wooden slatted container for storing linen whose worm-eaten holes looked positively medieval.

A full bottle of whisky rested on its top.

What sane person, whatever his hurry, abandoned such a fine malt, Jorge wondered? He set the bottle aside, pulled on a pair of white plastic gloves and opened the chest's lid.

Lying inside was a large scrapbook which turned out to contain dozens of reports from local newspapers.

Something called The Gazette described how a dead whale had been found stranded a few miles away at Littleton-on-Severn in 1885. Traction engines dragged the leviathan ashore and special trains had been laid on by the Midland Railway Company to deposit sightseers at the nearest station. So many people had arrived to see the monster that they had formed a queue three miles long.

Next minute something outside the house caught Jorge's attention.

He felt compelled to go to the window. Look out.

A shadow was creeping across the face of the sundial on the lawn near the lake, as if some dark hand would mark the day's first hours with its claws.

Sasha barked. Scratched the door.

'Really?' said Jorge, carrying his newly found bottle into the kitchen. 'You literally want to go for another bloody walk already? That's not we agreed. This is what you did with your real owner, I suppose? You liked to go for a run with Luke at the crack of dawn? You still do? Okay. Okay. Just let me find a clean glass for my whisky, will you?'

Further research would have to wait. He had little interest in whales himself, even if his meticulous investigator had. Luke had assembled details of every bizarre sighting and disaster that had occurred up and down the Severn estuary going back a hundred years.

But why?

Revenant himself, Jorge drank a toast to the ghost of his friend who had decided to return home only to disappear again.

Chapter 16

'You really want to do this, Frank?'

'Believe me, I'm your friend, reverend.'

'You're wrong about that.'

'You have it with you? You do, don't you, Luke? Wow, I knew you'd be the answer to all our prayers.'

'Honestly I don't think I am.'

'I just need to see it for myself.'

Luke responded with a glance that he had no time for speculation – with a growl that he did not want to indulge in any. The frantic tapping of his fingers on the pew in the chapel of HMPL…. went unnoticed, however.

To encourage Frank Cordell in his obsession was only to delay his own busy day still further. A twenty-year-old prisoner had already come to him because he couldn't cope. Whenever this man used the toilet his cellmate sat on his bed. Watched him defecate. The cell was so small and the lack of privacy so bad that he had told him, 'Reverend, I can't fucking breathe, I feel as if I'm drowning.' He'd been very highly strung, like someone at the edge of a cliff. It was his job to talk the poor bastard down.

Instead here he was indulging some fool's fantasies.

As he produced the Bible from his pocket Cordell's eyes fell upon it not so much in greed but in reverence.

'What's wrong, reverend? You getting cold feet already?'

'So tell me your theory.'

'Trust me, I saw Rex write things in these very pages.'

'Then start at the beginning.'

'What's wrong? Don't tell me you don't want to get rich, too? Or would

97

that somehow be against your nature now?'

'Meaning?'

'The thing is, reverend, some of the prison officers aren't too thrilled to see you here. To them you'll always be 'Lucky' Luke Lyons, son of Rex Lyons the ram-raider who liked to rob the rich. You're the offspring of one of the most successful Robin Hoods in the country.'

'I've had all my pre-appointment checks and security clearances ready to start work.'

'You know what they say, the leopard can't change its...'

'I have written permission from my faith leader.'

'Yes, of course, I know that, Luke, but what are people in here expected to think? You yourself did time inside not that long ago.'

'Doesn't mean God can't save a bad person.'

'To some, your clerical clothes are the Devil's disguise.'

'We've grown that cynical, have we Frank?'

'So what did make you decide to become a prison chaplain?'

'I grew up.'

Cordell only laughed. Then, undaunted and childishly excited as ever he began to thumb hurriedly through more pages.

'Rex recited certain passages over and over when he was high on drugs. He raved a great deal about his hidden fortune.'

'And how exactly do you intend making sense of it all, Frank?'

'There has to be a clue or key of some kind.'

'Why would I pay any attention to the ravings of a recovering druggy like you?'

'Hard to believe they were random and meaningless ramblings, reverend.'

'You have a plan?'

'I need to know what Rex knew, so why disappoint me?'

The confidence was chilling. So much so that Luke did not doubt for a moment that, by sharing a cell with his father day and night, Cordell had somehow seen into his soul. He'd found his attitude peculiarly hypnotic and spellbinding.

'What would you have me do exactly, Frank?'

'I would urge you to help me find the right pages in this fucking Bible.'

'Astonishing.'

'Fact is, I've had certain lines in my head for years now. For instance, Rex would murmur something like the following: *If thou seekest her as silver, and searchest for her as hid treasures...*'

'*Then shalt thou understand the fear of the LORD, and find the knowledge of God.* It's from Proverbs 2: 4-5.'

'Find it, reverend. Find it for me now.'

'Anything to oblige.'

Luke felt commanded. How could he resist? But, dazzled by the flickering strip light in the ceiling, he saw absolutely nothing about the quotation that was at all useful.

Cordell was disappointed, too. His good eye scanned pages in a frenzy.

'Again, reverend: *For where your treasure is, there will your heart be also.*'

'Luke 12: 34.'

'Look it up. Look it up.'

He located the quotation in the text easily enough.

Cordell leaned forwards again, his good eye blinking.

'Nothing?'

Luke shook his head.

'So I have to ask myself, what would Rex say if he were here today?'

'It's a clue, I tell you, reverend.'

'And we're doing so well, so far?'

'Try this then,' said Cordell and with difficulty recited something from The Book of Revelation.

As with Proverbs, so with the rest.

Cordell was now strangely calm but in reality his agitation had not abated.

'Look here, reverend. Are those not hand-written numbers inside the cover?'

'Where?'

'There! 678 034. They must refer to something, surely?'

But numbers of that combination could not be found anywhere. They both sat where they were for a minute or two, then, casting aside the Good Book, Luke extended one hand to the prisoner across the pews. He meant the gesture to be conciliatory but Cordell only looked aghast – his good eye grew wider, confused and unfocused. He rolled his head.

A lot depended on finding that treasure.

Cordell was experiencing a stroke, as well as some serious pain in his chest – all intelligible speech immediately became slurred.

Not even when medical help was urgently summoned would he consent to go quietly to hospital. Kept wailing about El Dorado. Temporarily lost his reason.

Luke placed the Bible back in his pocket. Their meeting had proved fruitless but he hated to tell himself, 'I told you so'.

*

This overgrown, former railway was not the easiest place to walk in the warm spring evening. Luke trod the overgrown trackbed to a point high above the River Severn. He pushed past the last few trees and bushes – saw hundreds of silvery snakes uncoil among the black, gleaming mudflats far below. Such currents resembled the blazing backs of living creatures from his unusually high vantage point. He could not help but wonder at their incorporeity and strangeness. Moreover, he was inclined to make out not simply wavering, sunlit channels but gently unravelling hair as though of someone living.

He stared at the retreating sea and felt the air around him grow suddenly colder. A flaming red sun hung heavily on the horizon and in two hours' time the ebb-tide would be at its lowest. His view embraced beach as much as bank, estuary as much as river, so expansive did the seamless meeting of sky and water seem – so tirelessly bracing. Only curlews and shelducks appeared to appreciate the contradiction. Then a bark from Sasha broke the spell.

They were at the end of the line just outside Sharpness. The unguarded drop into the ship canal lay at the tip of his toes. This was the place where the now truncated railway had once continued across the water; this was where it took 6,800 tons of iron to bridge the estuary. Being vertiginous, it soon gave him vertigo.

'A sad end, here, to a great achievement,' he said aloud.

'You got that right, reverend.'

He was not alone, Luke realised with a shock.

A man who had to be in his eighties emerged from the spindly ash trees directly behind him.

He was, frankly, horrified to see him lean so far over the viaduct's ruined parapet, since only space spanned then and now. He could embrace the seemingly infinite but not the void.

'Sorry, what did you just say to me?'

'Hard to believe, isn't it, reverend? How can something so solid simply vanish?'

Pressed for an answer, Luke had none to give.

How should he react? He'd already made the mistake of replying.

His companion's attitude was that of a tedious and talkative local. Something blazed in his bright brown eyes. This was *his* spot and he was intruding?

Luke decided to assert his right to the vista, too.

'River looks magnificent on a day like this, doesn't it?'

The other man instantly raised his hand by way of objection.

'Why then should everything feel so soulless? Is it just because something horrific happened here?'

'Such sad remains stand testimony to human folly or bad luck, I suppose.'

'Bad luck?'

'Some would call it the Devil's work.'

'Would you?'

'No.'

That this haggard, unshaven bore still sought to detain him was obvious. To cap it all, he stank of beer and urine.

'Surely you haven't forgotten those days when you and I went fishing, reverend? Surely you'd recall an old acquaintance if you met him after so many years?'

'I can't say. You?'

'The name is Ian Grey. I used to buy elvers from your grandfather to sell to restaurants in Gloucester. He and young Slim Jim Jackson were my best suppliers. You remember Jackson? Of course you do. Later on, it was Jackson who took you and that chubby vicar's boy – I forget his name –

poaching when you were ten or so. Your grandfather showed Jackson where to hide his boat in Berkeley Pill. Then Jackson showed you the same thing. Thus does one inherit a little bit of the river to pass on. It was Jackson who gave you his cap to wear. Called you 'Captain'.'

Jackson. Why should it of all the names in the world resurface now?

It was like a stab with a blade to his heart.

It rang alarm bells, but in starting backwards Luke found his path blocked again.

Crazy thoughts rushed into his head. They wanted to hurtle him into the nearby void like a runaway train.

'You done here, Mr Grey?'

'Take it easy, reverend. No reason to get on your high horse with me.'

'Sorry, I have to go. Duty calls.'

'First Jackson then you. If this isn't fate I don't know what is.'

'You think?'

'I ran into the lousy bastard only a week ago in Gloucester. Who'd have thought it, reverend, after all this time? I'm enjoying a quiet beer in my local and in strolls Slim Jim. Bold as brass he was.'

This time Luke's blood positively froze. How could this be? Somehow he had convinced himself that the subject of their conversation had to be in the twilight of his life. Like Ian. Because that's how he remembered him from long ago. A child will always consider an adult to be old. He counted the years on his fingers. In fact, Jackson was probably only in his mid-sixties now. Hardly a ghost, then, after all.

'Slim Jim Jackson's alive and well?'

'Still up to his former tricks, reverend. Ask anyone.'

'An old man like that?'

'His age is not the problem.'

'Somehow I don't doubt it.'

'He and I had a chat about old times. Sank a few pints together.'

'Bad choice.'

'I've got to be honest with you Luke, in the end I told him he wasn't welcome.'

'Is this little chat of ours meant to be going somewhere?'

'I know he was a bit of a wrong'un but I'm not here to muddy those particular waters. That's just the way things were in those days.'

'Question for you. Tell me what the hell it is you want with me, if it isn't to do me some sort of harm?'

'I really don't.'

'Just catching up?'

'Love to talk about old times, reverend, but I need your help.'

Confronted head-on, Luke chose to confront. He braced himself. Had he not already burnt his bridges to be done with the past? He was angry and dismayed. This was nothing less than a vile ambush.

'As I said, we're done here.'

'It's about your grandfather Sean Lyons. Now, reverend, will you wait awhile and listen to me or not?'

Luke stopped dead in his tracks.

'Sean Lyons? Whatever do you mean?'

'You're the only one who might give a shit about what really happened to him.'

'I'm sorry, but I honestly don't have time for this.'

Ian buried his heavily veined fists in his coat in a manner that could only be described as incorrigibly unpleasant. His whole attitude was sly and devious.

'It all took place here at about 10.30 at night on the 25th October, fifty-six years ago, if you recall, reverend? Two oil tankers, the Wastdale H and the Arkendale H got caught in the tide. Some accounts state that a member of the crew lashed the boats together to try to save them both, though that's disputed. So many died that night it is hard to get the full picture. All we can say is that for some reason neither boat could get free of the other. Going full steam ahead on port or starboard helm didn't release them from their fatal embrace. Crews only had a few minutes to correct course before they struck one of the railway bridge's vital piers.'

'No one will ever forget that terrible night, Mr Grey. The death of five tanker crew is commemorated on two fine memorial stones. They're touchstones, so to speak. Already many a person will refer to something as being 'before' or 'after' the bridge came down. Such markers along the way are rightly part of who we are.'

'But they don't celebrate Sean Lyons, do they?'

'Facts speak for themselves. My grandfather disappeared in the fog as he tried to row out to the burning barges in mid-river, right opposite where we are now standing, only to have them explode in his face.'

Ian paled. It had to be conjectured from the look in his eyes that he, too, had come here to pay his respects today. The screams of gulls still echoed those of men?

'They found Sean's boat the next day – what was left of it.'

'So tell me something else I don't already know.'

'Might be nothing, reverend.'

Luke demurred. He was unresponsive for a while and stared into space. For such a panorama, the light was getting poorer.

The aftermath of the sun's heat on the sandbanks, mud and water served to generate an uneasy shimmer.

It was enough to imagine that he saw the troublesome shapes of poor lost souls as they waded forever forlornly among the treacherous shoals.

Suddenly he turned and said angrily: 'My grandfather died a hero, I tell you. There were other valiant men who set sail in small boats that night, too, but that doesn't diminish the part he played. You know any different?'

'I don't. Nor did I see him drown.'

'So which is it?'

'No one else found him drowned, either.'

'That's because the river washed him straight out to sea when the tide turned.'

'That's one version of events.'

'You have another?'

'Will you hear me out or not?'

'What choice do I have?'

'None – unless you want to go on living a terrible lie.'

Ian was offering him the chance to listen to him very carefully. Besides, had he not just told him that Slim Jim Jackson lived? Not everyone got to resurrect the one person they murdered every day, in their own mind.

Clearly just wishing someone dead was not nearly the same as dying.

Chapter 17

Jorge pulled his black cap lower down his brow to shield his eyes from the hard glint off the water. There was, this far upstream, a most unusual graveyard for boats that had been 'hulked' to shore up the dyke between the river and the ship canal where he and Luke had once played as boys.

He caught up with Sasha as she ran round the wrecks.

This early in the morning it was as lonely a place as the sorriest soul might wish to see.

Many of the graves were mere grassy humps, while elsewhere a rusty bilge pump or broken bow marked the place. In places the rising sun lit names such as ADA, HARRIET and SALLY that protruded above the sand and grass like tombstones.

Here, schooners, trows, bird barges and numbered lighters full of mud rose from the ground like the blackened, prehistoric remains of the trees from which they had once been hewn.

Still others had been reduced to bleached and jagged spikes of timber that resembled bones.

It was from the beached wreck of the two-masted schooner Island Maid that Luke's grandfather Sean had gleaned valuable scrap metal in 1953, but Luke had not been like his family. He had openly revered the wrecks. Told Jorge that he must do so, too. Together they used to re-enact the journey 20,000 leagues under the sea in Jules Verne's journey to Atlantis – they had renamed one of the wrecks the Nautilus while he played Professor Aronnax and Luke was Captain Nemo.

It was wishful thinking, of course, but he could almost see Luke framed against the river. Atop a hulk. Telling tall tales.

It was Luke who told him the real-life story of the captain who had shot himself in the head in his cabin, only to be found years later walking up and down the slanting deck of one of these very same shipwrecks.

Even if the boats did not come with a ghost they were haunting enough for the screech of a gull to scare him now, thought Jorge.

There was history to be learnt, too, if you knew where to look. The 127ft schooner Catherine Ellen might be lost from sight today but in 1921 she had been impounded for running guns to the IRA in Ireland.

This was a treacherous place where the unwary might be tempted to forget that the tide could come racing round the corner like a steam train.

The last time he was here he had been that careless, Jorge recalled, in an amateurish attempt to wade into the river to fish for salmon.

He had miscalculated the speed of the bore and spring tide in the darkness while Luke went off to collect firewood. When he looked back to shore the shipwrecks lay askew and broken as water fed fresh silt through their smashed ribs, singing and sighing the strangest of songs.

Next minute, the level of water was three or four feet up the bank and rising. All ways back to land were suddenly deceptive.

He tried to wade a hidden gulley. Got struck in its quicksand – the path to safety was a mockery of the bravest, a contempt for the living, a blasphemous invitation to the already dead only.

'Help! Luke! I'm sinking!'

The expanse of clear night sky added to the silvery silence in which the river appealed, siren-like, to all he had ever liked or loved. Ripples sparkled through the maze of sandbanks and mudflats in jewel-like ribbons. Their sweet melody promised him something most beautiful in the starry reflections if he took another step out to sea; the gathering currents offered him immense riches of dazzling import if he went that little bit further....

He could not take another step backwards or forwards.

Surging towards him there emerged four seahorses at the head of a glittering chariot all made of water.

He had to brace himself for when the glassy cavalcade struck his chest, even as the rush of foaming steeds ran him down to the sound of much hissing and spitting.

'Help! For Christ's sake, somebody help me! I can't move my legs.'

He thought in all the confusion that he heard the sound of his own name.

Felt himself scooped up. He screamed even as a glistening face shone through spray and spume to peer down and take him.

Next minute someone was plunging at him through the flood. Never before had he seen such flagrant neglect of their own safety. They took a deep breath and dived for him regardless of any tsunami; they half swam and half surfed through swirling silt and currents. They swept their arms left and right in front of them as they burrowed deep into the sea wave. If they had fallen flat in the mud they would most likely have got stuck, too. If they had panicked or ingested too much salt water, they would have been lost like him when the bore crashed over them both with its watery avalanche.

Seconds later a long thin hand grasped his arm. It pulled him upwards and backwards. It was Luke!

The year was 1991.

They were both ten.

*

Of the foaming chariot he had hesitated to say much at all. His mind felt forever fixed on that moment when, during his near-drowning, he had seen a red-headed charioteer ride by high above him in the water. How could he be mistaken about a vision so clear on her white crest of a wave? Yet it had been but a mirage?

Luke stood next to him, dripping water by the seawall.

'Wow, Jorge. That was close. Thought I'd lost you. Can't you swim at all?'

'No way.'

'Relax, I'll teach you one day.'

'Aye, aye, Captain Nemo.'

'You okay?'

'Why are you asking?'

'You look bloody awful. What's wrong? What did you see?'

'It was nothing.'

'Jorge, you're ashen. Or is it just the cold?'

'You got that right.'

'You can't be too careful. My grandmother says that on a spring tide Sabrina rides the bore as far as Gloucester.'

'Who's Sabrina?'

'She's the guardian goddess of the Severn, silly. She lives in a palace built of dead men's bones deep underwater.'

'What's that got to do with me?'

'Tonight's a full moon. That's when you'll most likely see her.'

It was only another of Luke's scary stories.

'You see, Sasha, I swear he wanted me to believe that nonsense he told me that evening.'

The taste and smell of the sea still took his memory by storm and to this day he didn't know how much faith Luke put in a legend that could never be proved.

But from that moment on they had considered themselves blood brothers.

He still did, even if they had, years later, gone their separate ways.

Chapter 18

'You seem upset and fearful, Mr Grey.'

'Damn right I am, reverend.'

There came into Ian's bright eyes something wild and disconcerting. His mention of a living lie excited him terribly, thought Luke. This high above canal and river he found himself sweating. Who was to say that his unexpected companion would not hurl them both from the ledge at any moment?

'If you have anything to tell me, Ian, now's the time.'

'Trust me, reverend, what happened on the night of 25th October 1960 leaves a lot of questions.'

'You suppose?'

'Come see for yourself.'

Ian drew from his pocket a number of black and white photographs and placed them side by side on the broken parapet.

The first picture depicted a length of fallen railway line whose crumpled end had come to rest on a stretch of sandbank exposed at low tide. Pinched and kinked, each buckled rail looked as if it had been torn from its bridge by the vindictive hand of some enraged giant.

Luke studied the scene in detail: a black mass of wreckage turned out to be girders and barges that were inextricably entangled. Another picture showed the reason why. Some intrepid photographer had ventured to the very edge of the yawning gap in the sky where two iron spans had gone missing high above the River Severn. An impenetrable mist shrouded the distant shore at this point in something discernibly preternatural.

Track vanished into void.

'It's a shock to see pictures taken so soon after the event.'

'Totally.'

'It's as if it happened yesterday.'

'See here, reverend. People were cut off from each other on both shores; they had to sit shivering in their unheated homes for days because a gas pipe that was bolted to the bridge was also severed.'

Luke gave a shudder.

'The first time I saw such horrifying depictions of the disaster was in a scrapbook that my grandmother kept in Chapel Cottage. She collected newspaper cuttings from the local Echo, too.'

But Ian had only just started.

In another photograph a thick pall of smoke filled the sky against which were silhouetted the hulks of two burning barges. The name WASTDALE H was clearly visible while the other barge sat grounded close beside it. The black and white image conveyed very starkly the aftermath of the tragic accident as the wrecks lay exposed but still smoking on the sands drained by the tide. Less like seagoing boats than stranded whales, the smooth, curving hull and flat bottom of the WASTDALE H in particular spoke again of some monstrous act of detestable violence.

The rest of the pictures showed the bridge being dismantled and cut up for scrap years later.

He sensed something disquieting stir inside him.

'I wasn't even born when the collision happened, yet many a night I relive my grandfather's efforts to save dying men in my dreams. Why is that, I wonder? Honestly, I don't want to know.'

'What can I say, reverend? As a young boy your father Rex Lyons saw *his* father Sean row out to the bridge as it fell into flames, never to be seen again. The whole catastrophe was imprinted so deeply on his psyche that he must have bequeathed it to you? The terror of that night is forever part of your genetic make-up?'

'It's true my grandmother never stopped referring to it. She called it our family curse.'

'One person's curse is another's blessing.'

'Yeah. You're probably right. But you've got to admit it all happened a long time ago.'

'Doesn't mean there aren't still consequences.'

'The photographs are so black and bleak.'

'Like them or not, reverend, it makes no difference.'

'Sorry, you're not making much sense.'

'That's because nothing does.'

Ian pointed upriver towards the snaking bend in the Severn called The Noose.

'Those barges are still out there, reverend. You'd see them right now if you had binoculars. Some people walk out to them at low tides despite the quicksand. After the collision the boats drifted together upstream where it's largely unnavigable and had to be blown up with hundreds of tons of gelignite to render them harmless. They belong to the river now. A scary place is the Severn, don't you agree? I do. Perhaps it's because I can't swim.'

Luke fixed his eyes on the awful focus of the other's gaze and did, he thought, see the skeletal shells of two hulks gleam white in the dying light.

It was the mud.

Every ebb tide recoated the hulls in slime that dried so ghastly pale.

Next moment Ian offered him his hand.

'Take a good look, reverend.'

'Sorry, you've lost me.'

'Please, I need you to see this.'

'Ian. You're panting?'

A gold pocket watch and chain lay in his shaky palm. A key on whose round disc a horse's head had been engraved hung from its chatelaine, while its not dissimilar fob's stiff neck and curly tail suggested more seahorse than stallion.

The cylinder bar key wind was working because they could both hear it ticking, although it was, by the time on his phone, ten minutes fast.

Before he could take a closer look its possessor snapped shut its cover.

It was now rapidly getting dark, but some strange light did gleam on the circle of solid gold.

Ian pressed his forearm with urgent fingers.

'This watch belonged to your grandfather, Sean. How it looks is how I found it.'

111

'You asking me?'

'It's not a question, reverend.'

'How long has it been in your possession?'

'I found it on the riverbank.'

'What made it wash up there, I wonder?'

'Sean Lyons dropped it.'

'In 1960, you mean?'

'I mean in 1981.'

'No, no, I already told you, my grandfather died a hero on the night the bridge came down. He drowned in the river trying to save the crew of those burning barges.'

'Keep telling yourself that.'

'I'm definitely not listening to you now, Ian. How many times do I have to say it? He's the one good thing about my family that I can cherish.'

'And if it's all an evil lie?'

'Who says?'

'What is this watch worth to you, Luke? Is it worth anything to you, at all?'

'Yes, it is. It's absolutely priceless.'

'Good, because the proof of what you need to know lies inside.'

'What do you want in return?'

'As you say, reverend, to the right person the most treasured possession has no value. It's the truth that counts. Without that, how do we know what to feel? In our hearts.'

'Sorry. What?'

'It's yours. Take it.'

'Why would you do that?'

Ian retreated round the curve in the railway cutting – he beat his way through its trees and bushes up the gradient towards town and docks where he paused only to call back briefly with a nervous laugh.

'Fact is, Luke, I've kept silent far too long. That curse can be yours now. Meet me at the tin tabernacle. Come alone.'

'Why wait until then?'

Ian's right arm described in the air some dismissive semaphore. It was an unsettling, heartfelt, joyous wave as if in relief he felt reprieved.

'First I have to see someone else. Don't forget to look inside the watch, like I said.'

Luke stood motionless before the drop into the canal where, with pounding heart, he scanned the grey horizon for more signs of wreckage. Ian Grey was purporting to be his long lost friend. He really wasn't. The old man was correct when he'd hinted earlier how he hadn't cared much at all for Slim Jim Jackson's behaviour years ago, but he hadn't saved him from his attentions, either.

The unexpected donation of his grandfather's watch temporarily drove all darker thoughts from his head, however. He pressed its cold, glass face hard against his ear whereupon its rapid ticking, like his heart's, grew louder and more urgent.

*

That night in Hill House Sasha kept vigil while Luke closed his eyes by the fire.

In truth, there was little sleep in him.

He took up his new acquisition and looked for a hinge in the rim. He found it at the 6 o'clock position. Then he inserted the point of the four-inch blade of his flick knife into a little notch. Opened the watch's back. The previous owner had obviously been in the habit of snapping the case-lid shut far too quickly. As a result, the steel latch, being harder than the solid gold, had worn out the spot on the rim where the latch engaged.

Inside the cover was the portrait of a young woman.

He could see by way of his magnifying glass that she was dressed in a jet black taffeta gown which was both very voluminous and nipped at the waist. The front yoke had a scrollwork pattern beaded with glistening clear bugle beads or something very similar. It was apparent, even in miniature, that the dress's brief bodice was boned and shaped with panels in the bust cups in a style that had to date to the 1940's.

His eyes fastened next on her hair: a crocheted bag kept the back of its black curls neat in a snood while the fringe was left out and rolled.

He prised free the photograph and on its back were a few words penned in black ink: **To Sean with love from O.**

113

He studied the face again and her large, ebony coloured eyes peered right through him. Her long nose, stiff neck and jutting chin suggested a stuffy aristocratic air of entitlement that was belied by her wild stare. The defiant curl of her lip was openly rebellious as he estimated her age to be the early twenties.

Ian was right, the pocket watch had never been exposed long to the elements. Certainly it had not spent years at the bottom of any river. And yet, what it managed to do was to bridge, from then till now, the gap between the missing and the found.

*

And so at midnight, surrounded by his mummified fish and model ships in glass cases, Luke dozed off in his chair.

He dreamt that he was his grandfather on the night the bridge came down.

Must row harder…

Flames as high as the bridge.

…in and out of pools of burning petroleum. Looks like one barge has hit another. I can see someone in the water.

Can't get near the fallen girders.

Tonight burns like hell.

All this fog is fire.

Are those cries I can hear from the riverbank?

It's no use, I'm literally too late already.

Or am I?

'Is anyone there?'

'Yes.'

The answer comes back very faintly.

'Where are you in the water?'

'I can't say. I just am.'

The blaze is so fierce, not even the firemen can get near. Can just about make out the crackle of radios and flash of lights through the red glow. No sign of the fireboat from Sharpness Docks. No wonder. It's built for the ship canal, not river. In these conditions it doesn't stand a chance.

The water must be alight from shore to shore in a wall of fire for nearly a mile...

At last! There! Beyond my rowboat's bow.

...straight ahead beneath the burning oil.

Swing the boat hard around.

That's where they could yet resurface...

That beautiful face.

Visible suddenly...

Time to ship the oars and call again.

Beneath the slick of iridescent oil shine agate, Turkish blue and emerald green...

'Give me your hand, Sean.'

'What makes you think you can save me?'

'What makes you think I can't?'

'But I'm not wearing any life jacket.'

'Be quick, I tell you, or you'll burn me with you.'

'You go, my boat could sink at any moment.'

'Better to come with me to the bottom.'

Again, those other, distant voices of frantic concern.

A red navigation light flashes its bloody eye on the bridge's double pier seventy feet above me.

That siren voice from beneath the waves is so luring and tempting.

Tomorrow dark water will disgorge its deadly flotsam.

*

Luke opened his eyes with a start, still convinced that he waded dead men's bones at the bottom of the river.

Sasha pawed at his chest. Barked and growled. She urged him to hurry up and take notice.

It was pouring with rain outside Hill House – he was listening to rain, not drowning.

'What is it? What's wrong?'

The fire beside him was reduced to glowing ashes which was why he felt so cold? He stood up sharply in almost total darkness. Then he felt his way cautiously across the floor as far as the door.

Sasha followed.

If someone else was in the house, then they had just entered while he was dreaming?

Violent gusts of rain flooded the patio doors that stood open at the very end of the corridor that divided the house from east to west on its ground floor.

Sasha awaited his command but as a precaution he kept his hand on her collar. She would, once unleashed, be unstoppable.

Before a bookshelf stood a man in a camel coat. Somebody urgently thumbed pages. He glanced at them through his wire-rimmed spectacles.

Long, thick fingers were dreadfully pale.

Luke guessed at once that he was not reading but looking for something.

Of his face he saw only the misshapen jaw and twisted nose of a street fighter who'd suffered more than a few brutal knocks in his heyday. The large, bullet-head had a cap drawn low over its brow. A strap over his shoulder went to a bag at his hip into which he was ready to press some vital volume or other.

His breath condensed white in the cold air that blew through the doors that he had forced open from the terrace.

If the bibliomaniac had looked beyond the flash of his torch then he might have noticed them. As it was, he sighed aloud in obvious frustration which struck Luke as dishearteningly often.

Sasha understood his alarm but not his caution.

Something prohibited him from challenging or retreating, a strange edict born of the dream from which he had just woken. They shared the house with a ghost?

Chapter 19

Day 5 was a day of delight.

According to his cabbage soup diet, he was permitted to devour a sizeable piece of chicken, Jorge noted.

He could also eat several fresh tomatoes.

The downside was that he was supposed to drink lots and lots of very boring water. The minimum, apparently, was eight glasses. This was to flush out something called uric acid.

Honestly, until now he hadn't even known he had uric acid.

The best diets, doubtlessly, were those which engendered just the right level of fear by feeding off a person's ignorance.

'I mean, uric acid!' he said. 'It can't be good. Can it?'

Sasha rested her chin on her paws and flattened one ear while he added two tablespoons of olive oil to a large pot which simmered over medium heat in the vicarage's newly cleaned kitchen. The future, he resolved, had to be a fresh start. He would from now on be more of a grazer than a feaster. Gone from the freezer were ten tubs of ice cream that he had bought only yesterday.

Next he added onions, bell peppers and carrots. His intention was to saute them until tender, after which he would stir in some garlic. A chicken broth lay beside him ready for the cabbage.

He bared both arms. Donned his spotless white apron.

He was, in the guise of some bold alchemist, striving to experiment – which went some way to explain the horror of his creation.

'Large I may be but I will not be demonised. The real demon is sugar. It's the new Satan.'

He reached for his recently acquired spiraliser which was particularly useful for ruining perfectly good courgettes that all food bloggers were now eating. Were these not the same young, beautiful people who wanted him to eat chia seeds by the handful? Such bird food set him thinking.

'If I had to hazard a guess, Sasha, I'd say that should Luke ever come back to life he'll return home here. To Hill House. What else can I say? Do the dead even need food and drink to sustain them?'

On the shelves were the missing man's cans of fruit and baked beans whose expiry dates had years to run.

Sasha whined. Wrinkled her nose. Flicked an ear.

'Yes, of course I can smell it, but where is it coming from? Who's the culprit here?'

Next minute he was striding, still draped in his apron, as far as the main reception room where he looked in.

No spark had leapt from the enormous gilded chimney piece to set fire to rug or furniture, thank goodness. Still the smell of smoke intensified. He continued along the corridor to its end. He rattled double doors. Worked their wonky handles.

Sasha whined to be let out to the terrace beyond. Jorge followed. Big, fluttering, grey and white petals immediately stuck to his blue NATO-style sweater and crisply ironed black trousers. They were whisked his way on the wind like the last cherry blossoms off the trees in the garden – they stuck, most annoyingly, to his highly polished black boots and even his apron.

It was hot ash.

Sasha hurried past the clipped pyramids of yew that flanked one corner of the house.

He shared her dogged indignation.

'Not so fast. Be careful.'

The midday sun had yet to shine through the smoky fir trees, he discovered, with a shiver.

His parents might have emigrated to Portugal in 2005, but the 18th century sundial still stood on the lawn covered in daisies and a pair of equally old, stone piers supported metal gates of a former carriage entrance. Tall urns stood atop the garden walls and commemorated in their patterns of stone and yellow lichen the union of ancient families by marriage. Hill House boasted a history far beyond that of a simple vicarage which, even while growing up here, he had never bothered to unravel.

The unnatural ambivalence that he felt towards his gloomy childhood home was as nothing to the outrage that gripped him now.

Volcanic red flame erupted within the brick confines of the kitchen garden. Sure enough, a man dressed in old clothes and Wellingtons stood by a large black oil drum in which the blaze was imprisoned.

A captain's cap shaded the arsonist's eyes as he went on picking things out of a large wheelbarrow. Paintings of shipwrecks came apart from their frames in his hands. Stuffed fish lay half out of their cases at his feet.

Before each bout of firing he took a swig from his silver flask.

'Luke, dear friend? That you?' cried Jorge.

The stoker removed his cap and scratched his broad forehead. Long white hair hung in a ponytail at the back of his neck. His beard was equally white, his large eyes very alert, his skin a mass of wrinkles which the smoke was busy tanning the colour of old leather. In height he was not very tall with very straight shoulders – not an old salt of the sea, after all, as he resorted to his wheelbarrow for more fuel.

'My name is Sam Rooke. Who are you?'

Jorge covered his nose and mouth with a tissue to combat the fumes.

'Never mind who I am, what are you doing in Reverend Lyons's garden?'

'I'm his gardener.'

'Doesn't explain why you are burning his books and pictures?'

'Mind your own business.'

'He tell you to do it?'

'What gives you the right to interfere?'

'How did you get into the house?'

'I have a key. You?'

'I'm Inspector Jorge Winter and I'm here to investigate Reverend Lyons's disappearance.'

'You working for God or the Devil?'

'If you're so keen to listen to idle gossip then you'll know that I'm in charge of Gloucester Cathedral's private police force. I'll investigate *you*, if necessary.'

'Doesn't mean you can stop me doing my job, Inspector.'

'Doesn't mean you can destroy Reverend Luke's things.'

'Well, you're too late. I'm doing all that needs to be done right now. It's going up in flames as we speak.'

Jorge flinched at the pyromaniac's hostile gaze.

'Fact is, Mr Rooke, Rev. Luke Lyons and I grew up together around here.'

Rooke extended his hand to the fire and dangled a book over it with a momentary pause of apparent anguish.

'He ever bring you here, at all, Inspector?'

'*I* brought *him*. Back then, I was the local vicar's son. This was my home, not his.'

'And now he's not here any more, what are you going to do about it?'

'I'm here to establish whether anyone contributed to his untimely demise.'

'Oh, so you do think there was foul play, then, do you?'

He smiled vaguely. The notion that Luke might have been murdered was still a consideration of his.

'It is important for the Church to know for certain that no claims can be brought against it in the light of some sort of preventable accident.'

With that, Rooke let slip the book he was holding.

'Give the Devil his due is more like it.'

'No one wants to be accused of vicarious liability, let alone contributory or criminal negligence.'

The book burned bright in the flames.

'You really do think it was murder not accident or suicide, Inspector?'

'For the sake of Reverend Lyons's soul, I hope to prove something.'

Rooke scratched his nose somewhat violently.

'Sounds ambitious.'

'It all comes down to burden of proof. Normally one thing that might assist me would be the doctrine of res ipsa loquitor. It means 'the matter speaks for itself'.'

'Sorry, Inspector, you've lost me there.'

'If Reverend Lyons was killed through the gross negligence of another it may constitute the criminal offence of manslaughter. However, since the police have no evidence to suggest that he was 'murdered' any proof of how he did come to die must be on the balance of probabilities. If he was not pushed and he did not mean to kill himself, something else must have induced him to venture too close to the river?'

'Damn it, Inspector. A man like that does as he likes.'

'You last saw him when, exactly?'

Wood, glass and varnish crackled as the stuffed fish joined the inferno. Then, seeing that his job had been fatally interrupted, Rooke backed away from the hellish inferno.

'I last saw Reverend Lyons with Barbara Jennings on the morning of the day he disappeared. I was watering plants in the greenhouse over there when they walked together through the garden. She was very agitated about something. I didn't distinctly hear what she said but she was asking for some kind of forgiveness.'

'His or God's?'

'Ask her yourself, Inspector. She rents a place in the village by the name of Angel Cottage.'

'How did Reverend Lyons appear to you in the weeks or days before he vanished? Was he upset or ill? Did he have financial troubles? Was he, by any chance, a gambler or womaniser? More significantly, how strong was his faith, do you think? Had he begun to doubt his own calling?'

Rooke's eyes were evasive, his gait awkward, his fingers flexed as if to re-enforce his own calm.

'I'd say he was a man possessed.'

'Interesting. Was it connected to what Barbara Jennings told him?'

'Reverend Lyons had become preoccupied with something about the River Severn – or the Severn Sea, as he liked to call it. Then Sabrina visited the vicarage.'

'Would that be the shipping magnate Sabrina ap Loegres, by any chance?'

'You know her?'

'I read about her in a magazine.'

'Honestly, I don't know what she saw in him apart from their shared interest in sailing ships.'

Jorge picked ash off his sweater. Whatever he did it would now stink of smoke forever, he feared.

'Loegres is an unusual name, is it not?'

Rooke raised a finger to stab his point home.

'That's not the most mysterious thing about her, if you ask me.'

'So where can I find her?'

'You can't. She lives abroad or sails the oceans.'

'Does she have flaming red hair?'

'Why do you ask?'

'Never mind that now.'

'Intend to stay here long, do you, Inspector?'

'What about you?'

'Not me,' said Rooke with a shudder. 'I moved out of my cottage in the grounds two weeks ago. Doubt if any man can live here by himself, now.'

'Too bad.'

At that moment Rooke's phone rang in his pocket.

'I'll be back later, Inspector, to dig the celery trenches.'

'Celery?'

'You can say. It should have been sown by now. There's nothing like food you love, is there? This garden should be kept alive, if nothing else.'

'Why bother if Reverend Lyons has gone forever?'

'You don't like celery, Inspector? The Captain does. He absolutely loves it. This year he wants me to grow the old-fashioned type. It's not self-blanching.'

So saying, Rooke stepped through the doorway in the kitchen garden's red brick wall and vanished.

Jorge gave a whistle. He'd come to Berkeley intending to perform a miracle. Since he now knew that he could not simply summon Luke out of thin air, he began to worry in earnest that he had not only performed a remarkable vanishing act but something almost supernatural. Outside the ordinary operation of cause and effect.

'This way, Sasha. You and I need to take another look at Hill House before our gardener friend deliberately destroys any more clues with his crazy exorcisms.'

Sasha cocked her head on one side and shook ash off her ears. Suddenly the senseless, risky bravado was all his. He did try to justify himself to her, but straightway was he subjected to her scornful silence.

It was the same dubious look she gave him when he announced a new diet, except for one thing: she was aware, like him, that for all Sam Rooke's talk of Rev. Luke Lyons's murder, he still spoke about him in the present tense.

Chapter 20

The frustration in the burglar's voice was plain to hear.

'It *has* to be here, damn it. Was he not always banging on about fucking 'Treasure Island'?'

He was baffled by the sheer number of books in front of him, Luke observed as he took a cautious step forward along the vicarage's wide, dark corridor.

Sasha's growl broke the otherwise profound silence.

Next moment he issued his own separate challenge.

'Do me a favour. Tell me what you think you're doing in my home?'

The response was immediate.

The bullet-headed phantom dived for the icy rain through the open doorway – his sprint into the wet night was a professional exit with a knowledge of Hill House that was a dire test of his hospitality.

'Now! Go get him, Sash!'

The moon cleared black clouds as Luke heard the fugitive's fading cries. In the meantime he began to retrieve books getting wet on the floor in the corridor.

First in his hand was 'Coral Island' by R.M. Ballantyne complete with coloured plates of 'the wonderful cavern' and pirates on board the mission schooner.

'Captain Singleton' came next, a tale of piracy and unexplored Africa by Daniel Defoe.

Hemingway's 'The Old Man And The Sea' was more realistic.

He soon discovered that Herman Melville's 'Moby Dick', alone of the scattered volumes, had not been torn apart in mindless rage.

But before he could attempt to explain such wanton destruction, he was recalled to the patio door by Sasha who stood whining on the terrace. She had returned empty-handed.

When he rang the police and told them that so far as he could tell nothing had been stolen, all they would do was consent to log the crime.

Who was he to say whom he'd seen, anyway? Had he not been half asleep when it happened?

Luke felt a sudden sense of restless motion that was not unlike the shifting of a boat on water. He had to sit down in his chair by the fireside for as long as the nauseating rocking of the walls all round him reduced the room to waves.

After that, he stared at his 10,000-piece jigsaw. Pondered why so much refused to fit together.

But it would, he vowed. He'd get to the bottom of it, no matter what.

Sasha, meanwhile, kept one ear open for the slap, slap, slap of any more wet footsteps in the hallway. His unwelcome visitor had shivered in body and soul like a very cold man until the chill suggested a death rattle. No one made such a noise unless he was dying or half frozen to the bone. He favoured the latter. It was the man's teeth that he'd heard chattering. To say it was Sean Lyons risen from the river might be a step too far?

Chapter 21

'Since when were these steps so steep?' said Jorge, as he trod Hill House's old oak staircase. Had he not run up them with ease when he was a boy, though he had not been exactly thin then, either?

Breathlessness overtook him and sweating was no less evident as his podgy fingers stuck to the dusty banister. His pounding heart was less heroic than horrendous.

He felt the need to give his beer belly a rest at the first twist in the treads. Dabbed his brow with his sleeve.

'Too many barbecued burgers. Too many pot noodles and pork belly bao buns for brunch,' he gasped.

Whereas the ground floor had felt claustrophobic and dark, up here was altogether different. The stained glass window, at least, had not changed since his childhood as he threw back its shutters to let in some light.

'What the devil!' said Jorge and stood open-mouthed on the landing.

So many copies of famous seafaring paintings hung on the walls that he, too, could have been all at sea at that moment as he became aware of his earnest desire to share the drama.

That Luke had felt the call of the ocean from the very depths of his heart was indisputable – he had collected all things nautical when sailing all over the world.

Such a siren-like calling was not necessarily the opposite of everything religious, not when the theme of such a great accumulation of relics concentrated on the sea's power of destruction and redemption.

He was drawn to one dramatic picture in particular. It was a reproduction of JMW Turner's wreck of the Minotaur. The Royal Navy 74-gun ship of the line was breaking up on the Haak Bank off the Netherlands in darkness and heavy weather. She had already rolled over on the sand. Was making water. Too late, the crew had cut all the masts to lighten the load only to see their ship flood its forecastle. Now the hull split under the relentless pounding of the waves as men took to a broken and rudderless launch and yawl to try to make it back to land.

He was familiar with the event of 1810 since the painting was so famous, but never before had he heard men's actual screams sound in his ears.

The mariners were so distressed and miserable and yet so tenacious that their howls filled the house with a heart-felt plea for their very souls.

Could Luke have heard the same thing?

Dangerously fascinating was how he found it, as if his friend chose to celebrate that moment of suspended animation when lives hung in the balance between heaven and hell.

'What had you in its spell, Luke? Was it literally that moment which decides someone's fate forever for good or ill? Or did you simply fall in love with death itself?'

Poor, lost Luke. He must remember he was not forgotten. Still had a friend. Perhaps then he could come home. Reach shore.

The whole collection he could view only as heart-rending and disturbing.

*

Jorge very much began to suppose that to ignore such calamitous seascapes was to miss some other heinous wickedness or devilish atrocity.

Ships' bells carried the names of lost vessels while antique compasses, sextants, telescopes, binnacles and diving helmets lined the wide corridor at the very top of the house with items gleaned from dead captains' cabins. It all ran contrary to those distant days when Luke had forbidden him to salvage a single thing from the wrecks beside the River Severn.

Sasha was not usually one to bother that a house could have its own special atmosphere, but next moment she began to bark furiously at a half-naked, red-haired figure propped on a chair.

He only thought the carved woman superbly defiant.

The bare-breasted beauty leaned his way with earnest intensity. One outstretched arm forged a path ahead with her burning lamp until he could not but thank her for her welcome light.

127

But how enigmatic seemed her face to him then – she'd come from a real shipwreck, to be sure.

Sasha advanced to the silent, immobile chatelaine and sniffed her grey, sculpted skirt. The sentinel slept with slits for eyes but with sufficient smile on her face that Jorge felt sure she dreamed of distant oceans. Her cheeks were bleached as white as bone from wind and water. Her black-painted and varnished lips retained their gloss, as if she might one day placate the high seas again by commanding the waves?

Whereupon he became aware of a nervous prickling on his skin – a frisson of apprehension at some inhuman presence, scarcely identifiable at first, but whose proximity grew more and more offensive.

It was not the ship's figurehead. Instead, he put out his hand to the brass knob on the door alongside her and the shiver subsided – withdrew it and it resumed. No other door was the same.

He chose not to test his childhood fears, however.

Passed on.

'Am I not the victim of my own worst hopes?' said Jorge irritably, as he entered the last room along the corridor and rushed to open its shutters.

There rested on a table beside a four-poster bed an old copy of the Bible. He took a tissue in his hand to examine his find. The name of one of Her Majesty's prisons was stamped inside the cover. Written next to it were the initials RL.

Years had passed and its spell in captivity was over but as the sky outside darkened he found himself strangely bound to this book and time.

Surely this had to be the very Bible for which Frank Cordell had grasped him with his dying hand? More to the point, this could hold the secret to why Rev. Luke Lyons had sunk without trace?

*

Back in the corridor, Jorge came again to the door that he had, a moment ago, declined to try.

Its carved wooden guardian sat stiff and still. Listening.

He could not be sure how long he delayed. His fanatically devout father had once administered his vicious beatings in the dark beyond. He gave the doorknob a quick turn. Found it locked.

A secret sigh of relief escaped his lips.

He might struggle to admit it but his search for Rev. Luke Lyons also meant exorcising a ghost of his own.

Chapter 22

'Look who's here to see you, Gwendolen. It's Reverend Luke Lyons.'

'I don't know any damned reverend.'

'Don't be silly, Gwendolen, of course you do,' said the nurse with her strong Polish accent. 'He's your grandson. He's come all the way from London, especially to visit you.'

The blonde, willowy nurse came to a halt before a grey-haired woman who was sitting in the dayroom of Severnside House for the care of the elderly.

Luke did the same.

The retiree was staring out of two big glass doors that overlooked immaculate lawns within sight of the River Severn. Her almond eyes were unblinking. Her face turned immovably towards the horizon. She appeared to register none of his physical presence.

'Hallo gran. I very much hope you're well.'

She was dressed in a ridiculously thick overcoat which inspired in him an unexpected emotion, something that anyone else might have regarded as feebly sentimental. Today she had gone to some considerable trouble to apply bright, red gloss to her lips as if she expected to go somewhere very important.

'Somehow I doubt it.'

'Let me take your coat?'

'I shouldn't be here is all that matters.'

'But you'll feel so much more comfortable without it in this hot room.'

'Take your hands off me!'

'Don't you want any visitors?'

'Today's the day I go home.'

'Take your time,' said the nurse in Luke's ear. 'Don't worry if she doesn't recognise you at first, but under no circumstances should you open the doors to the grounds. She'll be straight out.'

'Got it.'

Unidentified himself, Luke was slow to identify.

Because he doubted what he saw he began to wonder if he could trust himself to talk to this stranger at all. She was horribly altered. Shrunken, shrivelled and bowed, she exuded none of the benevolent authority over which they had once clashed. Her hairy chin was slightly stained with milk from breakfast that morning. Her long, almost white fringe, refused to remain where she had combed it. Sleeplessness had taken as great a toll. She appeared, at eighty-six, the perfect candidate for incarceration in a place that was warm, safe and most of all secure.

Then, as he stretched out hesitant fingers to her veined and wrinkled hand, on whose finger there still shone a bright gold wedding ring, he did see in her some evidence of the person who had once done her best to save his childish soul.

But he was in forgiving mood.

'Fuck it, Gwendolen, you look great.'

'Shouldn't you be in school?'

'Huh?'

'Keep it to yourself.'

'I'm sorry?'

'Haven't you heard? The bridge is down.'

'What bridge?'

'You can't take the train over the river to the Grammar School any more?'

'No, you're right, I can't.'

'Lucky day, then.'

Gwendolen shot him a sweet smile. It all came back to her very clearly and sharply, as having happened yesterday but to someone else.

Luke drew his chair quietly into line with hers.

'What a nice place this is. I'm so happy for you.'

In Gwendolen's twilight world something ghostlike, even phantasmal, stirred.

'Shit happens,' she said and gazed again through the locked glass door. 'It makes you think, doesn't it? I mean, a train passed over all right not long before those barges struck and there were men due to work on the bridge that very hour. So why not them? Why did your poor father have to suffer along with the boats' crews? What fateful hand struck them down and spared the others? Can something that big ever be rebuilt? It will take an act of faith from us all.'

It immediately struck him that, to her eyes, he was her son Rex – they were back in 1960 and his father had just started secondary school across the river.

'I'm Luke, gran. I've come home a changed man to live a new life. This is your grandson reborn in the eyes of the Lord.'

A tear rolled from one of Gwendolen's eyes.

'I knew a Luke once,' she said, suddenly reiterating what the nurse had said a moment ago. 'He was that very thin baby. I had to raise him for years because his mum and dad went to prison. A wild boy he turned out to be. He was born so bad he went to the devil.'

'Not quite, gran. He endeavours to be a good man now.'

'*The Devil's child the devil's luck.*'

'He's not that wild child any longer.'

His declaration derived, strange to say, from one of the few sensations of his otherwise dead heart.

'*The Devil never sent a wind out of hell, but he would sail with it.*'

He felt its serpent-like coil uncurl its claws.

Gwendolen remained stubbornly wild-eyed. Her pupils burned with a strict and powerful vigilance. She always had been *so* very awfully evangelical. The minder of a feral child – she whose bitter job it had been to keep him safe from sin – was this other and haunted person now.

Suddenly the ugly old woman beckoned him nearer. She would hiss something urgently in his ear.

'I had to send him away, didn't I? Had to give him up to a young offenders' home. By the time he was eleven he was already out of control, you see. They couldn't do much with him there, either. A rat, he was, reverend, and you know what we do with those.'

She chuckled.

Luke shuddered.

'I remember. It was my birthday. Dozens of them set up home under Chapel Cottage. The pest control man went down into the cellar. He placed poisoned blue grain called DieAlone in all the holes and left us a jar of it in case they ever returned. Never did find out why they chose us particularly.'

'Hundreds of them migrate along the riverbank every spring and autumn.'

'You let me live with you for those early years, gran. For that I'm very grateful. You were a mother to me while my parents rotted in jail.'

'Shame, no sunshine, I'd hoped there'd be sunshine today.'

Luke prepared to get down to business.

'I'm back in Berkeley, gran, in time for Ellie's wedding.'

'Who's Ellie?'

'You haven't forgotten your own granddaughter, have you gran?'

'We've no food in the fridge. Oh dear, ever since Sean went away it's been such a struggle. I can't explain it, but I'm practically certain something dreadful has happened to him. Aren't you?'

He gently squeezed her bony fingers with both hands. Gwendolen now knew who he was but in another time?

He could endure the awful misunderstanding, if not the continued cruelty of it in her eyes.

'Sean's dead, gran. He vanished into the river.'

'You not worried?'

'Should I be?'

'I fancy I'll see, O Lord, such awful sights tonight. My mind will be full of monsters! I'm sure I'll see him standing all dripping wet before my bed as the clock strikes midnight.'

'Do try to concentrate, gran. I've come to talk to you about something very important, not some silly dream.'

Robbed of her full mind, Gwendolen resisted the bad-tempered nature of his.

'You heard the terrible news?'

'What news?'

'They say... They say...'

'Listen to me gran, you're safe here. In fact, it's the only place for you. As a result, you can no longer be expected to manage your own affairs. I'm sorry, but Ellie and I have come to a decision about Chapel House.'

'I want to go out into the garden. I want to lay flowers by the river.'

'I'm not talking about refusing you certain treatments or telling you what to eat or what to wear, I'm talking about your property and finances. Let me handle all your affairs. I can pay your bills, collect your benefits and sell your home. You've not yet altogether lost the mental capacity to appoint a Lasting Power of Attorney or LPA.'

'The blackbirds will be nesting in the honeysuckle above the porch by now.'

'Listen to me, gran, if you don't appoint someone soon and you become unable to decide important things for yourself, then who will pay the bills or make choices about your future care as you become increasingly ill?'

'No, absolutely bloody not. Take me home right now. That is why you're here, isn't it?'

Gwendolen addressed their joint reflection in the triple-glazed door before them. Even a ghost in glass made more sense to her than he did, such were the mysterious depths to which her mind dived now.

'Why not sign Chapel Cottage over to me today, gran? It'll be mine and Ellie's one day anyway.'

'Everyone says the swallows are going to arrive late this year. Is that true?'

'I've brought some of the papers with me.'

'Don't be so sure.'

'Fact is, grandpa is long gone. There is no one else but me and Ellie to inherit anything from you.'

'Doesn't mean the dead won't come knocking.'

'Why would they do that when they've been gone so long?'

'Perhaps they've grown cold in the water and want to come home.'

'Problem is, gran, you can no longer distinguish between fact and fiction.'

'That is what I would expect you to say, reverend. It is 'reverend', is it?'

'It's good you understand something,' he muttered, but had to admit that even the sanest person might struggle to reconcile a teenage delinquent called 'Lucky' Luke Lyons with Luke, a man of the cloth, now.

Gwendolen plucked at her coat to fasten its buttons and then looked round for her hat.

'Not everything people choose to remember can be said to be true. Can it?'

'No, gran, but facts are facts. Sean drowned fifty-six years ago. At least, we must presume he did because his body was never found. Sometimes the absence of proof is so strong we have to consider it a presumption of fact until the contrary is proved.'

'That's easier.'

'Listen to me, gran, you can limit the decisions I make or place conditions on what I do. An empty house can't be left to rot indefinitely.'

She took his pen. Considered the documents.

'But the dead must have somewhere to go.'

'That's it, just scribble your name here and here.'

'The dead bear witness to us all.'

'Please let me steady your hand.'

'I want my solicitor.'

'You don't need a solicitor for this.'

'If I sign you'll have control.'

'Yes and no.'

'You want to get rid of me?'

'Says who?'

'You do. Are you even my grandson? Nurse? Who is this man?'

No sooner had she cried out than the nurse came running.

'What is it, Gwendolen? Whatever's wrong?'

'This man – he shouldn't be here. He's making me sign things I don't know.'

'Believe me, gran, I'm on your side.'

'He says that, but when the Devil prays he has a booty in his eye. Don't you think, nurse?'

The nurse stared hard his way.

'I'm sorry, reverend. Gwendolen finds your presence upsetting.'

'But I only want to put her affairs in order.'

'Sometimes even help can seem like a threat.'

Luke cared not for the nurse's scurrilous insinuation while the form that he needed to take to the Office of the Public Guardian flapped uselessly in his hand.

'We'll settle this later, when we see how she is.'

Whereupon Gwendolen turned her head his way. Her almond-coloured irises blazed at him. Her face was one mean and sly grin.

All this he witnessed, then fell back before her utterly gleeful horror, as if at his own malice aforethought.

She didn't seem the slightest bit crazed but he felt crazy being there.

She was staring in utter disbelief at the newly acquired gold pocket watch that he wore on his waistcoat, Luke realised.

Next moment she let out an ear-splitting scream. It was half hurt child and half ghoulish jinn.

She could have been a vixen cornered by hounds.

'Nurse! I want Barbara. Where is she? I need to talk to my old friend Barbara Jennings right away. It's a matter of life and death.'

Suddenly Gwendolen hurled herself at the locked doors that led to the terrace. She worked their handles hard and pointed. She was, Luke realised, looking upriver to where the massive iron railway bridge had once crossed the canal and estuary. Together, they gazed beyond the daffodils in bloom on the lawn all the way to the water, but hers was the stance of a person forever on the look for an expected, desired or feared occurrence. Clearly she clung to that day in 1960 like a ship to its anchor. Thus she reassured herself with some mental fixedness that something at least remained real.

'Look, he's coming! He's coming!'

The nurse hurried to her side.

'Who is, dear?'

'You'll see soon enough. The river always gives up its own.'

Chapter 23

'Not too short over the ears.'

Even a vicar with a chequered past was obliged to keep up his godly appearance, thought Luke, as he sat back in the chair of a barber's shop in Berkeley.

He took a moment to remove his clerical collar.

The most reticent of men liked to chat while having his hair cut. Things were looking up, to the point where he was beginning to feel at home again in his very own parish. He had delivered his first sermon on the sins of corporate greed which had been very enthusiastically received by his new congregation of St. Mary's. It was a fresh start as planned.

Continue like this and people might begin to give him the benefit of the doubt? He had even arranged to hire a gardener to tend to the vicarage's overgrown garden and vegetable plots.

What, then, could possibly go wrong?

The barber, a rotund but amiable Italian called Tony, shuffled about on the shop's greasy floor with feet as stiff as wood.

'Diabetes,' he explained and sipped tea from a cup on a bench littered with scissors and combs. 'It plays havoc with my toes.'

Luke looked through the window. Two men were shaking hands enthusiastically on the pavement, not ten feet from him.

Neither profile was at first familiar, but the jewellery and tattoos were. The person dressed in a camel coat laughed and a glass bauble on a chain shook in his right ear. That picture of a malign water spirit that coiled under his chin matched his own.

No face could be that face he saw right now, thought Luke, but memory was not such a terrible liar. Every hair rose on his neck. In short, he was all gooseflesh and pimples. His eyes expanded beyond disbelief until he was a pathetic prisoner trapped beneath his taut, blue dustsheet in his barber's chair.

A name resurfaced. It was Mel McAtree. He looked somewhat professorial in his wire spectacles – had to be in his late sixties now?

The only time they had truly met before was at his father's funeral, twenty-six years ago.

Most of Rex Lyons's former members of the Severn Sea Gang had been there, fresh out of jail, which made Luke think that he would in a while get a view of his companion, too. He saw the latter bend down and pat Sasha affectionately on the head as she sat guarding his bicycle. Next minute she put her front paws on the stranger's knee to lick his face, which was unusual for her. When Mel tried to do the same she growled and went wild. The other man smiled where his front teeth should have been, after which he stood up and sliced the ends off two six-inch-long, straight-sided cigars. He held one for himself and one for his friend.

Tony leaned closer.

'Please, reverend, keep still.'

The electric razor skated noisily up and down the back of Luke's neck as he tried not to wriggle.

Instead, he watched the two men turn his way as though to peer in through the window. Was he even the subject of their observation?

Mel raised his finger and pointed out something to his companion. They could have been aware of his presence or oblivious. Most likely they were discussing what to do next, or even whether they had time for a trim, like him.

'All finished,' said Tony, handing him a tissue.

'Yes, of course. Thank you.'

'Something wrong, reverend?'

'Absolutely not,' replied Luke and promptly paid him over the odds to escape at the double.

He soon had hold of his bicycle but his two observers were gone. Then, quite by chance, he saw them head for the tearooms.

He also crossed the street.

As the taller man let out an ugly laugh, Luke recalled the name that he had sworn never to repeat, not since he had renounced his own criminal ways in favour of his new career as God's obedient servant. That name was Slim Jim Jackson. But he was horribly withered, pale, breathless and unwell. Alcohol or drugs had left him very shaky as he tried to match mouth and cigar at his lips. His suit was shiny, his shoes needed a polish, although a new black hat sat high on his greasy grey hair. The fedora, set at a jaunty angle, was part Cavalier and part gangster. Most of all he recognised the sunken eyes. Their glint of green was as hard as jade or did he imagine it? At this distance his mind ran riot.

Like Mel McAtree in his Homburg, Slim Jim was no spring chicken.

Both ex-cons behaved as if they were about to embark on some tense vacation.

Luke tracked them shop by shop as they strolled along.

'Stay close, Sash.'

Neither man seemed to know where they wanted to go. They looked in numerous doorways and windows. Then, at last, they entered a newsagent's shop. When they re-emerged they walked as far as an old red Mercedes. Once seated inside, they spread their newly bought map across its steering wheel.

They wanted to re-acquaint themselves with the local area, Luke decided, as he ducked quickly by.

In particular he saw the hand that did the pointing. Those ugly blue letters that were tattooed on those powerful knuckles were as fresh to him now as they had been twenty-five years ago.

Mel started the car's engine.

Drove off towards the river.

*

The moment Luke began to ride his bicycle, blood burst from his nose. It bled so copiously that he felt obliged to dismount.

Each annoying red splash on the pavement added to his already peculiar disequilibrium.

That he was now in dire need of a coffee went without saying.

That reassuring sense of feeling at home in Berkeley evaporated as he quickly became aware of the alarmed look that people were giving him as he pushed his bicycle along.

Each time he saw them whisper to each other he was secretly enraged. It was not his fault if they chose to see in his red-smeared face only a certain disdain for their provincial nervousness. No man of God should have to endure such disagreeable and blundering gawkers.

He dived into the only place that he knew to settle his shattered nerves.

The waitress looked up the moment he walked into the tearooms.

'Americano. Half a shot. Am I right?'

'Please.'

'You got a problem, reverend? You're all bloody.'

He put a hand to his face.

'It's nothing.'

So saying, he took his phone from his pocket ready to ring Ellie. The numbers danced as he dithered then changed his mind. Better not rock the boat for the moment until he could work out what the hell to do.

'If it's nothing, reverend, then why are you shaking?'

'Forget it. You wouldn't understand.'

The waitress fixed her hazel-coloured eyes on his as she took his credit card.

'You really grow up round here, reverend?'

'Sort of.'

It occurred to him that her question had all the charm of an inquisitor.

'The name's Sandy by the way.'

The colour of her hair matched her name.

'Nice to meet you, Sandy.'

'This is a quiet town. Very quiet. And these are quiet tearooms. Doesn't mean I don't get to hear disquieting things, though.'

'Really?'

Sandy lowered her voice.

'Somebody in the next room has been asking after you.'

'Who?'

'Eva Greene. She's the crime reporter for the local Echo.'

'I don't care who she is.'

Sandy smeared her hands on her apron. Shot him a smile.

'Better watch that one. She's like a dog with a bone when she scents a story.'

'Thanks, I'll bear that in mind.'

Luke took Sasha a bowl of water in the cobbled yard. He returned to think about the revenants that he had so narrowly avoided from the murky depths of his past. Or, to be exact, from his parents' past. He clenched both fists on the counter. His stomach heaved. Thought he was going to have to run to the toilet. Throw up into its bowl.

His liver secreted a bitterness deep inside him that went far beyond any bile.

The only other customer continued to sit quietly at her table. She observed him past the archway that divided the tearooms into two.

Meanwhile Sandy grew chattier.

'My mum liked your sermon on Sunday.'

'Thanks.'

'Let's hope you fare better than the last vicar.'

'Why? What happened to him?'

'Did no one tell you? He quit in a hurry.'

'Yeah. Why was that exactly?'

Sandy inspected her nails.

'A Fisheries patrol boat found his lover dead in the river. They buried him last week in St. Mary's graveyard.'

'What was his name?'

'Stephen Rivers. Ironic, huh. Rivers drowns in a river. After their civil marriage, he and Reverend James were due to have their reception at the castle on the 6th of August. Still no one knows how he came to fall out of his boat.'

Luke sipped his coffee.

'As it happens, I ran into the funeral.'

'The poor soul was only twenty-eight but some people will be glad to see him go.'

'Surely not?'

'Stephen was in favour of the new nuclear power station near here. So was

Reverend James, come to that.'

'To which he said nothing.

'What's up, reverend? Cat get your tongue?'

'Why should it?'

'Some people say you plan to sell your grandmother's home to the developers? Is that right?'

'It's complicated.'

'Yeah, so tell us your real plan, reverend,' said a voice behind him.

Luke glanced over his shoulder. His eavesdropper had decided to join him, after all.

'Doesn't mean I can't drink my coffee in peace.'

Light from the room's chandelier lit the woman's face in sly little shadows. Her jet coloured eyes nurtured all kinds of conspiracies attributing characteristics of the darkest kind.

'Come, reverend, don't be rude. I just want to say hi.'

'Who are you, anyway?'

'Didn't Sandy tell you? I'm Eva Greene.'

'I remember now. I saw you at the head of Stephen's funeral procession? You and and another woman were helping Reverend James walk along.'

'It's a tragedy.'

'You knew Stephen well?'

'I should say so. He worked in my office as a reporter, like me. We even went running together every Sunday.'

Eva's profile was that of a young person in widow's weeds, Luke noted. Everything about her black boots, gloves and jet necklace sought to express her Gothic grief. Her long hair and fingernails were black, her thin cheeks colourless, her mouth similarly withered with dry, cracked lips which seemed forever on the defensive. She was small and lean but with broad shoulders – an athlete, no less. He was annoyed, too, when her eyes grew moist – annoyed and a trifle alarmed. Surely no one should shed tears for the dead in public?

'Forgive me, reverend, it's all been such a shock.'

'I'm sorry for your loss.'

'Oh, spare me the platitudes. You think the world has ended because I miss him? I've put him in the ground and now I'm ready to move on. He's dead, unfortunately, but that's as it should be. I can never bring him back. Nothing can be allowed to be worse than it is.'

'Damn right.'

Eva lifted her face. Her look was haggard but in her dark, bewitching eyes a light burned bright.

'You're 'Lucky' Luke Lyons, all right. You're Rex Lyons's and Jess Kennedy's son.'

'You don't want to go there. Believe me. That's a very bad idea.'

Eva leaned on the counter.

'What's not to like, reverend? I wish I had parents who robbed stately homes. Most days nothing exciting ever happens round here.'

'I'd love to talk about me but I have to go.'

'Hell. Relax, reverend, what is it with you? I'm just messing with you. Your parents were a real Bonnie and Clyde. Just think, all those stolen antiques have never been retrieved. All that gold and silver is still waiting to be found. I wonder where?'

'Why are you even asking? My father was most likely murdered because of it. My mother abandoned me and moved to Spain and can't resist bragging about it. Isn't that bad enough?'

'Still, you must ask yourself what it would feel like to be really, really rich? You must at least want to believe in the treasure's existence?'

Luke went to move his cup of coffee to a distant table.

'What would I get if I did?'

Eva winked.

'Perhaps you'd get divine inspiration.'

He resolved not to be intimidated by any reporter's unwelcome presence, yet he did start at her impertinence. True, he would have been insulted had such a spy chosen *not* to take any interest in someone like him; he also assumed that she would not have had the presumption.

She really should have guessed with whom she was dealing, though.

He would have held a gun to her face not so long ago for merely alluding to that treasure.

Never was it wise to give someone like him dangerous ideas.

It was best to collect Sasha and cycle home with his head held high while he still could, Luke decided.

On the way he would call in to see Ellie at Floodgates Farm.

The grieving reporter stood at the window to watch him go, he noted, as he glanced back at the teashops.

And then into his thoughts came the unbidden certainty that something was going to happen, that he should soon see her again as now, but not accidentally. Eva's gaze logged his course automatically without a word, in its own special dead reckoning which only saw him peddle harder.

He seldom knew whether or when to respond to friendship, anyway, since he was always happier with silence rather than heartily voiced feelings. He never knew how correctly to size up the sincerity of the offer.

That night the telephone rang in the gloomy hall in the vicarage.

'Who's this?' said Luke, raising the heavy, old-fashioned receiver to his ear.

'The tin tabernacle. Friday night. Eight o'clock.'

Chapter 24

Naked, he was somewhat miffed. The more he confirmed that his girth was still fifty-one inches, the less he could deny that he had eaten far too much yesterday.

'Why am I being so hard on myself?' Jorge asked himself airily. 'Why listen to self-styled experts on dieting when they are so moralising? It's like a new Grand Inquisition conducted via television, books and social media. I will be my own person.'

But being his own person did not result from protesting, 'I will not give into the Fat Fascists,' or from binning his sloppy white chia pudding and hazelnut and raisin energy balls.

He felt guilty at his own guilt, no matter how many times he denied all the extempore or written discourses delivered from Instagram by way of semi-religious instruction and exhortation.

Food nowadays was almost a religious or moral subject.

A present day Sermon on the Mount would, he was sure, include the Eleventh Commandment: 'Thou shalt not eat nice things'.

He fiddled with the eel-like tape measure, icy cold as it was against his skin, but could not 'lose' more than half an inch.

'Really?' he said to his mirror in the vicarage's antiquated bathroom. 'Must a few extra kilos of abdominal fat cells mean that I mess up all the insulin in my body when I have no sign of cardiovascular diseases, rheumatism, asthma or cancer? Once in heaven, everyone can surely eat what they jolly well like, anyway? Should I literally make myself miserable in this life just to earn as much food as I can in the next?'

Slowly, undeniably, he became aware of the steady pattering of paws outside the bathroom – prowling, impatient, progressively angrier.

'All right Sasha. I'm coming.'

It was mid-afternoon when, with some peculiar intuition that he could not yet fathom, Jorge arrived at the door of Angel Cottage in the village of Hill.

He could discount his feeling of apprehension but not of foreboding as he opened a blue wooden gate to an overgrown lawn that was littered with rotting fir cones.

Sasha stopped to wee against an overturned bucket. Aimed at its galvanised sides in an attitude that had nothing less than contempt in it.

'That bitch yours, officer?'

Jorge spun round. Called Sasha to heel. The speaker who had voiced the complaint was spectacularly lame. She could also have been said to be very striking, despite being in her eighties, with dyed pink hair, very bony features, long nose and pointed chin. Her eyes narrowed at the sight of the peaked cap on his head and then at the insignia on his shirt's epaulettes, so similar to that worn by a regular police inspector.

'Barbara Jennings, I presume?'

'Don't know about that.'

Jorge was of the instant opinion that she did not suffer fools lightly. Her dark, rose-coloured pashmina coat folded at her waist over her long moleskin riding skirt. Her bare, muddy knuckles were a sea of veins as she held a long-handled axe in both her hands. She glared at him with bright azure eyes.

It was a look to be ignored at his peril.

'I'm sorry to disturb you. My name is Inspector Jorge Winter. You remember me?'

'You that vicar's son?'

'It was many years ago.'

'You're Tom Winter's boy.'

'I'm here to investigate the disappearance of Reverend Luke Lyons. The thing is, I'm feeling a bit of a stranger in my own village. Perhaps you can help me?'

'You got that wrong, Inspector.'

'I've been told that you were one of the last people to see Reverend Lyons alive. Am I right?'

'You asking me?'

'You did meet him in the vicarage garden, did you not?'

'No one said a word to me about you coming.'

'I've been hired by the Bishop of Gloucester to lead a new force of constables to guard its Cathedral.'

'You a policeman now?'

'Consider it official Church business.'

Barbara redoubled her grip on her axe.

'Keep that dog off my bluebells! If you crush the leaves they won't flower.'

'Come back here Sasha,' said Jorge firmly.

Sasha wrinkled her nose at him. Sat down. Scratched a flea in her ear.

'You want to talk to me, Inspector?' said Barbara. 'Make yourself useful. Fetch me some wood off that wheelbarrow. My hip's playing me up something awful today.'

Jorge feared for his coat. That load of old logs by the front door looked messy and full of snails.

'How well were you acquainted with Reverend Lyons?'

'You don't want to know.'

'But you did like him, right? In the beginning?'

'A man like that can inspire a lot of devotion, Inspector. He exuded charisma when he spoke to us in St. Mary's on Sundays. He shared stories of his violent past with us. God had saved him and shown him the way, he said. As such he was an example to us all.'

'He been in touch at all? Any phone calls? Any postcards?'

She lowered her axe and leaned on its long, tapered handle; used it to prop her worn-out hip to keep herself upright.

'Seriously?'

'You think he's dead, do you?'

'Who knows? Who cares? I hope he drowns in hell. I don't know why I wasted my time on someone so fraudulent and cruel.'

Her change of tone was startling.

'It really is important that I find out how he came to vanish.'

'What can I say? He left us all in the lurch. You coming in, or what?'

Barbara pointed again at the freshly chopped logs in the rusty wheelbarrow.

147

No firewood, no entry.

Suffocatingly smoky the cottage smelt, too, beneath its very low ceilings. A polished brass shell casing from the Second World War served as both umbrella and walking stick stand in the narrow hallway. The living room's bare floorboards creaked under his boots while in its ancient and blackened fireplace a fire gently smouldered.

Centuries of dirt were engrained in the ceiling's exposed beams. It was like being below decks in a very old ship.

Sasha, however, went straight to the hearth with its pile of chopped wood and sniffed something.

'You let that awful dog in,' complained Barbara, snarling at Sasha, but declined to go anywhere near her.

'Now that we're all inside and being friendly, did Reverend Lyons ever mention to you that he was looking for buried treasure?'

'You want some tea, Inspector?'

'That would be nice.'

'You haven't tasted my tea.'

Barbara ducked worm-eaten rafters into a modern but untidy kitchen that had been built on to the back of the cottage.

Jorge followed as far as the door. Pots and pans needed a good clean. Through the large window he could just see the serpentine glint of the River Severn snaking beyond the fields.

'Did you notice anything odd about Reverend Lyons in his final days?' he asked upon their return to the fireside. He failed to see anywhere suitable to sit down.

'Most definitely something came to obsess him, Inspector. He *changed*.'

'For the better or worse?'

Barbara set a tray down on a table in front of them both.

'Mary Brenner knew more about it than me.'

Jorge dusted a chair with his sleeve.

'Mary Brenner? Who's she?'

'Another one of our congregation. She had great hopes of the reverend, too, in the beginning.'

'You can tell me. It'll be all right.'

Barbara wrinkled her nose.

'It can't be, though, can it? It was Mary who came across Reverend Lyons down by the river. His hair and clothes were all wet. There was something wrong about the way he staggered about on the muddy foreshore, she said, which had a very great effect on her. She saw how white his hands were. The other most prominent aspect of his appearance was the pallor of his face. Its bloodlessness indicated to her that he was already a ghost.'

'Was she sure it was him?'

'Absolutely. It was a full moon.'

He ignored the cup of tea on the table. Inhaled sharply. No priest worth his salt believed in that sort of premonition. Rationally, he resisted. Irrationally, he yielded.

'What was Mary Brenner doing at the riverside after dark?'

Barbara looked defensive.

'She was walking her dog.'

'And Reverend Lyons? What was he doing?'

'He was frantically digging for something in the mud.'

His cup had a crack in it, Jorge noted with dismay.

'Can we trust her?'

'Trust me,' replied Barbara in a voice which came across as oddly confiding, as if it were very important that he believed every last thing she told him. 'That night Mary was shaking all over. Terrified she was, because she always said that a river will give up its dead.'

'Where can I find her?'

'You can't unless you know how to talk to ghosts, too. She was found floating face down in the Severn at Whirls End shortly after Reverend Lyons went missing. Some say she fell into the water but that's not right. She wasn't that irresponsible. Ros heard Mary's dog barking frantically. It took her straight to the place where it happened. Then again, people say a lot of strange things about the river round here.'

'And Ros is?'

'Ian Grey's daughter. Runs the Pumpkin Bridal Shop in Berkeley.'

'Can we be absolutely sure that Reverend Lyons was searching for something that night?'

'And other nights, by all accounts.'

'I see.'

Barbara's grey eyebrows twitched with each blink of her eyelids. Off their lashes rolled a tear. It might have been sorrow or something else.

'Can you keep a secret, Inspector? If you ask me, Reverend Lyons ran off because of that damned redhead. She put him up to it, at the very least. Everything was fine until she showed up. After that, he lost all interest in Church matters. It's as if his congregation ceased to exist. Had eyes only for her. That's why I submitted a written complaint to the diocese. I wasn't the only one to fear her manipulative ways, I know that for a fact.'

'This redhead have a name?'

'Why, it's Sabrina ap Loegres, of course.'

'Were they lovers?'

'Huh!'

'So when they met how did you feel?'

'Concerned.'

'You imagined he was in danger and then he was gone?'

'Pretty much.'

'Just to recap, why was Sabrina so interested in Reverend Lyons, in your opinion?'

'Because she can't resist making waves.'

'You never heard of anything that lives in the River Severn, at all?'

Barbara's face paled.

'Lives? No.'

'But people say strange things about it?'

'Did I say that? Whatever next?'

'It just seems odd that Reverend Lyons, Stephen Rivers and Mary Brenner have all come to a bad end in the water within such a short space of time, as if they were taken by something.'

'My mother warned me never to go near the estuary because its mood can change in an instant. I've always been scared of its tidal currents.'

'Me, too. You smoke cigars, at all?'

Barbara looked indignant.

150

'I should think not, Inspector.'

'Someone does. Looks like the end off a Montecristo,' said Jorge, using a tissue to retrieve the shrivelled evidence from the corner of the hearth where Sasha had been sniffing.

Such a Parejo had an open foot for lighting and needed to be cut before smoking. From its diameter it had originally been five to six inches long, which made it a Montecristo.

Probably a number 3, he thought, a trifle wistfully.

And to think he'd given up smoking for the sake of his health. Hence the weight.

'I really don't know what you mean, Inspector.'

'Here's a thing. I know for certain that you were upset when you spoke to Reverend Lyons in the vicarage gardens on the day he disappeared because Sam Rooke told me. Were you and Luke arguing about his infatuation with Sabrina, by any chance?'

'I think you'd better leave now, Inspector.'

'You didn't kill him, did you, Barbara, in a jealous rage?'

'Get out.'

'I wouldn't blame you if you did.'

'*I'm* no murderer.'

'Perhaps you didn't see it coming?'

'Get out, damn you!'

'Okay, if that's what you want.'

'I do.'

'Sorry Sasha, we lose.'

Sasha growled. She gave a withering look. Bared her teeth at the angry perpetrator of their rude eviction.

Barbara jumped up and clawed frantically for her walking stick. Then, frightened by her own frightfulness, she made strange shooing noises.

'Better hope the dead don't come for you as well, Inspector. Better hope they stay where they belong.'

'That makes no sense at all.'

'Tell yourself that, Inspector.'

Yet fooling about Barbara was not, as she stationed herself in the porch. She watched them go down the garden path all the way to the gate. She waved her walking stick at them as if she would annihilate them both.

He could only guess what had passed between her and Luke on the day of his disappearance, but he deduced one thing at least from the way she behaved. Whoever had left the end of their Montecristo in her house had made a big impression on her. Someone had done more than ask her a few awkward questions, they had implied some terrible threat to her life, character and reputation.

They were hard on the heels of a dead man, too.

Chapter 25

'You steal it, or what?' said Ellie with a laugh.

Luke wobbled to a halt in the stable yard at Floodgates Farm on his squeaky black bicycle.

'No, but I'm kind of grateful I found it.'

'You look ridiculous.'

'Can't believe you just said that.'

Ellie was leading Molly by the mane.

'I could do with a bike to meet Randal from school every day. So how did you come by it?'

Luke propped the antiquated machine by its basket against the farmhouse wall and smoothed his long black coat.

'I found it in a shed in the vicarage garden.'

Ellie had him hold the gate open for her into the field.

'Hill House? That old place? They say it's haunted.'

'They're not far wrong.'

'You met its ghost already?'

'What if I have?'

'I take it that's a 'yes', then?'

'You don't want to know anything about it.'

'Has something happened? You look drained. When was the last time you slept properly?'

'The place gives me the creeps, that's all.'

Ellie watched Molly trot into the field and put her head down to graze.

'Would it surprise you to know that monks built a monastery there in the twelfth century?'

'Why would they do that?'

'At fifty metres above sea level Hill House has always been somewhere to go to avoid floods of biblical proportions. It still has the air of being a natural refuge.'

Luke cast his eye over the flat landscape in the lee of the castle.

'So much of what we see round here really belongs to the river, let's face it.'

'Trust me, brother, were it not for the seawall these fields that we're standing in right now would be invaded every year. In 1607 a tsunami killed two thousand people all along the Severn estuary as far north as Gloucester. You should have been here when the floods came again in 2007. We all thought that we were going to be washed out to the Atlantic.'

He shut the gate to the meadow as the pony's hot breath blew like dragons' smoke from her snorting nostrils.

'Really, twelfth century?'

'Older, probably. Hill House marks the place where ancient Britons worshipped the Severn. That's because its tides once flowed past the foot of the hill from which Queen Estrildis and her daughter Habren were thrown to their deaths by the rival Queen Gwendolen.'

'You don't say?'

'She ordered that the river be forever named after the innocent Habren in tribute. She did it out of guilt, I suppose. That's Habren or Hafren in Welsh, Sabrina in Latin and Severn in English. Sabrina became the presiding deity of the water and rules it still. But you know all that already, don't you?'

'Or maybe the fact that everyone wants it to be true says everything?'

'No, it can't be. Can it?'

'Honestly, I can't imagine why people cling to these old legends. There's lots to love in such outlandish tales but not that much.'

'Seriously, Luke, you don't want to believe?'

'I did once, but everyone knows it's mere superstition.'

Ellie raised her eyebrows.

'Because you are, like, now a man of God?'

'Never would have expected to feel like a stranger in my own home.'

'Maybe that's where the drowned still go for refuge?'

'You think?'

'What can I tell you? They say a river will always give up its...'

'*Dead?* That's funny, Gwendolen told me the same thing.'

That he did not elaborate Ellie took for granted. They were still virtually strangers, after all. She thrust her hand into his. Bemused as ever. Then she led him back to the farmhouse with the same disarming scepticism that she had shown him since he had strayed back into her life wearing a dog collar.

'You hungry, brother? You want some breakfast?'

'Please.'

He called Sasha.

'Must that bitch come into the house?' said Ellie.

He frowned.

Ellie frowned back.

'*Stubborn.*'

*

There was in the farmhouse's large kitchen an old wooden table. It stood on uneven, stone slabs and was littered with bills and other papers that related to the farm's business. Yet here was as warm a refuge as the coldest of men could ever wish to find. Luke drew up a chair close by an Aga on which Ellie banged about with a pan to fry them both some bacon.

Suddenly her phone rang.

She went off into another room where, very soon, he heard her utter a wail.

She stormed back into the kitchen a moment later. Swore loudly.

'What's wrong?' asked Luke.

'It's the wedding reception. You won't fucking believe it. That hotel Jeremy found last week for our reception is a no-go.'

'You don't like it?'

'No, it's more than that. The Severn bore burst its banks last night right opposite the hotel and inundated the kitchen. Everything will be out of action for months, all thanks to a freak spring tide. It's like an act of God.

Or Devil? What did I just say about flooding round here? The Severn Sea secretly wants to sink us all.'

'I thought you wanted to hold the reception in Berkeley Castle?'

'I did but they're fully booked.'

'Okay, it's just that it might be worth trying them again.'

'Why?'

'I've met someone who can help.'

This was not firm knowledge. He knew next-to-nothing about the castle, but had not the mysterious Sabrina ap Loegres given him good reason to be hopeful?

'Listen Luke, the castle has no vacancies all summer. I've tried begging them to fit me in. It can't be done. What good will it do me to go through all that again?'

'No, yeah, I don't know. It is what one might choose to call intuition.'

Half an hour later, Jeremy walked in.

'Oh there you are,' said Ellie. 'Say hi to Luke, my twin brother. Luke, meet Jeremy Lawrence-Hamilton. This is the man I'm going to marry in St. Mary's.'

Jeremy stiffened. By the look on his face he was manifestly held in disfavour, thought Luke. How could he disagree? He had forgotten everything to his credit.

'Welcome to the parish, reverend. Sorry I missed you in church on Sunday. I've heard a lot about you.'

'Pleased to meet you. It's high time I got to know the bridegroom.'

As for Jeremy, his bearing was that of a strong and muscled farmer. He had slate-grey eyes, a round face, ample chin, an untidy mop of blond hair tied in a small ponytail, as well as broad hands. He looked as if he could bang in fence posts all day. He acknowledged his guest while he made himself at home but with none of the warmth of some imminent new relation. They barely shook hands as he slapped his tweed cap on the table.

'We should try to book the wedding reception at Berkeley Castle again,' said Ellie hopefully.

'The castle? Who says?'

'Luke says.'

With no audible apology Jeremy ate a slice of bacon off the Aga. He narrowed his eyes and stared straight at him, Luke noted. He had no explanation for the shiver that convulsed him other than it was a tremor of alarm at the discovery of an ex-gangster in the family.

Next moment he refuted his own silly moroseness and jealousy and began to edge his way to the door with a few feeble excuses. He did his best not to feel too peeved.

'I should be going.'

Jeremy was a little edgy, too.

'That man been back here? Have you caught him poking about, at all?'

Ellie shook her head.

'Stop worrying.'

'If he comes again, get my gun.'

'Wow. That's your plan?'

'It can't hurt to be prepared.'

'Relax. I've told you a hundred times. He only wanted to know if we had any scrap metal lying about on the farm.'

'What did he look like again?'

'I'm just not sure there's much more to say. There was something a bit odd about him, that's all, as if he were after something other than a few pieces of rusty metal. Barbara Jennings met him poking about her place, too, in Hill.'

'You weren't scared, were you?'

'I didn't like the tattoos across his knuckles,' said Ellie. 'They made him look like a real bruiser.'

That declaration brought Luke to a sudden halt in the doorway.

'You remember what those tattoos were?' he asked.

'They spelt SLIM on one hand, I know that.'

'Like hell they did.'

'Did I say something wrong?'

Luke frowned heavily. He tried not to indicate that he was picturing someone he knew.

Instead he patted Sasha vigorously. She, too, was confused. He had seemingly forgotten that they were leaving.

Actually, he decided to say nothing. But that mention of tattoos could not be denied.

Not for the first time Slim Jim Jackson had been caught snooping around since he had set foot back in Berkeley.

Had Jackson not recently tracked down Ian Grey to a pub in Gloucester?

Come this evening, at the tin tabernacle, he would demand to know what else was said. And why.

Chapter 26

Jorge sat down next to the enormous, gold-painted chimney piece in the reception room in Hill House and opened his laptop.

'Fact is, Sasha, we have no idea what has driven Luke to disappear. What secret? Is it love or hate? If so, is it for himself or somebody else?'

Sasha lay down at his feet and sighed. She already knew him reasonably well. She could share glances or even read his thoughts with the minimum of difficulty.

His eye fixed on the angel shark, blue skate and spiny butterfly ray lovingly mounted in glass cases along the wall.

No doubt it was a cast too far, but it struck him forcibly that the most heavily hooked and baited end of any fishing line was the ultimate piece of detective work – it sometimes paid to take a shot in the dark.

People spoke of Luke changing. But he had changed once already. From criminal to priest. So what made him change his mind again? Was he always secretly downright bad, as Frank Cordell believed? Or perhaps something else wouldn't let him change for good – something more like the Luke of old, less like the new.

To know the son you had to know the father, he decided.

He googled 'Severn Sea Gang' and up came the lurid headline, **Rex Lyons: Head Of England's No. 1 Crime Family**.

Rex was, as evidenced in this 1980s prison TV documentary by the BBC, the head of a notorious gang, some of whom he had recruited from a feared traveller community. His lean, closely shaven but slightly haggard face stared out of the screen with an affable expression that nevertheless seemed cheerless in its cheerfulness. There was something forbidding about his dark pupils while his very black, neatly cut hair only served to reveal how pale he looked in reality. There were great shadows under his bold eyes, which, being so watchful, afforded him a certain seriousness, cleverness, even importance. This was someone who was accustomed to getting his own way, who did, curiously enough, think he deserved celebrity status.

'Is it because of you that Luke is dead?' thought Jorge aloud.

The Lyons family's origins in Gloucestershire dated back to 1946 when sixteen-year-old Gwendolen Ryan married twenty-seven-year-old itinerant Irish labourer Sean Lyons, Rex revealed. Together they'd had three children. The first two died, which left him as the only survivor. 'It was a sad time. My mum nearly died having me. She couldn't have any more children, she kept miscarrying. By then my father was helping to build the nuclear power station at Berkeley, but we didn't have a bean. That's why I started stealing things when I was nine or ten. It was the only way I could see to help put food on the table. Otherwise it was picking fruit for local farmers. Mum and I used to go to the Vale of Evesham. Do you know how many damned black currents you had to pick to earn a shilling in those days? Then they'd dock us sixpence for having too many leaves in our bucket. It was akin to slave labour. Every day my fingers turned blue from the juice. The landowners just saw us as cheap labour. Losing my dad when I was ten made no difference to people like that, not even when they owned so much. Even with a house of our own no one could forget my father's origins. But it wasn't us who were abnormal, it was everyone else. It was the same later on. When I got sent to borstal it was full of bullies and weirdoes. They were the ones trying to say I was crazy. They talked as if I was some kind of psychopath just because I would take no shit from no one. Of course I absconded several times. Ever since then people have treated me like a wild animal.'

Jorge fretted and frowned, not just because of what Rex said but because he did not dislike the face that said it. This crook had loved his family very much. He saw not a thing to disprove it. Discount the wild disregard and contemptuous callousness and he could have been looking at Luke himself. Father and son shared the same good looks. Rex was a powerful thug, with muscles well honed by exercise and bodybuilding drugs. He saw the gang's trademark tattoo of a giant, serpent-like Sabrina round his neck, just inside his smart shirt collar.

His face was jokey and jovial when he chatted to the pretty waitress in the Berkeley tearooms, but dark and agitated as soon as the door opened and someone else entered.

'I don't want Luke or Ellie to have it as hard as I did,' said Rex. 'I don't want them to be seen as somehow non-people because their parents have behaved a little bit differently.'

While he could not help but dismiss Rex's complaints as the selective recollections of a criminal mind, Jorge did raise his eyebrows when he came to his criminal record. Rex had set fire to the dormitory while in a youth custody centre. Acquired twenty convictions for fifty-six offences in a few years. After that, snuffboxes worth £5.5 million were taken from a National Trust property in Buckinghamshire. Silverware, porcelain and clocks worth £800,000 were stolen from a Formula One tycoon's house near Swindon.

Other burglaries followed. Right from the start he and his fellow thieves called themselves the Severn Sea Gang. Sheer daring gave him his appalling cockiness, while all the time the base from which his fearless raids were launched remained a modest caravan site in Gloucestershire.

Jorge curled his lip a trifle grimly. Rex's favourite way of breaking and entering was to tie a section of telegraph pole to the roof rack of a Land Rover and batter his way into a manor house as if it were a castle. Nor had he been indifferent to his hauls: 'I love old things. I went to all sorts of museums and auctions and collected their catalogues.'

When the end came, it came swiftly. Police forces from Gloucestershire, Thames Valley, Warwickshire and West Mercia joined forces to hunt the robbers down.

That's when the Lyons's family caravan was raided next to the River Severn. 'Armed cops burst in everywhere,' said Rex. 'They shoved a gun in my mouth. My mother as well as my girlfriend, Jess, were terrified. The press never gave me and the rest of the gang a chance. We were all named and shamed before it got to trial. It was all a conspiracy by the upper classes to bring us down. I was afraid that Jess would miscarry with the twins, just like my mum.'

Rex was convinced that someone had betrayed them. He had no idea who it was but one day he and Jess would get even: 'The courts should never have believed a word that snitch said. They used him to get at me. It was unfair.'

The interview ended abruptly, but not before the journalist managed to elicit details of how Lady Sara Greene had come to be shot dead in Rex's last, botched burglary in Wiltshire. 'Imagine, if you can, that you're in some rich mansion and you see a burglar rush at the lady of the house and shoot her. What just happened, you wonder? You think he's killing her in cold blood in order to escape. Well, you haven't nearly seen it all. In fact, the burglar with the gun has noticed the lady about to fire at his girlfriend and kill her. He rushes between them and saves her life. The unfortunate thing is, in all the tussle, the gun goes off and fatally wounds the lady. Context is everything. The courts were totally against me and Jess and all because Lady Greene was nine months pregnant, but Jess was pregnant, too, and that should have been taken into consideration. Jess had to have her babies, Luke and Ellie, in prison. But no, it was a callous, heartless act on our part, apparently. No one in the court gave her a single thought.'

If Luke had been his childhood friend, thought Jorge, it was because Luke had been the next generation of the Lyons family. Gone was his father's self-righteous accusations of constant persecution. Mostly. In their place he had met a lonely boy whose mother wanted nothing to do with him and whose father was in prison.

When Luke had visited Hill House vicarage all silver had been locked away. He had come with the burden of his father's reputation – anyone foolish enough to give evidence against the Lyons family was forced into witness protection for their own safety. Those less brave were sworn to silence.

Yet Luke had held *him* in some esteem, thought Jorge. How could he explain it? Back then he saw nothing in himself to indicate any godly calling. They had once stolen a wheelchair from outside a house and thrown it in the river.

Asked to justify himself, Luke had said nothing while *he'd* sobbed in fear of his father's next savage beating.

This was the same Luke who'd won a place at Lydney Grammar School in time for his eleventh birthday, only to drop out of classes after little more than a month or two. Rex had by then been murdered in prison. Thus did history repeat itself: at about the same age, Rex had 'gone off the rails' when *his* father had disappeared in the river in 1960.

Still no adult then could entirely account for Luke's change in character.

But he could, thought Jorge, he had an idea why he had turned so violent, so suddenly.

It had little to do with *like father, like son.*

Once, when he had found Luke sobbing alone by the hulks on the riverbank, he hinted at something that had 'fucking shipwrecked' his life.

He should have tried to get more out of him but he was a child then, too.

When he asked him what he meant, Luke cut short his inquiry with a cry of his own. He spat three words, only:

'It's a secret.'

Chapter 27

The sun set on his rusty Land Rover as Luke drove along the winding lanes that led the short distance from Hill House to the hamlet of Shepperdine.

No fond memory should have such splendid views across the Severn and yet be so shattering. The vista was a cruel dream.

Why choose to resurrect childish recollections by a return so reckless?

Yet it all looked so beautiful as a great flock of dunlin and knot wheeled and turned like smoke across the River Severn before they chose to roost for the night along its shore.

He was in a half-remembered land of grassy fields next to reed beds and silt lagoons as he took his bearings from a big white building. It was said that it had started life as a fisherman's cottage but later became The New Inn. Bargees had moored their boats there to drink their beer. Not that it had kept its first name for long. Given a strong north westerly wind it could be nigh impossible to leave the shore again.

According to his grandmother's stories many a bargee had stayed for 'one more pint, please'. They claimed that the wind was far too strong to set sail on the river.

So much so that the pub had changed its name to The Windbound. It had been a local joke for years.

He, too, had gone there to slake his thirst, long ago.

But there would be no beer for him tonight. The land was earmarked for Oldbury B station and its new reactors.

On one of the derelict inn's walls there resided a very large red and white sign that said FOR SALE, although he knew for a fact that the site had already been sold to H – Nuclear Power.

Rumour had it that the former inn would be a pile of rubble by December.

As would nearby Chapel Cottage, if he had his way.

'Come along Sash. Be quick. Let's get this over with.'

Several placards said **No To Nuclear** in the fields. A lot of good people had reason to hate him now. All he had to do was to sign on the dotted line and his grandmother's home would join the vast site for redevelopment. No need to delay further since the last piece in a very valuable jigsaw lay within his grasp.

It was one reason why he had thought twice before coming here tonight. It would do no good to advertise his presence to hostile neighbours.

He glanced at his newly acquired pocket watch after a few strides.

There was still time.

*

The Church of St. Mary the Virgin at Shepperdine had never lost its walls of corrugated galvanized iron, although originally it had been designed to be rebuilt in solid brick or stone. Its sides resembled tin, hence the church's other name of 'the tin tabernacle'. It resembled the tents once used as a sanctuary before the final settlement of Jews in Palestine; it had been erected hurriedly about a hundred years ago to cater for an upsurge in religious belief. Such huts had also been shipped out to the colonies.

With its three fancy finials, red tiles and freshly painted weather boarding, it made a cheerful refuge in the gloom.

Luke found a cluster of old-fashioned Bakelite switches which worked the lights and wiped his feet on a rug on his way in.

'Ian Grey? You there? It's me, Reverend Lyons.'

Two bulbs glowed in white shades in the three-sided roof whose brown, varnished planks resembled the hull of a capsized boat not far above his head. Conversely, bare boards creaked beneath his heels. It was, in reality, more like boarding a very old tram.

He looked quickly round. Seven rows of hard wooden seats lined the walls whose square, plain glass windows gave little sign that he was anywhere overtly religious. Another blue and white rug covered part of the floor at the other end of the 'car'. He was deeply impressed by its simplicity, but being conscious of the actual reason why he was there, he struggled to explain the uneasy feeling with which it filled him now. He could only say for certain that so far he was altogether alone.

A very plain altar with a cross and a pair of candlesticks was draped in a pale, floral cloth. Someone had filled two blue vases with fresh, wet seaweed and mistletoe.

With them came the smell of a pungent perfume whose briny taste dissolved salt on his tongue.

He walked past the blue satin cloth that dangled down the front of a lectern-cum-pulpit when something else caught his eye.

On a front pew rested a wooden collection plate. Devoid of coins, it contained a little piece of rolled paper.

On the scroll was a name.

*

The tiny church immediately turned unbearably claustrophobic. Luke hurried outside. There, he found Sasha sniffing at a line of stepping stones that led across the grass.

He could see muddy footprints lit by the glow of the lamp above the chapel's porch. Whoever had entered and then left the church had done so just before him. They'd headed towards the river.

He decided to follow. There was a stillness in the air which came with the darker side of twilight.

It was, he told himself, simply because everything was so quiet.

At his back lay the grassy fields, hedges and orchards full of mistletoe, but a few yards before him stretched another, entirely different world of reed beds and silt lagoons. Dangerous routes led across the River Severn at such places and times as this, that's to say at low tide. The Romans, too, had learnt to wade in and out of the shifting sandbanks and gravel beds long before any proper bridges had been built. They had followed the local cattle drovers as they herded their animals from one side of the estuary to the other in order to shorten their journey to market.

The sensation was uncanny. The longer he stood in silence under the vast night sky, the more he convinced himself that someone else passed by. He heard in front of him the tread of footsteps, steady, purposeful, into the estuary!

'Ian? Is that you? It's me, Luke Lyons.'

Someone was wading mud and water?

He heard them rattle dead bulrushes.

Whoever knew such secret ways could walk across the river on the remains of weed-covered 'fencing' woven from hazel, he fancied. It was into such conical traps that men had once driven salmon. Built to catch fish on the ebb tide, oak, larch or elm staves were driven into the riverbed to build weir-like hedges that were twice the height of a human being and stretched far out into the estuary. Such traditions went back to the 5th century. Then, with a shiver, he gave a nervous cough. He gave up trying to listen to 'nothing'.

Sasha, too, suddenly barked at the vast emptiness.

Luke gave her a pat on the back. Whoever walked on water in the dark was not Ian Grey.

Tonight would not be the night that he learnt the significance of his grandfather's pocket watch? Nor could he ask about Slim Jim Jackson.

He opened his hand. Unrolled the piece of paper that bore his name.

On it were four hastily written words:

RUN FROM THIS PLACE

Chapter 28

If food were a drug then it was also his best friend, thought Jorge as he sat up in bed, sweating. He was in need of some sort of detox.

Definitely was he missing his classic full English breakfast.

There was something addictive about the sight of pork sausages, eggs, thick-cut bacon, grilled tomato, hash brown, beans and sourdough bread.

Of one thing he was cruelly aware: such hallucinations of good food still visited him in his dreams. His favourite start to the day, when living in York, had been a particularly mouth-watering combination of orange and cinnamon sugar torrijas with smoked bacon, crème fraiche, toasted almonds and maple syrup.

Right now he could taste wonderful things in his chewed up pillow.

Instead of which it was Day Six of his cabbage soup diet.

No wonder he didn't want to leave his bed.

Today was the day he could eat as much protein as he liked, though, which meant steak and leafy greens.

Praise be.

He stumbled into Hill House's bathroom to shave where, critically, he regarded himself in the mirror. His fat jowls looked like a squirrel's. Their entire disposition struck an attitude that was of smug but unsettling defiance.

'You think I look a bit thinner today?'

At his feet Sasha rolled her eyes. Her look, her stance, the droop in her tail, these were all sympathetic demonstrations of the subtle difference between a whine and a whimper.

Sam Rooke's messianic bonfire of Luke's effects suggested that the gardener knew more than he cared to admit about why he wanted to destroy such valuable evidence, Jorge concluded.

The pyromaniac had in no way misunderstood some vague instruction to tidy the house, but had set about it with a fiery vengeance as if to eradicate some definite evil. Surely it was the thought of not finishing the task that had filled his eyes with such obstreperousness, which explained why he had not yet returned to dig the celery trenches, as promised.

Next minute the phone rang.

It was Hammond.

'Guess what, Inspector? The police in Bristol are convinced that Frank Cordell leapt off that roof all by himself. He was high on Black Mamba, apparently.'

Jorge gave a snort.

'Frank was in a very bad way but trust me, the only leap he ever meant to make was into the dark by meeting me. I arrived too late to save him, thanks to a real suicide off Clifton Suspension Bridge. There's something more we need to know, I'm sure of it.'

'I did some digging like you said, Inspector.'

'Very well, let's hear it.'

'It seems Frank did a bit of excavating himself.'

'How come?'

'Seriously, he was twice fined and then 'sent down' for digging up archaeologically important wrecks along the River Severn. He's been at it for years, on and off, between spells in prison.'

'I know the place very well, at Purton. Did he say what he was really doing there, at all?'

'Nothing was found on him but he'd cleared a very deep trench next to one of the keels.'

'Interesting.'

'It seems the fool really did believe in buried treasure.'

'Did you get to look in HMPL...'s visitors' book for me?'

'Honestly, Inspector, I don't know what to say.'

'Please do.'

'The woman who visited Cordell early last year signed her name all right. Guess what?'

'What?'

'It was Jessica Kennedy.'

A sharp intake of breath hit the back of his throat.

'Not a redhead, then?'

'No.'

'Rex's ex-girlfriend visited Frank in prison? What for? I thought she spent all her time sunning herself on the Costa Del Sol?'

'It must have been for old times' sake?'

'No, she wanted you to think that.'

'Does it matter?'

'Jessica Kennedy wouldn't bother to visit an old lag like Frank Cordell without a very good reason all of her own.'

'She did that interview last year on TV, remember, Inspector. She bragged about all the loot that she and her hubby stole.'

'She's not the only one in the Lyons family to crave celebrity status.'

'Better ask her yourself, then.'

'Her villa in Spain won't answer my calls.'

'Sounds like sour grapes.'

A curse died on his lips.

*

Jorge donned his black cap and blue sweater as he and Sasha set out to walk the extensive estate that surrounded the vicarage.

Windblown branches of several fir trees began to scratch, rub and groan at their approach. The sound somehow made him uneasy, but no one on a manhunt with God's rich bounty in mind could permit himself to baulk at the gloominess of somewhere quite so secluded.

Sasha's head hung low. Her tail did the same. Clearly she could not escape the sensation that, merely by exploring the grounds with him, they were inviting some colossal catastrophe or mortal calamity?

They followed the edge of the tree-lined lake until a substantial, brick-built garage caught his attention.

Sasha sniffed and growled.

A stag's white, empty-eyed skull hung over double doors while a little blue and white wooden sailor with a black cap stood guard at the apex of the roof.

'You asking me?' said Jorge and tugged pointlessly at a rusty padlock.

It was then that he thought to fetch a crowbar from the greenhouse. As for the actual business of breaking and entering, he did try not to do any damage, though naturally he did.

A ten-foot-long dinghy was parked inside the shed on a trailer.

This had to be the craft in which Luke had been seen exploring the river so thoroughly last summer? He clambered over the gunwale and crouched down at the stern. It had room for three adults and was a versatile day vessel with a good turn of speed under sail – if there was no wind it could be rowed or a small outboard would push it along.

The biggest elver net that he had ever seen lay concertinaed at his feet, as if ready to be extended and towed behind the boat.

Strictly illegal, it could have caught a person.

A flute lay gathering dust on one of its seats, Jorge noticed. Had his friend sought to charm his catch with music? His sense of glee was soon overtaken by the sight of something bright sparkling at his feet.

Such a find was both unnerving and forbidding.

Few people could buy such saltwater pearls anywhere in the world any longer.

It was an antique earring.

He began moving all sorts of spares for navigating treacherous channels in the River Severn, should any more treasure lay concealed underneath.

Here were torches with spare batteries, a navigating light, spare fuel and engine oils, bilge pumps, hand bailer and flares. His hands touched upon a sound signalling device and spare full filter element.

For, while the boat could be sailed or rowed, it needed its trustworthy outboard motor to negotiate the river's powerful tides.

A muddy spade lay on the transom.

Sasha suddenly let out a bark and ran outside to sniff the air.

Jorge followed, wondering why on earth she was staring at some invisible presence beyond the gardens.

An excited howl issued from her throat that responded to something only she could see or hear.

Meanwhile, the roof's watchful sailor waved his white paddles. He signalled a cold blast of wind from the estuary. Performed urgent semaphores with both arms.

'What's wrong, Sasha? What are you doing? Why are you behaving so weirdly?'

Her whole behaviour he recognised only as worryingly fretful.

Still could he scarcely believe the evidence in his hand. By what strange occurrence had someone sought to wear such a precious earring in Luke's boat, anyway? What dangerous circumstances?

Why sail at all to meet whom on the river?

It wouldn't be until he searched a lot further that he'd learn more.

*

Next morning, as a pair of snow-white egrets flew past him like ghosts, Jorge sat on the vicarage's terrace and unfolded the local newspaper that he now had delivered daily from Berkeley.

He focused at once on its black headlines: **Missing Man Identified**.

Beneath the headline he read: "A man found in the River Severn has been named as long-term resident of Berkeley Ian Grey (84). So badly decomposed was the skeleton that it had to be identified by its teeth. Police have not ruled out foul play."

'*He that takes the devil into his boat, must carry him over the sound,*' whispered Jorge gravely, but so quietly that only Sasha, who sat at his feet, caught his drift.

She breathed as great a sigh of relief as he did.

By all accounts that body should have been Rev. Luke Lyons.

Chapter 29

'Saturday, August 6th it is, then?' said Sabrina, looking resplendent in her long pale gown on their way into the keep at Berkeley Castle. She stroked the spine of the little silver sea-serpent in her ear as she spoke.

Ellie was ecstatic.

'At last I can send out my wedding invitations. I'm so lucky.'

Sabrina turned her head with curiosity. A little smile, for him alone, curled one corner of her mouth, Luke noticed.

'Lucky? Is that what you believe?'

Ellie beamed.

'Sounds great. Agreed, brother?'

He beamed a thin smile back.

'One person's loss is another's gain, it seems.'

Ellie stiffened.

'Sorry, what?'

'Stephen Rivers's death saves the day, is all.'

'You think?'

'He and Reverend James were going to have their reception at the castle on the 6th of August, after their civil ceremony. All of a sudden there's a vacancy. It's as if it was meant to be.'

Ellie gave him a quick dig in his ribs.

'Shit, Luke, I'll gladly take another bride's place to get what I want.'

'Don't thank me, thank Sabrina. She did it all.'

'Somehow I don't think so.'

'Always.'

'If there's anything else you need to tell me, brother, please do?'

He put his hand to his head and hot veins throbbed in his temples.

'I'm fine.'

'Honestly Luke, you look like death today.'

'Don't be silly. It's nothing. Really.'

'What's that nasty red spot on your clerical collar?'

'I had another nosebleed this morning.'

Sabrina trailed her heady perfume whose ocean fragrance dissolved something briny in the air. It smelt of salt-filled breeze, rock pools and sun-bleached driftwood as she beckoned them to follow her up a narrow, spiral staircase.

'Mind your heads on the low doorway.'

'I've always wanted to have a wedding in a castle,' said Ellie, 'but my first husband wasn't so keen.'

'You divorced?' said Sabrina.

'Widowed. My husband drowned when our car skidded into a lake in Scotland. The road was icy. I lost control. Saved my son but not him.'

'Drowned, you say?'

'Okay, I'd been drinking which didn't help. He didn't stand a chance.'

Sabrina shed some of her haughtiness in favour of agitated concern, even as she assumed a pace more reckless than before.

'People say drowning is painless but what do they know? How can they possibly understand what it is to suffocate so cruelly? Can anyone really anticipate what it is to feel fear at the last moment of our lives, knowing that the next breath we take will be full of water?'

'I imagine what my sister is trying to say is that she wants her wedding day to be a truly fresh start,' said Luke. 'Just the way she has always dreamed.'

The oddly emphatic way in which Sabrina reacted seemed on a par with his own disturbed state.

He had little idea what to make of her sudden discomfort. He could only rightly gauge the strength of his own.

Ellie kept firm hold of Randal's hand round each bend in the cold, stone corridor as he skated after her in his shiny black school shoes.

The boy's enthusiasm came as a welcome distraction.

'Oh, my! Isn't this place fantastic? It must be such fun living here.'

'This is the castle in which King Edward II met his fate hundreds of years ago,' said Sabrina. 'Sometimes you hear his ghost scream at night.'

'Why was he killed? Was he a bad person?'

'Come, shall I show you where it happened?'

Sabrina welcomed them all into the King's Gallery where she led them to the grille in the wall of the Guard Room.

There she lowered her eyes as if the thought of wanton cruelty to someone of truly royal blood still filled her with horror.

'Edward's evil queen had him imprisoned while her lover wrongly claimed descent from ancient kings.'

Randal looked over the wooden rail into a dark pit.

'Is it very deep?'

'Thirty feet at least. Edward was up to his knees in water into which all the channels of the castle ran. On some days it smells of the sea.'

Randal called into the gloom; listened for the echo.

'Did he drown down there, then?'

'Not exactly. When the pit failed to kill him his traitorous queen had him murdered.'

'I bet they chopped his head off.'

'No, legend has it that someone inserted a red-hot iron into his anus by way of a drenching horn.'

'Wow. He must have suffered horribly.'

'Such is the savagery of vengeful lovers when they usurp someone else's kingdom. They show no mercy, no matter how ancient the lineage.'

'Sounds about right,' said Luke, laughing. 'Do we care, is all that matters?'

At which moment he pictured the crooked body of a man fatally broken and writhing in agony.

He was lying on his back with his legs wide apart while his eyes sought help from heaven.

His coat was torn open and his head propped in someone else's hands, as confused voices bent over him to confirm he was dying.

That man was him.

'Oh bloody hell.'

Ellie seized his arm.

'Luke? What's wrong?'

Too late. The room went blank.

It blackened and blistered.

*

'What happened?'

Ellie was cradling his head on her knees when Luke opened his eyes at the floor.

'You fell.'

'I really didn't.'

'Went out like a light…'

'How long for?'

'A minute, at least. Did I not say you looked ill? You should see a doctor.'

'Sorry.'

'You only just missed hitting your head on that metal handrail beside you by a couple of inches.'

Sabrina came back with a glass of water.

'Here, drink this.'

'Thanks.'

'Too long on your feet,' said Ellie. 'Not enough blood being pumped to your head. Soldiers on sentry duty suffer the same fate.'

Luke tried to focus on things around him in a daze.

'Where's Sabrina?'

'Gone to get more water.'

His outstretched hand came to rest on a very large, very elaborately engraved cypress chest on whose lid some ships floated by in full sail.

Galleons rode the waves in formation. They were bedecked with dozens of red and white ensigns as if at some great regatta.

He leaned on it for vital support.

To his swimming brain the ships appeared to see-saw on the waves at a great rate of knots.

Sabrina returned.

'Here, reverend, drink this. Is not water also the life-blood of our existence?'

This time their hands touched briefly round the glass. He felt something course through him that took all his senses by storm. The coldness, the boniness, the slenderness of her hand, all together were they nowhere so appropriate as in the living dead. Yet they shocked and stung him awake, too.

It was no good, he would have to sit on the seaman's chest for a while longer.

At which point Sabrina scrutinised his face rather searchingly. He had, in fact, no answer to the unexpected pity she would feel for him now.

'Is this chest full of treasure?' asked Randal as he traced its elaborate curves of dark wood with the end of his finger. 'I love it. I want to climb in. I bet it has sailed to the end of the world and back.'

Sabrina laughed. She drew Randal gently aside. Narrowed her eyes at him.

'It's thought that this particular chest belonged to Sir Francis Drake who visited the castle in the sixteenth century. Such sea-rovers extended the borders of the known world, they embarked on great adventures beyond all known boundaries, both on land and sea, and into their own souls. Yet the dark, unfathomable caves of ocean are still the last places on Earth of which mere mortals know very little. Monsters and mysteries still exist, don't you think, in the immense expanses of water that surround the lands of this globe?'

Randal grinned.

'I'd like to be a famous sea captain, one day.'

Sabrina again reached beneath the lace and pleated chiffon on her arm. She scratched skin with sharp nails. She shot Luke that critical and partial smile that was peculiarly her own.

'We say of Sir Francis Drake that he was a great explorer but really he was a buccaneer, slaver and pirate. He traded in African men and women and robbed the Spanish of their gold. Has it not always been the same? Have not men always set sail with the highest hopes, only to sink very low in their own estimation? Yet still they would rather scuttle their own ship than surrender, *such is their insatiable longing for treasure.'*

She curled her long, sharp nails ready at any moment to claw sore skin inside the net's undersleeve and so draw more blood.

She felt driven to do it out of habit, but Luke wondered if it were not also a sign of something truly impatient with the shortcomings of them all.

He stood up, a little unsteadily.

'H'm, well, yeah, I'm feeling fine now. Please show us where all the guests will dine on Ellie's big day.'

*

Sabrina did not so much as offer them a cheerful wave as pass on the sombre stares of the gloomy royal portraits on the wall.

She glided steadily along the darkest passageways as if her favourite places were those in which the history of the castle was most evident.

Her cream silk gown, lavishly decorated with lace, tassels and trimmings gave her the appearance of a frustrated bride herself.

As they went in single file up one level and down another in the labyrinthine stone corridors, Ellie held back slightly.

'Hey, Luke. Notice anything unusual about our guide?'

'Such as?'

'Well, she smells divine for a start.'

'What should she smell like?'

'I'm talking perfume. That could be Sargasso Oscar de la Renta or Wood Sage and Sea Salt by Jo Malone.'

'Well done, you.'

'I wish that was all.'

'What then?'

'That dress of hers is rotten under her armpits.'

'I'm not smelling that.'

'Look closely,' said Ellie. 'The silk chiffon that lines the lace yoke area has deteriorated with age. There might not be any underarm staining that you usually get with vintage dresses, but beneath both sleeves that lining is so fragile that it could tear at any moment. I'd stake my life on it.'

Sabrina trod the great hall's cavernous interior with an air of authority which seemed rather chilling but also enthralling, since she now had room to swish her antique gown across the wide, blue and grey stone floor.

She appeared to deplore the person she herself had never been allowed to become; she regretted not being rightful queen of a mighty fortress like this one.

Her toes, all the while, flexed restlessly inside her sharkskin shoes.

'Come Randal,' said Sabrina and extended her long bony hand his way. 'For a day you'll be able to live in your very own castle.'

Ellie clutched her faux fox fur cashmere poncho to her throat and shivered. 'Will it be this cold?'

Sabrina looked surprised.

'Cold? I hardly noticed.'

'I should say so. It's positively freezing.'

'Then on the day we will light you a great fire.'

*

Sabrina flung open the door to the castle's Inner Bailey. Gave a gasp. It was both appreciation of the fresh, salty air that blew up from the river and something else.

She rattled the dangling skulls of seabirds on a bracelet while, with sleight of hand, she adjusted a slide made of white whale bone in her fine red hair.

Her silvery green eyes flashed like waves. Such was her steely gaze that Luke soon found himself hanging upon her every look and word as she led the way to ancient terraces from which they could all gaze down at the lawns below.

Randal admired four ancient cannons that stood high above the bowling green and pointed towards the River Severn.

'Aren't children wonderful?' said Sabrina. 'They are so new and innocent in this world, such welcome fresh blood. What better way to secure one's legacy than to nurse one's own?'

'I suppose so, yeah,' said Luke. 'Do you have children?'

'Really brother,' said Ellie, 'whatever do you mean? Please forgive him, your ladyship.'

179

Sabrina smiled her thin smile.

'No, I don't have children but I can trace my history back to Troy. You've heard of Troy, haven't you, Randal?'

'I once drew a picture of the Trojan Horse at school.'

'Well, it's said that such ancient kings once ruled these lands, too… Perhaps you've told Randal this famous story before, reverend?'

'Not at all.'

In truth, his mind was still in a whir as her voice quickly gathered momentum.

'Well, my boy, I get my name by way of Locrinus, who was one of the sons of the Trojan Brutus who founded Britain. Locrinus ruled part of Britain called Loegria. When the Huns defeated his brother Albanactus, King of Scotland, brave Locrinus led an army there and defeated them. With the invaders scattered, he fell in love with one of his prisoners, a German girl called Estrildis. He visited her secretly in a subterranean palace in New Troy, or London as we know it now. Soon she fell pregnant. Bore him a daughter called Habren or Hafren. It's a Welsh name which, in Roman times, came to mean Sabrina.'

Randal wriggled.

'Sabrina is a nice name.'

'But Locrinus, you see, was already promised to Gwendolen, daughter of Brutus's second-in-command Corineus. For honour's sake, he was forced to marry her, but his passion for his true love never diminished. When Corineus died seven years later, Locrinus left his wife to marry Estrildis. I rejoice that I was born of such great devotion. Blood is thicker than water, even though the tide keeps its course.'

If Sabrina's proud-hearted celebration of her name sat well with her evident haughtiness, it did not spell complete happiness, thought Luke, but filled her eyes with a certain cold insouciance.

Once more she very much gave him to believe that she would have his approval especially. He felt flattered.

Ellie stood over her son and gently smoothed his fair hair.

'What do you think, Randal? Should mummy get married in a spooky old castle, or what?'

Randal's almond eyes grew wider.

'I should say so.'

'Next time you come you must meet Freya and Varg, my two Elkhounds,' said Sabrina at once.

'Those are funny names.'

'I suppose.'

'Why did you call them that?'

'Well, I named Freya after myself.'

Luke interrupted.

'But Freya isn't your name.'

'No, but in Scandinavia where my dogs come from Freya means noble woman.'

'And Varg?'

'That's an old Norse word for wolf.'

*

Thus did Sabrina offer everyone her heartfelt aid which, within the not too distant future, led Luke to place his absolute trust in her with such strange results.

Chapter 30

Luke crossed the bridge that spanned the moat, ready to exit the castle.

Suddenly a shout penetrated the cackles and caws that came from the rooks in the trees above him.

'Reverend Luke Lyons? Can I have a brief word, please?'

Sure enough, a young woman approached him with a loud click of her boots.

'I know who you are. You're Eva Greene. You ambushed me in the tearooms in Berkeley.'

It struck him as odd that once more she should single him out for her special attention.

'Have you started to look for the hidden treasure yet, reverend? You have, haven't you?'

'You spying on me, or what?'

'I told you, I intend to write your life story.'

'Doesn't mean I'm interested.'

'Doesn't mean you have a choice.'

She was even ruder than he remembered. No older than he was, she hid much of her face behind her very large, black C-thru sunglasses.

Equally black crosses hung from her ears.

The crooked smile on her lips was excessively self-assertive and determined, like most investigative journalists.

A black notebook and pencil rested between her fingers, on one of which she wore a coffin ring.

'You really ought to know better, Ms Greene. Who says there is any treasure, anyway?'

'Your mother, Jess Kennedy, spoke about it on TV. Are you two in league?'

'Goodbye, Ms Greene.'

'What's the hurry?'

'I must drive my sister and nephew back to their farm.'

'But what if I can help you?'

'I very much doubt that.'

'At least let me give you something,' said Eva, hurriedly handing him a large brown envelope from her pocket.

'What is it?'

'Believe me, you need to see this.'

'Busy day, Ms Greene. Busy day.'

'Call me. My number is on the back.'

*

'Good grief, Luke, who was that awful woman?' said Ellie, with a laugh. 'Doesn't she know how difficult it is to take anyone seriously when they dress like an undertaker while at work?'

'Quite difficult?'

'You got that right.'

'She's a damned hack who wants to write my life story or some such rubbish. You know the sort of thing: *Gangster Priest Returns Home.*'

'We should read what she gave you.'

He passed her the envelope to open.

'It looks like the front page of today's Echo,' said Ellie.

With that, Luke climbed into the Land Rover and started its engine.

Ellie and Randal followed suit.

'What does it say?' he asked as he drove the short distance to Floodgates Farm.

Ellie cleared her throat.

'*Police confirm that the remains of a severed foot have been found inside a steel-capped leather boot that washed up in the River Severn. Due to the hermetic seal caused by the leather, some fatty acids have been converted to soap by a process of saponification. A toe or two have been preserved. Police think the mud might continue to throw up more bones.'*

'They don't suggest whose it might be, then?'

'Forensic tests will follow. The gruesome find was made by a woman walking her two dogs along the river near Severn House Farm, half way between the redundant power stations of Oldbury and Berkeley. It's a vintage oxblood, steel toecap type from the 1970s or early '80s with a sole plate to guard against punctures from below. It did have laces but they have all been eaten by the fishes.'

'What does a boot have to do with me?'

'If you want to know that you shouldn't have told Ms Greene to bugger off quite so quickly.'

'Ignore her. Clearly she likes to make a big fuss about nothing.'

As they approached the farmyard's gate, Ellie shot him a different look altogether.

'How's it going with grandma? What did Gwendolen say to you?'

'She thinks we mean to rob her blind.'

'I feel so much happier now that you're here to help sort it all out, that we can all pull together from now on.'

'I suppose.'

Luke sat tight in his Land Rover.

'You coming in or what?' said Ellie. 'I have beans on toast.'

'Next time.'

'Do please bring your dirty clothes. They can go in the washing machine, if you like?'

'You'll do my smalls?'

'No, brother, but you can.'

'In prison I once had all mine done for me.'

'Spoken like a man.'

'Freedom was a high price to pay for my weekly wash, I have to admit.'

He waited for Ellie and Randal to go through the yard's heavy metal gate, then went to restart the Land Rover's engine.

Seconds later there was a tap on his window.

It was his sister again.

He wound down the dirty glass.

'What is it?'

'You lost this when you took that tumble in the castle.'

In Ellie's hand was a gold pocket watch.

'I never even missed it.'

'Sorry, my fault. I put it in my bag. Forgot all about it until now.'

'Fact is, I'm certain it belonged to our grandfather.'

'Wow Luke, really? What on earth makes you say that?'

'Ian Grey gave it to me.'

'After all these years? How come?'

'He said he found it on the riverbank in 1981 which is strange in itself.'

'I should say. Did you know that there is something hidden inside its fob?'

'Not the fob, no.'

'It split apart when you hit the floor.'

'Show me.'

Ellie slid her nail into the rim of the decorative seahorse. Sprang it apart. Sure enough, a lock of hair curled neatly inside.

'Whose is it, Luke? It can't be grandma's. Gwendolen never had black hair.'

'The hair must, I think, belong to this woman.'

He took the watch from her and showed her the tiny photograph lodged in the back of its cover.

'Who is she?' said Ellie, marvelling.

'There's a message written on the back that says **To Sean with love from O**.'

'Whoever she is – or was – she's quite a beauty.'

'Don't you see, Ellie, a find like this could change everything.'

'Sorry Luke, but I disagree. So what if our grandfather was a dark horse? What does it matter?'

'It could matter a great deal.'

'Sean Lyons drowned on the night the railway bridge came down,' Ellie protested, in a deeply earnest voice for which he was least prepared. 'Must I tell you not to muddy the issue?'

'Here's what I admit. Ian Grey desperately wanted to unburden himself to me. He was doing some private detective work, during which he uncovered something unsavoury about our grandfather. He was going to enlist my help, I'm sure of it. Since when he's disappeared off the face of the Earth.'

'Disappeared? How come?'

'Ian was due to meet me at the tin tabernacle. Instead he left me a note warning me to stay away. Someone frightened him off? If so, who doesn't want *what* to resurface?'

'Fact is, brother, you've got some crazy notion into your head. Even if our grandfather was still alive today, he'd be 97.'

'And if we can't rule it out?'

'It's simple. We end up in very deep water.'

'Someone has to know why this watch isn't lying in a submerged grave along with its owner.'

'Wrong. You should resist the siren call of the river.'

∗

Sasha lay along the top edge of her seat and peered through the Land Rover's back window as they drove down narrow, twisting lanes back to the vicarage.

For some reason she kept watch on the road as it uncoiled behind them, Luke noticed.

Her sense of being followed would not go away?

Then came a feeling no less strange and faint than the one he had experienced when he heard about the death of King Edward II in the King's Gallery. Most of all it felt both virtual and visceral, as if occurring in another time and world but to nobody else but him. Somehow Sabrina's voice had been hypnotic and dangerous.

It still was.

Suddenly he looked in his mirror again, ready to hit the brake.

But it was all right.

That old red Mercedes had taken another turning.

∗

The moment he arrived at Hill House, Luke rushed to prise apart the pocket watch's seahorse fob like a stubborn clam. He scooped out its lock of jet black hair. Watched it uncoil twice round his finger.

He was sure that it belonged to **O** in the photograph.

Did she have her hair cut and styled specially for her studio picture but saved a curl for her lover's token?

He quickly closed the seahorse again and with it its secret.

Chapter 31

It was Day Seven of his cabbage soup diet.

Today he could consume as much unsweetened fruit juice, brown rice and vegetables as he wished, Jorge told himself happily on his last day in hell.

Seconds later, Sasha deposited a dead rabbit at his feet on the vicarage's cold stone floor.

He stood up too quickly and wobbled, whereupon there floated into his covetous mind a most tantalising vision. That was the trouble with dieting, it could leave you slightly light-headed, weak and even impair your concentration.

He was licking his lips at the thought of rabbit pie.

Instead, the sound of canine teeth cracking bone filled the kitchen, accompanied by loud growls whenever he tried to go too near.

'Unbelievable. You've no idea how that gets on my nerves.'

Upstairs was no better.

The perpetual darkness of its cluttered corridor caused him to proceed cautiously, a caution reinforced by the ominous silhouette of the ship's figurehead outside its shut door.

He had already gone over the house with a fine toothcomb in the hope that something would shed light on Luke's disappearance, but still there remained this one last room that he dared not try.

However long the red-haired sentinel had been removed from the ocean, nothing could diminish her ability to appeal to him with some sort of plea, although nothing audible passed her lips.

Her eyes flashed a silvery sea-green glint between her eyelids by way of attention. Such irises were two unclouded vaults of heaven or lapis lazuli.

It confused him, then, to confess in what way a lump of sculpted wood deserved his fear.

Then he saw it. The hitherto forbidden door stood ajar beside her.

'Sam Rooke again?' said Jorge with feeling.

Sasha caught up with him. She pawed at black wooden panels with irrepressible bravado and bloody claws.

He followed her in to his father's claustrophobic office.

The tall cupboard, on top of which Rev. Thomas Winter had once kept his cane, was still there but not the offending item.

Gone, too, was the chair over which he had been told to bend to receive his punishments.

The room now looked more like a cabin since, laid out on its immense table, there were all sorts of charts that related to sea and sailing.

That the so-called gardener had been poking about in here behind his back, he could be absolutely certain.

A large painting had been unhooked from its pale patch on the wall and left propped against the room's dark oak desk, ready for the next bonfire. Sailing ships worked to windward in this faded but still fine Victorian picture which was a depiction of the Severn Railway Bridge in all its glory.

He turned it over and a cardboard train ticket had been tucked into a wooden slat of the frame on its back. It turned out to be a pass for a reporter from the Dean Forest Guardian newspaper, permitting him to ride on the first train over the bridge on the 17th October 1879.

The picture was as old as the structure.

If there were so many things to burn there had to be a reason, he conjectured and turned back to the desk.

Someone had been writing copious notes in a large leather bound ledger.

'The way I see it, Luke, old friend, you were engaged in some very thorough work shortly before you disappeared.'

Jorge turned a page in the book and his eyes fixed on an entry dated March 23, 1951. The Egyptian registered ship Ramses II was bound for Sharpness loaded with thousands of tons of maize from Russia when she ran aground on Lydney Sand. She was a total loss.

A neat annotation in pencil stated that the wreck could still be seen occasionally above the mud at low tide.

A second entry had been circled in blue as if it deserved special attention. On 16th February 1961 the BP Explorer was heading for Sharpness from Swansea when, inexplicably, she turned over in the water. She was seen the next day floating upside down through the wreckage of the Severn Railway Bridge. Five men drowned.

Since the wrecks were all in the Severn estuary but years apart, it had to be locality, not time, that was especially significant.

The list ran to dozens of wrecks.

Jorge turned his eyes briefly to the half open door and fancied that its guardian had turned her eyes slightly his way.

Surely she had just heard him sigh very deeply?

'Whatever induced you, Luke old friend, to act on your desire, fear or circumstance, there can be no doubt that you were in the middle of investigating some link between the drowned and the living.'

A room this full of books, maps, charts and nautical relics amounted to a vast accumulation of conclusive and corroborated evidence.

'You were seeking to establish how the river works, weren't you?' Jorge said aloud, fingering binnacles and sextants. 'You were learning the secret of the Severn Sea for a purpose, to see where things washed up? Why was that, I wonder?'

He gazed at a large chart of the estuary all the way to the Atlantic and saw that crosses had been marked along its bank upstream and downstream of the site of the missing railway bridge.

They could have been crosses on some pirate's treasure map or the places at which bodies, boats or wreckage regularly came ashore as far north as Purton and as far south as Oldbury-On-Severn.

In another drawer lay a newspaper cutting from October 1960: **Missing Boat Found In River.**

He read on: 'Sean Lyons (41) was seen to set sail in his dinghy on the night of 25th October to rescue survivors after the tanker barges Wastdale H and Arkendale H collided in heavy fog and brought two spans of the railway bridge crashing down. He was last observed launching his boat at high water from marshy land at Purton. Yesterday his upturned dinghy was discovered at Frampton-on-Severn. Police believe it highly likely that he has been buried in mud or washed out to sea by the tide. People are saying he died a hero.'

A gold pocket watch lay in the drawer's left hand corner, Jorge discovered.

It weighed heavily in the palm of his hand and began to tick as soon as he wound it.

With it was something else.

'What the hell, Luke? What were you intending to do with a gun?'

It was then that a few lines from Revelation formed involuntarily on his lips: *And the sea gave up the dead which were in it, and death and Hades gave up the dead which were in them, and they were judged, everyone of them according to their deeds.*

Chapter 32

'First Molly tries to jump the wall. Now this. I literally don't know what to make of it,' said Ellie, grasping a heavy steel mallet firmly in both hands.

They were standing before a gap in a hedge that bordered one side of the paddock on Floodgates Farm.

Luke frowned.

'It's not as if there was any thunder or lightning…'

'What can I say? I woke up at midnight. Heard her galloping round her field like a mad thing.'

'…I know, because I sat up until 3 a.m. doing my jigsaw.'

He offered up a sharpened stake to the hole that he had just dug in the ground.

'Thank God the cut on her front leg isn't too bad. This ointment will at least keep off the flies.'

'Lucky you know what to do.'

Ellie retied her red scarf on her head.

'Good of you to help me with the fence, Luke. I really appreciate it. Jeremy never wants to waste time on my 'pet' at the best of times.'

'Too bad.'

'You don't like him, do you?'

So saying, Luke slipped a metal rammer over the top of the post and held on to the cylinder's two steel handles. He shut his eyes as he let Ellie take first swing at it with the mallet.

His arms juddered horribly with the violent shock of each blow while the stake sank inch by inch into the stony ground. By striking metal, not wood, they saw to it that they did not split the post apart down the middle.

He tried to answer over the succession of loud dongs that rang like bells in his ears.

'It's like this, Ellie. Having found you at last I feel as if I'm about to lose you again to someone else, I suppose.'

'Don't tell me my gangster brother has feelings, after all?'

'Ex-gangster.'

'You mixed with some pretty dodgy people in London?'

'What do you expect? I had parents for criminals.'

'Very funny. Jess rang last night. She thinks you and she should talk.'

'Say again?'

'Really, Luke, give her a chance, will you?'

'Open your eyes. She's bad luck.'

'You're making her sound like a witch.'

'She's the curse of our lives, all right? Ever since she resurfaced there's been nothing but trouble.'

'That's you being irrational.'

'Twice your pony has been frightened silly. You might think about going to the police. What if, next time, Molly gets seriously attacked or something?'

'Nonsense. I put it down to the spring grass.'

Sasha had set about exploring the ground by the gate, Luke noticed.

He said nothing at first, then gave her a whistle.

Sasha looked up. Raised her ears. She thought him rather impertinent before she redirected her investigation earnestly elsewhere.

He went over to see what she was sniffing at and found boot prints left behind in the mud.

'See here. Your dubious scrap dealers have been back, I reckon.'

'Don't worry, I keep all doors and windows locked at night.'

'I'm glad to hear it.'

'You sound like Jeremy.'

'I don't like it. Something is going on.'

'The sooner you hold this last post straight for me the sooner we'll get the job done.'

'I wasn't going to tell you but I've seen two of our mother's old friends here, in Berkeley.'

'So? It's a free country.'

'One of them is Slim Jim Jackson. The person with him is Mel McAtree. Last time I met them was at our father's funeral.'

'Not me. I was in hospital with an acute appendicitis.'

'What the hell are they doing back here, anyway?'

'They probably say the same about you.'

'Doesn't mean they aren't dangerous.'

'Keep still or I might hit your trigger finger.'

Luke helped wrap stiff silver wire round a solid-looking railway sleeper at the end of the fence; he kept twisting his pliers tighter until the wire mesh straightened under tension against this most solid of wooden anchors.

Ellie wiped her brow with a dirty glove.

'You and I need to have a serious talk, Luke.'

'Damn right we do.'

'Not about ageing burglars.'

'What, then?'

'It's grandmother. She wandered off from the care home last night.'

'Oh bloody hell. Where did she go?'

'A nurse found her by the river. I assume she was trying to go back to Chapel Cottage.'

'Is that so surprising? She must feel very disorientated at the moment.'

'You can say. Gwendolen has started to spout all sorts of strange things. She keeps seeing someone at the glass doors of the dayroom. Says she's being haunted.'

'I don't see what we can do about it. She'll be on psychotropic drugs, either sedatives or antipsychotics. Someone with the mind of a child will imagine anything.'

'But Luke, it's so real to her. She can even smell him, she says.'

'And what does this man smell like, exactly?'

'He smells of the sea.'

'And his name is?'

At which point Ellie began to bluster. She was conscious of relating her innermost fears to a near stranger or, perhaps, like him, she still did not yet entirely trust what it was to be a blood relation?

She worked doubly hard on the fence like someone trying to keep something out as much as in.

'She says it's Sean Lyons.'

'That's dementia for you.'

'Yes, of course, I know that, but why keep referring to him with such conviction? What's the significance here? Does she literally think he has come back from the river?'

'You asking me?'

'I fear someone has been putting horrible ideas into her head.'

'I really haven't.'

'Tell me that you've not been quizzing her about that gold pocket watch that Ian Grey gave you. Have you, brother?'

'Not exactly, no.'

'That a promise?'

'You bet.'

'Be careful, because she never asked for all this.'

The fencing finished, Luke picked his way distastefully around a pile of cowpat.

Honestly, the countryside could be overrated, he thought, as he inspected his black boots for gloppy brown muck on his heels.

'What do you mean? Is something else going on?'

Ellie chained the field's gate shut behind them.

'Right after the matron at Severnside House rang me I went to see Gwendolen who burst into tears the moment she saw me. She's scared, Luke, really scared. So much so, she was desperate to tell me all about it.'

'And you're going to tell me – what, exactly? A ghost story?'

'The point is, she sounded totally lucid. When Sean went missing on the night of 25 October 1960, a story went round that some *thing* helped cause the two tankers to crash into the bridge. One evening in the Windbound Inn, a surviving crewman told her that a red-headed figure had risen up out of the water to bind the boats together. No matter how hard the Wastdale H went full astern or the Arkendale H went full ahead, nothing could break the boats apart. It was like a human sea-serpent, apparently. When she tried to question the same bargee about it again later he said that he must have been in a state of shock, or totally inebriated, to talk such rot and ran off.'

'H'm, yeah, well, it could be anything. Once someone as ill as Gwendolen gets an idea into their head, then their brain replays the tape over and over. It just won't let go or ever stop. Doesn't mean it isn't all nonsense.'

'If she is, as we suppose, reliving the collapse of the railway bridge all those years ago, then what is it about it that makes her so afraid now?'

'Ellie, I have no idea.'

'I only know one thing.'

'Which is?'

'The answer to it all lies in the river.'

He laughed.

'You want me to believe that Sean Lyons was taken by a monster?'

'Something won't let grandma rest easy. Something has happened to stir her subconscious, at least.'

'Then let it stay there, Ellie. Is not the mind like a river anyway? All our thoughts and emotions stream through it like currents. Sometimes they flow easily, or break over weirs or crash down rapids. They plunge over precipices in spectacular falls. Thanks to the horrendous dementia and equally ruinous drugs, she's navigating a very deep sea of memory.'

'Problem. Whatever was down there isn't down there any longer.'

There followed a very awkward pause. Both of them gazed across the fields towards the River Severn, as if neither could wait to finish their walk, a slightly longer way back to the farmhouse.

'More to the point, how are the wedding preparations coming along? Do you still want me to bollock that hire car firm in Bristol for you?'

But Ellie barely heard him, Luke realised.

She had come to a halt not far from the stables.

Nailed to a wooden electricity pole was a flyer: **SAY NO TO NUCLEAR.**

Whoever had invaded the farm by way of the pony's field late last night had done so to leave them a message.

'Who would do such a thing?' said Ellie, truly perplexed.

Luke tore the flyer down.

'It means somebody doesn't trust us to do what's best with our own. This is a warning not to sell Chapel Cottage to the developers.'

'What else can we do? Who wants to live next door to a new nuclear power station, anyway? Not me, for sure.'

'This is wrong. This is really wrong.'

'People round here wouldn't do such a thing. They're my friends.'

Where the Devil cannot come, he will send, thought Luke. The fact that someone was whipping up hostility against his sister had to be because of him.

Or something else was going on.

Sometimes there was just no way of knowing what people would do next.

A dead rook hung from the same nail as the placard; from its bloody beak swung its twisted tongue.

Chapter 33

That night Luke dreamt he was back in 1990.

He was secretly putting on warm clothes and Wellingtons and letting himself out of Chapel Cottage.

Next minute he was climbing over the stone seawall to the foreshore of the River Severn where he was due to meet friends to go fishing.

A firm hand pulled him quickly aboard their boat.

'Quietly does it, Captain.'

Newly tattooed letters adorned the big hand's knuckles, he noticed enviously, which said SLIM JIM.

'Where's Jorge?' asked Luke.

'He hasn't shown up yet.'

'But, Slim, he promised.'

'Sorry, can't wait.'

'Not even for a minute?'

'You sure you weren't followed, is all?'

'I left gran snoring in her chair.'

That same tattooed hand sat him down at the tiller.

'Can't be too careful, Captain, seeing as it's a full moon.'

'Not cops?'

'Could be. Officers from the Environment Agency served a warrant at the docks in Gloucester on Saturday. They seized a boat. Damn them.'

'Hope they don't catch us.'

'If anyone ever asks, you know nothing about me.'

'You bet.'

Shooting stars reflected on the river's silvery surface, beneath which lurked dark currents. You could easily attribute some living soul to the flood's animated flow, thought Luke, with a thrill.

Such a massive volume of liquid had the power to inspire or terrorize in equal measure; he could feel it secretly stir his blood as it raced to and from his heart along its dark, arterial highway.

He'd so hoped that Jorge could go with them tonight but his father had no doubt locked him in a room again as punishment for some trivial misdemeanour.

Jorge had probably failed to polish his shoes. Or he'd wet the bed which merited ten lashes of the cane.

His best friend was always getting punished for the most minor things.

A baseball bat lay in the bottom of the boat's narrow hull in case of trouble. From what he knew of Slim Jim's behaviour so far, he guessed that he would never surrender easily to any patrol boat tonight. Since their last voyage on the river together, he had broken one of his front teeth, Luke noted, either from another fight at the Windbound Inn or from an accident on the tugboats on which he worked very hard.

Slim pulled a cigar from his pocket. Lit it slowly.

'That's it, Captain. Keep your hand on the tiller and you can have a smoke, too. Your grandfather took me on trips like this when I was your age.'

A river in spate could soon burst its banks. Not that Slim seemed too concerned as he trimmed the sail and steered the dinghy past sandy shoals. It wasn't Slim who sensed how easily the water might rise and drown them.

All sorts of debris and strange things rose to the surface at such dangerous times.

Monstrous things.

From the darkest water.

Instead, Slim remained in ebullient mood and a piratical glint flashed in his eyes – he thrilled to all things immensely profitable.

'People in Hong Kong will pay thousands of pounds for what we catch tonight, Captain. I'll buy you those new trainers you need because I know your grandma can't afford them.'

'Wow. You promise?'

'I promise.'

'Thanks, Slim. That'll be great.'

'Don't thank me, boy, thank the bounty of the river.'

'I've heard that elvers are born in the Sargasso Sea.'

'You're not wrong.'

'I wish I could go there. Will you take me one day?'

'Many a boat has fallen foul of the island-like masses of seaweed that cover that part of the North Atlantic, Captain. Many a derelict sailing ship has been found floating there, their crew all dead or simply vanished. A slaver was discovered totally intact but, when boarded, it yielded up only the bones of the crew and their human cargo. It's bordered on all sides by very strong currents and no real wind ever blows there. It is a place of the dead.'

'So, please, Slim, can you tell me why the eels come all the way here, to us?'

Slim furled the boat's sail, better to wield a huge fishing net on its white pole and scanned the water with a lamp. He searched in the moonlight for the dark, wriggling mass that would be baby eels.

'Well, it's like this, Captain, if they don't leave the saltwater sea they won't grow into adults. They must find the shelter of small freshwater streams and ditches to mature, you see.'

Slim thought it his duty to instruct him in the lore of the river. He set about showing him how to trawl the net in the water against the flow of the currents. He looked over his shoulder at him with a black-toothed smile of devilish pride and concentration.

Diverted himself, Luke chose not to deviate from the task in hand.

He couldn't wait to tell his father of his great adventure when he next visited him in prison.

Why else would he override his… what? It wasn't fear of the water.

'Look Captain, you can see right through them.'

'Wow, Slim, that's amazing.'

'See how they all mass together in the water.'

'They sparkle like diamonds.'

'They're not called glass eels for nothing.'

'Let me,' said Luke and helped pour elvers into buckets.

'Two years it has taken them to drift here from the other side of the world.

Sailors say that they grow from dead men's hair.'

'Lots of dead men must fill the ocean.'

'Only the dead know how to keep a secret.'

The elvers' translucency rendered them strangely fragile, while their wriggling mass fringed the muddy riverbank in a dense ascending band that was forever in frantic motion.

'And to think, once upon a time, people caught so many of them in April and May that farmers used them to fertilise their fields. Don't worry, Captain, we'll catch millions more tonight. We're looking at £200 a kilo. That done, we'll share a plate of smoked bacon and elvers with egg and toast just like your grandpa did with me years ago.'

'Grandma says they're poisonous.'

Slim laughed out loud.

'Only if eaten raw. It's their blood, you see. It contains a toxin which cooking kills.'

'She says the Witch of Berkeley uses it to mix her spells.'

'Somehow I believe it.'

His friend's eyes darted left and right. Spotted lights on the southern shore.

'What is it, Slim?'

'Elvermen!'

Sure enough, they could see shadowy figures gathering on the riverbank.

Oddly shaped nets were being lifted from the roofs of cars and carried to the water.

Fishermen were choosing 'stumps' from which to do their fishing as they walked along by the light of their lanterns.

Slim sank lower in the boat.

'Lazy buggers.'

Luke did the same.

'How come?'

'They won't even have to fish for them. They'll just let the elvers drop off the bore into their nets.'

Such words filled Luke with awe. He had seen the Severn Bore in action, he had seen how the water flowing upstream collided with the river coming downstream, until it overrode it in one big reverse tsunami – he'd heard it hissing like a sea snake as it rounded the nearest bend before which every bird fell silent.

As soon as they reached the beacon at The Paddock, they turned into the twisting, tidal inlet that led up Berkley Pill which kept them out of sight of the lights of the nearby nuclear power station.

There they hauled their catch ashore.

Slim stood over the buckets in the moonlight, stirring the seething mass of elvers with his hand. He felt them wriggle and squirm. He talked to them admiringly. Did it with worshipful tenderness.

Then again, to Luke's own lips came the burning question as if something were wrong, that it did not make up for things that really were.

Not everything had been told him so far?

'What did happen on the river, Slim, that night the railway bridge came down? Is it true that my grandfather just disappeared into the water?'

The directness and simplicity of the question left Slim all aquiver. He was delighted, though, that he cared at all, astonished and a trifle embarrassed. Surely it was unnatural for such a young boy to speak of the dead like that?

'Shush, keep your voice down, Captain.'

'But I don't like the dark.'

'Coming after me, or what?'

Slim signalled him to help move the nets and buckets to their hiding place.

Reeds rattled in the wind as the two of them progressed up the tributary to within sight of the shadowy castle below which stood a boathouse.

'You lie down there, Captain, and I'll tell you how Sean Lyons died a hero that night.'

'On this mattress?'

'One day we'll dig a grave for your grandpa and honour him when he is back among us. The river always gives up its own.'

Luke could have had no notion of how prescient Slim's promise would prove to be. He relaxed beside the boathouse's solitary lantern and soaked up its fickle warmth. Felt the bitter whiff of paraffin suddenly flood his nose...

Suddenly he sat up with a gasp.

He was awake again in bed in the vicarage; he was wheezing and retching before he suffocated.

He was struggling like a diver to regain the surface. Was back in that moment when Slim Jim blew out the lamp in the dark boatshed.

A tattooed hand sealed his mouth to stifle all protest while into his ears came those never to be forgotten words:

'Remember Luke, if anyone asks, you know nothing about me. It's our secret.'

*

Luke dressed hurriedly and stood trembling at his bedroom window. The sun had yet to penetrate all the shadows across the vicarage's lawn, but there was no going back to sleep now, as he watched mist rise from the river.

He thought he saw for a moment one particular patch of ground fog separate from another, as if some visitor or other would approach the house...

He could afford to peer at the baffling absence of something so basic as a human figure, since there was none, but braced himself even so.

...waited to hear their peremptory knocking on the glass doors overlooking the stone terrace, like a revenant?

Next minute he set off along the landing in a hurry.

The ship's figurehead, the pride of his collection, was all dark presence outside Reverend Winter's former office.

The red-haired effigy's chiselled eyes stared in the direction he was going, her head appeared to move for an instant as he brushed against her.

As did her silvery, sea-green irises.

Suddenly from downstairs there came the sound of frantic barking.

'Whatever is it, Sash?'

She had already reached the bottom of the stairs ahead of him.

It was a shock to see how she stood so still like that, just inside the front door, in the hallway.

Between her paws lay an envelope.

'Can it be true?' said Luke. 'Look here, it's addressed to Olivia Lyons.'

Chapter 34

To follow a diet was to feed himself special food akin to a medical regimen or punishment, but to end one was to feel even worse, thought Jorge.

Right now he could have been a prisoner out on bail.

He had to promise himself that he would refrain from eating chocolates in bed for the foreseeable future. He had to give his solemn word of honour.

So why did there come into his head an inordinate need for marinated kipper fillets, as he cycled briskly into Berkeley?

Even all-green miso soup with brown rice seemed like a good idea this morning.

He had found the bicycle when rooting about in the shed in the grounds of the vicarage and already he was attracting strange looks from local people, as if he were some sort of reincarnation of its previous owner.

He dismounted outside the tearooms and an invisible vulture immediately perched on his shoulder – told him to go inside in search of all the honey and almond macaroons that were on offer on the colourful cake-stand in the window.

Instead he turned heroically on his heels to push his bicycle as far as the Pumpkin Bridal Shop.

A brunette in her thirties looked up the second he entered. She was dressed all in black, which made her appearance somewhat ominous among so many antique white wedding dresses and accessories.

Her heavy eyelids blinked quickly, defying her pain, until she greeted him with a face that was pale and drawn.

'Oh shit.'

The sight of his black peaked cap with its blue and white-diced band startled her.

'Forgive me, I'm Inspector Jorge Winter from Gloucester Cathedral police force. I'm investigating the disappearance of Reverend Luke Lyons on behalf of the Church.'

'For a moment I thought you were just another cop come to give me bad news.'

He took off his cap to appear less formal.

'You Ros? You Ian Grey's daughter?'

'I am.'

'I just read about the recovery of your father's body from the River Severn. May I say how sorry I am for your loss.'

'There'll have to be an inquest, of course,' began Ros, but then hastily broke off to rearrange several yards of Brussels applique lace flounce on the counter – seemed to take heart from its pretty floral design of forget-me-nots and daisies at her fingertips. 'It's a dreadful, dreadful business…'

He shut the door carefully behind him to silence its jangling bell.

'A strange one, certainly.'

Ros sniffed loudly.

'Of course, in my heart of hearts I was convinced my dad was alive. We all were, even though he's been missing for months.'

'How many, exactly?'

'It was not long after Reverend Lyons arrived in Berkeley last spring. My father's spade was found dug into the bank by the Severn. His cigarette lighter lay at the foot of the seawall. He was taken while searching for something, it seems.'

Jorge shivered. Again there was that word *taken*.

'Please. Tell me more.'

Ros lifted a corner of a fifteen-inch square, hand-embroidered wedding handkerchief. She started to fold and refold its scalloped edges.

'Fact is, Inspector, the sanctity of the river has been violated and its goddess is angry. It's up to us to pay her greater respect and tribute. You should join us one night at the tin tabernacle.'

'Would that be the Goddess Sabrina by any chance?'

'We go to the River Severn to honour the ancient ways of the Celts and the

205

Romans. At our next gathering I will scatter my father's ashes to the currents and ask her for forgiveness, I will give him back to her World of the Waters to be reborn.'

'Huh?'

Ros shot him a stern look.

'Ever read Milton, Inspector? Then know that Sabrina is a sea nymph not just of the waves but of the fishes, caves, sandbanks, rocks and shores. More particularly, she is a Naiad who guides the freshwater Severn through the deepest oceans to the other side of the world. Born of the local river, she is like the daughters of the Earth-encircling river Oceanus on which the glass eels ride to and from the Sargasso Sea every year. She can walk on land but she'll die if she ever falls in love with a man.'

'Yeah, well, but…'

'Milton best tells her story in his Masque 'Comus':

The water-nymphs, that in the bottom played,

Held up their pearled wrists, and took her in,

Bearing her straight to aged Nereus' hall;

Who, piteous of her woes, reared her lank head,

And gave her to his daughters to imbathe

In nectared lavers strewed with asphodel,

And through the porch and inlet of every sense

Dropped in ambrosial oils, till she revived,

And underwent a quick immortal change,

Made Goddess of the river.'

'I know the poem. Whenever my father considered me bad, which was quite often, he locked me in his office and insisted that I read Milton for hours on end to improve my mind. It was his idea of mental torture.'

'Then you'll know that it should be the hall of Nodens, not Nereus. Nereus is the name for the Old Man of the Sea before Poseidon, whereas Nodens is the Celtic name for the king of the Severn Sea.'

This was pagan superstition of the worst kind, thought Jorge or the grief-stricken Ros was raving.

His eyes followed her nervous hands, step by step, while she drew tight the string on a pretty bag decorated with Irish crochet lace trim.

She would break it if she pulled any harder.

'Did Reverend Lyons participate in these so-called rituals?'

'Oh no, Inspector, he was vehemently opposed to them.'

'In his capacity as local vicar he tried to interfere?'

'As such, he felt it was his duty.'

'Did it earn him any enemies, at all?'

'Let's face it, ancient pagan spirits and religious absolutes can make strange bedfellows. He and Reverend Anne Buck had a great argument about what constitutes belief in the 21st century.'

'Who is Reverend Buck?'

'She preaches in the Church of St. Mary The Virgin at Shepperdine, though I can see you set no great store by the funny ways of us locals?'

'On the contrary, I very much want to speak to you all.'

'Truth is, Inspector, Reverend Lyons was a threat,' said Ros. 'The more political among us didn't have much time for him.'

'Meaning?'

'You must have heard that we're against the building of Oldbury B station on the River Severn.'

'I have it on record that Reverend Lyons's grandmother owned Chapel Cottage, which is just outside Shepperdine? Am I right?'

'The nuclear power company still needs it to complete a jigsaw of land to build its new power station.'

'And Reverend Lyons was willing to sell it to them?'

'Now that the existing reactors have been decommissioned at Berkeley and Oldbury-on-Severn, many people hoped that they had seen the back of them forever. Reverend Lyons's sudden arrival changed all that.'

He listened to Ros's voice turn shrill. It was rash, fanatical, inspired and idealistic. She really did not want the river blighted by something which she considered a threat to its spiritual environment.

'So did someone go out of their way to 'stop' Reverend Lyons, or what?'

'Your guess is as good as mine.'

'He probably didn't even consider the power plant a threat, he probably saw it as a desperately needed necessity for the future production of electricity. He may, as a man of God, have considered it outside his remit?'

'The point is, Inspector, he lost sight of his mission. He changed. You ask his sister Ellie at Floodgates Farm. She'll tell you the same.'

Again there came that other crucial word, thought Jorge. *Changed.*

A delivery man entered the shop carrying two rolls of silk.

Jorge was about to follow him out when Sasha's presence on the pavement recalled his other reason for being there.

'You found Mary Brenner's dog, didn't you, Ros, on the night she drowned?'

'Who told you that?'

'Barbara Jennings.'

'Since when does she care?'

'Ever since she became aware of some preternatural presence in the river?'

'You sceptical?'

'Shouldn't I be?'

'Then know this, Inspector. When I came across Mary's black and white pointer on the riverbank, it wouldn't move. It behaved as though it were scenting game as all pointers do. It raised its front paw at the slithery footprints on the mudflats and looked straight towards their slimy trail.'

'Are you saying that Mary met something coming or going from the river?'

There came no answer or none that made any sense. During the sudden lull, Ros unrolled the new delivery of lace in the same way she might unravel a mystery.

'I really don't know much more about it than you do, Inspector. I can only assume that she ventured too far from the shore in a frantic search for her drowning pet, because I found him all wet and muddy.'

'Or the loyal pointer went into the water after her.'

'It was too late to tell. The tide was rushing in and obscuring all the tracks. What does Mary Brenner's death have to do with Reverend Lyons, anyway? Or my father, for that matter?'

His smile was impeccable, his posture relaxed and friendly, the reassurance he gave her sincere, plausible and without a trace of subterfuge.

'Absolutely nothing, yet.'

'Then please go now, Inspector.'

'Unless, that is, the worshipping of your river goddess requires regular, ritual sacrifices of the human kind?'

He left without further explanation but secretly wondered the wildest thing. Had Sabrina taken Luke?

Chapter 35

Luke tore open the envelope in Hill House's dirty hallway and recited aloud the letter's hastily written words:

'My darling Olivia, I have found a way to keep my promise to you. Soon I will let you know time and place. Must lie low until then, as faraway as possible from Berkeley. *There will be no more unhappiness.* I'll explain everything the moment it is safe to resurface. Your loving husband, Sean.'

The letter was dated: October 31st 1960.

It was enough to make anyone's head spin.

An address in Scotland lay at the top of the page.

For his grandfather to send a message six days after the River Severn's Railway Bridge had crashed in pieces defied the logic of his death.

As to Olivia's identity, that, too, was just plain wrong. Was Sean not married to Gwendolen?

If asked, he had to say that only his grandfather could answer, but *he should have been food for the fishes.*

The vicarage suddenly felt terribly altered. His collection of maritime relics proved a timely reminder: what he most needed to do now was to redouble his efforts to investigate, via authentic, empirical evidence all the dead men and women who had ever washed up along the shores of the Severn Sea. He must find out how anyone could disappear and come back to life again. Must discover their secret.

That meant discovering where the treacherous currents usually deposited their remains?

Sasha placed a paw on his knee and whined.

'What is it?' Luke asked irritably.

Next moment he saw the page spill red in his hand in the hall.

It was his bloody nose again.

He should listen to Ellie. Should see a doctor.

He was bleeding in the house of the drowned.

Chapter 36

The sun had almost set when Jorge left the vicarage to take Sasha for a walk in the evening rain.

He had to maintain a brisk pace for thirty minutes in order to lose 150 calories per day – to lose a pound a week he had to shed 500.

While he very much wished to strengthen his bones and muscles, no one should ever overdo it. It was all very well saying that regular exercise alone helped to stave off high blood pressure, heart disease and type 2 diabetes, but everyone had to be reasonable. Should not risk burnout, as he trotted along.

Sasha, forever alert and inquisitive, was remarkably excited despite the worsening weather. She soon set so rapid a pace that he could hardly keep up with her.

It was his fault for not having yet bought a lead for her collar. She ran straight to the river despite each high-voltage electrical discharge between cloud and ground while he grew wetter and wetter.

He had not intended to go so far on such a night.

'Sasha, slow down, damn it.'

To come upon the river at high tide in the gathering darkness was to feel his heart begin to race.

Such was the expanse of water travelling fast upstream that land and sky seemed to slide apart.

He could not wholly dismiss its serpentine sense of peril, even if he was not yet actually imperilled. He looked into dark water. Was Luke down there? Was he dissolving in tides that were even now carrying his remains out to sea? Carrying him to the far side of the globe on some secret current?

Sasha stood atop the seawall, insensible to the icy spray and savage gusts of wind that blew off the briny water. She barked a single bark. Let the water know she was there. She listened very intensely.

Not to any voice but to its silence.

Jorge seized hold of her collar and uttered dire imprecations as they both peered harder into the gloom.

Sure enough, a ship lit up in the next flash of lightning.

It steered between the shore and Lydney Sand in order to avoid sunken islands at Hills Flats and Hayward Rock, all the time coming nearer and nearer to where they waited in the rain.

A thin stream of smoke trailed from its funnel while ragged sails helped propel it towards the open gates of the ship canal at Sharpness.

The vessel's not unfamiliar black-painted hull with its imitation gun ports sailed so close that Sasha began to yelp excitedly.

Already they heard rigging, chains and lanyards creak and groan while the masts flexed slightly in the wind. The vessel could have been steering itself since no one appeared to be resetting yards and sails.

Unwelcome words formed on his frozen lips: *The Devil never sent a wind out of hell, but he would sail with it.*

The rain-lashed figurehead at the vessel's bow rattled its skeletal body. It proffered them its drinking cup at the end of its claw-like arm. The skull's gibbering grin celebrated its awful toast while on the doomster's back danced three bony children.

No lamps showed in the vessel's cabin windows, but from her unseen helm the clear resonant notes of her bell reached his ears to proclaim her passing.

For hers was a TRUE course, with no need to adjust it for magnetic variation or change in compass.

The next zigzag of lightning lit letters of gold as the ship dissolved again into clouds of mist and rain.

In that brief and awful illumination he read the name painted on the stern.

It was **Amatheia**.

Chapter 37

If he made the mistake of trying to sail beyond Narlwood Rocks he might yet go aground on Oldbury Sands, Luke calculated.

The tide would soon come storming towards him past Whirls End and Slimeroad Sand.

With his mud-encrusted spade lodged in the bottom of his boat, he scanned the shore with his torch. He had to be quick if he wanted to go ashore and dig at the next place marked on his map.

Lights suddenly flashed on land. He was not alone. People were leaving their cars at the ruins of the Windbound Inn to make their way past Chapel Cottage as far as the seawall.

He was inclined to sail quietly past when, from the riverbank, there came a scream. It was a ferocious, protracted shriek as of some poor lost soul at the edge of the water. It might also have been an owl.

Luke's hand tightened on the tiller. He was, for a moment, a boy again on Slim Jim Jackson's boat – he was trawling illegally for glass eels in defiance of licensed fishermen on their 'stumps'.

Already he was expecting to see those familiar buckets that counterbalanced poles on each fisherman's shoulder; he strained to make out the dipping nets that reminded him of oversized butterfly bags by the glow of their lanterns.

The regular fishermen would think he was out here on the water to poach the baby eels that were about to hitch a ride on the bore.

Except it was much too late in the season for elvers now.

He dropped his boat's sail and took up the oars. A firm aft skeg provided lateral stability as he corrected course with each dip of the blades.

That cry had aroused his interest.

Next minute lamps were placed on the shore to designate a circle, even as people stepped forward and opened their arms to the river.

'Definitely *not* elvermen,' thought Luke.

He made his boat doubly secure among the tall bulrushes and crept closer to the crowd.

Someone rang a ship's bell.

Already, a dozen people were walking the circle. The ones dressed in creamy white hoods and habits could be mistaken for monks.

From this Luke immediately felt totally alienated, as though from this moment the circle already had sufficient magic to exclude all outside interference.

Flaming torches fuelled a bonfire as a monk-priest cried out:

'O goddess, whose spirit lives in the river, please be here with us tonight for our offering.'

'No, absolutely bloody not! It can't be. Can it?' thought Luke.

But already he made out with some certainty the square jaw and little blond ponytail of his sister's future husband, Jeremy. To the sound of ceremonial singing, the naked young man was then led to the water. A garland of bladderwrack and seashells hung round his neck.

Other people's features showed in shadow and flame when, with a gesture from the priest, they turned and gazed at the stars.

One such person was Barbara Jennings. Another was Ros Grey whose voice reached his ears loud and clear the instant she broke into a chant:

'Sabrina fair.

Listen where thou art sitting

Under the glassy, cool, translucent wave,

In twisted braids of lilies knitting

The loose train of thy amber-dropping hair;

Listen for dear honour's sake,

Goddess of the silver lake,

Listen and save.'

Her recital from Milton's masque 'Comus' was impeccable, her posture confident and elegant. It filled Luke with an uneasiness which he was inclined to call fear.

Ros's chant was taken up by Mary Brenner. Luke could distinguish more faces but not yet name them all, having passed them in the hamlet of Hill or been served by them in shops in Berkeley. Others he recalled from Sunday services in St. Mary's.

Last to read was the vicarage's very own gardener, Sam Rooke.

Next minute, the monk-priest calmed the gathering with a chant of his own:

'O River Goddess!

We praise you:

For currents that flow

From the far side of the world. We praise you,

For all things, O Water Spirit,

Who bringeth life!'

The shaman certainly believed in the power of his own plainchant as he relaxed his posture rather as a yoga teacher might centre himself on his mat.

'Remember, brothers and sisters, we are here to coordinate all our inner energy for a common cause. We are here to call on Sabrina's help in our time of need. Ground yourself to the mud and sand of the foreshore. Bridge the gap between you and the water.'

With that, Jeremy had his head pushed down into the current, he was held underwater in a way that left him choking and spluttering. He was being baptised to be reborn.

So it was that their leader calmly encouraged everyone with his hypnotic words: 'Remember all those lost to the dark water and feel yourselves take strength from its ancient currents. Let its psychic forces flow through your veins…'

Each devotee appeared for a moment to be swimming as they opened their arms.

Then, at the very last moment, Jeremy was lifted from the river, gasping and coughing. He was dragged on shore at the very point of expiring – he had been compelled to peer deep into the underworld, to see through a crack in its secret door to the abode where only the dead resided.

Luke felt obliged to admit that it was powerfully enacted, yet still a pang of repugnance returned.

After the 'sacrifice' came a chant:

'We invoke you, Sabrina,

Spirit of the river.

So shall you sail to us,

So shall you advise us,

To reveal our future

From the deepest currents.'

A young woman appeared at the edge of the river and held aloft a banner: 'You are the spirit now in our midst. Water god, inspire us. O spring of love, O source of life, please, Nodens, send us Sabrina!'

The voice was familiar but scarcely imaginable in this context. It had to belong to the same Sandy who served him coffee in Berkeley's tearooms.

With a growing acknowledgement that he might be succumbing to the spell of the ceremony, Luke felt compelled to spy further on her ardent incantation before the makeshift water altar.

Thus, a golden cup of liquid taken from the Severn passed from person to person. Each turned a full circle. They lifted their arms slowly up and down in synchronised slow motion.

Three times the water from the Severn passed from mouth to mouth while Luke did his best to record it all with the camera on his phone, when suddenly he heard the bleating of a sheep.

That the poor animal's presence boded ill was obvious as soon as the monk-priest made his appeal, 'Now let us pay tribute to our lady of the river.'

Everyone at once began to dance in a circle at the sacred edge of land and water as Ros recited from 'Comus':

'Sabrina fair,

Listen where thou art sitting

Under the glassy, cool, translucent wave,

In twisted braids of lilies knitting

The loose train of thy amber-dropping hair;

Listen for dear honour's sake,

Goddess of the silver lake,

Listen, and save.

Listen, and appear to us,

In name of great Oceanus.'

The chant began softly, then grew in volume and speed. The beat of a drum did the same.

'Goddess Sabrina, do you accept the sacrifice?'

As if on cue, there rose a snake-like whisper, more hiss than intelligible sound, whose voice travelled fast upstream between sky and river.

There came with it a wall of water. Luke went to shout a warning, conscious of the worshippers' unnatural stillness. But they were watching the shock wave, too. Something like a collective paralysis gripped them all. Then, with one utterance they proclaimed their grief, fear, pain and joy with perfect timing.

As surf climbed the bank at ten miles per hour the monk-priest stepped up to name the Omen:

'Sabrina. Help us.

Help us to prevail.

Lady, help us save our river

From Reverend Lyons and all things nuclear.'

The spectral stampede of the bore swept past everyone with its cloak of surf bedecked with slivers of moonlight. Air filled with brine like some heady perfume.

Common sense dictated the need to get back in his boat in a hurry.

Some might have expected to see a keel split the waves, anyone else might have sought to explain the dark shape that rose up from the deep in such a resurgent rush as a wreck or fish, or something.

Into Luke's head came everything his grandmother had ever told him. The hoary old sea-god Nodens rode by in his great scallop shell, drawn by four seahorses, all galloping along on the crest of the sea surge.

His adopted daughter stood at his side.

She alone cracked the whip to steer their chariot.

Streaming red and gold currents were hair-like and human.

Boiling river broke apart with shards of water, fused again like liquid glass. It could have been Sabrina ap Loegres, but not as he knew her. Living serpents of water yielded to some uncanny pressure to coalesce and form the vision. This was someone who could command sea monsters?

Then, just as molten glass could be shaped by air alone, the translucent goddess 'blew' upriver across Saniger Sands.

He had been drawn to the riverside rites by sheer chance, but now Luke considered it his Christian duty to investigate such an act of dangerous observance.

On the beach the sheep bled its river of red.

*

The seeing of the Omen brought everyone to their knees in a state of receptivity, they wished to absorb the divine power which had just come to them by way of the bore.

Each person rushed to scoop surf from swirls left behind by Sabrina's glittering deluge as it bridged the void between the living and the dead.

They spilt glassy streams through their fingers in a hazardous gesture of humility and subservience.

One wrong step or lean too far and the bore could still sweep them off their feet. They could be carried upstream or simply drowned as the river went on swelling.

One old man whom Luke had last seen seated in the dayroom of Severnside House had clearly made his way here with relatives to cure his arthritis. Other people were simply filled with what amounted to a holy joy at communing with a deity they could actually see and feel. Thus did they continue to have visions peculiar to themselves or hoped to heal their particular ailments.

The monk-priest threw back his hood. Began a celebratory chant. That man was Andy Bridgeman. He used his divinely enhanced power in talismans and gestures.

'Lady Sabrina has blessed us. Every time we invoke her she becomes stronger and more aware of the needs of her people. With her strength we will prevail against the likes of all false prophets and their obscene ambitions.'

When Bridgeman spoke it signalled the closure of a gateway.

People slowly began to move and think more as individuals in so far as the collective spirit waned.

Any water that remained in the ceremonial gold cup was returned to the river in a gesture that was full of respect and gratitude, even love.

The bonfire on the riverbank, so nearly flooded, was now extinguished as the ship's bell rang again to deconsecrate the holy circle.

Its slow, uniform strokes were ordinary enough as bells went, but in no way did its beat recall anything Christian. Rather, there echoed faintly to the measured sound some far-off but unseen answering knell from the bottom of the nearest ocean.

A ship's bell would always ring underwater like that when part of a wreck, thought Luke and turned back to his boat even as it was about to break its moorings.

Tonight Jeremy had gone over to the side of those who opposed the building of the new nuclear power station. That put him at loggerheads with him and Ellie when it came to selling Chapel Cottage.

He questioned what Ellie would make of the initiation tonight? What else did it signify and what would she do, should he decide to tell her about her fiancé's cruel betrayal? He could think of nothing worse than having to justify the hideous pursuit of someone else's ignorant ritual.

Suddenly Exodus, Chapter 20, came into his head: *'Thou shalt not make to thyself a graven thing, nor the likeness of any thing that is in heaven above, or in the earth beneath,* **nor of those things that are in the waters under the earth.**'

Chapter 38

'Hallo, is that the journalist Eva Greene?'

'Sorry, reverend, the line's pretty poor. You're breaking up.'

Luke threw open the double doors to the vicarage's stone terrace that overlooked the garden – ever since his unwelcome visit he had done his best to fix their damaged handles without much success.

In so doing he set Sasha free to dig for moles in the lawn.

'Can you hear me now?'

'That's better.'

'Fact is, Ms Greene, some time ago you gave me a newspaper article about a severed foot found in the River Severn. Why? You had no cause.'

'Oh, but I did, reverend. So do you.'

'You think?'

'Really? Must I spell it out? That boot and its bones could belong to your grandfather Sean Lyons. More of him might yet show up in the mud any day now.'

'You can say.'

'I've already had a look for myself.'

'Same.'

'So are we fellow mudlarks, or what?'

There followed a long pause during which he considered his options.

'I have in my possession my grandfather's gold pocket watch. There's a photograph inside its cover that reads: **To Sean with love from O**. Its gilded seahorse fob also splits apart like a brooch. Inside that is a lock of hair which I'm pretty sure belongs to someone called Olivia Lyons.'

'Lyons?'

'It seems that Sean was married to a woman about whom I know nothing.'

'Then you should let me have it.'

'Huh?'

'How can I put this? Allow me to use my influence with the police. I know someone in Forensics.'

'Who do you think you are, Columbo? These days, it's all DNA testing.'

'True, but new techniques can determine a lot. It's all to do with calculating the ratios of isotopes in keratin, the protein that gives a single strand of hair its structure. It should be possible to find out what Olivia ate, drank, smoked, where she lived and how old she was when she handed over her keepsake.'

'Honestly? You'd do that for me?'

'It's why you've rung me, isn't it, reverend? You need my contacts?'

Luke could not deny her good will.

'I need to find the name Olivia Lyons on a census right away.'

'Of course,' said Eva. 'Once you know where she lived, you can discover the parish where she got married to your grandfather. Anything else you have that might be a clue? If so, tell me now.'

'Honestly?'

'Trust me, reverend. We have more in common than you might imagine.'

'Still not sure.'

'Be that as it may, we ought to talk.'

'It's against my nature.'

'Yet here we are, talking.'

'Okay. Stop by St. Mary's Church at your earliest convenience.'

'And if I have better things to do than go on a wild goose chase?'

'You'd like another story for your newspaper, wouldn't you?'

'So *that's* why you rang me? It's a trade-off?'

'How would you like to expose a pagan practice on your very own doorstep?'

'Oh, shit.'

He rang off and didn't mention his grandfather's mysterious

correspondence that had arrived through his door.

Eva's spontaneous interest in his private affairs struck him as obviously more than a little coincidental, but he dismissed his slight misgiving. After all, family history was her speciality.

Was she not forever demanding that she write his story?

She still looked to him for her next big scoop and he was going to give her one.

Chapter 39

'Please confirm your name?'

'Reverend Luke Lyons.'

'Your address?'

'Hill House vicarage in Hill near Berkeley in Gloucestershire.'

'Very good, reverend. Now please lie down on the couch and place your head on the rest. If your shoulders feel at all uncomfortable, then wriggle down a bit further.'

The radiographer had an exceptionally spare frame, a haggard face, a mop of grey hair and eyes that were wild-looking as a result of fatigue or something. The fact that he was dressed in ordinary clothes and not in some scary white coat rendered him impressively amiable as well as a little disconcerting.

It was as if he were about to be experimented on by his best friend, thought Luke.

Today was the day he was due to have a CT scan done on his skull in Gloucestershire Royal Hospital.

As he lay on his back he heard the radiographer rattle off many functions of Computed Tomography, but the machine was too noisy and it was hard to hold a proper conversation.

He was both alarmed and reassured, not by what he was told, but by the circumstances which prevented him from hearing it. An automated voice in the room sounded a warning. Obviously, X-rays carried some risk with their ionising radiation? He did not expect the warning to be repeated in Walloon, however.

'It's fine the first time you hear it, reverend, but after a while it grates.'

'I assume the scanner was made in Belgium?' said Luke.

'You got it. Today I'll be taking diagnostic images of your brain. Do you need any eye or ear plugs?'

'No.'

'Good.'

Next moment Luke felt himself sliding into the scanner, then back again, as the radiographer made some slightly jerky adjustments to the angle of his chin.

A contrast could be established between anything anomalous and the surrounding blood vessels inside his head, thanks to the dye that had just been injected into his bloodstream via the cannula in his left arm.

He felt a hot flush which made him want to pee.

'Don't move!' warned the radiologist, repositioning his chin at the correct angle.

'Do I keep my eyes open or shut?'

'It doesn't matter.'

He was inside the doughnut-shaped gantry from which a narrow fan-shaped beam of X-rays would rotate in a complete circle around him.

'It's like being in a submarine.'

'Please keep absolutely still, reverend. I will be in the control room next door, but you will be able to talk to me via the intercom at any time. As the X-ray produces an image of a cross-section or 'slice' of your head, the information will pass to my computer which then produces a picture. I'll be able to see inside you on my TV screen.'

'Nice.'

By now the noise was almost deafening.

Purple lights gathered speed around the circular glass 'wheel' directly above him.

It took less than a second to produce each slice of his brain which could vary in thickness from one millimetre to a centimetre. One thousand images could be generated in less than a minute. But that was little consolation when you were trapped in a machine. Lying on his back he felt curiously weightless, but it was less like being in space than Atlantis.

In surrendering to the bluish-purple lights that rippled across his face, he could sense himself beginning to float in another dimension, halfway between the physical and the mental.

The vortex of flashing currents whisked him round and round.

He could have been in Captain Nemo's Nautilus as it disappeared down the biggest ever whirlpool.

Instead he was back in a dark boathouse. He was trying to shut out the smell of slimy eels on a man's bare flesh as he tunnelled into him. He was counting the waves of dark water that lapped the hut's wooden piles beneath floor and mattress on which he lay. He listened to the smack of each ripple in order to numb the pain's dull rhythm...

It was not a human feeling but more animal suffocation, much as a diver resurfaced too quickly in his diving bell.

...in agony.

The X-rays passed through his skull like a living force, guided by electronic sensors on the other side of the gantry.

It was what he imagined dying was like.

If souls did exist, they had to be this most secret of currents.

Never before had he sunk so far into himself.

'Reverend Lyons?'

He opened his eyes. The radiographer was back at his side and holding his arm.

'Yes?'

'Are you all right, reverend?'

'What happened?'

'You let out a scream.'

'Did I?'

'Why is that, sir?'

Luke flexed his trembling fingers one by one in slow and painful motion. He did it the same way the nauseous diver fought cramp in his limbs after he rose from the deepest ocean.

'I relived something.'

Chapter 40

It was all about portion control, Jorge decided, as he cycled through narrow lanes in the shadow of Berkeley Castle.

The solution was simple: diet boxes. To have ready-to-eat, calorie-controlled meals delivered to his door had to be an advantage – it put the onus on someone else to make him thin.

All he had to do was to overcome his instinctive dislike of rice, fruit and low-fat cream cheese that came in plastic pots so small that they looked more suitable for newborns.

Never before had he realised what choice there was in such miserable food. While one box offered a leek frittata breakfast, another would have him eat stewed fruit and granola-topped yoghurt. Lunch was no better. Should he opt for raw mooli and chicken or settle for more cheese on his oatcakes?

How else, though, could he ever feel more vibrant, lighter and brighter?

Actually, he felt empty.

Anyone who began the day with raw cacao chia with coconut yoghurt and a few blueberries was, by definition, going to be desperate for his lunchtime ration of shiitake mushrooms in miso broth.

Sasha looked at him wide-eyed from his bicycle basket.

'Here we are,' he said, taking his feet off the pedals, 'this is the dairy farm I was telling you about. Looks pleasant enough, doesn't it? Today we stand to learn more about Reverend Luke Lyons and his decision to disappear without so much as a goodbye.'

Chapter 41

As Luke coaxed Sasha towards the crowded quays in Gloucester Docks the sound of music grew louder and louder.

Excited families converged on the waterside at the start of the Tall Ships Festival and she was not happy about all the noise.

'Don't be silly, Sash. Didn't we agree that you must learn to get used to new things?'

She gave him a baleful look and kept close to his side while he paid £6 to enter.

Sufficient tall, brick warehousing survived next to the water-filled basins to remind him of the vast quantities of timber, grain, wines and even lemons that had once been offloaded from ships at these wharfs. This had been the beating heart of the city's trade and commerce for hundreds of years or more. Some of that hustle and bustle was being re-enacted today, just for fun.

In his hand was the latest copy of Porthole Cruise Magazine.

The first boats he could rule out immediately, such as the small, Bristol pilot cutter replicas called Kochi and Ezra of Lerwick or the classic yacht Sceptre.

Determined but impatient, he joined the crowds to walk past the three-masted Earl of Pembroke and the Danish schooner Den Store Bjorn.

A new inshore lifeboat for the Severn Area Rescue Association at Sharpness was being shown off rather impressively on the water.

Then, under Sasha's fearful eye, he paused at a stall selling curried goat, rice and peas.

The idea was to put them both at ease with a bite to eat. As he did so, two heavily bearded and swashbuckling pirates tipped their hats to a party of pretty girls, before one of them – the taller – turned his smile Luke's way.

A heavy cutlass swung wide from his belt and struck his leg.

Some rice and a few peas went flying.

'Good day, reverend.'

'Do I know you?'

'Wouldn't that be lovely?'

Sasha growled.

Luke glowered menacingly, too, but both Jack Sparrow lookalikes quickly melted back into the crowd.

A little later, with a glass of cider in his hand, he dodged soldiers in red uniforms and plumed hats; he instinctively shrank from the truncheon bearing peelers dressed in their carefully reconstructed uniforms of long blue coats and stove-pipe hats, who ran round the docks in pursuit of a 'thief' as the air reverberated to live battles on the waterfront.

He was beginning to have doubts about the wisdom of his quest when a black, three-masted ship met his eyes, high and dry in Nielsen's ship repair yard.

The closer he went the louder sounded the thumping in his heart.

'Honestly?' thought Luke. 'Must I stake everything on one mad throw of the dice today?'

She looked every bit the ocean going vessel, even if she was a replica of some long lost schooner.

Here was a ship that could transport its passenger halfway round the world with ease.

A skeleton hung from chains fixed to the bowsprit where its withered arm proffered a rusty drinking cup to the water. The grinning skull looked real enough. Three smaller skeletons rode the figurehead's back and looked like those of actual children.

He was looking at the Amatheia.

'Can I help you, reverend?'

A man of middling height who wore a grubby eyepatch approached him. He had on a crinkled, black, silver-washed stovepipe hat and a grey scarf while inside his shabby jacket a watch chain dangled from his buff-coloured waistcoat.

He belonged to a lost age, apparently, with his boots, dark brown trousers and very long sideburns.

'My name is Luke Lyons. I was just admiring the ship. It said in my magazine that she would be here in time for the Tall Ships Festival.'

'She's in dock for a quick refit, if that's what you mean.'

'It's Sabrina ap Loegres's ship, right? Registered in Sweden.'

'Yes, it is.'

'Where will she sail to next, do you think?'

'Honestly, the whole thing is a bit of a mystery.'

A gangplank bridged the yawning gap between dock and deck.

'I'd really hoped to go aboard.'

'Then you should know that it's considered unlucky for a priest to set foot on any ship, reverend, even in dry dock.'

'I used to be a ship's chaplain.'

'Like it or not, it's for the owner to say, not me. Something to do with Health and Safety.'

'Isn't it always?'

'My name's Ray by the way. I work in the repair yard here.'

Luke could not but wonder at the ship's beauty and mysterious presence.

'Since you can't tell me where, perhaps you can say *when* the Amatheia will next sail, to your knowledge?'

Ray shot him a peculiar smile.

'*Can* she, is all that matters.'

'That a problem?'

'First a new crew will have to be found.'

'What happened to the old one?'

'Most deserted as soon as she docked and vowed never to return.'

'How come?'

'They say she's the Devil's ship.'

'Why Devil?'

'I really don't know any more about it.'

'Will she be ready to set sail by, say, the end of July or the beginning of

August?'

'Maybe not even then?'

Emptiness and silence crowded upon them. The ship was deserted but this was more than simple absence, it really did feel possible that no one would ever come back to sail her. Right now it felt as jinxed as the Mary Celeste. But he didn't despair, it might yet be the answer to all his prayers. The mood he was in, he would sail the ship all by himself to the other side of the world if he had to.

He'd do it with Godspeed.

But before anything remotely like that could happen, there were other, equally vital things he must resolve, thought Luke, such as whether to marry Ellie and Jeremy in church in Berkeley.

He must decide if her fiancé's pagan 'baptism' ruled out a real one?

Chapter 42

Ellie Kennedy could not believe her eyes. She took her time to unbolt the gate to the yard of Floodgates Farm and focused on Jorge's blue NATO-style sweater with its Gloucester Cathedral Police patch worn on the left side of his chest.

'Really? You serious, Inspector? The Church has finally decided to take an interest in one of its own?'

Jorge gave his peaked cap a pat and smiled politely. He was trying not to get mud on his shiny black boots.

'I appreciate you agreeing to speak to me at such short notice.'

Ellie's black hair had acquired a streak of grey. Her face was thin and tired, her posture awkward with no sign that she wished to shake his gloved hand. Her voice, surprisingly hoarse, growled at him with a mixture of relief and hostility that were difficult to reconcile.

'When you rang I nearly put the phone down.'

'It really is important I ask you some questions.'

'I will talk to you, Inspector, but only because you're not the local police.'

'Any truly significant new evidence I will refer on if necessary. For now, though, this is strictly between you and me.'

'Is that my brother's dog? Is that Sasha?'

'It is.'

Ellie did not invite him into the farmhouse, but began busily to push her wheelbarrow towards the cowsheds. He could only guess how she was feeling. Surely some definitive clue to her brother's true fate should have come to light by now?

Not that he disbelieved the police when they said that they had looked into

Luke's 'vanishing' absolutely thoroughly.

After considerable pressure from the Bishop of Gloucester, detectives had checked hospitals, friends, lovers, plane departures, phone records, everything. His own visit was hardly going to add much, only renew her sense of frustration and misery?

'As I explained on the phone, Luke and I were the very best of friends for the first twelve years or more of our lives. He once fished me out of the river in the nick of time. I could easily have drowned.'

Ellie waved her pitchfork past his face.

'Thanks to him everything is a bloody mess, Inspector. Because of his selfishness I can't sleep at night wondering why he did it. Did he really come back to Berkeley just to spite me?'

Her accusation took him by surprise, not least its vehemence. He covered his mouth as she forked more straw vigorously across the shed's concrete floor.

There followed an awkward silence in which they both watched Sasha hunt cats round the cattle pens.

'How well did you and he know each other?' Jorge asked at last.

Ellie stepped back and laughed.

'Honestly?'

'I really have no idea.'

'Luke and I were born twins in prison. We were both more or less 'abandoned' by our parents at birth, if you like. He went to live with our grandmother by the river and I was brought up by an aunt and only later by my mother, Jessica, in Spain. Luke, she said, reminded her too much of Rex, our father, who was murdered in prison in 1990. Rex and Jessica never married. Because Luke chose to call himself 'Lyons' after his father and I grew up 'Kennedy' like my mother, we didn't even share the same surname, let alone country. Then, suddenly Luke rang me out of the blue. He'd found out from social media that I was back home in England and getting married for the second time and it so happened that he was returning to his roots in Berkeley, too. We kept in touch via Skype. Ever since the death of my first husband, I have been absolutely determined to recreate a family both for my own sake and that of my son Randal. Having my twin brother back in my life was the icing on the cake – I'd always felt that a part of me was missing. I soon learnt that he had gone off the rails like his father, at least for a time.

He'd been the leader of some gang or other in London. Carried a gun to keep others off his turf. He had the tattoo of Sabrina on his neck and an old bullet wound in his right shoulder to prove it. But here he was, a priest, prison chaplain, man of God, call him what you will! He said he was a reformed person and I believed him. That's how he came to help me arrange my wedding. As I say, he was going to officiate on my big day in St. Mary's but something changed his mind. I always sensed that he didn't like Jeremy, my fiancé, for some reason, but mother was right: the sins of the father are soon visited on the son.'

'How so, exactly?'

'Where do I begin? One day, last summer, Luke arrived on my doorstep all battered and bruised. Even Sasha was limping. He told me that he had gone to see some sailing ship or other in Gloucester Docks during the Tall Ships Festival when he was set upon by two old mates of our parents.'

'These men, did he name them, at all?'

Ellie nodded.

'Slim Jim Jackson and Mel something or other. It was Slim who came snooping round Floodgates Farm in search of scrap metal.'

'What did they want with Luke?'

'They were convinced that he knew where to look for something that the Severn Sea Gang stole forty odd years ago, they were sure it was buried in or near the River Severn. The whole county was talking about it – still is – ever since our mother foolishly mentioned the word 'treasure' on TV. They accused him of moving back to Gloucestershire with the specific aim of digging up millions of pounds' worth of antiques.'

'And did he? Did he know where to dig?'

'Who knows? Then, in his last phone call to me, Luke said he had a plan to get us all out of trouble.'

'Tell me more about the two men who ambushed him. Where can I find them?'

'No one's seen them round here since last summer.'

'Those antiques have been buried for years. Who put Luke's attackers up to it, do you think, after so long?'

'Ask my mother. They're her cronies, not mine. She's still in Spain with her Costa Del Sol waiter.'

'She won't answer my calls.'

'It's because of her that Luke is dead. She set those crooks on to him, I know she did. Is it any wonder that she won't speak to me now?'

'Did he say anything else about his assailants?'

'I forget. Believe me, my mind is shot to pieces…'

'You're doing fine so far.'

'You think?'

'Sometimes not knowing the truth can be worse than the thing itself.'

Ellie threw down her pitchfork. The job in hand seemed to lose its urgency finally.

'You do realise that my grandmother is dead because of all this? Do you, Inspector?'

'Please call me Jorge.'

'Luke's return to Berkeley proved too much for her in the end.'

'I'm sorry to hear it.'

'Know this, then, Jorge, that Gwendolen left half Chapel Cottage to me and half to my brother. Now everyone's saying that I can't sell it. Surely there is some way out of this impasse? What if Luke is never found?'

Jorge whistled Sasha and she returned with a rat whose back she'd broken.

'Without a body there can be no Coroner's investigation and no death certificate. Therefore, no Grant can be obtained to allow the Executors or Administrators to distribute your brother's assets, let alone deal with any liabilities. Those assets will remain frozen and no one can claim any inheritance or sell anything he owns.'

'Oh shit.'

He tried in vain not to dwell on what Sasha was doing.

'See here, Ms Kennedy, if I can show that I have done all I can to find your brother, perhaps then you will be able to obtain a Presumption of Death and/or a Leave to Swear Death Order.'

'A what, Inspector?'

'Such a court ruling would state that Luke is deceased in the absence of a body or remains. Once there is a presumption of death, the Leave to Swear Death Order will allow you to deal with the assets.'

'I can't understand why we can't just say he's dead. Someone found his hat and coat by the river, for God's sake. Please, I just need some form of closure. I have a child to raise.'

'The reality is that the Coroner, so far, has refused to apply to hold an inquest under S.15 of the Coroner's Act 1988. Put simply, the Home Office will not consider any application which has not allowed time for the body to be recovered.'

'It's been over eight months.'

'At present it is not at all clear what is regarded as 'sufficient time' since this is open to each Coroner to interpret.'

Ellie watched Sasha crunch the head off the rat and swallow it whole.

'Suppose Luke is still alive? Suppose he's lying crippled somewhere in some foreign country? How can it be so bloody difficult to find someone? Surely he must be recorded on some street or shop CCTV somewhere? Has someone used his credit card? I know we were not exactly close. You probably knew him better than I did, but it wasn't our fault that we grew up strangers. As I said, all that was about to change, we were going to be a family again. He'd even begun helping me to mend fences in the fields, for God's sake. It's inconceivably selfish that he would simply do himself in, that he'd leave me alone *a few days before my wedding*. Have you any idea how painful that feels?'

'I'm sure the police are doing their best but, as you may be aware, around 200,000 people go missing in the UK every year. Okay, most turn up again after two days but that doesn't mean we should give up on him just yet.'

Ellie stared at Sasha's bloody fangs in another attack of numbness.

'It's the helplessness I can't stand. I simply don't know what else to do. Jeremy feels the same.'

Jorge loosened his black tie at his throat to breathe deeper.

'I understand, I really do. The thing is, I need to piece together your brother's state of mind. There had been genuine concerns for his mental health according to a report that the Church was compiling just prior to his disappearance. His work as prison chaplain had tailed off to virtually nothing while his sermons in St. Mary's in Berkeley became wilder and wilder. He'd begun to shun his parishioners. Since neither phone nor computer have been found so far, it is difficult to estimate what most occupied his mind in his final days. He seems to have become friends with the Welsh shipping magnate Sabrina ap Loegres, but so far her office won't forward my enquiries. Apparently she's on vacation abroad. Can't be disturbed until she returns. Was Luke stressed? Happy? Ill? Got any ideas?'

Ellie's eyes narrowed, but as she closed and bolted the cowshed door she suddenly remembered something else.

'Luke convinced himself that Sean, our drowned grandfather, came back from the dead a few months after Rex was jailed for murder in 1981. How strange is that? He had a theory that Sean visited his son in prison, that he was charged by Rex to safeguard the stolen antiques while he saw out his sentence. That would be a minimum of fifteen years. Who else could Rex trust if not his own father? But Sean simply vanished again.'

'It's the man, not the treasure, I'm after.'

'Find one and you'll most likely find the other, Inspector.'

'You think?'

'Luke showed me a gold pocket watch and swore it was Sean's.'

'Is this it?' said Jorge, producing watch and fob from his pocket. 'I found it in a drawer in the vicarage.'

'Yes, that's it. When pressed, Luke told me that someone had simply walked up to him and given it to him at the site of the old railway bridge at Sharpness.'

'This person have a name?'

'It was Ian Grey.'

'What else?'

'I'm just not sure there's much more to say, Inspector. All I know is that Luke became a different person as soon as he acquired that watch. He took to wearing it on his waistcoat as a reminder of the one person in whom he had always believed so completely: the brave grandfather he never met but hoped to emulate. He kept saying that Sean must have died a hero on the night of the 25th October 1960 when the railway bridge fell into the river and he would prove it. Luke trusted no one. Never truly loved man or woman, I don't think. Sean was his answer to all that fear deep within him, proof that people could be generous and good despite their upbringing.'

'Did he have any other reason to think Sean faked his own death?'

'Eva Greene certainly encouraged him to think so.'

'I haven't been able to find her, either.'

'She's the one who helped Luke investigate his family history. Without her and Sabrina things might have been very different, believe me.'

'You sound as if you disapprove of them both.'

'Hard to believe it was a random and selfless act when they showed up, Inspector. You want someone to blame? In Eva's case I think she was after something for herself and Sabrina decided to help. Since then they've both skipped town in a hurry.'

'I'm interested to hear that.'

'You should be.'

'Got any more ideas?'

'Here's what I think. Eva Greene offered my brother something he couldn't refuse.'

'What's that?'

'The truth. In return I think he told her something he would never tell me.'

'That'll be the 'secretiveness' to which you just alluded?'

In the absence of all the evidence Ellie found it hard to be rational, an emotion which did its best to elude him, too. He felt as hurt as she did. Had Luke turned to him at the eleventh hour might he not have been the one to save him?

'Please, Jorge, I've begun to think that it all has to do with something from his own boyhood.'

'Me, too.'

Chapter 43

Those two Captain Jack Sparrow lookalikes were advancing his way again, Luke noted, as he turned his back on the Amatheia's ghastly figurehead and its mocking skull.

They were definitely following him through the noisy crowds on Gloucester Docks' busy quayside.

Meanwhile, children cheered peelers who pretended to catch their thief, mothers pointed out boats' pretty flags to their babies and a sea shanty rang out over a loudspeaker in the carnival atmosphere:

'What shall we do with a drunken sailor?

What shall we do with a drunken sailor?

What shall we do with a drunken sailor?

Early in the morning?'

The pirates amused him with their ridiculous, black leather boots and greasy hair in rat's tails. Each marched along with his hand clasped firmly on the handle of his cutlass on his belt.

When they finally drew level with him, Luke heard a laugh. Some unthinking impulse caused him to turn his head.

At once he saw one pirate smear a black gauntlet across his twisted grin.

It shocked and disgusted him.

The swashbuckler's kohl-blackened eyelids narrowed cynically.

'Reverend! You look troubled.'

'Just enjoying a day out, that's all.'

'Too bad it's at our expense.'

'Huh?'

'Surely you recognise two of your old shipmates?'

'What do you want?'

'You know that very well.'

'Piss off.'

'How am I? Oh, thanks for asking.'

To anyone else, they were simply acting out a costumed role like those peelers in plain view just now. Perhaps it really was all part of the day's fun after all? He had already seen other fearsome looking muskets and pistols and noticed nothing inappropriate or untoward about them. Yet something in the shape and size of these buccaneers' firearms now – something in the brace of fancy flintlocks tucked into their colourful sashes – suggested to him that they were not mere toys and surprise turned to alarm.

He ordered Sasha to be still.

'I don't know you, I tell you.'

'It's been a few years, reverend. We last spoke at your father's funeral, remember.'

'That was years ago.'

'Seriously. You still acting stupid?'

This pirate wore more than a few piratical embellishments to help him blend in with the day's re-enactments, but fixed to his ear beneath his mane of false black hair was a familiar glass bauble on a chain. Also, a serpentine tattoo slid down his neck.

There was no mistaking the man that he had seen outside the barbershop. It was one of The Severn Sea Gang.

'I really can't imagine what you want with me, Mr McAtree.'

'That's funny.'

'I mean it. I'm no criminal any more.'

'Get this,' said Mel. 'We know where your sister Ellie lives on Floodgates Farm. You wouldn't want anything bad to happen to her little boy, would you? Personally, I'd hate to raise a child so close to a river, it's so fucking dangerous.'

'The hell if I know what Randal has to do with you.'

'Don't you, my old friend? Don't you really?'

To the other, taller man, it was no joke.

240

'Time to cut the crap, Mel.'

This other pirate appeared particularly ill-suited to his false beard as he pulled his pistol from his sash and held it wrong way round by the muzzle.

It was now more club than gun.

At the same time the gap-toothed buccaneer wheezed terribly. Such a lean, pale veteran looked unwell. There was a hole through his nostrils into which a ring could easily have fitted, except this was no piercing for any jewellery but something more serious – snorting cocaine had destroyed his septum long ago.

Those crow eyes belonged to Slim Jim Jackson.

Mel McAtree laughed.

'Now that we're officially all mates again, what can you tell me about your father's stolen antiques?'

The question stuck in Luke's craw.

'Not my call.'

'Come now, reverend, tell us your plan.'

'Yeah, what is it?' snapped Slim Jim.

'God knows. You're the ones doing all the talking.'

'But we've seen you digging!'

'Someone hid the treasure near Berkeley, I'm sure, but that was the year I was born. How can I possibly know where it is now?'

'Because Frank Cordell has given you a clue.'

'Cordell is a fantasist. Anything he has told you is untrue.'

'We don't believe you.'

'He's a blabber and a boaster.'

Mel leaned closer.

'You and Cordell intend to divide the loot and cut out us of it. Do you?'

'I don't have it, that's the truth.'

'Then how are you going to pay for your sister's wedding?'

'Who says I am?'

'Never mind that. It's Cordell we want to know about. He says he's going to be a rich man when he gets out of jail. You and he have done a deal. Am I correct?'

'What if we have?'

'So you admit it?'

Slim Jim turned his head and spat in the dock.

'Didn't I fucking tell you? He's planning to go off with it all.'

The unhealthy, dished cheeks, the mean lips, the soulless eyes, lent this washed-up crook the hue of some pathetic bird.

'Suppose my father did inadvertently tell Cordell something in his drug-addled dreams?' said Luke. 'What is it you think I have, exactly?'

'A fucking map. What else?'

He played dumb, while into his head there floated a frantic scheme.

'Seriously? You want to play pirates?'

'Running out of patience here, Luke.'

As soon as he saw his chance he scooped Sasha under his arm. He did it for her own safety.

'For real?'

Slim Jim weighed his pistol in his hand.

'You're massively disappointing me, Luke. You and I used to be, like, so close.'

'How can I forget?'

'We know Frank Cordell gave you something, reverend. We think it might have been one of his paintings. Or a book? We've searched the vicarage once already and we'll do so again, so why don't you save us and yourself a lot of trouble? Tell us what he told you.'

'What happens if I don't?'

'Ellie's little boy fails to come home from school.'

Sasha barked. She wanted to go for both men's throats. Obviously such a meeting could not end well.

'You stay away from that child.'

Slim Jim smirked.

'But you and I know how gentle and caring I can be, don't we, Captain?'

'Don't you dare touch him, do you hear? Nobody loves that boy like I do.'

Not nearly all of Slim Jim's leer did Luke rebuke at first, faced as he was with such a sly, lascivious and malign expression.

He was going down – he was a sinking ship as inky black water closed over his head.

Disarmed briefly, he felt tears well in his eyes. He was back in that boatshed near Berkeley Castle, listening to the dark waves slap the piles beneath the rocking floorboards. If he had always felt guilty about what had happened in that riverside shack it was because he had sometimes had an erection, too. If he had sometimes had an erection, then there must have been complicity on his part, he must have somehow wanted it to happen?

Then came the anger. *That sense of being at the bottom of the deepest ocean where even the fish swam blind.*

'Why don't you simply fuck off and leave me alone?'

Mel objected.

'You don't think you can rat on your best mates, do you, reverend? Are we not all family, so to speak?'

'Not to me.'

'Just tell us where to dig, Luke and we'll leave you alone.'

'You know I can't do that.'

Slim Jim was scathing.

'You heard him, he's lying.'

Luke narrowed his eyes.

'That's the way it is, fellas. Now bugger off, both of you.'

It seemed impossibly unfair that this wanton, lustful man should have power over him still, but he did, he half crippled him with shame and regret.

He shook in every limb. Hot beads of perspiration chilled his skin as he screamed inside with dismay.

He was not scared exactly – he was utterly devastated.

This was his chance to confront his tormentor, this was the face-to-face meeting that he had envisaged ever since he had grown old enough to contemplate murder instead of self-harm.

Yet he could scarcely move a muscle, he was nine years old again, somehow, as if this decrepit thief still exercised all his former control over him with impunity.

Slim Jim frothed at the mouth.

'I don't think he's getting the message.'

Mel agreed.

'Do yourself a favour, reverend, tell us everything about the river and its likely hiding places.'

'Keep working on it.'

Suddenly Sasha leapt at Slim Jim and bit his shin. Luke had his arms free, even as the whole quayside, with its Devil's ship, did a spin.

A fist slammed into his stomach.

The next fast undercut struck his jaw.

'Hit the bastard, Mel! Hit him!'

Shock met pain. Back in the day, he would have shot them both dead in a flash, except that would be no plan at all.

'I can't... won't... tell you a thing.'

'Fuck you, reverend. Here's what I think,' said Mel. 'Somewhere there's a clue to millions of pounds' worth of clocks, china and snuffboxes. Make the choice that Rex Lyons never did.'

Sasha entered into a perilous tug of war with the fractious Jim at the edge of the quay.

'He's right, you know, Luke. Give us the treasure that we helped your father to acquire, or never get to enjoy your share.'

'Oh, so its 'share' now, is it? And what about my sister, Ellie? Doesn't she deserve something, too?'

'Very well, we'll cut her in. Just get this damned dog off me!'

'And Jess? My mother helped steal those antiques. She was one of the gang. Or are you doing all this behind her back, too?'

'Whose idea do you think this is?' said Mel.

'So my own mother aims to sell me out, after all? I thought so. But I haven't said I know where any treasure is.'

'No, but you're on its trail. We need to know what you know so far. And you're going to tell us.'

'You think?'

Advancing along the quay, Slim Jim gave Sasha a vicious sideswipe with his boot. A yelp and the awful sound of splashing water ensued; the horror and disgust of it turned Luke's stomach.

He rushed to the edge of the flooded basin and grabbed Slim Jim's cutlass from his hand. Then he turned with a wail like a banshee. He was going to use the side of its short, broad blade as a cudgel.

'No one hurts my dog.'

Then his world exploded. He swayed and toppled like a tree. Fell flat on his face. Lay prone.

Next he felt himself being dragged backwards. He dug his fingernails in vain into the quay's cobbles; he slid along inside his bloodied black coat, even as the surrounding festivities beyond the Amatheia sounded close by, but with an alien medley of distant voices.

The cries of actors and audience completed their own peculiar drama, but no longer for him, apparently. Their shouts were filled with hideous, demonic gabble like the sudden rush of water in his ears.

He opened his eyes to see a man's face meet him eyeball to eyeball. His cutlass had gone flying.

'As soon as you have the treasure, Luke, dear boy, make sure you tell us. Or you get more of the same.'

'Son of a bitch…'

Mel had come at him from behind…

'H'm, yeah, I would urge you to worry about Ellie's son from now on. You have until the end of the week, max. Come up with the map or I can't answer for what will happen to Randal.'

…that blur was a brick.

Next second Luke closed his eyes.

Someone else was screaming obscenities at them?

But everything was so painful and dizzy – he was in a long, downward plunge, with never a chance of recovery into darkness deep, unfathomable, extreme.

That new voice was not a man's, yet sounded familiar.

It could have been the Devil himself, if the Devil had long red hair and the face of an angel.

*

Beneath his blood-soaked face lay solid ground. He hadn't been thrown into the dock, after all, Luke realised.

He was somehow off his knees and staggering through the crowd. Children and parents alike hardly gave him a second glance as peelers chased more vagrants and buxom women clad in long cream dresses reeled about giving everyone drunken embraces.

He was a good act at which to scream and laugh as he winced at every move he made.

He was at the door of a building that stood in the shadow of the looming gables of Reynolds Warehouse. Wherever he was, he was being sat down inside a pale stone, Gothic archway as a fresh set of hands closed firmly round his shoulders.

He was in the cool, white interior of – what, exactly? He opened one bruised eye but not the other and there came into focus a white oblong board that was fixed to the wall just above some pews:

GOD IS OUR REFUGE AND STRENGTH

A VERY PRESENT HELP IN TROUBLE

Then the world turned bloodier and blurrier.

'It's all right. I'm here to help you, reverend. My name is Gabriela Meireles.'

He clasped his benefactor's hand. Pressed it the same way a penitent did a priest's.

Then he groaned.

Had he not visited the docks today simply to find the Amatheia? But even the best plan could turn out to have the direst consequences.

Sometimes in order to bait a trap you had to *be* the part, not act it.

'Forget me. Save my dog, save Sasha. She's in the water, drowning…'

Chapter 44

Jorge listened to the violent storm that raged over the River Severn as he struggled to concentrate on the enormous and unfinished jigsaw left behind by his predecessor.

How could thousands of pieces of blue sky and water be so bafflingly similar?

At his feet, Sasha raised her head and growled at a particularly loud roll of thunder from her rug by the vicarage's fire.

Not only did Hill House's leaky windows rattle glass in the rain, but the wind caused shutters and doors to squeak on their hinges.

It was as if someone were searching the house from top to bottom, yet not a drawer or cupboard was opened – there appeared to be a fitful, uneasy visitor who left by one entrance, only to return by another.

'Frank Cordell wanted to unlock the secret of the treasure,' said Jorge aloud while wracking his brains. 'But the fool had only half an idea of what he was looking for.'

After a while he abandoned his chair. He completed a slow tour of the room. Inspected its nautical relics. Arrived back at the fire.

He stood there, jaw dropping, his face bathed in shadows caused by sudden flickers of flame.

Rex Lyons's Bible lay open on the table where he had left off studying it, some time ago.

'The Devil!' cried Jorge, a trifle inappropriately and seized the Good Book in both hands.

He immediately sensed a nervous tingling in his fingers. A shiver took hold of him. It was barely a prickle to begin with, but less and less controllable.

He turned the Bible at an angle to the light of the fire and his shiver was gone; tilted it back again and it returned.

Someone had circled letters with red pencil and then rubbed it out again long ago. The remaining indentations reacted to a certain gleam and just the right amount of shadow.

Here, then, was one of the biblical passages to which Frank Cordell had been so desperate to draw his attention.

By tipping the page to the flames certain letters shone in Revelation at just the right angle: 'and before **the** th-**r**-one there was something like a sea of glass, l-**i**-ke crystal, an-**d** in the centre and round the throne, four livin-**g** creatur-**e**-s, full of eye-**s** in front **and** back'.

Then it was that he noticed the fire's elaborate mantelpiece and its head of a woman.

She widened her eyes when a sudden explosion of sparks in the grate seemingly set her gilded hair aglow.

She stared straight at the page, too?

At his fingertips he spelt three words: **the ridge sand.**

He did his best to look up what else the dead man had mentioned. In particular, he discovered: 'She will give you the tre-**a**-sures of darkness.'

This time only one letter was ringed with red like fire.

Undeterred, he crossed the room and seized the collection of canvases that he had rescued from HMPL....

Then he spread them side by side over the floor and looked for more biblical phrases recorded by the obsessed Cordell on the rear of his drawings.

He cross-referenced two of them to Luke and Proverbs: 'For where your **t**-reasure is, **the**-re will your heart **b**-e also.' 'If thou seekest he-**r** as s-**i**-lver, and searchest for her as hid treasures; Then shalt thou understand the fear of the LORD, and find the knowle-**dge** of God.'

All the straining and banging in the house, so like a storm-tossed ship at sea, could not divert his gaze from what the letters spelt.

Rearranged, they made a message.

His mixture of excitement and terror redoubled, they rose to the surface of his consciousness as if from the deepest sea floor. There, they began to fuel one conviction, or promise another. He was being dangerously tempted, he was certain of that, *as had Luke Lyons?*

248

But he aimed very soon to solve the puzzle:

The ridge sand
She will give you the treasures of darkness
at the bridge.

Chapter 45

Ellie was furious.

'Christ, Luke, how bad is it?'

'Quite bad.'

'Let me drive you to hospital.'

'That won't be necessary. Besides, I'm used to looking after myself.'

'Shit. What have you got yourself into?'

'It's complicated.'

'Which makes you a damned fool.'

Another surge of pain coursed through his body. How safe he was now he didn't know, but what had happened to him in Gloucester Docks had been a wake-up call.

He gently patted his swollen ear which bled again as Ellie's anger turned to panic down the phone.

'Where are you now, Luke?'

'At the vicarage.'

'Stay there, I'll come to you.'

'You don't want to do that. Trust me, Ellie. That's not necessary.'

'Fine. Yes. Whatever. Go get yourself killed.'

'How is it my fault?'

He could hear his sister kicking furniture about at the other end of the line. She was furious at him for being so careless and stupid.

'They ambushed you at the Tall Ships Festival? Why?'

'Why do you suppose? Slim Jim Jackson and Mel McAtree really do think

I know where our parents hid those antiques years ago.'

'You were right. I should have gone to the police when I first caught them sniffing around the farm.'

'I think I can handle it.'

'You think? You *think*!'

'We need a plan.'

'Tell me your plan.'

'Then, again, there's justice.'

'Can you be any *less* specific?'

'Better if you don't know.'

'Can't believe I just heard that.'

'What can I tell you? The sooner someone acts decisively the sooner this will be over.'

'Over, in whose opinion?'

'I'm sorry, Ellie. I didn't mean to scare you.'

'Of course you're scaring me. This is my family we're talking about here.'

'What if I were to offer to dig up the treasure myself?'

Ellie caught her breath.

'Are you mad? No one knows where that shit is.'

'Suppose I do.'

'Really, Luke, I don't have time for this. I've been driving a tractor since six a.m. I have a farm to run.'

'Don't tell Jeremy I called, don't tell anyone. Not yet. Trust me, I'll sort it.'

'That it? You ring me with some bullshit story about our father's thugs beating the shit out of you and...'

'I wanted to warn you to be on your guard, that's all.'

'Yes, of course I'll be careful. But what is this new scheme of yours all about? What's the point here?'

'The point is, you and Randal won't have to live in fear of the past any longer. Let me offer to give everyone what they want.'

'Sorry Luke, but I'm worried.'

'Don't be. These men are messing with the wrong person. You hear me?

The wrong person.'

Ellie fell silent.

In the end, he spoke first. In the forefront of his mind was Slim Jim Jackson's threat to harm Randal. He hoped *that* was all hot air. He couldn't take the chance, though, he had to act fast. But to tell Ellie everything now would only worry her too much.

He changed tack instead.

'How's Jeremy?'

'He's as weak as a kitten with the flu ever since he stayed out all night 'with the boys'. Apparently he went swimming in the river.'

'Give him my regards.'

Obviously Jeremy had not yet confessed to Ellie about the riverside ritual, or she was covering for him.

'Wait, Luke! I forgot, Jess rang.'

'She did?'

'Mother will arrive two days before the wedding.'

'That doesn't give us long.'

*

That night in Hill House Luke sat by the grinning, gilded face carved over the fire and dreamt the strangest of dreams – she would have him relive his father's last raid on the country house in Wiltshire which went so terribly wrong.

According to Rex, it should have been 'a piece of piss'.

Stay calm.

Fuck it, Rex. Can't see a thing in all this fog.

Shut up, Jess, it's the perfect cover.

Go fast. Turn through the big iron gates. Steer up the la-di-da driveway with its big beech trees.

You definitely want to do this?

What do you think?

Trust me. It's a great idea.

I'm feeling jubilant.

Like playing the best of jokes on the richest of people.

Christ, Rex, my heart is racing.

I feel like fucking Robin Hood tonight.

Nothing too subtle. We're not cat burglars. It's in and out.

I could shit myself.

Press my foot flat on the accelerator.

We're gonna be rich tonight.

Slim Jim and the rest had better keep up because I'm going straight through the fucking window in our 4x4.

What if the lord of the manor has a gun?

How should I know?

What if they put up a fight?

Just do what you have to do.

He woke up all hot and flustered, but it was all right, the vicarage was as quiet as the grave and the face on the overmantel no longer seemed alive.

Time to open a fresh bottle of whisky.

It might have been a short dream but he shared his father's jubilation and excitement.

As a boy he had felt the allure of something hideously criminal, even murderous.

A little piece of him still hankered after its glorious finality, since there was nothing like staring down the barrel of a gun to focus all your thoughts.

He returned to his fireside chair and used his stiff, bruised fingers to juggle more pieces on the table to fit his jigsaw puzzle. He tried to see the bigger picture. After all, he'd been holed up here for quite a while – long enough for all the wild garlic to lose its white, starry petals and wither under the trees by the lake in the garden.

Sasha lay down at his feet with a whine.

'What is it Sash? What have you got there, for Christ's sake?'

In her teeth was another envelope. Someone must have slipped it through the letterbox in the front door while he'd been dreaming. It was with mounting expectation that he took it from her mouth to read the contents:

'My dear Sean, I still feel angry at all the anguish you caused me, all those years ago. I can't understand it, not when you loved and cherished me so much in those early married days. I wanted to be with you 'in sickness and in health, richer or poorer'. Now I feel I betrayed you by not telling you I was pregnant. Either way, we managed to ruin something very precious. As you say, we'll not make the same mistake again. Come to me, darling, as soon as you can and meet your lovely daughter Sara at last. Love, Olivia.'

The destination on the envelope was 1 Terrace Gardens, Edinburgh, while the address at the head of the page was Chelsea in London.

The letter, written in blue ink on faded cream paper was dated 30th November 1960 and was in response to the October one that he already had in his possession.

Clearly it had been a whole month before Olivia had taken the heart-stopping decision to reply.

His hands trembled. Whoever was feeding him such old correspondence wanted him to know something truly momentous?

Olivia had to be the missing piece of the greater puzzle or it was all lies.

There was a thrill to evil you never saw coming.

Chapter 46

It was all so simple, thought Jorge, as he cycled along the narrow lanes towards the River Severn with Sasha for company. According to the free app on his phone, all he had to do was absolutely nothing when a hamburger flashed up on the screen.

A banana showed next and he pressed a key to approve.

Then came a bar of chocolate. His stomach at once told him to stop at the next shop and buy something in an automatic motor response.

Instead he pedalled faster with Sasha running beside him.

It was called response inhibition training. Alcoholics could, in a similar fashion, train themselves to ignore the urge to reach for a drink apparently.

His phone had in it an element of distraction akin to mesmerism. As he steered one-handed towards the shore, he nearly missed the ninety-degree bend in the road.

'Wow, that was close.'

Sasha managed to stay upright in his bicycle's basket. Turned her head to keep a worrisome eye on him. She considered him better acrobat than cyclist.

It was a bumpy ride through the edge of Shepperdine when they came to the little green and black church of St. Mary the Virgin. Seconds later, he was aware of the proximity of the wide grey waterway before him, more sea than river. To be in the presence of such an impressive vista filled him with wonder. He felt humbled, but not necessarily only in a religious sense.

Rather, the need to submit to the great force of Nature almost took his breath away.

'Can I help you, officer?'

A woman blocked the porch of the tin tabernacle. She was exceptionally thin, with a dark brown tan, wind-blown brown hair, pale and somewhat cracked lips that gave her the appearance of a young but experienced sea gazer. She was dressed in black with a clerical collar.

Her entire attitude Jorge could regard only as guardedly suspicious. Her grey-flecked eyes blazed with defiance.

He held on to Sasha's collar very firmly.

'My name is Inspector Jorge Winter. I'm investigating possible poor performance and conduct issues concerning Reverend Luke Lyons prior to his disappearance last summer...'

'I know who you are. You're that Church detective guy? Right? God's Mr Nosy Parker from Gloucester Cathedral?'

Jorge straightened his shoulders inside his long black coat.

'You Reverend Anne Buck?'

'Since when do you care?'

'You were one of the last people to see Reverend Lyons alive.'

'Don't be ridiculous.'

'You not concerned, at all?'

'Should I be?'

'It'll soon be nine months and no one knows a thing about him.'

'But that's what people do when they get themselves into trouble,' said Rev. Buck confidently. 'They lie low.'

He leaned his gloved hand on the porch. Blocked her exit.

'I really need to talk to you about rumours of a cult that worships the goddess of the river.'

'Do you now, Inspector?'

'Because of the sensitivity of the allegation I would prefer to keep this between ourselves.'

'I see. You've come filled with a lot of hot gossip?'

'As a relevant witness, you are required to co-operate with my investigative interview as dictated by rules upheld by your Senior Deacon.'

'For God's sake come in and shut the bloody door.'

The tin tabernacle was a single room just as Jorge remembered it from his childhood. That's to say it was a very basic shed with a few pews and some rather faded blue rugs on its wooden floor.

Such a place was kit-built for the convenience of worshippers, a temporary refuge for prayer, a prefab just for God.

The flimsy, replacement windows resembled those of a very modest bungalow which could, but never did, fly away on the frequent gusts of wind that blew up from the Bristol Channel.

He dusted a pew with a tissue, took off his peaked cap and sat down beside it. He took out his notebook and pencil.

'It's my belief that Reverend Lyons uncovered the worship hereabouts of the goddess Sabrina. Is that true in your estimation?'

'Reverend Luke did come here to tell me about something that he had witnessed one night by the river,' confessed Rev. Buck, choosing a pew of her own.

Jorge gave Sasha a reassuring pat and she lay down at his feet on a patch of bare boards.

'What did you say to him?'

'I suggested we say a prayer together, Inspector.'

'Did you not know of these pagan practices, at all?'

'Naturally I hear rumours.'

'You ever investigate them or what?'

Rev. Buck's gaze came to rest on a pretty, hand-sewn picture of three playful badgers which adorned the wooden kneeler at her feet.

'I've been here long enough to delve deep into local history, Inspector. I like to understand my parishioners' roots, so to speak. This stretch of river has always been a remote, forgotten sort of place. Why else do you think that two nuclear power stations once operated here? Even as the former Magnox station was being decommissioned at Oldbury, many people became vehemently opposed to building another in its place. They still are. And who can blame them? The proposed new 3,300 megawatt station will be four times bigger than its predecessor. It's not like it's a simple exchange. It will take five thousand workers to construct it and there could be 1500 lorry movements a day for almost two years which will make many people's lives a misery. Most protesters have been content to lobby their MPs and DECC consultation, but who am I to criticise those few who have chosen to harness the spirit of the river, no matter how monstrous? They want to defeat the plan through a different kind of power, not least because it's the river that is most at risk from possible pollution.'

'That means direct action of a preternatural kind?'

'If nothing else it has stiffened people's resolve by bringing them all together.'

'So what did Reverend Luke say about it exactly?'

'He wanted to expose what he said could only be a form of devil worship. I told him to tread carefully.'

'Did he?'

Rev. Buck frowned heavily.

'The thing is, Inspector, he had too much to gain personally. The nuclear power company needed additional land for temporary construction facilities – land he proposed to sell to them if only he could wrest it from his ailing grandmother in time.'

'Wrest is a strong word.'

'You think you know better?'

'It's my guess that Reverend Luke wanted your help to wrong-foot his critics to help push through the sale. Am I right?'

'Naturally I refused. I might not believe in water-nymphs who can take human form to walk on land, Inspector, but I'm loyal to my parishioners. Once a month I listen to their worries in this church. As a newcomer I do not share all their concerns about the advanced boiling water reactor. As far as I'm concerned any radiological detriment to health from the generation of much needed power or any risk from the management of associated waste will be low. This being a flood zone worries me more! But I have seen the toll that this shadow has cast over people's hearts and minds, I worry for their spiritual well-being when God seems to have turned a blind eye to their cause.'

'Greed gained Luke enemies, I see that now.'

'That,' replied Rev. Buck, 'is all greed will do. But I really can't say that Reverend Luke Lyons struck me as particularly avaricious, Inspector. On the contrary, the more times I reminded him how much the river meant to other people, the more he apologized for selling his soul to the highest bidder. In his heart of hearts he loved its goddess, too. After all, is not a river the ancient source and origin of life itself, a timeless place to baptise newborns as a sign of purification and initiation, especially into the Christian Church? When Sabrina was drowned by her evil stepmother, many centuries ago, she was transformed into the guardian of the water. It would be a mistake to equate her with the Devil, however. Yes, this tidal estuary was once also considered a gateway to the abode of the dead and, if you went fishing on the Severn on Sunday, you might hook Satan, but it was never all bad. With the sea comes fertility. The river is where life and belief intermingle and Sabrina is its natural nurturer and custodian.'

He could have done without the sermon, thought Jorge and looked out a window. He breathed the smell of bladderwrack and brine that blew his way on the breeze.

Did he not still share a love of the river, too? As boys, he and Luke had learnt so much from its mysterious ways.

Was it not the one thing which would forever link them together, for good or evil, in life and death?

For a moment a voice seemed to come to him *on the air*.

'Suppose somebody wanted to persuade Reverend Luke not to sell his grandmother's property? What if they decided to give him the fright of his life? What if they ambushed him by the river in a mock 'baptism'? It wouldn't be the first time that somebody was dunked in the river and it went wrong.'

'Is that your theory?' said Rev. Buck, scathingly. 'You think somebody local killed him *by accident*?'

'I think you'd protect your parishioners no matter what.'

She widened her eyes at him.

'Reverend Luke came to me because he said he felt tempted to do something truly wrong.'

'By wrong, you mean the disposal of the 'cottage'?'

'Okay, that's what we talked about at first, along with the cult as you call it, but later on he seemed to be talking about something else altogether. He appeared to clutch at straws like a drowning man. Looking back, I see how he literally wanted to know if one wrong could ever justify doing another?'

'A person secure in their own faith can confront the Devil and still win.'

'But if that devil is himself?'

Jorge gazed again out the window towards the river. He could sense its twisting currents glide past in one long, glassy serpent.

His great weight caused the floorboards to sag under his heels.

'Isn't it always?' he said softly.

Rev. Buck lit herself a cigarette.

'Whatever it was, it was tearing him apart.'

*

Myth and superstition would have to wait. Jorge left the little church in order to cycle along the bank of the Severn where, soon, there rose up before him the silent, empty building called Chapel Cottage.

To call it a cottage was a complete misnomer. Instead he leaned his bicycle against a very substantial stone building that was the size of a barn with a high central gable. Winter honeysuckle sagged from its porch while a sign read UNDER OFFER in fast fading letters on black iron railings. A steep set of steps led up to a locked Gothic door at which he knocked very loudly.

No answer, as expected.

So he descended to the gravelled yard again where he let Sasha go off to explore a garden. Then he walked round the courtyard. Discovered a locked garage.

He could by pulling at its big, badly fitting double doors, peer in through a gap.

His heart missed a beat. Gathering dust inside was a rusty Land Rover.

It was with such a vehicle that Luke had towed his boat.

Next, he walked round to the other side of the house and removed a brick from the edge of the path. As Sasha was still happily hunting rabbits in the garden's overgrown grass nearby, his gaze went beyond her to the edge of the river. To the vast estuary. To the ocean where one current met another. To where Luke had gone, he now felt certain, dead or alive. And from where he must inevitably return. At the resurrection.

Moments later the shrill piping sound of two oyster catchers reached his ears. The presence of the birds did not distract him from his brutal intentions. He whistled Sasha and picked her up. Then he hurled the brick through the condemned building's picture window. Stepped over shards of glass.

It did him good to vent his anger.

It had always been said about Sean Lyons that he made a lot of money from scrapping tanks and planes at the end of World War II, which had enabled him to buy Chapel Cottage. Other people said that he won it in a game of poker one night in The Windbound Inn. Most likely this house had been too much of an empty ruin for anyone else to take on in the 1950s.

Jorge paused to don white plastic gloves and a face mask. With a retch or two he proceeded with caution among spiders' webs and mouse droppings.

Sasha sniffed chairs and tables with indifference. More rabbits, she intimated, were worthy of her attention outside.

Someone had been placing Gwendolen Lyons's possessions carefully into black bin bags. A real attempt months ago had been made to sort her personal effects from room to room.

One bag was full of photographs, letters, ornaments and books of poetry. Others contained sheets, blankets and pillows.

Certain useful or sentimental things had been destined for Severnside House care home, without a doubt, while others were due to be thrown away?

Whatever Luke's good intentions something had happened to make him abandon the project to help his grandmother in her new life; he had walked out on everything he had come here to do in order to end his own past one?

Or had he?

Every day Jorge trembled in case this was the day that he recognised his lost friend on the National Crime Agency UK Missing Persons Bureau's website. He could imagine the cadaver that he would be invited to identify on the screen by its number: *03-001258. Gloucestershire, Berkeley. Male. Date 31 July 2016, 35. White European.* He could anticipate his shock and horror when he clicked on 'case detail'. What had once been the most intimate characteristics of a living human being soon bore all the hallmarks of a 'thing' in a catalogue. *Hair: black. Facial hair: none. Eye colour: blue-black. Distinguishing features: old bullet wound in right shoulder. Tattoo of the goddess Sabrina on neck. Clothing: coat, black. Shirt: black. Collar: white, clerical. Footwear: boots, black, size 10. Trousers: black. Hat: black. Jewellery: none.*

It was the worst case scenario. A dreadful, horrific imagining of the quite plausible, of everything he wanted so hard to deny. Not only had his friend somehow died, but their friendship would never be restored?

A photograph lay on a table which showed a young woman dressed in a red and white polka dot, one-piece swimsuit. Two other women linked hands with her, all posing provocatively but playfully on a hot beach somewhere in their elegant halter neck monokinis from the 1950s. He removed the print from its frame. Written on the back were their names: Barbara, Mary and Gwendolen.

More photographs loose in a box showed the three friends as schoolchildren, Girl Guides, would-be ballet dancers and bridesmaids. Not only had they grown up together, they had been a team and ridden to hounds together. One photograph showed them sitting smiling and triumphant on horseback beside a bloodied fox in the snow at Christmas time.

Another photograph showed Luke and Gwendolen by the river.

'You came home to make a new life for yourself, Luke, old friend. It was all here, your job, sister, grandmother and parishioners. So where did you go at the last minute? What was it that suddenly turned your world on its head and wrecked everything? What sudden storm? What bitter secret?'

*

Back at the vicarage Jorge went again to his father's old office where he began to study everything Luke had been working on.

He reluctantly concluded from the river charts and newspaper clippings that he could learn little more. Not so, Sasha. After a thorough reconnaissance of the hopelessly cluttered room, she did circles and wagged her tail while refusing to move far from the painting that stood propped by the room's stone fireplace. It was the Victorian picture of the river and its railway bridge.

She could smell her lost master on the canvas?

Seconds later Jorge was staring hard at the composition that he held squarely in both hands.

Luke had exiled this particular seascape from the rest of his beloved collection of nautical scenes elsewhere in the house, as if it represented some sort of – what? Reminder? Temptation? He had hung it in the office-cum-library as a visual complement to his researches?

He turned it over. Someone had used their knife to cut something into the back of the frame.

The painting displayed the vast curve in the river as a pointer to something?

678 and 034 were carved into the back of the canvas.

Hairs rose on the back of his neck when a chill shot up his spine. Something electric tingled in the tips of his fingers to shock and sear him to his core.

It was the same combination of numbers recorded inside the cover of Rex Lyons's Bible.

While they might yet turn out to signify some secret code, they struck him more as a map's Eastings and Northings.

Chapter 47

Curiosity diverted Luke to the grassy plain at the foot of Berkeley Castle's vertiginous battlements.

A jousting match was in full swing, he observed on his way to the Church of St. Mary's. Parents and children loudly booed Black Knight Lord Pendragon on his black charger as he attempted to score points off his opponent with his twelve-foot-long lance.

Thundering hooves shook the ground in a breathtaking show of speed and courage in the pale summer sunshine.

Suddenly he was overtaken by a gaudily attired figure who danced in and out the crowds, even as they both stopped to bow politely to King Henry VIII and Anne Boleyn. His fellow reveller was dressed from head-to-toe in a bright red top and trousers, while on his head he wore a floppy three-cornered hat from which three bells jingled each time he nodded to his admirers.

It had to be the Earl of Suffolk's jester, thought Luke. All smiles, he danced past him with a wave of a human skull that adorned his marotte.

Murdered in revels at the castle in 1728, Dicky Pearce had been resurrected from his tomb in the nearby church graveyard to play The Fool for the day to the delight of the visitors.

'Sash, stay close. Don't run off where I can't see you.'

Sasha shrank to the ground and whined at his side. The presence of so many people was almost too much for her.

Seconds later, she licked a toddler's ice cream from its cornet with a quick click of her tongue. Lapped it all up before the mother noticed.

Cracked ribs still made breathing difficult as Luke stood on his toes somewhat nervously to see more jousting. He felt a bit like Sasha did.

However, it was no bad thing for a priest to mingle with people from his parish.

Even the most duplicitous vicar should be seen to have fun sometimes.

He was limping along the edge of the grassy tilt-yard at the foot of the castle's grey walls when he chanced to look up.

Four terraces above him someone stood beside the row of cannons near the entrance to the Outer Bailey.

She was clothed appropriately for the festivities in a close-fitting medieval white gown with a belt of gold.

Her head was wrapped in a wimple from crown to chin, as though it were unseemly to show any part of her hair in public.

She folded her arms tightly against her chest and gazed at him directly. She might have been shedding tears of frustration or it could be rage.

Instead, she uttered a laugh that chilled him to the marrow. In the time it took Luke to run back up to the Outer Bailey she no longer stood by the guns.

When he happened to look through the iron railings of the tree-lined graveyard immediately beside him, however, he caught sight of the court jester again.

The Fool stood by a table tomb, talking to Sabrina ap Loegres who was in the process of removing her headdress – he was, by turns, provoking and calming her with cross little gestures and frantic kisses until her face glowed with rightful indignation. It could have been a lovers' tiff.

Some of their agitation wore off on him.

Overhead, young squabbling rooks blackened the air. All their screaming and cawing sounded less than natural; they seemed very enthused about something.

A witch could not have excited them more.

Pretty much.

When Luke entered the graveyard it was inexplicably deserted. At the tomb his eyes came to rest on a bizarre inscription that had been carved into one side:

HERE LIES THE EARL OF SUFFOLKS FOOL

MEN CALLED HIM DICKY PEARCE

HIS FOLLY SERVED TO MAKE FOLKS LAUGH

WHEN WIT AND MIRTH WERE SCARCE

POOR DICK ALAS! IS DEAD AND GONE

WHAT SIGNIFIES TO CRY!

DICKYS ENOUGH ARE STILL BEHIND

TO LAUGH AT BY-AND-BY.

Frankly, it was a relief to enter St. Mary's Church, however gloomy, thought Luke. Its sodium lamps really would play havoc with his sister's wedding photographs, should he ever choose to proceed with the ceremony?

He watched Sasha wander off to wee on a wall. This was his church from which he was expected to give his sermons. He had set foot, as a child, in this very nave to attend a funeral or two with his grandmother.

Back then, when feeling bored he had gazed endlessly at two gossiping heads topped by a toad that were carved on the wall directly above him.

A chill hung in the air as if the dead hand of history haunted dark corners. Had not soldiers fought very hard for this church during the English Civil War? The parliamentarians put cannons on its roof to blast down a wall of the neighbouring castle.

Sasha gave a growl at his side. Someone knelt before the entrance to the chancel straight in front of them.

'Sabrina? Is that you? It's me, Reverend Luke Lyons.'

'Leave me alone.'

'Can I help you?'

Shrouded in gloom, she continued to stare at something very high up on the wall. It was not toads.

He went closer and placed a hand impertinently upon the kneeler's right shoulder.

Angrily, her silvery sea-green eyes swirled in the yellow glow from the lamps – all manner of storms, whirlpools and vortexes surged tempestuously across her glistening pupils when she looked up at him.

Their violent nature appeared quite at one with the fretful figure he had glimpsed on the battlements fifteen minutes ago. Her voluminous red hair flowed freely down her back and over her shoulders.

He fancied he saw in her eyes dead sailors, fishermen, river and canal pilots, bridge builders, dock workers and suicides – all those who had ever come to grief in the River Severn.

Close by, her black dogs Varg and Freya waited impatiently for her command.

'Has something happened? Shall we pray together?'

'Do you think that this is what this is all about, reverend?'

By 'this' he was secretly intrigued but suspicious.

'What I mean to say is that everyone is welcome in St. Mary's. It even ministers to the prison at which I am chaplain.'

Sabrina rose to her feet and simultaneously stroked the silk brocade of her cotehardie dress encrusted with jewels. She swirled its voluminous train round her red velvet shoes while, with a hiss, she ordered both Elkhounds to stay still.

'Been in the wars, have we, reverend?'

He fingered the recently healed cuts on his face and smiled.

'Call it a bit of a misunderstanding. But you'd know all about that, wouldn't you?'

'Can't answer that.'

'But you were there in Gloucester Docks when it happened.'

'Believe me, I arrived in the nick of time to visit my ship.'

'If it hadn't been for you I would have come off even worse.'

But she wasn't listening.

'You believe in hell, reverend?'

It took him a while to see what exactly was still the object of her rapt attention. Slowly some indistinct shapes and colours emerged on the stonework high above the chancel arch until he saw Christ seated in Judgement. So worn away was the stone in places that wall and image flowed into each other like water.

He could quite see that nowadays most people, himself included, would forget all about its very existence if they never thought to look up. It was a mediaeval painting called a Doom.

'Hell is what we don't do for other people,' said Luke, somewhat coldly and watched the black hounds slaver.

'Sometimes I think hell would be a blessing,' said Sabrina. 'I don't know why I expected to find peace of mind in such a place as this anyway.'

'You not a Berkeley, at all?'

'Did I not tell you – my family predates any Fitzharding.'

'And yet they don't lie in this or any other church in the vicinity of the castle?'

'They do not, reverend.'

'How come?'

'Long ago, somebody did a very bad thing to us.'

'So where do they rest now?'

Sabrina's look met his and there floated in her pupils more faces whose bloodless, bloated lips struggled to call out to him.

He shook his head. Just recently his swimming brain had begun to play cruel tricks on him and this was another?

'Rest?' said Sabrina harshly. 'You speak as if you would have us lie up like some ship or other when for many of us the voyage never ends. But then, what does a priest really know about eternity, anyway? Would you even dare to set sail?'

Her odd, archaic turn of phrase was so vehemently delivered that Luke was at a loss to explain why she also grinned at him. Her look had something vengeful in it. He felt a distinctly awkward desire to give her a smile, too, but of a different sort. He could only say that in no way was she joking.

'I'm not entirely sure I understand what you mean?'

'There comes a time when the dead should be raised from their graves, judged and consigned to their fate once and for all, don't you think reverend?'

'Are you making some kind of threat?'

'Do I really have to say it?'

'I'm sorry?'

'Eva Greene has told me about the unexpected resurfacing of your grandfather's pocket watch. Did you bring it with you as promised?'

'Hey, slow down. Anyone could have stolen that watch before he vanished. Its significance remains unknown.'

'I may have a solution.'

'Solution?'

'We should combine forces to give us what we most want?'

'What's that?'

'Justice.'

His jaw dropped. Was not that the very word he himself had thought to invoke when last talking to Ellie? Sabrina could have been reading his blackest, most grievous thoughts.

Before the chancel he saw her do a slow twirl. Drawn by he knew not what compulsion, she danced below the Doom like a bride practising her waltz down the aisle.

Except her face exuded in its joy all the siren call, grace and beauty of one of the light stepping daughters of Oceanus.

'I'm not sure what you mean by justice. I'm a man of God now, not the vicious thug I grew up to be.'

'Come, come reverend, wouldn't you willingly trade everything you believe in for one last chance to put things right?'

'Whatever do you mean?'

At which point there came a little jingle. A door from a spiral staircase to the north of the west window opened on to a stone platform that had the faces of lady, knight and priest carved on the steps just below it.

It was Dicky Pearce.

'Sabrina means we have something to offer not threaten you, reverend.'

On closer examination Luke recognised Eva Greene, come to keep her rendezvous with him after all.

'What do you know about it? You agreed to conduct some research into my family, but instead you've been avoiding me for weeks. Obviously you can't help me.'

'Yeah, I think I can, reverend.'

'How's that?'

'For a start you and I are related.'

'That's madness.'

Eva looked out from what might once have been a pulpit even as she and Sabrina exchanged knowing glances.

'Say what you like but you and I share a big secret.'

'I doubt that very much.'

'Actually we're sort of brother and sister.'

'Why are you telling me this nonsense? What's in it for you?'

'That's for free.'

'What makes you think I'll believe you?'

'Hope you're ready for this, reverend?' said Eva firmly. 'Then I'll begin. My grandmother was called Olivia. She was very posh and well-connected but also very wild, which is why her secret love for a handsome Irish scrap dealer called Sean Lyons was such a disaster in terms of her social class. But she and Sean did marry – in 1939, to be exact, when she was just eighteen. The London Blitz drove them apart, I guess. Many a young couple had their nerves shattered during the Second World War by all the bombing. We can say that at least. According to lots of letters I inherited, Olivia and Sean separated after a few years but never divorced. Divorce in those days was never easy anyway. Sean didn't know it but Olivia was pregnant with his daughter Sara. Soon afterwards he bigamously married your grandmother Gwendolen. By then Sara was already growing up elsewhere to be a great beauty and, somewhat reconciled to her mother's former friends, she ignored her advice and recklessly married the much older Lord Henry Greene of Wiltshire. She did it for his money.'

'Not my call.'

'Oh, but it is, reverend. One night your father Rex Lyons broke into Lady Greene's Wiltshire home deep in the countryside. He shot and mortally wounded her on the night of his last, botched burglary. Sara gave birth to a child by emergency C-section before she passed away in Gloucester Hospital. Her husband died of a heart attack shortly afterwards. He was seventy. That baby torn from her womb was me, reverend. As a result I was brought up an orphan.'

'*You* put those two letters through my door.'

'When I began to dig into the circumstances of my birth I came across correspondence between Sean Lyons and my grandmother in the attic of our country house, since sold. It shows that he staged his disappearance in 1960 in order to leave Gwendolen and go back to Olivia. She never stopped loving him.'

Luke neither accepted nor refuted the allegation, but struggled to catch his breath in a heave of sore ribs.

'How long have you known this?'

'Fact is, our grandfather lived in Scotland and then in London until 1981. That pocket watch you promised to bring me today will confirm everything. Can I see it?'

'Some other time.'

'That's funny.'

'What now? What do you want?'

Eva rattled her bells.

'Like I said, I want justice. This is not a joke.'

'Do you know how difficult it is for me to understand a thing you're saying?'

'Then I'll be clear, reverend. Your fucking family robbed mine blind. Your father murdered my mother and, in most people's eyes, my father, too. Rex Lyons and his gang took my family heirlooms worth millions. I want them back. You're going to get them for me, not least because you and I share the same bad blood.'

He winced and turned to appeal to Sabrina. Something silver and serpentine writhed in the lobe of one ear beneath her red mane.

'No, absolutely bloody not.'

She circled him on the cold stone floor.

'Relax reverend. Eva has a point. You want to do the right thing and return the stolen loot to its lawful owner, don't you? Consider this, then, an offer. What can we do to help you make the honest, Christian decision?'

'Prove to me that I can trust you.'

'How can we do that?'

'There is one thing.'

'Do tell, reverend.'

'I want you to help me get rid of someone's body.'

'What body? Whose?'

'Mine.'

Sabrina's face darkened. For a moment she played with her necklace of priceless saltwater pearls. Then Eva spoke for them both from the pulpit.

'No way! Are you mad? That's a step too far.'

'And if I can do as you ask and make you as rich as Croesus?'

'Now you're talking.'

271

Chapter 48

'Almost too beautiful to be true, isn't it?' said Luke, as bright sunshine lit the Severn. 'Make the most of it while you can.'

Sasha sat on the seawall with her nose in the air and sniffed the view. She didn't respond when he called her name again, but gazed at the incoming tide intently as though she were also listening to its currents and gulls. Like him she was happier out here in wide open spaces. Together they watched a noisy bird hitch a ride on a log to go with the flow.

Suddenly she gave a bark not just at the gull but at a motorboat that wove its way along the river's snakelike channel between mud and shingle.

It could have been an Environment Agency launch or even a craft belonging to Severn Trent Water Company.

That he was the object of their rude attention was obvious, thought Luke, but he had the advantage: this side of Hayward Rock the sun had to be in the eyes of the two-man crew.

As the craft slowed the sunlight glinted on someone's binoculars.

Suddenly the mood of the river changed. Now it was less picturesque than slightly malevolent. Both men on board the motorboat were anxious to let him know that they were observing his regular morning walk along the riverbank as usual.

Not Environment Agency or water company, then.

He gave them a wave and the boat's engine roared back into action. A bullet-headed man raised a muddy spade in what amounted to a challenge.

Luke knew who he was, but he need not have bothered. That went for the other crew member, too. Clearly their digging had so far proved no more rewarding than his own?

Next minute his phone rang.

'Yes, Ellie?'

'Listen to me, Luke. Something bad has happened.'

The voice in his ear was puffing and blowing.

'Relax. What's with you?'

'It's grandma, stupid.'

'What about her?'

'She walked out of Severnside House at dawn this morning.'

'Honestly? Where is she now? Have they found her yet?'

'Thank God, she's back home.'

'Where did she go?'

'To the river.'

'Why there?'

'She won't say.'

'Doesn't anyone know anything?'

'She's very confused. As far as I can tell she found the gate open in the care home's gardens and kept going.'

He swore.

'Shouldn't the grounds be locked at night?'

'It's not a prison.'

'Good luck with that!'

'If you'd been a proper grandson to her, you'd know.'

'I really wouldn't.'

'Listen to me, Luke, why do you think I put her into care in the first place? You left me to make the decision, remember, so don't complain now. This isn't exactly new. Last Christmas Eve she wandered off to the old hospital in Berkeley. It's been closed for years, but she was convinced that you had an appointment there to see a doctor. It must have been some old memory of hers because she was behaving as if she were back in the 1980s or 90s.'

'Isn't she always?'

'She had to take you to hospital on account of some blood down your legs…'

'Sounds about right.'

'You remember?'

'I was nine at the time.'

'What happened to you?'

'Why go to the river, is all that matters?'

'Please, Luke, don't blame the matron.'

'On the contrary I need to speak to her right now.'

*

When Luke arrived in Severnside House Gwendolen stood as stiff as a sentry at the big glass doors of the dayroom. She stared at something in the extensive gardens beyond.

He paused before going any further. Didn't want to startle her.

'How is she?'

Matron referred to the watch pinned to her blue uniform.

'So far it's been two hours.'

'Has she explained why she went to the water, at all?'

'Not exactly.'

'Who's that with her, with the pink hair?'

'That's her best friend. That's Barbara Jennings.'

It was not until Luke crossed the room that he heard what they were saying.

'Seriously, Gwendolen, no one expects you to remember anything on account of your Alzheimer's.'

'But Barbara, he's in the river.'

'Shut up, you fool. Do you want to damn us all? Don't let them put words into your mouth.'

'How can I?'

'You forget.'

'Forget what exactly?' said Luke.

Barbara turned her head sharply and paled. She thrust her chin at him. Stiffened her shoulders. Glared. Her eyes were venomous between their rapid blinks, her teeth were clenched behind her bright red and partly open lips. Next moment she took a long, loud breath through her nose to vent her outrage.

A **NO TO NUCLEAR** badge was pinned to her collar.

'Reverend Lyons, I literally can't imagine why you are here?'

'Excuse me?'

'Thanks to you there seems to be some confusion over poor Gwendolen's home. By that, I mean Chapel Cottage.'

'That's none of your business.'

'Oh, but it is. Gwendolen and I are like sisters. We grew up together. We went to the same school. How can you sell something that is not yours to sell? And you seemed so nice when you moved into our parish in the spring! We all had such high hopes of you. Such fiery sermons!'

'So, can you please tell me what's going on here?'

Barbara kept hold of Gwendolen's waist. She pulled her close until they were joined at the hip.

'We all know who our real friends are round here, reverend.'

'Yeah, I see that.'

'I'm really disappointed in you. I thought you'd come home to do us some good.'

'I thought that, too. Now please leave us alone.'

Barbara blushed and withdrew her arm from Gwendolen's waist. Then she looked round for her coat.

'You won't get away with this, reverend. Who gave you the right to make trouble in Berkeley? I mean, should you even be here? I remember you as an angelic child. Your grandmother did such a good job raising you, given that your own parents were in prison. Then, when you turned ten you became a monster. Why is that, by the way?'

'I really don't have time for this.'

'By twelve you were drinking alcohol and taking drugs. Your behaviour became violent and unpredictable. Suddenly you wouldn't talk to any adult. In short, you made Gwendolen's life a complete misery from then on.'

'That's why you reported me to the police so often, is it?'

'Fat lot of good it did you! Next thing I heard you were in some teenage gang in London where you'd decided to take after your father. Gwendolen loved you, Luke, but you threw it all back in her face. And here you are again,

275

trying to ruin her life by selling her home behind her back. You should be ashamed of yourself.'

'You leaving now, or what?'

Barbara gave Gwendolen one last hug.

'Don't listen to him, my dear. Just because he's wearing a clerical collar doesn't mean he isn't the same old Luke underneath. He's not to be trusted, but he's powerless to do anything without your say-so.'

Luke handed Barbara her walking stick.

'What's the delay?'

Barbara held up her head. Limped off.

She paused at the dayroom's door to wave her stick in the air.

'Don't let anyone make a big, unnecessary splash, Gwendolen, don't let them stir up old times.'

She emphasised each syllable in a way that bordered on menace.

Gwendolen did not respond, but appeared to lose track of what was happening. The urgent, panicky desire to keep vigil at the glass doors took precedence.

Luke took her by the arm to break the silence.

'Gran? You seem restless and worried. Is this really about Chapel Cottage or something else?'

'Don't leave me. Don't go back to the river.'

'Stay calm.'

'I said don't go back. You don't belong in such cold, dark water.'

'Who doesn't?'

'I've told you a thousand times, she can't have you. *You're mine.*'

Luke had to listen hard to decipher all she said.

'Who are you talking to, gran? Who can you see in the glass? Is it Sean?'

'Do you honestly think I'll let you get away with this? Impossible. You've done a very bad thing. Right? *Right.* And me? What about my feelings, have you thought of that?'

Fearing that she might yet try to break the sliding doors with the palms of both hands, he did his best to draw her safely away.

'Come and sit down, gran. Please. In your chair.'

Gwendolen's cheeks paled and her face crumpled. Her lips trembled. Her voice broke as high as a child's with indignation.

'Think you can do better than me, do you? Listen to me, you bastard, that London bitch will get what's coming to her. Whatever it takes, Sean Lyons. Fuck her brat, too. Frankly, I don't care. Ironic, huh? Fact is, you want to use our son's stolen treasure to fund your new life with *her*. Do you? I can't even bring myself to speak her name. Just because she has rich friends you think she's better than me? You think you can waltz back into our lives after twenty-one years just because you went to see Rex in prison *behind my back*? Your own son might forgive your absence but I don't. So what, if he has given you the key to a few stolen antiques! Doesn't mean you have the right to use it to buy my silence. You touch one ruby or snuffbox from that hoard and, so help me God, I'll tell the world. What does that silly brass key of yours open, anyway? Pandora's box? I thought so.'

The dark and stormy memory was able to replay itself in her head, because to her, at that minute, he was the illusive likeness of her absent husband.

'You don't want to believe everything you see. Trust me, gran. It's the effect of all the pills you're taking. Sit down. Let us pray together.'

'Don't you realise what I've suffered? I thought you were dead. How can you do this to me? And all for her? Now you tell me she has a daughter called Sara. *Your* daughter. How do you think that makes *me* feel? Have you ever cared about *me*, at all? You married *me*, for Christ's sake. And all the time you were married to her. Does she even know about me? About Rex? About Luke and Ellie? You say now that you want to keep in touch for the sake of the grandchildren, but really you want to take baby Luke away from me, don't you? You've agreed this with Rex, you say? But you're 'dead', remember. You're a ghost in this world now. You really think you can do better than me when it comes to raising your newly born grandson? That so? But what about me, what about my love for my grandchild? For you? I've grieved for you thinking you died a hero.'

'Please, Gwendolen, come and sit down. You're upsetting other people. That old gentleman over there is positively shaking. I'm afraid he might have a fit or something.'

'Get your filthy hands off me.'

'Stay calm. It's all a mistake.'

'Damn you, Sean Lyons.'

She struck him in the face with her fist and screamed. The blow left him

277

dazed, not because it stunned him – at her age she was not so strong – but because of its vehemence and anger.

'Reverend Lyons!' The voice sounded right behind him. 'Whatever are you doing?'

'Forgive me, I was just trying to…'

The brisk, no-nonsense matron elbowed him aside in order to sit Gwendolen down with much gentle shushing and stroking.

'Please leave immediately, reverend. This is the second time that you've upset everyone in Severnside House and I won't have it.'

'But no one has exactly told me what happened this morning. How is it my grandmother came to be wandering alone by the river? How many more times is this going to happen?'

'She climbed out of a window.'

'Why?'

Matron rearranged two pens in her breast pocket.

'We're still investigating, reverend, I can assure you. It's a lapse on our part for which I can only apologise, but one of our residents suffered a heart attack in the night. As you can imagine all staff were mightily distracted.'

'My grandmother could be dead because of you.'

'Not because of me, reverend, but because of her fits of dementia.'

'Is there a difference?'

'Listen to me, Reverend Lyons, it is pointless asking Gwendolen where she was a few hours ago. She doesn't remember. Her short-term memory is virtually non-existent. Instead she relives events in great detail from years ago.'

'You mean she talks utter nonsense?'

'Whatever she recalls almost certainty did happen.'

'Does that go for conversations, too?'

'Absolutely.'

'Then why did she just try to claw my eyes out?'

'Imagine how you would feel, reverend, if you were condemned to relive some traumatic event over and over. Wouldn't you feel powerless and therefore frustrated? Wouldn't you do the same if you could see no other way to escape? Wouldn't you be that extreme?'

278

The questions so caught him unawares that he felt the sudden need to redirect the conversation.

'Or her disease has removed some inhibitions? What we are seeing is the real Gwendolen that, until now, she has kept a secret?'

'It's possible.'

'That's cruel.'

'You speak as if it's a burden reverend, but for her, right now, it's who she is.'

*

There was something compelling about his grandmother's one-track mind, about the pain she was reliving, thought Luke as he walked back to Sasha in his Land Rover. The more he heard, the more like the truth it sounded. She had become more coherent, not less?

'Good grief, Sash, is it any wonder that gran was so angry? In 1981 she came face to face with Sean again after twenty-one years' absence. He really did rise from the dead, but for how long? *He vanished again.*'

With that, he took out his phone to tell Ellie, then changed his mind.

The person blinded by loyalty or emotion too soon forgot what it was that they had to do next in this world of evil.

He couldn't afford to be one of those people.

He had to stick to his plan.

Chapter 49

That afternoon the stormy weather returned in earnest. Heavy rain lashed the vicarage's loose sash windows while trees creaked and groaned throughout the garden. The wind sounded like surf in the gutters and downpipes to the point where the whole of Hill House was in danger of sliding downhill, feared Luke.

He jumped up and went to the window. There could be no doubt about it, the river was rising.

Like a silver thread in the otherwise black landscape, the black water lit up each time there came a fresh flash of lightning.

It was that time of year when many eels chose to leave the Severn Sea – they crawled considerable distances to live on land whenever and wherever the soil was moist enough. They could slither from salt to fresh water along muddy ditches even though they were fish, not serpents.

Already he could sense ten million wriggling creatures sliding and gliding uphill to where he was standing within the walls of his sanctuary. They were, he fancied, ready to drag him back to their den deep underwater.

He suddenly slammed shut the shutters not just against the storm but on himself. It was as if the creaturely river, sensing its hold on him to be almost complete, had begun to work the greatest of its siren wiles. Would have him imagine the unimaginable.

Next minute his phone rang.

'Hi. It's me, Ellie. You seen the news?'

'What news?'

'Remember that severed foot that Eva Greene told you about?'

'I remember.'

'Well, the police just stopped by my farm. They're checking anyone who might be related to missing people. Get this: they say that the steel-capped boot might even belong to our grandfather Sean Lyons. They literally hope to be able to identify the remains.'

'But is that even remotely possible? The boot must have been in the water for ages.'

'Its mixture of steel and leather has mummified a toe, apparently. Forensics have found a greyish, fatty substance that is generated by dead bodies subjected to moisture. They're calling it adipocere. They want my DNA to run some comparisons. Get this, too. They'll be investigating whether his death was an accident or not.'

Luke leaned into his phone.

'What are the chances?'

'It's daft, really. Everyone knows that Sean died trying to rescue drowning sailors when the railway bridge collapsed in 1960.'

'May I speak freely?'

'Gladly.'

'All this might come as a bit of a surprise.'

'All this what?'

'I went to see Gwendolen in Severnside House. I know you warned me against it, but the sight of Sean's pocket watch on my waistcoat triggered something in her. I didn't take much notice before, but now I'm sure.'

'In what way?'

'Fact is, she already knew about its existence.'

'Don't kid yourself. Grandma would have told me.'

'Ian Grey paid her a visit, I reckon. He must have gone out of his way to tell her that he found her husband's watch in full working condition by the river. *In 1981*. She may not be the only one he told.'

'But Ian didn't want the watch for himself and now he's left town. So what's going on?'

'Since 1981 he has been waiting for the right moment for the truth to resurface.'

'Why not give it to Gwendolen years ago?'

'Perhaps he tried?'

'Don't be silly.'

'Seriously, is she to be trusted?'

'Now you're the one being silly.'

'Open your eyes, Ellie. In 1981 Sean visited his son in prison. Rex told him where to find the stolen antiques. But Sean came back to Berkeley to trade the treasure in exchange for his baby grandson. Only Gwendolen refused. So did he simply take the loot and vanish? What does someone do with £80 million anyway? Do you even spend it without attracting attention? Or did someone stop him? Did she? That would mean the treasure is still close by, *as Gwendolen knows full well?*'

Ellie fell silent for a moment.

He could hear her trying to work out the significance of what he was implying.

'You don't want to say that, Luke. Believe me. That's a wicked idea.'

'Is it? Is it, really?'

*

Luke walked all that evening along country lanes in the vicinity of the vicarage, unable to rest.

There came into his heart the desire to redress a great wrong.

The vindictive feeling grew and grew. For years had not God been trying to show him the way? Show him how to follow some secret current. Dive deeper, like a submarine?

Now he must change tack, not by any deviation of any compass, but according to some more moral purpose. He must plot a TRUE course through the darkest water.

Sasha's eyes shone with incredulity. Suddenly the uncanny stillness in the paths and lanes began to shiver and shake. Clouds of uneasy rooks and crows flew up from the fields. She was on guard immediately, Luke noticed, as she halted to sniff and listen.

Very soon the object of her alarm presented itself only half a field away. Someone was riding flat out along a bridle path past Appleridge Farm; they were racing towards Whitcliff Deer Park even as the sun slipped low below the horizon.

Rider and mount crossed a gap in the hedge. With all four feet briefly off the ground, the gleaming black thoroughbred leapt a ditch. Thundering hooves sent clods of mud flying.

'Stay, Sash. Stay.'

Flaming red hair streamed from the rider's hatless head.

She leaned low on the horse's neck as she made it gallop faster and faster with the urgent rhythm of her heels.

Luke heard how hard the gelding snorted as it outran the dying sun's all-devouring light – it was carrying Sabrina as quickly as possible back to Berkeley Castle.

Her two black Elkhounds seemed to float behind her, each one a silent shadow as they bounded along.

Soon, from beyond the deer park, troubled hounds uttered baleful howls. They grew doubly restless in their castle kennels.

Sabrina didn't fully realise it yet but she was to be his ticket of leave from this living hell.

Chapter 50

The further Luke steeled himself to advance along the tidal inlet, the more reason he had to feel his heart might burst. A loud drumbeat beat in his head. Feet were heavier than lead. Hands turned cold and clammy.

He had to remind himself to breathe when he saw Berkeley Pill's steep banks and oxbow bends turn pink in the sun's delicate afterglow.

He was following the tributary that medieval boats once sailed from the river to the castle with their cargoes of cloth and wine.

Sasha ran ahead of him, sniffing the grass. The days when she would have disturbed a mink or two were long gone, but he could remember the excitement of seeing hounds hunt them down in the 1980s.

Suddenly he halted. Having snaked for nearly one third of a mile along the Pill, they were at the formidable dam that now blocked the inlet.

His ears could already detect the roar of water as the fast flowing tributary poured through the regulating weir.

Thus the freshwater stream could flow into the salty Severn but high tides were blocked by the one-way valve which prevented flooding.

Beyond that, the Little Avon River joined the Pill at Floodgates Farm, not twenty minutes' walk further on.

'Not far now, Sash.'

As a boy of no more than seven or eight, he had first come here to fish for eels, trout, roach and chub. Gudgeon and flounder, too. He had fond memories of this watery byway when the world was a settled, peaceful place and Friesians grazed happily in the neighbouring fields. He could still smell the sweet scent of hay in summer or the strong taint of silage fed to dairy cows in winter while the twin edifices of Berkeley Power Station and Berkeley Castle stood guard over the land all around. Then one day he met

Slim Jim.

Luke took another deep breath and his knees almost gave way when, with his next step, he set eyes on the object of his dread.

They were at the old wooden boathouse almost too soon. Before the dam was built, Sean Lyons had used the tide to sail right up to the shed like those Tudor boats of old. After the dam's erection and the tides were tamed this far inland, the shack was abandoned and forgotten.

'Anyone there?' cried Luke.

He forced open a wooden door on rusty hinges. He struck a match and ignited the cobwebby wick of an old oil lamp. Its yellow flame soon revealed a few tools gathering dust on a nearby bench.

One of them was a large wooden mallet.

It was in this shed that Slim Jim had shown him how to bait traps, some of which still lay about on the floor. It had been his job to put earthworms through the door in the roof of converted lobster pots. That way the eels were lured into a tapering funnel of wire netting that led them into the cage. It took about eight hours to make one trap but cost next-to-nothing if made from stolen osiers. In addition, Slim Jim had known how to braid his own nets. Had been very keen to pass his knowledge on. Here was one of the spears that they had used to go hunting eels in shallow water, Luke discovered and weighed it in his hand. It was Slim Jim who'd taught him how to spot a fish as it lay half buried in mud and silt.

Thanks to him he knew how to look for the gleam of sun on fin or tail.

He relived the thrill of doing something bold and heroic as he sat for a moment on a pile of boxes. It was in these crates that the eels had been kept alive for up to two weeks in order to rid them of their muddy flavour and to clear their guts of any food. At the time he had greatly appreciated Slim Jim's interest, patience, apparent respect and attention to detail.

He pulled his grandfather's pocket watch from his waistcoat and opened its gold cover. Checked its Roman numerals. Eight o'clock.

It was time.

*

The first thing Luke did was to pick up the mallet.

If it was one thing that Slim Jim had instilled into him, it was that to spring a trap you had to be patient.

The longer he sat in the darkness, the greater the variety of odours: pungent, disgusting, peculiar.

Next minute there came the sound of voices.

Steadily, undoubtedly, Luke made out the rhythmic footfall of someone approaching the boathouse along the riverbank.

Each heavy step resonated inside his skull as if those same smells that he was inhaling – mud, brine, eel – conjured up some hideous revenant.

Through the boathouse's walls and its covering of ivy came a few intelligible words.

'You see anyone yet?'

'Not at all.'

'You with me, or what?'

'Suppose it's a trap, Slim?'

'He wouldn't dare. We have the boy.'

'Are you okay with this?'

'Listen to me, Mel, if you want to get rich, which I do, frankly, then you'll catch up.'

'It's all right for you, you don't have to keep hold of him. He's like a blinking eel.'

'This is the place, all right.'

'Got any ideas?'

'Take the boy inside.'

'What if Luke won't do us a deal?'

'I've told you a hundred times, he will.'

'I'm just not sure there's any way we can trust him.'

'Just do as I say, will you.'

Next moment the door burst open into the shed.

With the clatter came a cry. Mel followed. He flashed his torch at all sorts of discarded fish traps from kypes to putchers in a hurry.

'All clear, Slim.'

Luke's hand rose high. It fouled a few cobwebs in the eaves. Crashed down on the silhouette in the doorway.

The mallet's heavy wooden block met human skull with a resounding crack.

Mel groaned as much from shock as pain. He sank down. His wire spectacles went flying. His long camel coat became entangled with the live boxes; the glass bauble in his ear was shorn from his earlobe with the same blow.

'What the hell?' cried Slim Jim. 'Mel, you stupid fucker. Get up! Can't you look where you're going?'

Mel's torch hit the ground and lit a crimson bubble that ballooned from his skull. He wasn't dead, but he wouldn't wake up too soon.

'What the f...?' Slim Jim rushed to take hold of a shocked Randal as he retreated to the door. 'Who's there? Show yourself right now!'

Luke went to land him one in the eye, but his aim was off in the confined space of the cluttered doorway. Slim Jim ducked. The mallet bounced off the end of a putcher and buried itself in its tangle of split willow staves. Suddenly he reeled beneath successive hard blows to nose and chin. Slim was whipping him with something hard and metallic. It had to be a gun. He crashed backwards. Seized hold of some fish traps to stop his fall.

That light from Mel's spinning torch on the floor lit the pallid, terrified face of Randal; caused his blond hair to light up with a strange frizzy halo. He was still in his school jacket. His almond eyes, wild and strong, revealed in them a terror too great for a young boy to comprehend. Lips went to scream. Voice froze. It could have been himself, thought Luke, twenty-five years ago.

'Run Randal! Run!'

Slim levelled his pistol at the door.

'You aren't going anywhere, lad.'

No sooner had he spoken than Sasha leapt at Slim's arm. She sank her teeth into his wrist and bit hard. He let out a scream but her jaws locked on. Twice he fired as they both spun round but she was above the gun, not below. She might only have come up to his knee in height but she had sufficient weight – scissored her bite to the bone. This was the person who had kicked her into Gloucester Docks to drown. She hadn't forgotten.

Deafened by shots Luke saw his chance.

'Quick, Randal. With me. Now!'

Placing himself before the distracted Jim, he seized the boy by the arm.

Bundled him bodily through the hut's open doorway.

'Run Randal! Run for your life. Follow the stream to Floodgates Farm. Tell your mother. Raise the alarm.'

Randal stood there too confused, shocked and cold to respond. Then, blinking tears, he began to mumble. Suddenly Sasha appeared beside him.

This time Luke issued commands more calmly.

'Go Sash. Quick. Take Randal home.'

Randal saw his chance.

'Aren't you coming?'

'I've some business here that I must see to first.'

With that, he barged back into the hut to come face to face with the barrel of a gun.

'Fuck you,' said Slim Jim, blood dripping from his torn wrist. He'd delayed to bind his wound with his silk, polka-dotted scarf but it had yet to work very well. 'You have the boy. Now where's the gold?'

Chapter 51

If only food didn't look so damned pretty, thought Jorge, on his way out of the Co-op in Berkeley. All those lovely pale green Aeros, yellow Flakes and purple Twirls triggered something in his brain that he could not resist.

Every time he took a fresh bite he felt a small burst of pleasure as his neurotransmitters went wild. He should have put all the chocolate back on the shelf, but he didn't.

If people wanted him to stop gambling with his health they should wrap things in plainer packaging.

That's not say that he favoured anyone trying to be overprotective or unduly interfering with his personal choices. Being large was his prerogative, despite all the overworked devils stoking his dopamine. Who had the right to sneer at him, anyway? They would be telling him next that he couldn't add white wine and cream to his Bolognese sauce and cook it in the oven.

Perhaps it was a jealousy thing.

Such dire thoughts raged as he drove along with much forceful declutching of the camper van's troublesome gearbox. Sasha blinked at him while sitting on his Inspector's cap. He knew that look. She'd have him exist on pasta, vegetables and olives every day while she gorged on tinned beef.

The quayside road soon became a mixture of warehouses and cranes. Sharpness New Dock had opened its gates to allow the blue and white cargo ship Sormovskiy to sail into port. He parked the camper van and overtook the Russian vessel on foot. He and Luke had once watched ships like this ferry minerals, cement and fertilizer along the River Severn. He felt the same excitement now, as if by shutting his eyes for a moment he could relive their greatest dreams.

All the old warehouses had been rebuilt since his last visit here decades ago. Railway lines rusted but there were ambitious plans for smart dockside houses next to refurbished marinas, apparently.

Next minute he felt Rex Lyons's Bible fill his pocket and hurried.

*

He left the lock at Sharpness Old Dock and found himself on the raised towpath that divided river from canal where it continued north to Gloucester. He was staring at the vast expanse of glittering estuary over which trains had once steamed through the sky on twenty-one iron spans, high up above The Ridge Sand.

He had never seen the bridge with his own eyes, but he felt its presence now. He was following the gentle curve of the seawall.

Soon there rose up before him a peculiar, round stone tower. It looked like a watchtower or remnant of an ancient castle but he knew better. Years ago the railway line had pivoted on top of this freestanding structure where its last, twenty-second span had spanned the canal. It had revolved to allow tall ships to pass by safely on the waterway below.

Over there, he observed, stood the stone abutment to which the swing bridge had once joined, now almost lost in encroaching trees on the canal's landward side. It was as if his eye, on seeing the sudden plunge into the water, was ready to imagine back into existence the crossing's missing pieces.

'Here, Sasha. This has to be the right place.'

But Sasha was distracted by the smell of bacon that drifted from a nearby narrowboat. She didn't like being led on a wild goose chase?

The vista changed suddenly as dark cloud crossed the sun and sent a chill through his veins. Something struck him hard in his heart like a splinter of ice. The dazzle of the river died. He stood motionless for a moment with eyes half-closed and his ears attuned to the music of the darkening currents.

Some sweet voice appealed to him from – where?

He turned his head to study the waves. Saw a woman surface on the water. Like some great sailing ship's figurehead, she floated his way; her red hair streamed behind her in the wind even as she called his name:

'Jorge… Jorge… Jorge.'

Her smile looked cold, but still she managed to appeal directly to something akin to his soul. Her soaked white robes bedecked with jewels were worthy of some queen who lived in a palace underwater. Her glowing, yellow lamp glittered at the end of her outstretched arm.

Her offer, as ever, was to guide him deep beneath the waves.

He pinched himself and the chill in his bones alerted him to his fearful fancy.

Next moment the sun re-emerged and the figure sank back below the water.

Mellifluous words repeated faintly, even as the seamaid's music called very distantly:

'Join me Jorge… at the bottom of the river.'

The Bible weighed heavily in his hand, but it was his Ordnance Survey map to which he referred again most closely. He took a step forward and traced exactly where the bridge had crashed into the river.

The power of its alluring spell centred on the surviving round, stone pier at grid number SO 678 034.

'Come Sasha, let's go home and say a prayer for Reverend Luke Lyons. There's nothing here for the likes of you and me. We shouldn't even have tried whereas *I fear he did.*'

There resounded in his head again the sweet siren words from Rex Lyons's Bible:

The ridge sand

She will give you the treasures of darkness

at the bridge

*

Back home in the Vicarage, Jorge studied again one of the strange pictures painted in prison by Frank Cordell.

Had he shown them to Luke?

Almost certainly he did.

It was the crude depiction of a sailing ship adrift on a tempestuous ocean which was seemingly about to be dragged down into the depths by a huge sea-serpent. Her reefs were rolled on ragged sails, her heavy guns long cast overboard, but in one last-ditch attempt to save the vessel the mizzen-mast was being hewn away.

Jorge could almost hear the clash of creaking blocks and straining rigging as, from the canting deck, came the screams of men.

Their fate hung in the balance, should their next decision prove to be the right or wrong one. The crew clung for their lives to the rigging as the enormous silver and scaly sea creature wrapped its tail tighter and tighter around their vessel. From its head streamed long red hair.

While some truths lay in the eye of the beholder, absolute truth belonged to God alone?

What if that giant creature was not about to wreck but to rescue them?

His official task, he reminded himself, was to decide if Luke had done a good or evil thing, but it could never be sufficient to conclude of someone that they were either virtuous *or* villainous. He should never be too quick to be excessively judgemental. On the face of it his lost friend had abandoned his coat and hat and walked into the river.

What, though, if Luke had been trying not to kill but to save himself?

Chapter 52

'For God's sake, Jim, put the gun down.'

Luke felt his stomach turn.

He was inside the boathouse.

A deafening roar filled his ears. Eyes swam. Lungs failed to breathe.

Such painful cramps in his belly were not caused by impending danger so much as by an ill-judged confidence in his own strength which was about to fail him? Surely, being so much younger than this veteran, he should not feel in any way physically inferior now?

Slim bit the end off a large, straight-sided coronel cigar and spat it at his feet with cocky insouciance. Then he took a lighter from his shiny blue suit. All the while, with his other hand, he kept his grip on his revolver. His black fedora hid his disagreeably shrunken and anaemic-looking features half from view. When his pallid face resurfaced it was all smiles. With the casualness came a cloying sentimentality. He could not believe that his little boy did not want to exchange fond memories?

'You don't – what – trust me now?'

'You should go to A&E before you bleed out.'

'Not until I have the treasure.'

'That treasure, as you call it, is someone else's property.'

'What's the matter, Luke? You not comfortable with stolen goods?'

'No I'm not.'

'But your mother and father did the stealing.'

'Then it's up to me to put things right.'

'Problem is you're not a cop.'

'I have right on my side.'

'That clerical collar of yours means nothing to me.'

The sight of the modified 4mm gun kept Luke focused. It was not the more usual 9mm weapon that he had once used in London. Designed to fire percussion caps, it was what he termed a garden gun. Small but lethal. At close range.

'You forget one thing, Jim. I'm not my parents.'

'Don't tell me you really don't have anything to give me, or else.'

'Or else, what?'

'I'll have to deal with you the same way I dealt with Ian Grey. He thought he could dig up our treasure, too.'

'You killed Ian?'

'We caught him with a spade on the riverbank by the tin tabernacle. He was digging holes…'

'Yeah, but not for gold.'

'Don't kid yourself, Luke.'

'He was digging for bones, for Christ's sake, as was I, on account of something Mary Brenner told him…'

'They're all in it together, damn them.'

'Who are?'

'Gwendolen Lyons, Barbara Jennings, Mary Brenner…'

'Is that what he told you?'

'The point is, Luke, I don't care what Ian Grey was doing. He's dead now.'

'Somehow I believe you.'

'We could have settled this down the pub. Why don't we, by the way?'

'Shut up and put the revolver down.'

'Relax, Luke, that treasure was never yours to have.'

'The treasure is not why I'm here.'

'No? But you've got to admit it's kind of compelling.'

'Greed is your answer to everything. Is it?'

Slim Jim looked hurt. Hard green eyes appeared to soften for a moment as he sucked on his cigar until it glowed. Then he opened his mouth. Let drift a cloud of blue smoke. Eased his very real discomfort.

'You asking me? Sounds like you're the one who won't share, Captain. Me, I'm prepared to cut you in, in return for your silence.'

'My silence?'

'About me and you.'

'Don't you realise that I've kept silent all my life? It's my silence that has allowed you to go on doing whatever you like, to God knows whom, all these years.'

'Hey, Luke, guess what, you're right but that's not what you should be saying, you shouldn't be acting up so.'

Luke felt something stick in his craw.

'How should I be acting?'

'Like a man.'

'I don't feel like a man.'

'Honestly, Luke, I don't know what to make of you.'

'You think you can dismiss what you did to me and then at the flick of a switch it will all go away?'

'Stubborn.'

'The fact is, not a day goes by when I don't relive you raping me in this very boatshed. It didn't just happen twenty-six years ago, it's today. It never stops. I'm the boy who can't grow up. Can't kiss my own sister without feeling disgusted at myself. Can't bear to see perfect strangers hold hands. It terrifies me to watch a father take his son in his arms, give him a caress on the forehead. All my good feelings are buried in this sordid little shed that reeks of elvers. Their fishy smell is your smell – on my face, down my legs and in my hair. 'Pretty glass eel' you used to call me when you stripped me naked on that filthy mattress. Fact is, I might as well have been made of glass since you smashed me to pieces, *inside*. How many of us have there been?'

The smile faded from Slim's lips. Suddenly his eyes were narrower, meaner.

'Don't tell me you lured me here just to talk about old times?'

'Talk might not be the right word.'

'My poor sweet boy.'

'Stop calling me that. I'm not yours. Never was.'

Slim had lost none of his swagger. Nevertheless, wisps of greasy grey hair stuck to his face where he sweated profusely.

'You'll be saying next that you're a survivor as if I never gave you what you really wanted.'

'How dare you! I had respect for you, nothing else. That's why I couldn't understand why you did what you did to me.'

'What's not to like, Luke?'

'I've had to live in the shadows all my life because of you.'

'You finished with this bullshit or what?'

'You threatened me, Slim. You said I'd go to hell if I told anyone. You said that I would be removed from my grandmother's care if I so much as breathed one word about you. You knew I'd as good as lost my father to prison, knew that my criminal mother had disowned me at birth. You were like a new parent to me. I trusted you. When Rex was murdered you pretended to console me. I was barely ten years old, for Christ's sake.'

Slim took a step forwards. The gun in his hand seemed to weigh more heavily. Next moment there was an abrupt bang on the wooden floor. They were both equally startled. Mel McAtree's loose glass bauble earring had just popped. Under his foot. He sighed and ground into dust with his toe what remained.

'You and I had good times together, Luke. I have fond memories of us fishing on the Severn. We had something truly special. Damn it, I loved you.'

'My grandfather taught you all about the river when you were a child. And you were best mates with my mother and father. Hell, Slim, you were as good as family. You even took me mink hunting.'

'Did I not say I did my best to make you happy?'

'No, you abused me for nearly two years. It didn't stop until you went back to prison.'

'So? It's all a very long time ago.'

'That time my grandmother took me to hospital in Berkeley I lied and said that I had crashed my bike. Split my anus. How could you be so kind to me and then do what you did? Right from the start, you deliberately wormed your way into my head with your false kindness. I had absolutely no idea of what you were going to do to me. You baited your trap for me with the same care and patience that you did with the eels. Lured me in until there was no way back.'

Slim waved his gun ominously. The light from the fallen torch on the ground illuminated the splashes of blood that dripped from his wrist. His eyes grew restless. Betrayed something less bold than mere bravado. It was agony.

'Hey, Luke, time's up. Take me to the loot right now.'

He did not move a muscle.

'I realise that as a child I could never hope to understand what you did to me, but I understand now. It doesn't take away the terror. I still feel my head beating through my skull. I still feel every joint tear in my body with you inside me. Still hear the dark water lap beneath the boathouse as you rocked me on the sagging floorboards. Thanks to you I turned to crime, too. I lashed out at the world that left me to drown in sorrow. Mostly I did it to hurt myself because that's what I thought I deserved most.'

'Enough, reverend! You're a man of God now. You said it yourself.'

Luke barely flinched. He had thought that he would die at the hands of this man once already, long ago. He wouldn't let him scare him now, even if it did mean paying the ultimate price. In a flash he seized one of the fishing spears from the bench beside him. Slashed it like a blade...

Slim spat out his cigar as his cheek peeled apart like an orange.

...struck again.

Unbalanced him with a snarl of outrage – half avenging angel and half screaming jinn – a surprising, Godless, unholy creature, the image of a devil.

Slim dropped his revolver to clutch his larynx. Already he was beginning to gargle blood as he fought to breathe.

'Don't worry, Slim. If I'd wanted to kill you I would have brought my gun.'

Slim half stepped, half fell backwards through the boathouse doorway. He looked to be in a panic. Made it no further than the side of the hut. There his lips issued frantic whispers in his otherwise horrified calm.

'You don't... want to do this, Luke. Trust me. It's a bad idea.'

'What does it feel like to be so helpless? Where's all that power now? Did you really think you could terrify my sister and her son and get away with it? I don't think so.'

'For Christ's sake, Luke, have you gone mad?'

'They say that chemical castration is good for predators like you. Nothing like the real thing, I say. What was it you told me to look out for whenever we went fishing? Look in the mud for the glint of sun on fin or tail.'

With that, he drove home his spear. Stabbed with all the pinpoint accuracy with which his victim had once taught him to pierce live eels.

Chapter 53

The knocking grew louder and louder.

'All right! What's the hurry? I'm coming.'

Jorge threw open the vicarage's door and Barbara Jennings stared into his face with such fixed intention that it positively alarmed him. He had long since failed to make up his mind whether or not to distrust or admire this pink-haired old lady who lived so untidily in Angel Cottage, but who always dressed so correctly.

'Ms Jennings? What's wrong?'

Clearly the climb from the village had greatly fatigued her.

She fussed with scarf, handbag and little black gloves. She always had the air of someone who must run the show and make all the arrangements, yet today she looked grey in the face and had smeared her lipstick. Her eyelids looked red and her cheeks tear-stained, her mouth shut tight, her posture tense like someone in pain as she leaned heavily on her walking stick.

'There's something you need to know, Inspector.'

'Please. Come in. I was just packing some of my things into my camper van. I'll be leaving Berkeley in the next few days to go back to Gloucester.'

'Your work here is done?'

'Alas, I won't get to the bottom of it all but I'm confident that I will be able to write my report on Reverend Luke's state of mind when he vanished. I think I can do it to the Church's satisfaction.'

'Consider this then a timely visit.'

'Is it?'

'Please, Inspector, do please keep that dog of yours at a distance. I don't want hairs on my coat.'

Sasha eyed Barbara closely, snarled softly and with a grave and pronounced strut, walked back to her basket.

Jorge led his guest into Hill House's main reception room where he offered her a chair by its gilded fireplace.

More awkward adjustments of coat and skirt ensued, but mostly he was impressed by her quiet dignity.

It was less some stately elevation of manner than the desperate self-respect of a person who had exhausted all other options. She really hated having to come to see him like this.

He walked over to the drinks cabinet.

'Whisky?'

Barbara brightened considerably.

'If you please, Inspector.'

Jorge set their glasses on the table on which lay the very large jigsaw puzzle.

'You like puzzles, Ms Jennings?'

She shook her head somewhat abruptly.

'No, but I can see you do.'

'I don't know how many hours I've sat here piecing it all together. Reverend Luke Lyons left it behind for someone to finish. As it happens, that someone is me.'

'I recognise the scene, Inspector. That's the railway bridge that once crossed the River Severn at Sharpness.'

'So much blue sky and water can prove very tricky.'

'But only one piece remains.'

'That's true.'

'So why don't you finish it?' said Barbara and poked a slice of black and grey cardboard about with her pink fingernail. It featured a door.

He quickly stayed her hand.

'Here's the thing, I didn't even know that the tower had a door until I went there to see for myself.'

She pointed at the name: Sharpness Swing Bridge Cabin.

'How else do you think the signalman climbed up to work the controls, Inspector?'

'You can't see the entrance today. Not obviously.'

'That's because the tower was bricked up half a century ago after the bridge was removed. Inside it are stairs going nowhere.'

'Talk about hiding in plain sight!'

'Actually it's a sad and remarkable survivor.'

'Damn right.'

Barbara paused. Cleared her throat.

'Fact is, Inspector, it all begins and ends with that swing bridge.'

Jorge took a quick sip of whisky.

'I believe you. Now tell me why you're really here.'

'I'm here to carry out someone's last wish uttered on her deathbed.'

'Since when is that any of my business?'

It was Barbara's turn to sip some whisky.

'It's like this, Inspector. Gwendolen Lyons made me promise to tell you what really happened to her husband Sean in 1981.'

'How is that possible? She was too confused to remember anything properly. Her mental decline made her a very unreliable witness, I'm told.'

'This has nothing to do with Alzheimer's disease.'

Jorge's eyes came to rest on the seventeenth century gold face that adorned the overmantel above the room's fireplace. Suddenly he paid it very close attention.

'Yeah. Probably won't help now but it's my duty to listen, I suppose.'

Barbara drained her glass quickly.

'As everyone round here knows, Inspector, at about 10.30 on the 25th October 1960 the railway bridge over the River Severn was hit by two fuel tankers. I don't need to remind you that five good men died that night when Sean went missing. Soon afterwards his overturned boat was found in the mud upriver and everyone assumed that he had drowned trying to save the crew from their burning barges.'

'That much I've already put in my report.'

'You have? But how?'

'That really doesn't matter right now. Please continue.'

'Then know this, Inspector. In 1981 Mary Brenner and I walked into

301

Chapel Cottage to find Gwendolen talking to no other than Sean Lyons. He said he knew the location of their son's hoard of stolen antiques. That loot was – still is – worth millions. He showed us the key to its door in his pocket. With it he wanted to buy Gwendolen's silence about his bigamy, but most of all he wanted to take his grandson away with him. Well, Luke was not yet six months old and Gwendolen was in the process of adopting him because his parents would be in prison for the foreseeable future and could do nothing for him. But Sean's real wife came from a very good family. They thought Luke would fare better with them because Olivia knew all the 'right' people.'

'You walked in on Sean Lyons? How coincidental is that?'

'Once a month Gwendolen ran a reading club. The night that was our book night.'

'So what did you see, exactly?'

'Sean stood in the kitchen in his new steel-capped boots, leather coat and gloves. He boasted about how good a mother Olivia had been to their daughter Sara. But with Lady Sara Greene shot dead by Rex during the Severn Sea Gang's bungled burglary at her country house in Wiltshire, it seemed pretty obvious that they just wanted to fill a big hole in their lives. Or Sean felt genuine guilt and remorse for what his son had done to what was, in a very real sense, his own family? Perhaps he and Olivia wanted a brother for Sara's baby Eva who'd been born by Caesarean section in such traumatic circumstances.'

'Sounds logical.'

'But Gwendolen felt betrayed. Here was a man who had not only married her bigamously but who'd gone back to his war bride. She hadn't even realised that he and Olivia had had a child together, for Christ's sake. Sorry reverend – my language.'

'Fuck that, just tell me what happened next.'

Barbara sat up very straight. Wriggled her shoulders.

'Can I possibly have another whisky?'

'Honestly, I don't see why not. It belongs to Reverend Lyons.'

'The mention of a wartime baby with *that* woman was too much for Gwendolen, Inspector. She fell into a rage. She started calling Sean all sorts of terrible things. Told him that she regarded their marriage vows as still sacred, that digging up stolen treasure held no interest for her. She couldn't believe that someone she still loved had a whole other life to which she had been kept oblivious. The next minute they were fighting. I don't know who started it but that's when Sean lost his temper. They howled and tore at each other's faces. Banged and crashed all round the kitchen. Like wild animals.'

'You call the police, or what?'

'No, absolutely bloody not. No time. With a saucepan in his hand, Sean was beating Barbara about the head over and over again. She was down and dazed on the floor. Then he began to kick her as hard as he could in the ribs.'

'What did you do?'

'I yelled at him to stop, of course.'

'Good for you.'

'An argument lost on Sean. I tried to seize his arm but he was like a devil. He was calling Gwendolen every bad name under the sun, but most of all he was not going to let her ruin his future elsewhere, he said and threw me off. Told me to mind my own damned business. Didn't even notice Mary seize a knife from the kitchen drawer. I don't think she ever meant to do him serious harm, Inspector, she just wanted to stop him killing her best friend. The knife was very sharp and serrated. It cut through Sean's clothes in one blow. I doubt it would have killed him, though. Instead he turned enraged, tripped and fell against the kitchen sink. As he hit it hard he jammed the knife another inch into his heart and collapsed. We were all absolutely sure he was dead. At the time.'

'Pass me that bottle of whisky. I need another drink, too.'

That's when he noticed the face of the red-haired woman carved over the fireplace. She was grinning broadly.

*

Some time passed before either of them broke the silence, whereupon they both tried to speak at once.

'No, you first,' said Jorge. 'What did you do with Sean's body?'

Barbara took a deep breath.

'Mary wanted to call an ambulance, not to mention the police, but I wouldn't hear of it. I said: "That bastard has ruined enough lives already. He'll not put you in prison now." Mary simply burst into tears and Gwendolen and I had to make all the decisions.'

303

'Bold move.'

'In the end we decided to dig a shallow hole at low tide and drop the body into it in an old leather suitcase on the river's foreshore. After all, what did we have to lose? As far as everyone else was concerned Sean Lyons had already died twenty years ago when the bridge fell down. No one was looking for him anymore. As for Olivia, she'd more than likely assume that he had run off again with the money. He need not be found, not ever. Even the police had written him off.'

'So he died and you thought it was all over?'

Barbara swallowed hard and almost choked. To her sore eyes rose more tears.

'Except poor Mary began to convince herself that we had buried him alive. For years she had visions of him using that large brass key that he had shown us to dig his way out of his grave. Then, one day, Ian Grey told her about Sean's pocket watch that he had found on the riverbank at the time he went missing. It was the sort of thing the dead might come looking for, said Mary and convinced herself that Sean was back among us. In reality it must have fallen out of his coat when we bundled his body over the seawall. Mary and Ian were very close at the time. In the end she couldn't live with the secret. She as good as told him what she'd done, I think, because she was half out of her mind with guilt. I suppose you could call it post-traumatic stress. When Reverend Luke returned to Berkeley Ian decided to go digging for bones and I had to keep talking him out of it, but not before he scared us all rigid. That's when Sean's boot washed up. From that moment on Mary kept saying that the river was unhappy. We'd offended its spirit and it wanted justice. Said it wouldn't be content until it had taken us, too.'

'Which was all nonsense, of course.'

'Don't be so sure. Reverend Luke's disappearance sparked something. Even before then, two men came asking questions about Sean. They had an idea that he might have reburied the treasure somewhere. Then there was the sale of Chapel Cottage for the new nuclear power station. Would the bulldozers dig up Sean's last resting place when they built new flood defences? At last Mary did what she promised, she drowned herself at the place where we buried his body. More or less. I can't be sure. Since 1981 the river has seriously eroded that part of the bank which hampered Ian's searches as well. She couldn't accept that all he wanted to do was to get rid of the evidence to protect her most of all! In desperation he looked to Reverend Lyons as the only person he might trust because, as Sean's grandson, he had a shared interest in keeping the truth to himself.'

'Okay, I have more questions. Offending the river's goddess was *not* nonsense, you say?'

'Don't you see, Inspector, on the night Reverend Luke vanished Gwendolen heard the water call to her just like Mary. It wasn't the first time. She'd been called to the seawall before.'

'The real question is what did they say to each other?'

'He told her goodbye, Inspector. "You won't see me again," he said. "I'm leaving for good. I'm going on a very long journey." Of course, Gwendolen was confused.'

'Did she ask where to?'

'All he would tell her, Inspector, was that he was going to the end of the world where the eels go.'

'Are you sure? Are you quite certain that's what he said?'

'I swear.'

He liked to think that, no matter what, he could have been Luke's rock, thought Jorge, or his anchor. But he had to admit that he had no evidence that he could ever be anyone's saviour. Couldn't be that arrogant. Loyalty alone might not be that useful. It was on a rock that a ship might founder.

He reached for the whisky bottle to find it was empty.

Chapter 54

Luke sat on the seawall and watched the high tide flood the Severn. Slim Jim Jackson's convulsive gasps still rang in his ears. He felt neither mental distress nor physical exhaustion but only a strange euphoria at the sight of blood on his hands. It was as if he had just experienced a miracle.

That soon passed. Suddenly he could endure the wide empty horizon of sky and water, but not the emptiness in his heart.

How it had come to this, he did not rightly know. Yet some would say that there was not a single human being who could set themselves the simplest task, but that the eye of God or the Devil would bear upon it. There had always been, from the very beginning, a questionable side to the continued existence of Rex Lyons's so-called treasure, he thought. He was in great doubt about his father's secret. Had he not simply set out to prove the whole thing bogus both legendarily and factually to all his enemies – sad, defeated enemies, too apt to think that violence alone could buy them the thing they coveted most?

Clearly, in every sense, he had sat here crying for too long already. Deceptive was the shift in the river that drove its fickle currents.

He'd had his revenge but what now? His ears strained to hear past the water's moonlit, glassy surface when its siren call grew louder. He shivered inside his long black coat while in his boots his toes turned bitterly cold.

Berkeley Pill light beacons showed in line ahead bearing 187 degrees. They, too, would steer him into the river if they could?

He licked more blood off his lips as he failed to settle his stomach.

'I'll stay here a few minutes longer,' he told himself and flinched at the bitter taste on his tongue.

Because of surging water across mud and sandbanks he could not see how to navigate his way to the deepest channel; he worried that he would too soon become bogged down in swampy twists and turns. He was more apprehensive about choosing the best place to enter the water than his own apprehensiveness – he didn't deserve to drown too slowly.

Suddenly his phone rang with the call for which he'd been waiting.

'Luke? Thank God. It's me, Ellie. For Christ's sake, what's going on? Randal's come rushing home with Sasha. He says two men stopped him outside his school and told him they were friends of yours – that you were all going fishing.'

'Randal's unharmed? Thank God.'

'Jeremy and I have been worried sick. What do we tell the police?'

'Tell them there was trouble all right but it's all over now.'

'You okay? Randal says there was a fight.'

'Don't worry, I've taken care of it. No one will bother you or him ever again.'

'How can you be so sure?'

'Because without me no one can do a thing.'

'I'm really disappointed in you, Luke. You should never have got involved with any treasure.'

'No, obviously bloody not. No one should. It's a curse.'

'Are you quite sure you're not hurt?'

'Yeah, I think I am.'

'Admit it, these are the same men who attacked you in Gloucester Docks?'

'Damn right they are.'

'That's madness.'

'Hard to think they believed me when I said I'd give them the loot.'

'Where are they now?'

'Tell the police to check the hospitals.'

'What about you?'

'Forget about me. Hang on to Sasha.'

'She's run off somewhere.'

'I can't take her with me...'

'Listen here, Luke, you come home right now, do you hear me?'

'Home is where I'm going.'

'What do you mean?'

'You'll see.'

'Luke? You love me?'

'Always.'

He hung up. Then he lifted his eyes to the river and immediately the moonlight on the water seemed to dazzle. Knowing what he knew now, his mind was quick to discount the greatest doubt about what was out there, which was no mean feat in the current circumstances.

But he had grown up next to the estuary which made a big difference.

He chewed his lip. Unbuttoned his coat. In those tricks of the moon there was a suggestion of another living being close by? He had tried to deny everything else since finding God, but now the thing approaching him from downriver was all silvery back and scales.

His first thought was the bore.

It was too late for him to entertain any change of heart – the regret was too great; he was thoroughly disheartened.

Anyone else would have told him that, coming from the mouth of a determined suicide, any showing of the goddess Sabrina was always going to be the merest flight of fancy now. He couldn't be wrong, though, it was happening. Four seahorses were coming at him at full pelt. Their hooves rode the crest of the bore at a gallop with its surf. Each liquid rent in the quicksilver surface peeled back the inky depths beneath.

Others might state that no one would ever know for sure, that he was not a reliable witness. Naturally they were both right, but, as in some uncanny vision he did see loom before him a rider in a watery chariot of some kind.

To step upon its platform at last would be to embark on his final journey to the oblivion he now craved?

The red-haired charioteer turned and spoke, yet her lips hardly moved as her voice boomed in his ears. He noted then the appealing correlation between her commanding words and heartless smile as her sweet gaze bore down so hard upon him. He no more knew why she rendered him so spellbound than why he had so little willpower to resist. But he saw clearly that with all the mysteries of the ocean in her silvery sea-green eyes, there glinted something wonderfully tempting. With such cruel attitude, but with such beauty, she had come to offer him the world.

'Come, Luke, join me in the water. Come ride with me to my palace beneath the waves.'

Luke hastily divested himself of his coat.

Right now, the wide, extensive riverscape offered a fine, striking prospect as its water goddess held out her hand, dripping in jewels. He had none of the luxury of a wetsuit or drysuit. No latex seals at his neck, wrist and feet sealed the water from his cold body, only a little white clerical collar on his shiny black shirt. He listened eagerly while the golden hubs that lubricated the chariot's spinning wheels trod water as their charioteer tightened her grip upon the horses' reins. This reckless surfer was either witch or wonder, or both.

He went to take a step and immediately the river surged past his ankles.

Critics would argue afterwards whether, in his ill-founded role as a man of the cloth, he dared to observe some natural *phenomenon* as yet undefined by laws of the land. Were not such laws meant to place God reassuringly above Nature? As to that, others would have to decide. Necessity knew no law, which was why he was in no position to refuse. His sceptics would say that what he sought to see could not be found anyway. But what was to anyone else wholly nebulous was at this moment absolutely certain to him.

He tossed aside his hat.

'Wait for me, Sabrina. I'm coming.'

The estuary swelled with cold sea from the Atlantic. He had the promise of sufficient salvation to let it take him in. The water would sweep him away after another few paces, he knew for certain. He had to do it before Sasha returned. What he was about to do could not be considered sinful. He was not, even in the words of the Church of England's own code of law, about to commit suicide, only about to lay violent hands upon himself.

'Wait! Wait for me!'

Luke looked over his shoulder, surprised. At the nearby seawall stood an elderly woman whose grey hair blew about in the breeze and whose dressing gown fell open over her flimsy pink nightdress and cardigan.

She held out both arms to him urgently. Her sudden appearance was too illogical to be ignored.

'Gwendolen? Is that you?'

Shocking as her intervention was at that moment, he stopped wading deeper into the tide.

She stared at him with astonishment.

'Take me with you.'

So saying, Gwendolen climbed atop the seawall. She had, from there, nowhere else to go except into the river but that was no disincentive to her. Luke saw that her face was unusually animated for someone who was normally dismissed as so ill.

'For God's sake stay there, gran. Don't come any further. It's not safe.'

He crossed the few feet of foreshore even as the waves licked at his heels. He caught her in his arms. Held her tightly.

As she did him.

'Sean, my love.'

'Let me help you, Gwendolen. You're confused.'

He set her down on the wall and sat beside her. He took both her hands in his as if he would say a prayer with her to get her attention.

'What are you doing here, exactly, gran?'

Gwendolen squeezed his cold fingers and smiled.

'Whatever it takes, Sean, I'm with you now.'

'Now?'

She paused, then blinked rapidly at him.

'It's book club night, right?'

'I guess it is.'

She hung on to his arm and leaned her head on his shoulder. She still wore her wedding ring, Luke confirmed, even though legally it meant nothing.

'If only Mary and Barbara hadn't walked in on us in the kitchen.'

'You never did lock your door on Sundays, remember.'

'I left it open for you to return.'

'That's nice, in a way, to know.'

'Mary and Barbara thought you were a ghost but I knew different.'

'Sounds about right.'

'I could hardly make any sense of what you said, you were so excited.'

'Remind me. What did I say?'

'Never mind all that now.'

'What, then, do you want?' Luke asked as he led her safely away from the shore.

'Why, to ask your forgiveness, of course.'

'Forgiveness for what exactly?'

'If it wasn't for me you'd still be alive.'

'Please, Gwendolen, what did happen in 1981?'

'I'm feeling very tired.'

'You're right. Let's get you home.'

'Chapel Cottage?'

'There's no going back there, I'm afraid.'

'You mustn't talk like that. You must have faith.'

Luke gave a shudder and looked behind him. Serpentine bends of water swelled as they grew wider and wider. The course of the tide was positively writhing and twisting like a great monster, although the bore and its chariot and its frothing seahorses were long gone. A dark, silent highway stretched behind them now, fit only for those already dead or damned. Into this underworld and its fathomless depths he tossed his phone.

Chapter 55

If faddish diets were the new faith, then they were also sheer purgatory, thought Jorge. Consuming cabbage soup by the gallon had definitely challenged his impure thoughts, but still he needed to be cleansed of his sin of craving food. Nutritionists (the new confessors) might say he could eat vibrant and healthy meals that were fun and delicious but that was just another level of temptation. His contrition, unshrinking in theory, was elastic in practice. One act of self-mortification, such as giving up doughnuts, was soon balanced by a Cajun steak with a very healthy herb and lime slaw as an act of penance.

Right now, though, he straightened his shoulders and strode resolutely along the quays of Gloucester Docks. Not for him their contemporary all-day European dining, Italian café, or even the more casual pizza and pasta place with its funny name. The devil in his head was very persuasive: 'Study the proteins on offer and order a smaller portion,' was its subtle seduction of his self-control. 'Try the superb Thai cooking – it's not so fattening,' were similar weasel words.

Being medically obese could, frankly, soon turn into a life-sentence. On the other hand it was all about self-perception: no one suffered more than those who hated themselves. Any attempts to fat-shame him were, he thought with a smile, doomed to fail.

'Stay here, Sasha. Don't be nervous. I won't be long.'

To critics one and all he raised a finger.

*

Whereas the docks were largely new shops and apartments it was surprising to find such an odd little place of worship as this. He took off his Inspector's cap before he stepped through the open door and lodged it respectfully under his arm.

'Hallo? Is anyone there, at all? Where am I exactly?'

A woman dressed in black fixed her large honey-coloured eyes upon his, for her gaze was no less intense than his own. The unusual length of her narrow face, the unnatural pallor, the blood-red lipstick, gave this person of the cloth the look of a Gothic princess.

'I'm Gabriela Meireles. You are in the Mariners Chapel and I'm its chaplain.'

'How do you do? I'm Inspector Jorge Winter from Gloucester Cathedral Police. As I explained on the phone, the Church wishes to deal with the whole matter sensitively and with due respect for the reputation of the individual involved.'

'You heard about it on the news, then?'

'Is there even the slightest doubt that it's him?'

'Don't see how. His sister Ellie has identified him already.'

Gabriela shook his hand and led him into the little white church. The interior had very narrow, tall windows that were filled with red and blue stained glass – blue like the sea.

A coffin stood against a wall.

'No one told me that this place even existed.'

'This, Inspector, is a proprietary chapel which was originally built solely for the spiritual comfort of sailors and boatmen who visited the port of Gloucester. It's been here for the last one hundred and sixty-eight years. Spanish seamen brought onions to sell in the neighbouring streets while escaped slaves from America mixed with Norwegians, Danes, Dutchmen and Germans. I still have some of the religious tracts that my predecessors handed out in all sorts of languages, including Hindustani and Chinese, to benefit their souls.'

'That why Captain Singleton came straight to you and no one else?'

Gabriela rested one elegant hand on the lid of the chest. It was an ill-fashioned box built from very thin, reused planks, not like a proper coffin at all.

'Where better to bring it, Inspector?'

'You mean Captain Singleton was desperate to reach here and have you bless it?'

'As such it was my duty.'

'I just have to be sure that's all there is to the story.'

'What does it matter now?'

'Reverend Luke's last movements have yet to be verified.'

'Wait, Inspector, where are you going?'

'To look at the ship.'

'But his coffin?'

'So? It's empty. What use is that to me?'

'Wait, I'll come with you.'

Jorge settled his peaked cap on his head.

'Meet Sasha. She was Reverend Luke's dog. She's a bit shy.'

But Sasha had already barked. Wagged her tail. She rushed to lick Gabriela's hand and face.

'Don't worry, Inspector, we're old friends.'

*

Nielson's dry dock contained the totally exposed black hull of a familiar, three-masted schooner that was covered in barnacles, Jorge discovered. From its rigging hung dead seaweed. One sail hung in tatters. A painter's cradle hung off the stern ready to repaint her name in gold: **Amatheia.**

Sasha ran across a gangplank and began to sniff about on board.

'Did you know that the ship is named after a Greek sea nymph, Inspector? Amatheia was one of the fifty daughters of Nereus, god of the sea. It was her job to safeguard and preserve young fish. Her name means *nourisher.*'

'Where's she bound for next?'

'Better ask Sabrina. She owns her.'

'That'll be Sabrina ap Loegres, the Welsh shipping magnate?'

'You've heard of her?'

'I read about her in a magazine but she won't return my calls.'

'Then know this, she's a complete mystery. No one can even say for sure where she lives. Yet according to Captain Singleton there's nothing about tall ships that Sabrina doesn't know. It's she who is paying for the schooner's repainting and repairs.'

The deserted vessel, with its soaring masts, bare rigging and funnel, appeared strangely constrained by its dry, stone prison. As they trod the creaking wooden deck it felt odd not to be affected by the motions of sea and wind. Yet the ship was held captive but for a moment, it appeared, since a sinister impatience possessed it.

This Death ship wished to unfurl its sails. Light its furnace. Go on its way.

A silvery, green-eyed black cat leapt from hawser to hawser, glaring at Sasha and marking their progress.

'This was Reverend Luke's, too,' said Gabriela, pulling a crucifix by its chain from her pocket. 'Captain Singleton and his crew were most anxious to give it to me, should his ghost fail to rest in his grave.'

'Seriously. His ghost?'

'At the helm is where they saw him last, apparently.'

'You mean they fled the ship because it's haunted?'

'It seems Reverend Luke Lyons was desperate to reach England, dead or alive.'

'Did he explain to anyone the cause of his terror before he died?'

'No, but he said his soul depended on it. Uttered a few lines from a poem with his dying breath.'

'What poem?'

'I don't know its origins but the captain did his best to recite it to me:

Like one, that on a lonesome road

Doth walk in fear and dread,

And having once turned round walks on,

And turns no more his head;

Because he knows a frightful fiend

Doth close behind him tread.'

'It's from 'The Rime of the Ancient Mariner' by Samuel Coleridge, but why that somewhat melodramatic verse, I wonder?'

'He felt pursued by someone or something, Inspector.'

'Singing sea-shanties and reciting poems down the pub is many a seaman's party trick. Perhaps we shouldn't read too much into it.'

'Or he turned to poetry at the moment of his greatest distress. So say the crew.'

'But now they're afraid to admit it?'

'In a word, yes.'

'Doesn't rule out foul play.'

'I'd be spooked if a dead man sailed himself home at full speed. Wouldn't you?'

'You mustn't talk like that.'

Clearly unnerved Gabriela was annoyed at herself for showing it.

'After you, Inspector. Priests are not lucky to have on board, are they? We dress in black and perform funeral services. As such we are a bad omen since we make the crew think of death. Then again, I'm told you should avoid anyone with red hair when going on a long voyage. Redheads can bring bad luck to a ship, too.'

'So I have to ask you. What do you think actually happened here?'

Jorge trod more dead fish and shells among the seaweed on deck. The thick mass of berry-like air-vessels suggested some rampant invasion. Had the ship sailed the Gulf Stream and escaped entanglement in the Sargasso Sea, only to be savaged by storms on her way home from the Bahamas?

'According to the crew Reverend Luke was feeling ill when he set sail.'

Gabriela ducked her head down almost vertical steps to a series of cabins below deck. He and Sasha followed.

'So he died somewhere in mid-Atlantic?'

'Yes. The crew dismantled a cupboard and built him that crude coffin you saw in the chapel.'

'No signs of foul play, at all?'

'A contusion to his forehead.'

'So, yes.'

'You think he was murdered?'

'Which time?'

There were no broken fittings or furniture to suggest a violent struggle and most definitely were there no copious amounts of blood. Meanwhile all of Luke's newly acquired and very colourful Caribbean clothes hung in wardrobes in his quarters. Two dozen empty packets of paracetamol lay in a waste bin, Jorge noted, but not before he had donned a pair of white plastic gloves from his pocket with which to make close examination.

Gabriela went on to explain.

'According to the crew, Inspector, they left the Florida coast sixty days ago but ran into bad weather near the Azores. It seems that Reverend Luke became increasingly agitated and his behaviour more erratic. Stumbled about on deck like a drunken man. Complained that he was being chased by some monstrous creature worthy of the Devil itself. Twice the crew had to stop him from climbing the ship's rail and throwing himself overboard as he cried out that his head was about to burst.'

'How about the autopsy?'

'It's too soon to say.'

'But the police are mounting a thorough investigation?'

'Oh yes, all that began when the ship first docked in Bristol's Floating Harbour some days ago. That's where the Avon and Somerset Police recovered the body.'

'Of course.'

Having sniffed a pillow where Luke had slept, Sasha immediately turned her attention to some half open drawers in a bedside cupboard where, disappointingly, she found nothing.

'Anyone find a phone, laptop or tablet?' asked Jorge.

Gabriela looked blank.

'Captain Singleton didn't see the police take anything away. No personal effects.'

'No suspicious items in plastic bags?'

'If they were worried about anything they would not have released the ship so soon.'

'I suppose.'

Sasha, having redirected her search beneath the bed, rose quickly to her feet and growled.

'Hallo,' said Gabriela. 'It seems someone has found something after all.'

Jorge crouched low.

'Here, Sasha, let me see.'

From her teeth he prised a black and white sheet of paper.

Gabriela leaned low, too.

'What is it, Inspector?'

'It's a letter from a consultant at Gloucestershire Royal Hospital dated July 2016. It's all about not eating and drinking prior to admission to the wards. There's blood on it.'

'Reverend Luke must have dropped it when he fell.'

'Wow, what can I say? Our friend was due to have a biopsy done on a possibly malignant brain tumour the day after he disappeared.'

Gabriela frowned.

'You think he was so scared of the operation that he decided not to show up?'

'He wouldn't be the first.'

'What could he possibly gain by doing that?'

'Perhaps at the time he considered it his only option?'

Gabriela led their way back up on deck as Jorge again tried to imagine what unexpected turn of events had driven Luke to turn fugitive, only to try to return home less than a year later.

It wasn't as if any warrant had been issued for his arrest.

'There's something else you ought to know, Inspector. It might be irrelevant. Who knows?'

'Tell me.'

'Last summer I found Reverend Luke semi-conscious on the floor of my chapel.'

'Don't tell me. Two men by the name of Slim Jim Jackson and Mel McAtree attacked him during the Tall Ships Festival.'

'You know about that?'

'His sister related the sorry tale to me.'

'Then know this, Inspector. They threw Sasha into the dock and I had to dive in to rescue her. He loved that dog more than his own soul. So why didn't he take her with him?'

No sooner had he stepped back on deck than Jorge took a deep breath. He might have considered himself immune to the odd atmosphere in the cabin below but it felt good to shake his head and see daylight again. Sasha did the same.

'Seriously? You think he came back for his dog?'

'Even that wasn't as surprising as some other things he told me, Inspector.'

'What kind of other things?'

'He couldn't stop the monster uncoiling in his heart, he said. The superstitious fear and wonder with which the idea was awakening his feelings had all the ferocity of some crafty sea-snake. Told me that such a siren's call pre-dated his God and mine. What could I do about it? It was akin to the serpent that tempted Eve. He said the goddess of the river had spoken wondrous things to him and he had answered.'

'Such as?'

'Love. Retribution. Revenge.'

'So how did that make you feel?'

'Trust me, Inspector, I told him that no such heathen creature played any meaningful part in our lives any more. I believed that they were only ever silly legends. As did he, but now he was not so sure.'

'How so?'

'Because he'd twice seen her riding the bore on the River Severn.'

'That can't be right.'

'And now Sabrina was offering to help him put things right in exchange for a great treasure.'

'He was delirious, or what?'

'I said you really ought to go to A&E. Your concussion is making you say all sorts of blasphemous things.'

*

That evening, Jorge emailed Captain Singleton to inquire more about Luke's state of health while aboard the Amatheia.

As the ship battled heavy seas the captain felt honour bound to discharge his duty to his only passenger with compassionate care:

'I visited Reverend Lyons twice before he closed his eyes for the last time and more than once did he allude to the storm's siren voice, like his own sister calling. It conveyed such an impression to his mind as produced a rooted hatred for sin and a desire for holiness – thank God for it. More than once he called upon Jesus Christ to forgive him. His fears were such that he seemed to float on the brink of some mighty cataract. When I looked again

I gazed upon his lifeless face and his smile, even in horror, could not but hope he might yet be saved.'

Jorge emailed the captain straight back.

'Is that why Reverend Lyons tried to return home so unexpectedly? He was finally forced to admit that he was going to die without medical treatment that he had spurned previously?'

While no great revelation came by way of immediate reply, he did receive later that night a more detailed account of his friend's last hours.

'We all think we can outrun our most secret selves, don't we, Inspector, but what else awaits us at the end of the world?'

*

Waking early, Jorge took Sasha for a pleasant walk by the river. The sun was barely up but the jackdaws suddenly took off en masse from Berkeley Castle's pink-tinted walls to begin feeding in the meadows. A keen-eyed goshawk, meanwhile, waded water beside the reeds in a manner very unlike its usual method of catching ducks.

His presence failed to deter it.

The tide was on the turn and the river began to swirl. Currents thickened into arms and tentacles, beads of light burned in sunshine on the water's surface as it sparkled and glittered like jewels. From now on a restless excitement would grow and grow as the surge from the Atlantic came rushing home. Everything was waiting for its *genius loci*.

These serpentine rivulets could not settle for as long as its keeper and protector remained at sea, but back she'd come twice a day in her watery chariot.

In the wreckage of a man's life something had finally, irrevocably stirred among the deepest, darkest water.

In the forefront of his mind was Gabriela's strange suggestion of revenge. Even as Luke's resolve to seek retribution had lain undisturbed ever since childhood, so at last it had found a way to the surface like that monstrous growth inside his skull? Like Oceanus, like that secret freshwater stream that the eels followed every year to the Caribbean, the need to go with the flow had proved irresistible in the end? It had taken him with it when his dam of pain and silence had finally broken?

After so long Luke had sought to discover the one thing he'd lost as a boy.

320

The secret of happiness was the truth.

As for himself, thought Jorge, he had come to Berkeley fearing to confirm that his friend really had killed himself. Now he knew better. Luke's return to England was his last chance not to get even any more, but to face up to his past. His own and his family's. He had wanted to find the courage to fight that sinking feeling.

That's not to say he had finally gone crazy. He was not all at sea, just undergoing a sea-change. Finding his sea legs. Not drowning.

He smiled.

It was enough to satisfy his greatest hunger.

Chapter 56

To: cathredral_house@glosdioc.uk

Subject: Investigation into the disappearance of Rev. Luke Lyons.

From: Jorge Winter – jorgewinter484@gmail.

Dear archdeacon, herewith some explanatory observations and summary of my findings into the disappearance of Reverend Luke Lyons – named hereafter the respondent – on Sunday, 31 July 2016. As you are aware, the recent new Clergy Discipline Measure replaced the Ecclesiastical Jurisdiction Measure 1963 and has greatly simplified a process that was complex, expensive and slow. Nor was it particularly useful to treat the proceedings as criminal or semi-criminal. Certain terms such as 'the accused', 'ecclesiastical offence' and 'guilt' were not always helpful.

However, even though a full disciplinary tribunal by the Church might not use the language and practice of the criminal courts, but follow the disciplinary procedures of other professions, I feel I must draw on some legal language to explain certain points in full.

From my report (see attachment) you will note that I will seek to demonstrate that, just before the respondent went missing, he lured Slim Jim Jackson and Mel McAtree to the boathouse by Berkeley Pill on the pretext of giving them a treasure worth millions. For this information I am, in part, indebted to informal testimony from a young witness called Randal (the respondent's nephew.) Through such a ploy, the respondent sought to confront Mr Jackson with past crimes of a sexual nature which resulted in things spiralling out of control. I believe the respondent castrated his victim and left him to bleed out next to the water. In fact Mr Jackson survived his murderous amputation.

However, even if the assault had resulted in death I have no doubt that, were we the courts, we should consider this diminished responsibility. Such a thing is covered under section 2 of the Homicide Act 1957, which states: *where a person kills or is party to a killing of another, he shall not be convicted of murder if he was suffering from such abnormality of mind (whether arising from a condition of arrested or retarded development of mind or any inherent cause or **induced by disease** or injury) as substantially impaired his mental responsibility for his acts...*

The burden of proof in such extreme cases is on the defence who must prove it on a balance of probabilities and by calling evidence from at least two medical experts. As I say, there is some relevance here to our case.

What I have been able to ascertain is that the respondent was suffering from a growth on his brain which did, in all likelihood, result in an abnormality of behaviour in his last few months alive. Ironically his own worst fears have not been entirely borne out by the autopsy which has now proved the growth to be benign.

But many a person will lose their reason when they *think* that they might be about to die – the respondent's actions were driven by the terror that he would depart this life before he could 'set the record straight'. It is the task of the jury to decide this, not medical experts, though medical opinion may be taken note of.

The abnormality of mind does not have to be connected with madness.

Moreover, having spoken to many people in Berkeley, in particular the respondent's twin sister Ellie, I am of the firm opinion that by July last year he was in a doubly reckless mood on account of something that a prisoner called Frank Cordell had told him about his father Rex Lyons, in HMPL…. It was Cordell, thought to be a snitch by other members of the notorious Severn Sea Gang, who believed that the clue to the gang's hidden riches lay in an old Bible.

Indeed, for a while it seemed highly likely that a former gang member killed him for that very secret on the day of his release from prison, even as Ian Grey was drowned in the River Severn to silence him. Appearances can be deceptive, however, as I will explain shortly.

The whole effort to locate the stolen hoard of antiques amassed by the Severn Sea Gang was actually financed and masterminded by expat Jessica Kennedy from her villa in Spain.

Accordingly, she flew in to the UK briefly to visit Cordell in prison.

While her stint on Spanish TV was a brazen attempt to flush out clues to its whereabouts, her real intention was to set one person against another. She never even fully confided in her own daughter, Ellie. Instead, the latter's wedding proved convenient cover to keep tabs on the respondent, albeit by proxy. Jessica never could accept the painful truth that her dead lover Rex Lyons had entrusted the treasure's hiding place to anyone but her.

Thanks to the police investigation in Bristol we now know that Cordell actually met his death at the hands of someone whom he had abused years ago. It was my misfortune to witness the murderer's last moments on Clifton Suspension Bridge on the fateful day.

But my real point is this. The respondent was scheduled to have a biopsy done on his brain which left him with nothing to lose, *in his own mind*. Still nothing bad would ever have happened, I don't think, had it not been for the intervention of others. To say of him that he was very nearly seduced by some devilish creature not of his own making should never be sufficient. That he was secretly very angry, suffered from low self-esteem and blamed himself for what had happened to him years ago is, however, indisputable when a chance meeting with Sabrina ap Loegres, the mysterious Welsh shipping magnate, changed everything.

What began as a simple desire to sail abroad to escape two violent criminals became something quite different: he decided to 'die', apparently by drowning, just as his grandfather Sean Lyons had done in 1960.

In fact Sabrina gave him the chance to stow away aboard her ship, the Amatheia, wherein he made a terrible mistake. He was really running from himself.

To quote Isaiah: 'If only you had paid attention to my commands, your peace would have been like a river, your well-being like the waves of the sea.' I can say with some surety that Sabrina's uncanny influence over all parties in this extraordinary case has yet to be fully quantified.

Which brings me to the heart of the matter. In my report I have established beyond doubt that Eva Greene shared the same grandfather as the respondent. It was her family's very valuable antiques that were stolen by the Severn Sea Gang in 1981 when Eva's pregnant mother was fatally wounded by Rex Lyons, the respondent's father. Eva plotted to get even with the Lyons family. Sabrina agreed to help her. There is, however, no suggestion that either of them played any part in the mutilation of Mr Jackson. (The latter's total refusal even now to name his attacker says it all.)

On the contrary, the respondent alone made the decision to confront Mr Jackson on that awful night. He challenged the old man for the violence he had perpetrated against him when he was nine and ten years old. To this man's propensities I can, to some extent, attest myself since I, too, once had to fend off his clumsy attempts to touch, stroke and kiss me at the same age. Nor did the respondent ever tell me precisely what happened to him in that riverside hut; he only swore me to complete secrecy. He said he would kill himself if I ever so much as thought of speaking out. He never wanted his parents or grandmother to know.

Not only was the respondent incapable of making rational judgements on the night of the castration, but he could not exercise the will power to control any physical act in accordance with that rational judgement. He simply lashed out at last, since Jackson had the effrontery to resurface from the darkest part of his life as if nothing had ever happened between them.

Which brings us to the autopsy itself. The exact circumstances of the recent reappearance of the respondent's dead body aboard the Amatheia may never be determined. Certainly, though, he resided only a few months in Bermuda before his ill-fated attempts to hurry home. How to account for this risky volte-face? Could he not face a life on the run, after all? I can only think that he suffered from a fit of conscience: he really had murdered Slim Jim Jackson for all he knew. Truth is, he had never expected him to reappear in his life. This was the man who had done his best to destroy him. Left him wrecked and sinking. Becoming a priest had put him on a new course but now all that was in peril. He had to fix it once and for all. That meant payback. Once done, Sabrina gave him a way to sail away from it all – from the monster he'd become. But it was the wrong choice. He was in danger of going under again, of hiding another terrible secret.

To me his return smacks of panic – he had sinned before the eyes of our Lord? I haven't found the real reason. It seems frivolous to say of a man that food in the Caribbean didn't agree with him?

But here's a thing. The Coroner has been able to determine that a trace of eel blood resides in the corpse. Doctors confirm that such blood is poisonous to humans and other mammals. It is normally rendered harmless by cooking and the digestive process. However, a very small amount of eel blood when eaten raw is enough to kill a person, not unlike pips from an apple. The toxic protein cramps muscles, especially the heart, and is very dangerous to children. It is possible that the respondent, having ingested it in raw form, went into anaphylactic shock; he may have been allergic to glass eels in a way none of us ever knew.

Since he had convinced himself that he was dying anyway, it seems particularly vindictive that anyone should have gone to the trouble to murder him, unless of course he did, as I suspect, tell one too many lies about the supposed existence of the so-called treasure.

If he did know where it was he chose not to dig it up for whatever reason best known to himself. God moves in mysterious ways and although the respondent came to believe again in the goddess of the River Severn (to his terror) he never, in my opinion, lost his faith in doing the right thing at last.

Luke went in search of what he treasured most from the wreck of his life. He salvaged his sense of self-worth. His dignity.

Thus do men and women outdo the Devil in their carelessness.

See full report. Inspector Jorge Winter.

PS. Please excuse my unexpected absence from the cathedral this afternoon, but I really must attend Ellie Kennedy's and Jeremy Lawrence-Hamilton's wedding reception on this fine, sunny day in Berkeley Castle.

I have it on very good authority that there's going to be banoffee pie for desert.

Praise be!

Chapter 57

Tina fingered the bone-filled glove carefully inside the green biscuit tin. From its frozen grip she removed its prize. Sealed the tin's lid. Began to think, too, how fitting it was that it should take pride of place among all the other things in her collection. In fact, the presence of such an object seemed unlikely and absurd, it having belonged recently to a person of which nothing much else remained?

It was a very old, very large, brass key.

Brass did not rust in salt water.

As a result, words engraved on its gold-like, metal surface remained legible among the barnacles: SHARPNESS SWING BRIDGE CABIN.

In any case it was sensible to keep together everything she had so far gleaned from the River Severn in what constituted something of a shrine to its goddess and guardian. She had a fossilized sea urchin, thought to have come from a Bronze Age grave, a chiselled flint that once tipped a Stone Age fishing spear, a green octagonal ink bottle, two wig curlers, a First World War button and all sorts of blue and white delftware and pearlware as well as a circular pot lid from a Victorian pharmacy on which was painted a black ship in full sail.

The hand, however, surpassed everything that she had ever found in mud or sand.

No longer could her favourite doll take precedence, although she began fondly to recite the ballad that went with it. She knew a lot of bloodthirsty ballads. The doll was, according to Wikipedia, likely to be over a hundred years old.

She knew by heart the song by Seba Smith called 'A Corpse Going to a Ball' from which the cold, immobile figure had acquired its name of 'Frozen Charlotte'. In the poem Charlotte froze to death after she rejected her mother's offer of a blanket to keep her warm on a long sleigh ride to a party.

All because she wanted as many people as possible to see her pretty, new dress.

Tina could only reflect again on how strangely unresponsive and helpless its torso looked with its arms pressed flat to its side. The dark river had devoured its head and legs in the same way it had bitten pieces out of pots and snapped the necks off bottles.

Randal, meanwhile, watched geese fly over the ruins of the nearby railway bridge where its trackbed now ended in mid-air. Grew bored. Poked his stick about on the towpath between river and ship canal.

Suddenly his phone rang in his oversized tweed jacket.

'It's my mother.'

Tina frowned.

'Oh bloody hell.'

'Do I answer it, or not?'

'Don't bother.'

'What if someone sees us? I'm tired of keeping secrets.'

'I've warned you already. You'd better forget all about that. Telling people would ruin everything.'

Randal pouted.

'Don't see why. We'll be famous.'

'How can I trust you?'

'But you don't have a plan.'

'You have no idea what I'm thinking.'

Randal's phone rang again.

'It's mother. Do I answer it this time?'

'I suppose.'

Randal! Have you forgotten we have to be at the church in a few hours' time?'

'Oh, bloody hell,' said Tina again.

Ellie hadn't given anyone a moment's peace ever since her brother Luke's cremation in Bristol. Really, it was just pre-wedding nerves.

'Well?' said Randal. 'We going, or what?'

'Tell her to get lost.'

'You, too, Tina. I won't tell you again. You know I can't do without you today. Or have you forgotten that you're one of the bridesmaids?'

'Be right there, Ms. Kennedy.'

Instead she started singing:

'O where have you been, Lord Randal, my son?

O where have you been, my bonny young man?

I've been with my sweetheart, mother make my bed soon

For I'm sick to the heart and I fain would lie down.'

It was half a century since the bridge's last girders and piers had come crashing down. All but this one. Since then the entrance to the surviving tower's internal staircase had been sealed up with bricks which she could, she had just discovered, remove one by one.

Randal's phone rang again.

'Please, Tina, we have to go back to the farm. Get ready. Mum says.'

'Be right with you.'

Randal took a few steps along the towpath in the direction of Sharpness Docks. He managed to peep over the seawall at the sandbanks and ribbons of silvery water in the distance.

'How did my uncle Luke die again?' he said, scratching yellow lichen off the wall with his stick.

Tina frowned. A rumour was going round Berkeley that Reverend Lyons's death was somehow unnatural.

'In the end the coroner put it down to something he ate in Bermuda.'

'Not murder then?'

'Only the sea knows.'

'You not sad?'

'Should I be?'

'I liked him very much. He once gave me an Easter egg.'

With that, Tina broke into song:

'And what did she give you, Lord Randal, my son?

And what did she give you, my bonny young man?

Eels boiled in brew, mother make my bed soon

For I'm sick to the heart and I fain would lie down.'

'Boys at school say he was bewitched by the goddess of the river,' resumed Randal happily. 'They say Sabrina killed him for a great treasure. If only they knew! Can't wait to tell them it's all ours.'

'*Ours?*'

'It's half mine. I'm as rich as you are, remember.'

'Yes, of course, I know that, Randal. But what is all the fuss about now? What's your rush? You're just a boy.'

'I want my share, or else.'

'Or else what?'

'I tell.'

Tina finished her folksong:

'What will you leave your true love, Lord Randal, my son?

What will you leave your true love, my bonny young man?

The tow and the halter to hang on yon tree,

And let her hang there for the poisoning of me.'

She shunted the last brick to and fro in its hole. Nearly forgot to lock the door she was hiding.

Something gleamed through its keyhole – it sparkled and glittered from the place where it rested deep inside the pier, in its tomb.

'I want my breakfast,' said Randal, baulking at the two and a half mile walk back to Floodgates Farm.

Tina picked up her biscuit tin. She took her friend's hot little hand in hers. Strolled beside him. She had just sealed the derelict tower's forgotten doorway for the foreseeable future.

No one else, least of all him, would ever tell what it held.

'Don't worry, Randal. Look, I brought these specially for you. You can eat them on your way home.'

With that, she handed him a small plastic pot from her pocket.

'Thanks, Tina. What's in it?'

'Your favourite.'

'What is?'

'Glass eels.'

Epilogue

Two leggy sun-worshippers lay naked on the deck of their large white yacht. They let hot rays beat down on their oiled bodies. One was exceptionally pale, nearly washed out, with a thin jaw, no make-up, a profusion of long red hair somewhat tangled and an elegant nose. Her silvery sea-green eyes were the colour of the deepest ocean. Two black Norwegian Elkhounds lay panting at her feet.

'Mix me a Bermuda Rum Swizzle, will you?'

The other sunbather's eyes narrowed as if she might at first resent the order, but the moment passed without incidence. Slowly she rose from her towel, walked to the bar and began to gather together fruit juice, rum and bitters.

With some crushed ice she began to stir the mixture by inserting a pronged stick into her pewter pitcher.

She was soon rubbing it between the palms of her hands quite vigorously.

'Don't you ever tan, Sabrina?'

'It's a blessing you'll never know.'

'You look like one of those ivory-coloured mermaids that you see in those dreadful pictures painted by frustrated Victorian artists. You know, all shipwrecks and bare-breasted sirens in wet sea caves and slippery rock pools. You'd look good in a Burne-Jones.'

'You not sorry I got you into this, Eva?'

'Clearly that bastard priest outsmarted us both.'

'Forget the Swizzle. Bring me a Dark n' Stormy.'

She gave a smile that was peculiarly penetrating and provoking.

'Eva Greene at your service, Your Highness.'

'Don't scrimp on the ginger beer this time.'

'You know why it's called a Dark n' Stormy?'

'Does it matter?'

'It's said that a sailor invented the name because the drink is the colour of a hurricane. You wouldn't ever want to sail towards it.'

'That a fact?'

Eva licked cheese sauce off a chunk of lobster.

'Hey, Sabrina. You want some breakfast?'

'This slice of rum cake will do just fine.'

'Do you ever eat much at all?'

'I'm on a diet.'

'You look marvellous but even a belle like you can't live on air alone.'

'How long have you known me now?'

'You'll never look rosy about the gills.'

'Eva, my love, you're so amusingly tiresome.'

So saying, Sabrina, too, rose to her feet and walked to the front rail of the boat. Eva did ask her what she meant by that.

Instead Sabrina refused to look back at her rather stiffly as though she were spontaneously annoyed with something she'd done or failed to do.

She could be certain that at least it was not a rebuff.

'What now?' said Eva. 'Did he not say he'd make us rich?'

'As rich as Croesus.'

'I can't tell you what it means not to have what's rightfully mine.'

'A tedious point.'

'It was his plan, mostly.'

'What can I say?'

'You could say sorry.'

'Eva, that's not kind. That's not fair.'

'I just can't believe a man of the cloth could be so downright deceitful.'

'You got that right.'

'Of course we should never have believed him when he said the treasure was in Bermuda.'

'Men are such liars.'

'Don't forget he as good as stole your ship.'

'How was I to know he'd go back for his dog?'

'You have to forget all about that now.'

'Let it not be said that I, Sabrina ap Loegres, will ever fail to take unfair advantage of someone just because I suspect that he is particularly vulnerable, susceptible or downright ill.'

'Huh?'

'H'm, well, yeah, a woman has to be persistent, doesn't she? All's fish that come to her net, aren't they?'

Eva moved to the bow of the boat but Sabrina only stared ever harder at the water. Her lover's attitude forced her to concentrate her own attention on the brown weed that floated on the sea's surface and encased the side of the hull.

They'd been becalmed like this for a while now.

'According to legend many a sailor of yore was ensnared by the Sargasso Sea,' said Sabrina with a wry smile, 'never to be seen again. Columbus and his frightened men thought the weed was land when they were nowhere near.'

Eva said nothing at first – did not know how to justify anything she could say. She found the other's smile peculiarly penetrating and provoking. Yet it was no less so than her eyes, which were unblinking. In a few seconds she came to her senses. Stood her ground in the growing disturbance before the boat's bow.

'Shit. What is it?'

Sabrina extended one arm to the sea. She lowered a lantern into the pale shadows cast by the white hull where she began to scan the berry-like air bladders of the sargassum. Weed suddenly began to stir and gleam. Thousands upon thousands of eyes sparked sudden glints of glass – shiny black pupils stared up at her as a mass of snake-like heads broke surface, like jewels.

She was delighted.

'See, Eva. The eels are getting ready to spawn.'

Each gracefully thin, serpentine body that tapered to its tail slipped and slid against the next eel's slimy contours. They glided over one another with continuous, frictionless ease as they intertwined. They revolved like one big serpent.

Even Varg and Freya raised their heat-struck heads to sniff the sudden smell that rose from fish and weed.

'See how beautiful they are,' said Sabrina and pointed to the pairs of pectoral fins just behind each eel's shiny head. 'Watch them breathe through their gills.'

Eva made a face.

'Are you crazy?'

'Seriously, Eva, I don't know why you don't like them.'

'What should I like?'

'Their magic?'

'I'm not feeling that.'

Undeterred, Sabrina witnessed countless long back and anal fins merge with tail fins to create a mass of wriggling, soft-rayed fringes that madly fanned the sea. Silvery white bellies rolled over and over, as if doing her homage.

She smiled.

'The females are the biggest. They can be three or four feet long.'

Eva cast a cursory glance over the side of the boat.

'I don't see the difference.'

Sabrina grinned her peculiar grin.

'Look again. The females have the broader noses. They acquire those on account of their excessively developed jaw muscles due to voracious eating.'

'I'm happy for you.'

With that, the eels all opened their shark-like mouths in the gyre; they and the ocean stream became one seething mass of life and activity. Soon sharp little teeth bit the air as Sabrina swept her hand to and fro across the circulating currents on the otherwise calm blue water. Thus had eels been known to lay eggs in this mysterious sea, but rarely if ever had the exact moment ever been seen.

Her stance, as she leaned lower and lower over the boat's rail, impressed upon Eva some awful urgency. Her obsession appealed to her with a ruthlessness of purpose about which she knew nothing, yet she sensed that she would share it at her peril.

'Please come away from the rail, Sabrina and eat your breakfast.'

'Don't you see we're in the presence of something truly wondrous.'

'Yes, of course, I know that. But what is all the feverish commotion? What's the rush here?'

'These eels will all die. Their elvers, however, will float all the way back to England to grow into eels to repeat the cycle.'

'Really, Sabrina, I don't know how you can be so nonchalant. Reverend Luke Lyons promised us a fortune.'

'So what, he's dead by now for sure.'

'Tell yourself that.'

'You would have thought that he would have wanted what was rightfully his. Did he even know where to find any fucking treasure?'

'Never trust a man who can't trust himself.'

'What is true wealth, anyway?'

'As someone famous once said, *there is no wealth but life*.'

'They got that right.'

'You any good at cooking a Bermuda codfish breakfast?'

'I don't know. You?'

'Please, Sabrina, do help me peel these potatoes. I'm hopeless.'

'Give me a moment.'

'What now?'

Sabrina watched the eels' razor-sharp teeth snap at her fingers as she dangled her lamp a little lower to draw them closer. Suddenly those million eyes flashed again like diamonds. She peered into more spaces between the clumps of sargassum. Lit the seething dark water far below.

'Don't you just love the hidden riches of secret places? I do.'

*

Six months later Jorge stood high on the cliff overlooking the River Severn. He watched its silvery currents coil between the black, gleaming mudflats far below while Ellie and Randal called to him at the unfenced drop into the ship canal. He called back.

335

He saw the vista encompass sky and water for as far as his eye could see and listened to Sasha sniff the briny breeze beside him.

Then he advanced to the void where all twenty-two iron girders had once spanned the estuary. Braved his vertigo.

Before him Ellie held out a jar to him in a gesture both generous and kind.

She smiled wordlessly.

Jorge took it and returned the smile equally silently.

They faced the flaming red sunrise that anticipated high tide by less than an hour. They stood before the coming of the new day, shoulder to shoulder.

They watched noisy feral greylag and Canada geese fly by on the wind off the Atlantic. In their thoughts they recalled Luke's love for this wild place that had once been his home, as it was about to be again, forever.

Jorge held aloft the urn whose ashes Ellie had asked him to scatter. He held it up to sun, air and water as a final offering. And then he opened it.

39356232R00204

Printed in Poland
by Amazon Fulfillment
Poland Sp. z o.o., Wrocław